A MULTITUDE
OF SINS

D1231090

Also by Richard Ford and published by The Harvill Press

A PIECE OF MY HEART

THE ULTIMATE GOOD LUCK

THE SPORTSWRITER

ROCK SPRINGS

WILDLIFE

INDEPENDENCE DAY

WOMEN WITH MEN

Richard Ford

A MULTITUDE OF SINS

Stories

THE HARVILL PRESS
LONDON

First published in Great Britain in 2001 by
The Harvill Press
2 Aztec Row, Berners Road
London N1 0PW

www.harvill.com

1 3 5 7 9 8 6 4 2

These stories appeared first, in somewhat
different forms, in the following publications:
"Privacy", "Quality Time", "Calling", "Reunion", "Crèche",
"Under the Radar" (with the title "Issues"), "Puppy" (*New Yorker*);
"Dominion" (with the title "The Overreachers") (*Granta*); "Charity" (*Tin House*)
Richard Ford is grateful, in each instance, for the editors' permission
to reprint the stories here

A CIP catalogue record is available from the British Library

ISBN 1 86046 939 6

Designed and typeset in Galliard
at Libanus Press, Marlborough, Wiltshire

Printed and bound in Australia by
Griffin Press

Kristina

Acknowledgements

I wish to state, for the thousandth time, my gratitude to Gary L. Fistketjon, and also to Bill Buford, Meghan O'Rourke, Christopher MacLehose, Margaret Stead, Ian Jack and L. Rust Hills, for their generous efforts to make these stories better. I wish to thank, as well, Angela and Rea Hederman for their encouragement and long friendship. For being my acute reader and friend, I wish to thank Sarah MacLachlan. Finally, and again, my great gratitude goes to Amanda Urban.

RF

Contents

Privacy

This was at a time when my marriage was still happy.

We were living in a large city in the northeast. It was winter. February. The coldest month. I was, of course, still trying to write, and my wife was working as a translator for a small publishing company that specialized in Czech scientific papers. We had been married for ten years and were still enjoying that strange, exhilarating illusion that we had survived the worst of life's hardships.

The apartment we rented was in the old factory section on the south end of the city, the living space only a great, empty room with tall windows front and back, and almost no electric light. The natural light was all. A famous avant-garde theater director had lived in the room before and put on his jagged, nihilistic plays there, so that all the walls were painted black, and along one were still riser seats for his small disaffected audiences. Our bed – my wife's and mine – was in one dark corner where we'd arranged some of the tall, black-canvas scenery drops for our privacy. Though, of course, there was no one for us to need privacy from.

Each night when my wife came back from her work, we would go out into the cold, shining streets and find a restaurant to have our meal in. Later we would stop for an hour in a bar and have coffee or a brandy, and talk intensely about the translations my wife was working on, though never (blessedly) about the work I was by then already failing at.

Our wish, needless to say, was to stay out of the apartment as long as we could. For not only was there almost no light inside, but each night at seven the building's owner would turn off the heat, so that by ten – on our floor, the highest – it was too cold to be anywhere but in bed piled over with blankets, barely able to move. My wife, at that time, was working long hours and was always fatigued, and although sometimes we would come home a little drunk and make love in the dark bed under blankets, mostly she would fall straight into bed exhausted and be snoring before I could climb in beside her.

And so it happened that on many nights that winter, in the cold, large, nearly empty room, I would be awake, often wide awake from the strong coffee we'd drunk. And often I would walk the floor from window to window, looking out into the night, down to the vacant street or up into the ghostly sky that burned with the shimmery luminance of the city's buildings, buildings I couldn't even see. Often I had a blanket or sometimes two around my shoulders, and I wore the coarse heavy socks I'd kept from when I was a boy.

It was on such a cold night that – through the windows at the back of the flat, windows giving first onto an alley below, then farther across a space where a wire factory had been demolished, providing a view of buildings on the street parallel to ours – I saw, inside a long, yellow-lit apartment, the figure of a woman slowly undressing, from all appearances oblivious to the world outside the window glass.

Because of the distance, I could not see her well or at all clearly, could only see that she was small in stature and seemingly thin, with close-cropped dark hair – a petite woman in every sense. The yellow light in the room where she was seemed to blaze and made her skin bronze and shiny, and her movements, seen through the windows,

appeared stylized and slightly unreal, like the movements of a silhouette or in an old motion picture.

I, though, alone in the frigid dark, wrapped in blankets that covered
my head like a shawl, with my wife sleeping, oblivious, a few paces
away – I was rapt by this sight. At first I moved close to the window
glass, close enough to feel the cold on my cheeks. But then, sensing
I might be noticed even at that distance, I slipped back into the
room. Eventually I went to the corner and clicked off the small lamp
my wife kept beside our bed, so that I was totally hidden in the dark.
And after another few minutes I went to a drawer and found the pair
of silver opera glasses which the theater director had left, and took
them near the window and watched the woman across the space of
darkness from my own space of darkness.

I don't know all that I thought. Undoubtedly I was aroused.
Undoubtedly I was thrilled by the secrecy of watching out of the
dark. Undoubtedly I loved the very illicitness of it, of my wife sleeping
nearby and knowing nothing of what I was doing. It is also possible
I even liked the cold as it surrounded me, as complete as the night
itself, may even have felt that the sight of the woman – whom I took
to be young and lacking caution or discretion – held me somehow,
insulated me and made the world stop and be perfectly expressible
as two poles connected by my line of vision. I am sure now that all
of this had to do with my impending failures.

Nothing more happened. Though, in the nights to come I stayed
awake to watch the woman, letting my wife go off to sleep in her
fatigue. Each night, and for a week following, the woman would
appear at her window and slowly disrobe in her room (a room I never
tried to imagine, although on the wall behind her was what looked
like a drawing of a springing deer). Once her clothes were shed away,
exposing her bony shoulders and small breasts and thin legs and rib
cage and modest, rounded stomach, the woman would for a while
cast about the room in the bronze light, window to window, enacting
what seemed to me a kind of languid, ritual dance or a pattern of
possibly theatrical movements, rising and bowing and extending her

arms, arching her neck, while making her hands perform graceful lilting gestures I didn't understand and did not try to, taken as I was by her nakedness and by the sight on occasion of the dark swatch of hair between her legs. It was all arousal and secrecy and illicitness and really nothing else.

This I did for a week, as I said, and then I stopped. Simply one night, draped again in blankets, I went to the window with my opera glasses, saw the lights on across the vacant space. For a while I saw no one. And then for no particular reason I turned and got into bed with my wife, warm and smelling of brandy and sweat and sleep under her blankets, and went to sleep myself, never thinking to look through the window again.

Though one afternoon a week after I had stopped watching through the window, I left my desk in a moment of frustration and pointless despair, and stalked out into the winter daylight and up along the row of fashionable businesses where the old buildings were being restyled as dress shops and successful artists' galleries. I walked right to the river, clogged then with great squares of gray ice. I walked on to the university section, nearly to where my wife was at that hour working. And then, as the light was failing, I started back toward my street, my face hard with cold, my shoulders stiff, my gloveless hands frozen and red. As I turned a corner to take a quicker route back to my block, I found that I was unexpectedly passing before the building into which I had for days been spying. Something about it made me know it, though I'd never been aware of walking past there before, or even seen it in daylight. And just at that moment, letting herself into the building's tall front door, was the woman I had watched for those several nights and taken pleasure and undoubtedly secret consolation from. I knew her face, naturally – small and round and, as I saw, impassive. And to my surprise though not to my chagrin, she was old. Possibly she was seventy or even older. A Chinese, dressed in thin black trousers and a thin black coat, inside which she must've been as cold as I was. Indeed, she must've been freezing. She was carrying plastic bags of groceries slung to her arms and clutched in her hands. When I stopped and looked at her she turned and gazed down the steps at me with an expression I can only think now was indifference mingled with just the smallest recognition of threat. She was old, after all. I might suddenly have felt the urge to harm her, and easily could've. But of course that was not my thought. She turned back to the door and seemed to hurry her key into the lock. She looked my way once more, as I heard the bolt shoot profoundly back. I said nothing, did not even look at her again. I didn't want her to think my mind contained what it did and also what it did not. And I walked on then, feeling oddly but in no way surprisingly betrayed, simply passed on down the street toward my room and my own doors, my life entering, as it was at that moment, its first, long cycle of necessity.

Quality Time

Where he stopped for the red light on busy Sheridan Road, Wales watched a woman fall down in the snow. A sudden loss of footing on the slick, walked-over hummock the plows had left at the crosswalk. Must be old, Wales thought, though it was dark and he couldn't see her face, only her fall – backwards. She wore a long gray, man's coat and boots and a knitted cap pulled down. Or else, of course, she was drinking, he supposed, watching her through his salted windshield as he waited. She could be younger, too. Younger and drinking.

Wales was driving to The Drake to spend the night with a woman named Jena, a married woman whose husband had done colossally well in real estate. Jena had taken a suite in The Drake for a week – to paint. She was forty. She had her husband's permission. They – she and Wales – had done this five nights in a row now. He wanted it to go on.

Wales had worked abroad for fourteen years, writing for various outlets – in Barcelona, Stockholm, Berlin. Always in English. He'd lately realized he'd been away too long, had lost touch with things American. But a friend from years ago, a reporter he'd known in

London, had called and said, come back, come home, come to Chicago, teach a seminar on exactly what it's like to be James Wales. Just two days a week, for a couple of months, then back to Berlin. "The Literature of the Actual," his friend who'd become a professor had said, and laughed. It *was* funny. Like Hegel was funny. None of the students took it too seriously.

The woman who'd fallen – old, young, drunk, sober, he wasn't sure – had gotten to her feet now, and for some reason had put one hand on top of her head, as if the wind was blowing. Traffic rushed in front of her up Sheridan Road, accumulating speed behind head-lights. Tall sixties apartment blocks – a long file of them, all with nice views – separated the street from the lake. It was early March. Wintry.

The stoplight stayed red for Wales's lane, though the oncoming cars began turning in front of him in quick procession onto Ardmore Street. But the woman who'd fallen and had her hand on her head, took this moment to step out into the thoroughfare. And for some lucky reason the driver in the nearest lane, the lane by the curb, slowed and came to a stop for her. Though the woman never saw this, never sensed she had, by taking two, perhaps three unwise steps, put herself in danger. Who knows what's buzzing in that head, Wales thought, watching. A moment ago she was lying in the snow. A moment before that everything had been fine.

The cars opposite continued turning hurriedly onto Ardmore Street. And it was the cars in this lane – the middle turning lane – whose drivers did not see the woman as she stepped uncertainly, farther into the street. Though it seemed she *did* see them, because she extended the same hand that had been touching her head and held it palm outward, as if she expected the turning cars to stop as she stepped into their lane. And it was one of these cars, a dark van, resembling a small spaceship (and, Wales thought, moving too fast, much faster than reasonable under the conditions) one of *these* speed-ing cars that hit the woman flush-on, bore directly into her side like a boat ramming her, never thinking of brakes, and in so doing knocked her not up into the air or under the wheels or onto its non-existent hood, but sloughed her to the side and onto the road – changed her in an instant from an old, young, possibly drunk, possibly sober woman in a gray man's coat, into a collection of assorted remnants on a frozen pavement.

Dead, Wales thought – not five feet from where he and his lane now began to pass smartly by, the light having gone green and horns having commenced behind. In his side mirror he saw the woman's motionless body in the road (he was already a half block beyond the scene). The street was congested both ways, more car horns were blaring. He saw that the van, its taillights brilliant red, had stopped, a figure was rushing back into the road, arms waving crazily. People were hurrying from the bus stop, from the apartment buildings. Traffic was coming to a halt on that side.

He'd thought to stop, but stopping wouldn't have helped, Wales thought, looking again into the mirror from a half block farther on. A collection of shadowy people stood out on the pavement, peering down. He couldn't see the woman. Though no one was kneeling to assist her – which was a sure sign. His heart began rocketing. Cold sweat rose on his neck in the warm car. He was suddenly jittery. *It's always bad to die when you don't want to*. That had been the motto of a man named Peter Swayzee he'd known in Spain – a photographer, a silly man who was dead now, shot to pieces covering a skirmish in East Africa, someplace where the journalists expected to be pro-tected. He himself had never done that – covered a war or a skirmish or a border flare-up or a firefight. He had no wish for that. It was reckless. He preferred the parts that weren't war. Culture. And he was now in Chicago.

*

Turning south onto the Outer Drive along the lake, Wales began to go over what seemed remarkable about the death he'd just witnessed. Some way he felt now seemed to need resolving, unburdening. It was always important to tabulate one's responses.

The first thing: that she was dead; how certain he had been about that; how nothing less seemed thinkable. It wasn't a moral issue. Other people were helping in the event she *wasn't* dead. In any case, he'd helped people before – once, in the U-Bahn, when the Kurds had set off plastique at rush hour. No one in the station could see for the smoke, and he'd guided people out, led them by the hand up into the sunny street.

The other thing, of course – and perhaps this *was* a moral issue: he was moved by the woman as he'd *first* seen her, falling into the snow, almost gently, then standing and righting herself, getting her hand set properly onto the top of her head. Putting things right again. She'd been completely *in* her life then, in the fullest grip and perplex of it. And then – as he'd watched – three steps, possibly four, and that was all over. In his mind he broke it down: first, as though nothing that happened had been inevitable. And then as if it *all* was inevitable, a steady unfolding. In his line of work, no one had a use for this kind of inquiry. In his line of work, the actual was all.

The lake was on the left, dark as petroleum and invisible beyond the blazing lanes of northbound, homeward traffic. Friday night. Out ahead, the city center lit the low clouds shrouding the great buildings, the tallest tops of which had disappeared, igniting the sky from within. The actual jitters, he found, hadn't lasted so long. Though what was left was simply a disordered feeling – familiar enough – as if something had needed to be established by declaring someone he didn't even know to be dead, but it hadn't been. Of course, it could just be anticipation.

*

The Drake was jammed with people at six PM – even in the lower arcade, where there were expensive shops and an imitation Cape Cod restaurant he and Jena had dined in their first night, when they'd been so pleased with themselves to be together. Wales entered this way each night – the back entrance – and exited this way each morning. If Jena's husband employed a detective to watch for him, then a detective, he decided, would watch the front. He was not very good at deception, he knew. Deception was very American.

Men in suits and their wives in flowered dresses were everywhere in the lower lobby, hurrying one way and another, wearing nametags that said BIG TEN. He wanted past all this. But a man seemed to know him as he wove his way through the crowded arcade toward the elevator banks.

"Hey!" the man said, "Wales." The man bore through the crowd, a large, thick-necked, smiling man in a shiny blue suit. An ex-athlete, of course. His white plastic nametag said *Jim*, and below it, *President*. "Are you coming to our cocktail party?"

"I don't know. No." Wales smiled. People were all around, making too much noise. Couples were filtering into a large banquet room, where there were bright lights and loud piano music and laughter.

He had met this man, Jim. But that was all he remembered without really remembering that. At a college dinner, possibly. Now, though, here he was again, in the way. Chicago was large but not large enough. It was large in a small way.

"Well, you're invited in," the man Jim said jovially, moving in closer.

"Thanks," Wales said. "Good. Yes." They hadn't shaken hands. Neither wanted to hold the other too long.

"I mean, what better offer have you got, Wales?" the man, Jim, said. His skin was too white, too thick along its big jaw line.

"Well," Wales said, "I don't know." He'd almost said, "That depends," but didn't. He felt extremely conspicuous here.

"Did you get the tickets I sent you?" Jim said loudly.

"Of course." He didn't know what this Jim could be talking about. But he said, "I did. Thanks."

"I'm as good as my word, then, aren't I?" The man was shouting through the crowd noise, which was increasing.

Wales glanced toward the elevator banks farther on. Polished brass doors slowly opening, slowly closing. Pale green triangles – up. Pale red triangles – down. Faint, seductive chiming. "Thanks for the tickets." He wanted to shake the man's hand to make him go.

"Tell Franklin I say hello," the man said, as if he meant it sarcastically. By smiling he made his great unusual jaw look like Mussolini's jaw. Franklin, Wales wondered. Who was Franklin? He remembered no one at the college named Franklin. He felt drunk, although he hadn't been drinking. An hour before he'd been teaching. Trapped in a paneled room with students.

Bing . . . bing . . . bing. Elevators were departing.

"Oh yes," Wales said, "I will," and for a third time smiled.

"So," Jim said, "you be good now." All his front teeth were false teeth.

Jim wandered into the crowd that had begun moving more quickly toward the banquet room. Just at that moment Wales could smell a cigar, rich and dense and pungent. It made him think about the Paris Bar in Berlin. Something about smoke and this brassy amber arcade light was almost the same as there. He'd gone in one night with a woman friend for a drink and to buy condoms. When he'd stepped into the gents, he'd found the dispenser was beside the urinals, which were in constant use. And somehow – nervousness possibly, anticipation again – somehow he'd let drop his Deutsche Mark coin. And because he *had* been drinking then, and because he wanted to buy the condoms, badly wanted them, he'd squatted beside a man who was pissing and fetched the fugitive coin off the tiles from between the stranger's straddled legs. The man smiled down at him, unbothered, as if this kind of thing always happened. "I must have dropsy tonight," Wales said, fingering the hard little silver D-Mark, which was not at all dampened. And then he'd started to laugh, peals of loud laughing. No one in the gents could possibly have known what "dropsy" meant. It was very, very funny. A typical problem with the language.

"*Viel Glück, mein Freund*," the man said, zipping himself and looking around, pleased about everything.

"Yes well. *Der beste Glück. Natürlich*," Wales said, depositing the coin into the machine.

"Now everyone will know," his woman friend said as they exited the bar into the warm summer's night along Kantstrasse. She laughed about it. She knew everyone there.

"Surely no one cares," Wales said.

"No, of course not. No one cares a thing. It's all completely stupid."

Jena had given him the key, a crisp, white card which, when inserted in a slot, ignited a tiny green light, provoking a soft click, after which the door opened. Room 839.

"Oh, I've been dying for you to be here," Jena said, her voice rich, deeper than usual. He couldn't quite see her. The room was dark but for a candle Jena had set beside her easel, which was in shadows beside the window. It was a long L-shaped suite ending with a little step-up to tall windows that looked down onto the Drive. The desirable north view. The expensive view. The bed was at the other end, where there was no light, only the clock radio which said it was 6:05. A good, spacious American room, Wales thought. So much nicer than Europe. You could live an entire life in a room like this, and it would be an excellent life.

Jena was seated in one of two armchairs she'd placed by the windows. She'd been watching cars on the Drive. She extended her arm back to take his hand. She was irresistible. More attractive than anyone. "Aren't you late?" she said. "You feel very late."

"There was traffic," Wales said.

She turned her head toward him. He leaned to kiss her cheek, smelled her faint citrus breath.

Jena had the heat up. She was always cold. She was too thin, he thought, thinner than she looked in her clothes – a small, dark-haired woman with thin arms, not precisely pretty in every light, but pretty – her face slightly pointed, her soft, smiling lips slightly too thin. Yet so appealing – the sensation of incaution about her. She was quick-witted, unpredictable, thought of herself almost constantly, laughed at the wrong moments. She was rich and a wife and a mother, and so perhaps, Wales thought, she'd experienced little of the world, not enough to know what not to do, and so was only herself – a quality he also found appealing.

Wales had been invited to give a lecture to satisfy his college stay. And he'd decided to lecture on the death of Princess Diana as an event in the English press. He'd titled it "A Case of Failed Actuality." These, he'd said, were the easiest to cover: you simply made up the emotions, made up their consequence, invented what was important. It was usual in England. He'd quoted Henry James: "writing made importance." It was not exactly journalism, he admitted.

Jena had attended the lecture "from the community," driving down from her suburb up the lake. Afterward, she'd invited him for a drink. In the bar they'd talked until late about America losing its grip on the world; about the global need to feel more; about an enlarged sense of global grief; about the amusing coincidence of his surname – Wales. She was petite, forward, arousing, rarely stayed on any subject, laughed too much – the laugh, he thought, of a woman accustomed to being distrusted. But he'd thought: where did you come from? Where can I find you again? She had acted uncertain of herself at the beginning – though not shy, she wasn't shy in the least: she was protected, disengaged, careless, which allowed her to *seem* uncertain and thus, daring. This he also liked. It was exciting. He knew, of course, that when women came to lectures, they came wanting some-thing – conceivably something innocent – but something, always. That had been two weeks ago. As they left the bar, she'd taken his arm and said, "We'll have to hurry if we're going to do anything together. You're leaving soon." They had not quite talked about doing anything together. But he *was* leaving soon.

"Then we'll hurry," he said. And they had.

"Your hands are freezing." Jena took his hands. He liked her very much.

He knelt and put both his arms around her and held her so his cheek was against her hair. She was wearing a small black Chanel dress that revealed her neck, and he kissed her there, then kissed into her hair, which felt dry on his mouth. He could smell himself. He was sour. He should take a bath, he thought. A bath would be a relief.

"I saw a man in the lobby who knew me," he said. "He asked about someone named Franklin. I didn't know who he was."

"He probably thought you were somebody else," Jena said softly, her face beside his.

"May-be." Perhaps it was so, except the man had called him Wales. Though, my God, he realized, this was the drab news you would tell your wife when you had nothing else to say. Unimportant news. He didn't have a wife.

Each of the five nights they'd been at The Drake, Jena had wanted to make love the moment he arrived, as if it was this act that confirmed them both, and everything else should get out of its way; their time was serious, urgent, fast-disappearing. He wanted that act now very much, felt aroused but also slightly unstrung. He had, after all, seen a death tonight. Death unstrung everyone.

Only what Jena didn't like was weakness. Weakness anywhere. So he didn't want to seem unstrung. She was a woman who liked to be in control, but also to be kept off-balance, mystified, as though mystery were a form of interesting intelligence. Therefore she needed him to seem in control, even remote, opaque, possibly mysterious – anything but weak. It was her dream world.

And yet, remoteness was such a burden. Who finally worried about revealing yourself? You did it, whether you wanted to or not. He realized he was letting her play the interesting part in this. It was a form of generosity. What was most real to her, after all, were the things she wanted.

"I'd like to talk," Jena said. "Can we talk for a little first?"

"I was hoping we would," Wales said. This was opaque enough. Perhaps he would tell her about the woman he'd seen killed on Ardmore.

"Come sit in this chair beside me." She looked up, smiling. "We can watch the lights and talk. I missed you."

He didn't mind whatever he did with her; you could make a good evening in different ways. Making love would come along. Later they would walk out onto the wide, lighted Avenue in the cold and wind, and find dinner someplace. That would be excellent enough.

He sat between her and her worktable, where there were brushes, beakers of water and turpentine, tubes of pigment, pencils, erasers, swatches of felt cloth, razor blades, a vase containing three hyacinths. He had seen her paintings before – enlarged black-and-white photographs of a man and a woman, photographs from the nineteen-fifties. The people were nicely dressed, standing in the front yard of a small frame house in what seemed to be an open field. These were her parents. Jena had painted onto these photographs, giving the man and woman red or blue or green shadows around their bodies, smudging their faces, distorting them, making them look ugly but not comical. There was to be a series of these. They were depressing, Wales thought – unnecessary. "Bacon did this sort of thing first, of course," Jena had said confidently. "He didn't show his. But I'll show mine."

She took a long, red cashmere sweater off the back of her chair and put it on over her dress. The air was chilled by the window glass. It was exhilarating to be here, as though they were on the edge, waiting to jump.

Below them eight floors, the Drive was astream with cars – headlights and taillights – the lush apartments up the Gold Coast sumptuous and yellow-lit, though off-putting, inanimate. The pink gleam from the hotel's sign discolored the deep night air above. The lake itself was like a lightless precipice. Lakes were dull, Wales thought. Drama-less. He'd grown up near the ocean, which was never a disappointment, never compromised.

"There's something wonderful about the lake, isn't there?" Jena said, leaning close to the glass. Tiny motes of moisture floated through the tinted air beyond.

"It's always disappointing to me."

"Oh, no," Jena said sweetly and turned to smile at him. "I love the lake. It's so comforting. It's contained. I love Chicago, too." She turned back and put her nose to the windowpane. She was happy.

"What shall we speak about?" Wales said.

"My family," Jena said. "Is that all right?"

"I'll make an exception."

"I mean my parents," she said, "not my husband or my daughters." Jena had been married twenty years, though her two children were young. One was ten, he could remember, the other possibly six. She liked her rich husband, who encouraged her to do everything she wanted. Take flying lessons. Spend summers in Ibiza alone. Never consider employment. Know men. She needed only to stay married to him – that was the agreement. He was older – Wales's age. It was satisfactory. Merely not perfect.

She put ten slender fingertips onto the cold window glass and held them there as though against piano keys, then looked back at him and smiled. "Where are *your* parents?" she asked. She had asked this twice before and forgotten twice.

"Rhode Island," Wales said. "My father's eighty-four. My mother has, well . . . " He didn't care if he said this, but still he hesitated. "My mother has Alzheimer's."

"Would she recognize you?"

"Would?" Wales said. "She would if she could, I suppose."

"Does she?"

"No."

"And do you have siblings?" This she hadn't asked before. She often chose unlikeable words. Siblings. Interaction. Network. Bond. Words her friends said.

"One sister, who's older. In Arizona. We're not close. I don't like her very much."

"Hmm," Jena pulled her fingers away, just barely, then touched them back to the glass. Her legs were crossed. She was barelegged and barefoot and no doubt cold. She was being polite by asking. "My parents were essentially speechless," she said and exhaled wearily. "They were raised so poor in southern Ohio – where nobody really had anything to say, anyway – that they didn't know there were all these things you needed to be able to say to make the world work." She nodded, agreeing with herself. "My mother for instance. She wouldn't just walk up to you and just say, 'Hello, I'm Mary Burns.' She'd just start talking, just blurt out what she needed to get said.

Then she'd stare at you. And if you acted surprised, she'd dislike you for it."

Jena seemed to fix her gaze on the molten flow of cars below. This was *her* story, Wales thought; the one she couldn't get over from her past, the completely insignificant story that she believed cooperated in all her major failures: why she married who she'd married. Why she didn't go to a better college. Why she wasn't more successful as an artist. He'd had his own, years ago: 1958, an overcast day on Narragansett Bay with his father, in a dory. A fishing trip. His father had confessed to him about a half-Portuguese woman he loved down in Westerly – someone his mother and sister never heard about. The story stayed fixed in his mind for years, though he'd forgotten it until just now.

Still, these things were unimportant. You imagined the past, you didn't remember it. You could just imagine it differently. He would tell her that, tell her she was a wonderful woman. That's all that mattered.

"Is this okay?" Jena said, pulling her sweater sleeves up above her slender elbows. Her dark hair shone with the candle's flicker. The room was reflected out of kilter in the tall window. "I can't stand it if I bore you."

"No," Wales said. "Not at all."

"Okay, so my father," she went right on. "He couldn't go inside a restaurant and ask for a table. He'd just stand. Then they'd inch forward, expecting his wishes would be understood by whoever was in charge – as if his being there could only mean what he needed it to mean." Jena shook her head, breathed against the glass and mused at the fog her breath left. "So odd," she said. "They were like immigrants. Except they weren't. I guess it's a form of arrogance."

"Is that all?" Wales said.

"Yes." She looked at him and blinked.

"It doesn't seem very important," he said.

"It's just why they were unsuccessful human beings," Jena said calmly. "That's all."

"But does it mean very much to you?" It surprised him that this was what she wanted to talk about. It seemed so intimate and so irrelevant.

"They're my parents," she said.

"Do they like you?"

"Of course. I'm rich. They treat me like royalty. It's why I'm a painter," Jena said. "They didn't honor their duty to order the world in a responsible way. So I have to say things with my painting, because they didn't."

Perhaps all the time spent with children, he thought, making nothing into something, distorted your view. "But does it bother you," he asked.

"No," Jena said. "I'd like to put them in a novel, too. Do you think they would be believable in a novel?" She hoped to write a novel. She liked all media.

"I'm sure they would," he said. And he thought: how difficult could it be to write a novel? So many did it. He liked novels because they dealt with the incommensurable, with the things that couldn't be expressed any other way. What he did was so much the opposite. He dealt with things that happened. The wrapping of the Reichstag. The funeral of a phony princess. Failed actualities, with his reactions to make up for the failure.

Someone knocked loudly on the door at the end of the short, dark hallway, and then opened it. He'd forgotten to turn the lock.

"Housekee-*ping*?" a young woman's bright voice spoke. A bar of yellow light entered the room from the corridor outside.

"No!" Jena said loudly, her face, so close to his, startled, sharply unpretty. Her mouth could look surprisingly cruel, though she wasn't especially cruel that he had seen. "*No* housekeeping."

"Housekee-*ping*?" the voice said again, happily. "Would you like to be your bed turned down?"

"No!" Jena shouted. "*Not*. No bed turned down."

"Okay. Thank you." The door clicked closed.

Jena sat for a moment in her chair, in the candlelight, as if she was very displeased. Her hands were clasped, her mouth tightly shut.

He could sense her heart beating stern, insistent beats. He'd thought, naturally enough, that it was her husband. She must've thought so. And sometime, of course, it would be, long after it mattered. "Would you like *to be* your bed turned down," she said ruefully.

He looked around the darkened room. A tall wood-and-brass clock with a motionless brass pendulum stood in the shadows against the wall. There was a pretty decorative fireplace and a mantel. There was a print in a gold frame. Caravaggio. *The Calling of St. Michael*. He'd seen it in the Louvre. A glass of wine would be nice now, he thought. He looked around for a bottle on a table surface, but saw none. Jena's clothes were all put away, as though she'd lived here for months, which was how she liked things: ordered surfaces, an aura of permanence, as if everything, including herself, had a long history. It was *her* form of kindness: to make things appear solid, reliable.

"Have you ever killed anyone?" she said.

"No," Wales said. She liked to think of him not as a journalist but as a spy. It was her way to make him opaque, to keep herself off-balance. She had asked very little about what he did. At first, when they'd gone for a drink, she'd been interested. But after that she wasn't.

"Would you?"

"No," Wales said. "Do you have someone in mind?" He realized he still had on his coat and tie.

"No," Jena said and smiled and widened her eyes, as if it was a joke.

He thought for the second time in an hour about the woman's death he'd witnessed on Ardmore Street, about the progress of those events to their end. So much possibility, so much chance for a better outcome had been caught in that slow motion. It should make one able to see the ends of events before they happened, to forestall bad outcomes. It could be applied to love affairs.

"That's surprising," Jena said. "But it's because you're a journalist. If you were a real writer you'd be different."

She smiled at him again, and he caught the tiny faraway feeling that he could love her, could enter the mystery that way, though the opportunity would pass soon. But her willingness to say the wrong thing, to boast – he liked it. She wasn't jaded by experience, but freed by a lack of it.

"What do you do in Europe?" she said.

"I go see things and then write about them. That's all."

"Are you famous?"

"Journalists don't get famous," he said. "We make other people famous." She didn't know anything about journalists. He liked that, too.

"Someday you'll have to tell me what's the strangest thing you ever saw and then wrote about. I'd like to know about that."

"Someday I will," Wales said. "I promise."

*

Making love was eventful. At first she was almost dalliant, though selective, vaguely theatrical, practiced. And then after time – though all at once, really – engrossed, specific, unstinting, exactly as if it was all unscripted, all new ground, whatever they did. She could find the new with great naturalness, and he was moved by the sensation that something new could occur with someone: that self-awareness could take you on to immersion and then continue for a long while. He resisted nothing, abjured nothing, never lost touch with her in all of it. It was what he wanted.

And when it was over he was for a long time lost from words. She had turned on the lamp by the bed and slept with her hand covering her eyes. And he'd thought: where had this gone in my life? How would I keep this? And then: you don't. This doesn't keep. You take it when it's given.

The clock beneath the lamp said 9:19. Wales could smell the solvent and the hyacinths on her painter's table, sharp, murky aromas afloat in the warm room. Outside, voices spoke in the hall. Twice the phone rang. He showered, then walked to the window while she slept, and looked at the painted photograph, the two people, their smiling Midwestern features distorted. She must hate them. Then he remembered the Bacons in the Tate. The apes in agony.

What he wanted to think about then, was the funeral day in

London. It was a relief to think about it. The balmy Saturday with summer lasting on. He'd taken the train from some friends' outside of Oxford. The station – Paddington – had been empty, its long, echoing platforms hushed in the watery light, the streets outside the same. Though the tabloids had their tombstone headlines up. *WE MOURN! WE GRIEVE! THEY WEEP! GOOD-BYE.*

At the Russell Hotel, he'd stayed in and watched it all on TV. It was an event for TV anyway – his reactions were the story. Passing on the screen were the cortège, the acre of memorials, the soldiers, the bier, the Queen, the Prince. The awful brother. The boys with their perfect large teeth and the whites of their eyes too white. Through the open window, in with a breeze, he'd heard someone say – a woman, possibly in the next room, watching it all just as he was – "This'll never happen again, will it?" she'd said. "Ya can't say that about much, can ya? *Completely* unique, ya know? Well, not her, of course. She wasn't unique. She was a whoor. Well, sure, maybe not a whoor. But you know."

In America it was five AM. He wondered if anyone would be up watching.

And to all of it his reactions were: *How strange to have a royal family. She was never a beauty. What did it all cost? Death by automobile is always slightly trivial. People applauded the hearse. What does one write in a condolence book? It's really themselves they're pitying. How will they feel in a month? In a year? We magnify everything to learn if we're right. Someone* – and this is what he wrote finally, the crux of it, the literature of the failed actuality – *someone has to tell us what's important, because we no longer know.*

The next day he'd learned that his friend's wife had died in Oxford. An aneurysm. Very sudden. Very brief and painless. Only, no one could send flowers. All the flowers were spoken for, which seemed to point everything up badly. "The English. We've learned something about ourselves, haven't we, James?" his friend said bitterly, as they sat in his car outside the Oxford station, waiting for other friends to arrive. For the other funeral. The real-er one.

"What is it?" Wales said.

"That we're as stupid as the next bunch. As stupid as you are. That's all new to us, you see. We've never exactly known that until now."

Why that all came back to him he couldn't say. Stories he wrote usually didn't. Though later, it had been easy to write a lecture whose theme was, "Failed Actuality: How We Discover the Meaning of the Things We See." In it he'd retold the story of his friend's wife's death as a point of contrast. Which was when Jena had come into the picture, and they'd begun to hurry.

From the window, he watched onto the little wedge of public park between the hotel's back entrance and the Drive, still solid with cars this late. Taxis cruised past, their yellow roof-lights signaling *at liberty*. A jogger in bright orange bounced alone along the concrete beach that curved up to Lincoln Park. A man with two Weimaraners had stopped to sprinkle breadcrumbs on the park benches. All expelled soundless breaths into the night.

*

Outside on the cold Avenue they walked to the restaurant she preferred. Not far – Walton Street. She liked going to one place over and over until she tired of it and then would never go back. The wind was gusting. Lights up Michigan glittered. Traffic hummed but was thinner. The canyon of buildings seemed festive, a white background of night light and the startling half moon nearly lost in hazy distance. A skiff of snow had blown against the curbs. Heavy coats a must. Wales felt good, at ease with things. Unburdened. Not at all unstrung.

In the hotel lobby there'd been a wedding party with a bride, but no sign of Jim with the tickets. No sign of a detective when they passed out the main doors.

On the brisk walk, Jena's mind was loosened after making love, as if she couldn't match things right. She mentioned her husband and their therapy – all his idea, she said, her face hidden in a sable parka her husband had certainly paid for. She'd been fine with things, she said. But *he'd* wanted something more, something he couldn't quite describe but could feel vividly the lack of. A sense of locatedness was absent – his words – something she should somehow contribute to. "I thought a therapist would at least tell me something important, right?" Jena said. "'Forget marriage.' Or, 'Here's a better way to do it.' Why else go? Except that's not in the package. And the package gets expensive."

Wales thought about Jena's husband, about conversations he and the husband could have. How they might like each other. The husband would no doubt think Jena was out of her head just for being the way she was – so different, she would seem, from real estate. It made him happy that Jena had someone to feel certain about; someone willing to be complicit in his own deception; that there were these children. Her circle of affection. What else was marriage if not a circle of affection?

"It really seems so hopeless, doesn't it?" She laughed, too loud.

"Maybe no one could . . . " He started to say something extremely banal but stopped. He shook his head "no."

It made her smile. Her face was softened, so appealing even in the blasted air, her lips slightly bruised. She took his hand, which he found to be trembling. Again, the vigor of lovemaking, he thought. He had an urge, a strong one just then, to tell her he loved her – here on the street. But by stopping mid-sentence he once again curtailed revealing himself. She preferred that. A pledge of love was inappropriate, even if he'd felt it.

He wished, though, that his hands wouldn't tremble, since now was the best time, the moment after making love, when everything seemed possible, easy, when they could surprise each other with a look, change almost anything with an off-hand remark. It had nothing to do with revealing yourself.

"When you leave Chicago, where're you going?" Jena said. She took his arm as she had the first night, and they stepped out into Michigan Avenue at the light. The air was colder in the wide street. A group of young nuns hurried past, bound for The Drake in their bright blue habits. They were laughing about the cold. Jena smiled at them.

"London," Wales said, the wind biting in under his collar. He'd been thinking about London again, about his widowed friend in Oxford. He preferred returning to Europe through England. The easy entry.

"Do you still keep your flat in Berlin?" She was just talking still, not paying attention, light-headed after being with him. They were on the street in Chicago, in winter, going for supper late. Saying, "keep your flat" must feel good. He'd felt that way. It was like saying, "We live in the Sixth." Or, "It's just off the King's Road." Or, "We took rooms behind the Prado." Simple, harmless things.

"Yes. It's in Uhlandstrasse," he said.

"Is that in the East?"

"No. It's in the rich quarter. Near the Zoo and the Paris Bar. Ku-damm. Savignyplatz." She didn't know what these words meant, which was fine. She could hear them.

They were in sight of her restaurant. People were walking out the door, struggling into overcoats. Off the Avenue, the wind suddenly vanished, making the air feel almost spring-like. They passed the windows of a large, radiantly lit bookstore. People were having coffee and talking at high, round tables. All those books, Wales thought. It would be nice – he could suddenly feel it – to ride the train in from Gatwick, to have a morning to himself, read a book. There was a pure thought.

"If I asked you something important," Jena said, "would you not be shocked?" She held his arm, but slowed on the sidewalk, still beside the bookstore.

"I'd try not to be," Wales said, and looked at her with affection. This was not like her, to make a plea. But it was good. New.

"If I asked you to kill my husband, would you do it?" Jena looked up at him and blinked. Her hazel eyes were wide, swimming but dry. Two dark discs in white that seemed to grow larger. Her face was intent on him. "For me? If I'd love you? If I'd go away with you? At least for a while?"

Wales thought for just that instant about how they looked. A handsome, tall man dressed in a heavy camel hair coat. Hatless, with gray in his hair. Highly shined black shoes from Germany. And Jena, in a sable parka and wool trousers, expensive, heavy gloves. Expensive boots. They looked good together, even on the cold street. They made a pair. They could be in love.

"No, I guess I wouldn't," Wales said.

Jena turned and looked quickly back at the Avenue, where a driver had slammed on brakes and skidded over the frozen pavement. Two policemen in a white and blue cruiser waited at the curb, watching the car as it stopped sideways in the middle of the intersection. Perhaps she felt someone was following her. "We're doing exactly what we want to now, aren't we?" she said, distracted by the commotion.

"I am," Wales said.

She looked at him and smiled tightly. He never knew what she thought. Possibly she was more like her parents than she realized. "It was just something to say," she said and cleared her throat. "You shouldn't take me so seriously."

"Wonderful," Wales said, and smiled.

"Believe it, then," Jena said stiffly. "Everybody comes before somebody. Somebody always comes after." She paused as if she wanted to say something more about that but then didn't. "Why don't we eat," she said, and began to move along toward the restaurant's glass doors which were just at that moment opening again onto the street.

*

At dinner she talked about everything that came in her head. She said they should go dancing tonight, that she knew a place only a cab ride away. A black neighborhood. She asked if Wales liked dancing at all. He did, he said. She asked if he liked blues, and he said he did, though he didn't much. She looked pale now in her black turtleneck with a strand of small pearls. She was wearing her wedding ring and a great square emerald ring he'd never seen before. They drank red wine and ate squab and touched hands like lovers across the small window table. Someone would know her here, but she didn't mind. She was feeling reckless. What did it hurt?

She talked about a novel she was reading, which interested her. It was all about an English girl who'd once been an ingénue. There had been an influential film in France, and for a time the girl was famous. Then one thing and another went wrong. Eventually she came to live in Prague, alone, older, a former addict. Jena felt identification with her, she said, thought her story could be set in America. Somehow her parents could be in it, too.

After that she talked about her little girls, whom she loved, and then more about her husband whom she'd asked him to kill and who, she said, was at his best a mild but considerate lover. She talked about scratching her cornea in Munich once, about what a bad experience that'd been – finding an ophthalmologist with American training, one who spoke English, one who sterilized things properly, one whose assistants weren't heroin addicts or hemophiliacs. He realized that nothing he could do or say would have any effect on her now. Yet what kind of person would she be if he could so easily affect her. And being with her was such a pleasure. It made him feel wonderful, insulated. He wanted to see her again. Next week. Arrange something for then.

Only, he recognized, she was just now talking herself out of the last parts of being interested in him. Something must've seemed weak. Not being willing to kill someone, or at least say he would. She was raising the stakes, making it up as she went along until he failed.

"Tell me something that happened to *you*, Jimmy," she said. "You really haven't talked much tonight. I've just chattered on." She hadn't used the name "Jimmy" before. She was pale, but her dark eyes were sparkling.

"I was robbed tonight," Wales said. "On the way out to my car at school. A black man stopped me in the parking lot and asked to borrow a dollar, and when I brought my billfold out he grabbed at it. Knocked it out of my hand. Scattered money all around."

"My God," Jena said. "What happened then?"

"We scuffled. He tried to pick up the money, but I hit him, and then he just ran off. He got a few dollars. Not much." He stared at her across the table full of empty plates.

"You didn't tell me any of this before, did you?"

"No," Wales said. "I was happy to be with you and not to think about it."

"But weren't you hurt?" She extended one hand across the table's width and gently touched his.

"No, I wasn't," Wales said. "Not at all."

"Did it scare you?" she said. Interest rekindled in her eyes. She liked it that he was a man who withheld facts, who could make love, eat dinner, consider dancing and still keep all this to himself. She liked it that he would fight another man. Come to blows.

"It *did* scare me," Wales said. "But the thing I remember, and I don't remember very much, was how his hand felt when it hit *my* hand. There was terrible force in it. It wasn't like anything I'd ever felt. It was need and desperation at one time. It was attractive. I'm sure I won't ever forget it."

Wales took a sip of his wine and stared at her. All of this had happened to him two months ago, when he first came back to America. Not tonight. He hadn't fought such a man at all, but *had* been hit as he'd said and felt about it the way he'd just told her. Only, not now. He wished, for an instant, that he could feel that force again. How satisfying that had been. The certainty. She liked this story. Perhaps it would fix something.

"Are you sure you're not hurt?" Jena said, folding her napkin, her eyes lowered.

"Oh no," Wales said. "I'm not hurt. I'm perfectly fine."

"You're lucky to be alive, is what you are," she said, and glanced at him as her eyes sought the waiter.

"I know," Wales said. "I'll add it to my list of lucky things."

*

On the street, in front of The Drake, they stopped near the busy corner at Michigan, where taxis turned and idled past. It was after midnight, and seemed warmer. The wind had settled. In the curb gutters, ice was turning to murky water. The hotel glowed golden in the night above them.

They simply stood. Wales looked up the side street toward the lake as if he planned to hail a taxi.

"I'll be going home in the morning," she said and smiled at him, pulled her hair back on one side and held it there.

"Home, home," Wales said. "I'll be going too, then." He wished he could stay longer. He felt her room key card still in his pocket. That was over.

A man almost directly beside them on the street was talking into a pay phone. He had on a tuxedo jacket and a pair of nice patent leather shoes. He'd been to a party in The Drake, but now seemed desperate about something.

Wales had expected to tell her about the woman he had seen killed, about the astonishment of that, to retell it – the slowing of time, the stateliness of events, the sensation that the worst could be avoided, the future improved by a more gradual unfolding. But he had no wish now to reveal the things he could be made to think, how his mind worked, or what he could feel in response to events. Better to be a spy, to be close to her now, satisfied with her, think exclusively about her. He knew he was not yet distinguishing things perfectly, wasn't confident which feelings were his real ones, or how he would think about events later. It was not, perhaps, *so* easy to reveal yourself.

"Are you happy with these days?" he heard her say. She was smiling at him out on the cold sidewalk. "These were wonderful days, weren't they? Wouldn't it be nice to have a thousand of them?"

"I'm sorry they're over," Wales said. The man in the tuxedo jacket slammed the phone down and walked quickly away, toward the hotel's lighted marquee. "Could I ask you something," he said. He felt like he was shouting.

"Yes," she said. "Do ask me."

"Did this give you anything?" Wales said. "Did *I* give you anything you cared about? It seemed like you wanted there to be an outcome."

"What an odd thing to ask," Jena said, her eyes shining, growing large again. She seemed about to laugh, but then suddenly moved to him, stood on tiptoes and kissed him on the mouth, hard, put her cold cheek to his cheek and said, "Yes. You gave me *so* much. You gave me all there was. Didn't you? That's what I wanted."

"Yes," Wales said. "I did. That's right." He smiled at her.

"Good," she said. "Good." Then she turned away, and hurried toward the revolving doors as the man in the tuxedo had done, and quickly disappeared. Though he waited then for a time, just outside the yellow marquee – a man standing alone in a brown coat; waited until whatever disordered feelings he had about their moment of departure could be fully experienced and then diminish and become less a barrier. They were not bad feelings, not an unfamiliar moment, not the opening onto desolation. They were simply the outcome. And in a short while, possibly at some instant during his drive back up the lake, he would feel a small release, an unburdening, the sensation of events being completed, so that over time he would think less and less about it until it all seemed, upon reflection, to be almost perfect.

Calling

A year after my father departed, moved to St. Louis, and left my mother
and me behind in New Orleans to look after ourselves in whatever
manner we could, he called on the telephone one afternoon and asked
to speak to me. This was before Christmas, 1961. I was home from
military school in Florida. My mother had begun her new singing
career, which meant taking voice lessons at a local academy, and also
letting a tall black man who was her accompanist move into our house
and into her bedroom, while passing himself off to the neighborhood
as the yard man. William Dubinion was his name, and together he
and my mother drank far too much and filled up the ashtrays and played
jazz recordings too loud and made unwelcome noise until late, which
had not been how things were done when my father was there.
However, it was done *because* he was not there, and because he had gone
off to St. Louis with another man, an ophthalmologist named Francis
Carter, never to come back. I think it seemed to my mother that in view
of these facts it didn't matter what she did or how she lived, and that
doing the worst was finally not much different from doing the best.

They're all dead now. My father. My mother. Dr. Carter. The black accompanist, Dubinion. Though occasionally I'll still see a man on St. Charles Avenue, in the business district, a man entering one of the new office buildings they've built – a tall, handsome, long-strided, flaxen-haired, youthful, slightly ironic-looking man in a seersucker suit, bow tie and white shoes, who will remind me of my father, or how he looked, at least, when these events occurred. He must've looked that way, in fact, all of his years, into his sixties. New Orleans produces men like my father, or once did: club-men, racquets players, deft, balmy-day sailors, soft-handed Episcopalians with progressive attitudes, good educations, effortless manners, but with secrets. These men, when you meet them on the sidewalk or at some uptown dinner, seem like the very best damn old guys you could ever know. You want to call them up the very next day and set some plans going. It seems you always knew about them, that they were present in the city but you just hadn't seen a lot of them – a glimpse here and there. They seem exotic, and your heart expands with the thought of a long friendship's commencement and your mundane life taking a new and better turn. So you do call, and you do see them. You go *spec* fishing off Pointe à la Hache. You stage a dinner and meet their pretty wives. You take a long lunch together at Antoine's or Commander's and decide to do this every week from now on to never. Yet someplace along late in the lunch you hit a flat spot. A silent moment occurs, and your eyes meet in a way that could signal a deep human understanding you'd never ever have to speak about. But what you see is, suddenly – and it *is* sudden and fleeting – you see this man is far, far away from you, so far in fact as not even to realize it. A smile could be playing on his face. He may just have said something charming or incisive or flatteringly personal to you. But then the far, far away awareness dawns, and you know you're nothing to him and will probably never even see him again, never take the trouble. Or, if you do chance to see him, you'll cross streets mid-block, cast around for exits in crowded dining rooms, sit longer than you need to in the front seat of your car to let such a man go around a corner or disappear into the very building I mentioned. You avoid him. And it is not that there is anything so wrong with him, nothing unsavory or misaligned. Nothing sexual. You just know he's not for you. And that is an end to it. It's simple really. Though of course it's more complicated when the man in question is your father.

When I came to the telephone and my father's call – my mother had answered, and they had spoken some terse words – my father began right away to talk, "Well, let's see, is it Van Cliburn, or Mickey Mantle?" These were two heroes of the time whom I had gone on and on about and alternately wanted to be when my father was still in our lives. I had already forgotten them.

"Neither one," I said. I was in the big front hall, where the telephone alcove was. I could see outside through the glass door to where William Dubinion was on his knees in the monkey grass that bordered my mother's camellias. It was a fine situation, I thought – staring at my mother's colored boyfriend while talking to my father in his far-off city, living as he did. "Oh, of course," my father said. "Those were our last year's fascinations."

"It was longer ago," I said. My mother made a noise in the next room. I breathed her cigarette smoke, heard the newspaper crackle. She was listening to everything, and I didn't want to seem friendly to my father, which I did not in any case feel. I felt he was a bastard.

"Well now, see here, ole Buck Rogers," my father continued. "I'm calling up about an important matter to the future of mankind. I'd like to know if you'd care to go duck hunting in the fabled Grand Lake marsh. With me, that is. I have to come to town in two days to settle some legal business. My ancient father had a trusted family retainer named Renard Theriot, a disreputable old *Yat*. But Renard could unquestionably blow a duck call. So, I've arranged for his son, Mr. Renard, Jr., to put us both in a blind and call in several thousand ducks for our pleasure." My father cleared his throat in the stagy way he always did when he talked like this – high-falutin'. "I mean if you're not over-booked, of course," he said, and cleared his throat again.

"I might be," I said, and felt strange even to be talking to him. He occasionally called me at military school, where I had to converse with him in the orderly room. Naturally, he paid all my school bills, sent an allowance, and saw to my mother's expenses. He no doubt paid for William Dubinion's services, too, and wouldn't have cared what their true nature was. He had also conceded us the big, white Greek Revival raised cottage on McKendall Street in up-town. (McKendall is our family name – *my* name. It is such a family as that.) But still it was very odd to think that your father was living with another man in a distant city, and was calling up to ask you to go duck hunting. And then to have my mother listening, sitting and smoking and reading the *States Item*, in the very next room and thinking whatever she must've been thinking. It was nearly too much for me.

And yet, I *wanted* to go duck hunting, to go by boat out into the marsh that makes up the vast, brackish tidal land south and east of our city. I had always imagined I'd go with my father when I was old enough. And I *was* old enough now, and had been taught to fire a rifle – though not a shotgun – in my school. Also, when we spoke that day, he didn't sound to me like some man who was living with another man in St. Louis. He sounded much as he always had in our normal life when I had gone to Jesuit and he had practiced law in the Hibernia Bank building, and we were a family. Something I think about my father – whose name was Boatwright McKendall and who was only forty-one years old at the time – something about him must've wanted things to be as they had been before he met his great love, Dr. Carter. Though you could also say that my father just wanted not to have it be that he couldn't do whatever he wanted; wouldn't credit that anything he did might be deemed wrong, or be the cause of hard feeling or divorce or terrible scandal such as what sees you expelled from the law firm your family started a hundred years ago and that bears your name; or that you conceivably caused the early death of your own mother from sheer disappointment. And in fact if anything he did *had* caused someone difficulty, or ruined a life, or set someone on a downward course – well, then he just largely ignored it, or agreed to pay money about it, and afterward tried his level best to go on as if the world was a smashingly great place for everyone and we could all be wonderful friends. It was the absence I mentioned before, the skill he had to not be where he exactly was, but yet to seem to be present to any but the most practiced observer. A son, for instance.

"Well, now look-it here, Mr. Buck-a-roo," my father said over the telephone from – I guessed – St. Louis. Buck is what I was called and still am, to distinguish me from him (our name is the same). And I remember becoming nervous, as if by agreeing to go with him, and to see him for the first time since he'd left from a New Year's party at the Boston Club and gone away with Dr. Carter – as if by doing these altogether natural things (going hunting) I was crossing a line, putting myself at risk. And not the risk you might think, based on low instinct, but some risk you don't know exists until you feel it in your belly, the way you'd feel running down a steep hill and at the bottom there's a deep river or a canyon, and you realize you can't stop. Disappointment was what I risked, I know now. But I wanted what I wanted and would not let such a feeling stop me.

"I want you to know," my father said, "that I've cleared all this with your mother. She thinks it's a wonderful idea."

I pictured his yellow hair, his handsome, youthful, un-lined face talking animatedly into the receiver in some elegant, sunny, high-ceilinged room, beside an expensive French table with some fancy art objects on top, which he would be picking up and inspecting as he talked. In my picture he was wearing a purple smoking jacket and was happy to be doing what he was doing. "Is somebody else going?" I said.

"Oh, God no," my father said and laughed. "Like who? Francis is too refined to go duck hunting. He'd be afraid of getting his beautiful blue eyes put out. Wouldn't you, Francis?"

It shocked me to think Dr. Carter was right there in the room with him, listening. My mother, of course, was still listening to me.

"It'll just be you and me and Renard Junior," my father said, his voice going away from the receiver. I heard a second voice then, a soft, cultured voice, say something there where my father was, some possibly ironic comment about our plans. "Oh Christ," my father said in an irritated voice, a voice I didn't know any better than I knew Dr. Carter's. "Just don't say that. This is not that kind of conversation. This is Buck here." The voice said something else, and in my mind I suddenly saw Dr. Carter in a very unkind light, one I will not even describe. "Now you raise your bones at four AM on Thursday, Commander Rogers," my father said in his high-falutin' style. "Ducks are early risers. I'll collect you at your house. Wear your boots and your Dr. Dentons and nothing bright-colored. I'll supply our artillery."

It seemed odd to think that my father thought of the great house where we had all lived, and that his own father and grandfather had lived in since after the Civil War, as *my* house. It was not my house, I felt. The most it was was my mother's house, because she had married him in it and then taken it in their hasty divorce.

"How's school by the way," my father said distractedly.

"How's what?" I was so surprised to be asked that. My father sounded confused, as if he'd been reading something and lost his place on a page.

"School. You know? Grades? Did you get all A's? You should. You're smart. At least you have a smart mouth."

"I hate school," I said. I had liked Jesuit where I'd had friends. But my mother had made me go away to Sandhearst because of all the upset with my father's leaving. There I wore a khaki uniform with a blue stripe down the side of my pants' leg, and a stiff blue doorman's hat. I felt a fool at all times.

"Oh well, who cares," my father said. "You'll get into Harvard the same way I did."

"What way," I asked, because even at fifteen I wanted to go to Harvard.

"On looks," my father said. "That's how southerners get along. That's the great intelligence. Once you know that, the rest is pretty simple. The world *wants* to operate on looks. It only uses brains if looks aren't available. Ask your mother. It's why she married me when she shouldn't have. She'll admit it now."

"I think she's sorry about it," I said. I thought about my mother listening to half our conversation.

"Oh yes. I'm sure she is, Buck. We're all a little sorry *now*. I'll testify to that." The other voice in the room where he was spoke something then, again in an ironic tone. "Oh you shut up," my father said. "You just shut up that talk and stay out of this. I'll see you Thursday morning, son," my father said, and hung up before I could answer.

*

This conversation with my father occurred on Monday, the eighteenth of December, three days before we were supposed to go duck hunting. And for the days in between then and Thursday, my mother more or less avoided me, staying in her room upstairs with the door closed, often with William Dubinion, or going away in the car to her singing lessons with him driving and acting as her chauffeur (though she rode in the front seat). It was still the race times then, and colored people were being lynched and trampled on and burnt out all over the Southern states. And yet it was just as likely to cause no uproar if a proper white woman appeared in public with a Negro man in our city. There was no rule or logic to any of it. It was New Orleans, and if you could carry it off you did. Plus Dubinion didn't mind working in the camellia beds in front of our house, just for the record. In truth, I don't think he minded anything very much. He had grown up in the cotton patch in Pointe Coupeé Parish, between the rivers, had somehow made it to music school at Wilberforce in Ohio, been to Korea, and had played in the Army band. Later he barged around playing the clubs and juke joints in the city for a decade before he somehow met my mother at a society party where he was the paid entertainment, and she was putting herself into the public eye to make the case that when your husband abandons you for a rich queer, life will go on.

Mr. Dubinion never addressed a great deal to me. He had arrived in my mother's life after I had gone away to military school, and was simply a *fait accompli* when I came home for Thanksgiving. He was a tall, skinny, solemnly long-yellow-faced Negro with sallow, moist eyes, a soft lisp and enormous, bony, pink-nailed hands he could stretch up and down a piano keyboard. I don't think my mother could have thought he was handsome, but possibly that didn't matter. He often parked himself in our living room, drinking scotch whiskey, smoking cigarettes and playing tunes he made up right on my grandfather's Steinway concert grand. He would hum under his breath and grunt and sway up and back like the jazz-man Erroll Garner. He usually looked at me only out of the corner of his yellow Oriental-looking eye, as if neither of us really belonged in such a dignified place as my family's house. He knew, I suppose, he wouldn't be there forever and was happy for a reprieve from his usual life, and to have my mother as his temporary girlfriend. He also seemed to think I would not be there much longer either, and that we had this in common.

The one thing I remember him saying to me was during the two days before I went with my father to the marsh that Christmas – Dubinion's only Christmas with us, as it turned out. I came into the great shadowy living room where the piano sat beside the front window and where my mother had established a large Christmas tree with blinking lights and a gold star on top. I had a copy of *The Inferno*, which I'd decided I would read over the holidays because the next year I hoped to leave Sandhearst and be admitted to Lawrenceville, where my father had gone before Harvard. William Dubinion was again in his place at the piano, smoking and drinking. My mother had been singing "You've Changed" in her thin, pretty soprano and had left to take a rest because singing made her fatigued. When he saw the red jacket on my book he frowned and turned sideways on the bench and crossed one long thin leg over the other so his pale hairless skin showed above his black patent leather shoes. He was wearing black trousers with a white shirt, but no socks, which was his normal dress around the house.

"That's a pretty good book," he said in his soft lisping voice, and stared right at me in a way that felt accusatory.

"It's written in Italian," I said. "It's a poem about going to hell."

"So is that where you expect to go?"

"No," I said. "I don't."

"*Per me si va nella citta dolente. Per me si va nell'eterno dolore.*" That's all I remember," he said, and he played a chord in the bass clef, a spooky, rumbling chord like the scary part in a movie.

I assumed he was making this up, though of course he wasn't. "What's that supposed to mean?" I said.

"Same ole," he said, his cigarette still dangling in his mouth. "Watch your step when you take a guided tour of hell. Nothing new."

"When did you read this book?" I said standing between the two partly closed pocket doors. This man was my mother's boyfriend, her Svengali, her impresario, her seducer and corrupter (as it turned out). He was a strange, powerful man who had seen life I would never see. And I'm sure I was both afraid of him and equally afraid he would detect it, which probably made me appear superior and insolent and made him dislike me.

Dubinion looked above the keyboard at an arrangement of red pyracanthas my mother had placed there. "Well, I could say something nasty. But I won't." He took a breath and let it out heavily. "You just go ahead on with your readin'. I'll go on with my playin'." He nodded but did not look at me again. We didn't have too many more conversations after that. My mother sent him away in the winter. Once or twice he returned but, at some point, he disappeared. Though by then her life had changed in the bad way it probably had been bound to change.

*

The only time I remember my mother speaking directly to me during these two days, other than to inform me dinner was ready or that she was leaving at night to go out to some booking Dubinion had arranged, which I'm sure she paid him to arrange (and paid for the chance to sing as well), was on Wednesday afternoon, when

I was sitting on the back porch poring over the entrance require-
ment information I'd had sent from Lawrenceville. I had never seen
Lawrenceville, or been to New Jersey, never been farther away from
New Orleans than to Yankeetown, Florida, where my military school
was located in the buildings of a former Catholic hospital for sick
and crazy priests. But I thought that Lawrenceville – just the word
itself – could save me from the impossible situation I deemed myself
to be in. To go to Lawrenceville, to travel the many train miles,
and to enter whatever strange, complex place New Jersey was – all
that coupled to the fact that my father had gone there and my
name and background meant something – all that seemed to offer
escape and relief and a future better than the one I had at home in
New Orleans.

My mother had come out onto the back porch, which was glassed
in and gave a prospect down onto the back yard grass. On the manicured lawn was an arrangement of four wooden Adirondack chairs
and a wooden picnic table, all painted pink. The yard was completely
walled in and no one but our neighbors could see – if they chose to –
that William Dubinion was lying on top of the pink picnic table with
his shirt off, smoking a cigarette and staring sternly up at the warm
blue sky.

My mother stood for a while watching him. She was wearing a
pair of men's white silk pajamas, and her voice was husky. I'm sure
she was already taking the drugs that would eventually disrupt her
reasoning. She was holding a glass of milk, which was probably
not just milk but milk with gin or scotch or something in it to ease
whatever she felt terrible about.

"What a splendid idea to go hunting with your father," she said
sarcastically, as if we were continuing a conversation we'd been
having earlier, though in fact we had said nothing about it, despite
my wanting to talk about it, and despite thinking I ought to not
go and hoping she wouldn't permit it. "Do you even own a gun?" she
asked, though she knew I didn't. She knew what I did and didn't own.
I was fifteen.

"He's going to give me one," I said.

She glanced at me where I was sitting, but her expression didn't change. "I just wonder what it's like to take up with another man of your own social standing," my mother said as she ran her hand through her hair which was newly colored ash blond and done in a very neat bob, which had been Dubinion's idea. My mother's father had been a pharmacist on Prytania Street and had done well catering to the needs of rich families like the McKendalls. She had gone to Newcombe, married *up* and come to be at ease with the society my father introduced her into (though I have never thought she really cared about New Orleans society one way or the other – unlike my father, who cared about it enough to spit in its face).

"I always assume," she said, "that these escapades usually involve someone on a lower rung. A stevedore, or a towel attendant at your club." She was watching Dubinion. He must've qualified in her mind as a lower-rung personage. She and my father had been married twenty years, and at age thirty-nine, she had taken Dubinion into her life to wipe out any trace of the way she had previously conducted her affairs. I realize now, as I tell this, that she and Dubinion had just been in bed together, and he was enjoying the dreamy aftermath by lying half-naked out on our picnic table while she roamed around the house in her pajamas alone, and had to end up talking to me. It's sad to think that in a little more than a year, when I was just getting properly adjusted at Lawrenceville, she would be gone. Thinking of her now is like hearing the dead speak.

"But I don't hold it against your father. The *man* part anyway," my mother said. "Other things, of course, I do." She turned, then stepped over and took a seat on the striped-cushion wicker chair beside mine. She set her milk down and took my hand in her cool hands, and held it in her lap against her silky leg. "What if I became a very good singer and had to go on the road and play in Chicago and New York and possibly Paris? Would that be all right? You could come and see me perform. You could wear your school uniform." She pursed her lips and looked back at the yard, where

William Dubinion was laid out on the picnic table like a pharaoh.

"I wouldn't enjoy that," I said. I didn't lie to her. She was going out at night and humiliating herself and making me embarrassed and afraid. I wasn't going to say I thought this was all fine. It was a disaster and soon would be proved so.

"No?" she said. "You wouldn't come see me perform in the *Quartier Latin*?"

"No," I said. "I never would."

"Well." She let go of my hand, crossed her legs and propped her chin on her fist. "I'll have to live with that. Maybe you're right." She looked around at her glass of milk as if she'd forgotten where she'd left it.

"What other things do you hold against him?" I asked, referring to my father. The *man* part seemed enough to me.

"Oh," my mother said, "are we back to him now? Well, let's just say I hold his entire self against him. And not for my sake, certainly, but for yours. He could've kept things together here. Other men do. It's perfectly all right to have a lover of whatever category. So, he's no worse than a lot of other men. But that's what I hold against him. I hadn't really thought about it before. He fails to be any better than most men would be. That's a capital offense in marriage. You'll have to grow up some more before you understand that. But you will."

She picked up her glass of milk, rose, pulled her loose white pajamas up around her scant waist and walked back inside the house. In a while I heard a door slam, then her voice and Dubinion's, and I went back to preparing myself for Lawrenceville and saving my life. Though I think I knew what she meant. She meant my father did only what pleased him, and believed that doing so permitted others the equal freedom to do what they wanted. Only that isn't how the world works, as my mother's life and mine were living proof. Other people affect you. It's really no more complicated than that.

*

My father sat slumped in the bow of the empty skiff at the end of the plank dock. It was the hour before light. He was facing the silent, barely moving surface of Bayou Baptiste, beyond which (though I couldn't see it) was the vacant marshland that stretched as far as the Mississippi River itself, west of us and miles away. My father was bareheaded and seemed to be wearing a tan raincoat. I had not seen him in a year.

The place we were was called Reggio dock, and it was only a rough little boat camp from which fishermen took their charters out in the summer months, and duck hunters like us departed into the marsh by way of the bayou, and where a few shrimpers stored their big boats and nets when their season was off. I had never been to it, but I knew about it from boys at Jesuit who came here with their fathers, who leased parts of the marsh and had built wooden blinds and stayed in flimsy shacks and stilt-houses along the single-lane road down from Violet, Louisiana. It was a famous place to me in the way that hunting camps can be famously mysterious and have a danger about them, and represent the good and the unknown that so rarely combine in life.

My father had not come to get me as he'd said he would. Instead a yellow taxi with a light on top had stopped in front of our house and a driver came to the door and rang and told me that Mr. McKendall had sent him to drive me to Reggio – which was in St. Bernard Parish, and for all its wildness not really very far from the Garden District.

"And is that really you?" my father said from in the boat, turning around, after I had stood on the end of the dock for a minute waiting for him to notice me. A small stunted-looking man with a large square head and wavy black hair and wearing coveralls was hauling canvas bags full of duck decoys down to the boat. Around the camp there was activity. Cars were arriving out of the darkness, their taillights brightening. Men's voices were heard laughing. Someone had brought a dog that barked. And it was not cold, in spite of being the week before Christmas. The morning air felt heavy and velvety, and a light fog had risen off the bayou, which smelled as if oil or gasoline had been let into it. The mist clung to my hands and face, and made my hair under my cap feel soiled. "I'm sorry about the taxi ride," my father said from the bow of the aluminum skiff. He was smiling in an exaggerated way. His teeth were very white, though he looked thin. His pale, fine hair was cut shorter and seemed yellower than I remembered it, and had a wider part on the side. It was odd, but I remember thinking – standing looking down at my father – that if he'd had an older brother, this would be what that brother would look like. Not good. Not happy or whole-some. And of course I realized he was drinking, even at that hour. The man in the coveralls brought down three shotgun cases and laid them in the boat. "This little *yat* rascal is Mr. Rey-nard Theriot, Junior," my father said, motioning at the small, wavy-haired man. "There're some people, in New Orleans, who know him as Fabrice, or the Fox. Or Fabree-chay. Take your pick."

I didn't know what all this meant. But Renard Junior paused after setting the guns in the boat and looked at my father in an unfriendly way. He had a heavy, rucked brow, and even in the poor light, his dark complexion made his eyes seem small and penetrating. Under his coveralls he was wearing a red shirt with tiny gold stars on it.

"Fabree-chay is a duck caller of surprising subtlety," my father said too loudly. "Among, that is to say, his other talents. Isn't that right Mr. Fabrice? Did you say hello to my son, Buck, who's a very fine boy?" My father flashed his big white-toothed smile around at me, and I could tell he was taunting Renard Junior, who did not speak to me but continued his job to load the boat. I wondered how much he knew about my father, and what he thought if he knew everything.

"I couldn't locate my proper hunting attire," my father said, and looked down at the open front of his topcoat. He pulled it apart, and I could see he was wearing a tuxedo with a pink shirt, a bright-red bow tie and a pink carnation. He was also wearing white and black spectator shoes which were wrong for the Christmas season and in any case would be ruined once we were in the marsh. "I had them stored in the garage at mother's," he said, as if talking to himself. "This morning quite early I found I'd lost the key." He looked at me, still smiling. "You have on very good brown things," he said. I had just worn my khaki pants and shirt from school – minus the brass insignias – and black tennis shoes and an old canvas jacket and cap I found in a closet. This was not exactly duck hunting in the way I'd heard about from my school friends. My father had not even been to bed, and had been up drinking and having a good time. Probably he would've preferred staying wherever he'd been, with people who were his friends now.

"What important books have you been reading?" my father asked for some reason, from down in the skiff. He looked around as a boat full of hunters and the big black Labrador dog I'd heard barking motored slowly past us down Bayou Baptiste. Their guide had a sealed-beam light he was shining out on the water's misted surface. They were going to shoot ducks. Though I couldn't see where, since beyond the opposite bank of the bayou was only a flat black tree-less expanse that ended in darkness. I couldn't tell where ducks might be, or which way the city lay, or even which way East was.

"I'm reading *The Inferno*," I said and felt self-conscious for saying "Inferno" on a boat dock.

"Oh, that," my father said. "I believe that's Mr. Fabrice's favorite book. Canto Five: those who've lost the power of restraint. I think you should read Yeats's autobiography, though. I've been reading it in St. Louis. Yeats says in a letter to his friend the great John Synge that we should unite stoicism, asceticism and ecstasy. I think that would be good, don't you?" My father seemed to be assured and challenging, as if he expected me to know what he meant by these things, and who Yeats was, and Synge. But I didn't know. And I didn't care to pretend I did to a drunk wearing a tuxedo and a pink carnation, sitting in a duck boat.

"I don't know them. I don't know what those things are," I said and felt terrible to have to admit it.

"They're the perfect balance for life. All I've been able to arrange are two, however. Maybe one and a half. And how's your mother?" My father began buttoning his overcoat.

"She's fine," I lied.

"I understand she's taken on new household help." He didn't look up, just kept fiddling with his buttons.

"She's learning to sing," I said, leaving Dubinion out of it.

"Oh well," my father said, getting the last button done and brushing off the front of his coat. "She always had a nice little voice. A sweet church voice." He looked up at me and smiled as if he knew I didn't like what he was saying and didn't care.

"She's gotten much better now." I thought about going home right then, though of course there was no way to get home.

"I'm sure she has. Now get us going here, Fabree-chay," my father said suddenly.

Renard was behind me on the dock. Other boats full of hunters had already departed. I could see their lights flicking this way and that over the water, heading away from where we were still tied up, the soft putt-putts of their outboards muffled by the mist. I stepped down into the boat and sat on the middle thwart. But when Renard scooted into the stern, the boat tilted dramatically to one side just as my father was taking a long, uninterrupted drink out of a pint bottle he'd had stationed between his feet, out of sight.

"Don't go fallin' in, baby," Renard said to my father from the rear of the boat as he was giving the motor cord a strong pull. He had a deep, mellow voice, tinged with sarcasm. "I don't think nobody'll pull ya'll out."

My father, I think, didn't hear him. But I heard him. And I thought he was certainly right.

*

I cannot tell you how we went in Renard Junior's boat that morning, only that it was out into the dark marshy terrain that is the Grand Lake and is in Plaquemines Parish and seems the very end of the earth. Later, when the sun rose and the mist was extinguished, what I saw was a great surface of gray-brown water broken by low, yellow-grass islands where it smelled like tar and vegetation decomposing, and where the mud was blue-black and adhesive and rank-smelling. Though on the horizon, illuminated by the morning light were the visible buildings of the city – the Hibernia Bank where my father's office had been – nudged just above the earth's curve. It was strange to feel so outside of civilization, and yet to see it so clearly.

Of course at the beginning it was dark. Renard Junior, being small, could stand up in the rear of the skimming boat, and shine his own light over me in the middle and my father hunched in the boat's bow. My father's blond hair shone brightly and stayed back off his face in the breeze. We went for a ways down the bayou, then turned and went slowly under a wooden bridge and then out along a wide canal bordered by swamp hummocks where white herons were roosting and the first ducks of those we hoped to shoot went swimming away from the boat out of the light, suddenly springing up into the shadows and disappearing. My father pointed at these startled ducks, made a gun out of his fingers and jerked one-two-three silent shots as the skiff hurtled along through the marsh.

Naturally, I was thrilled to be there – even in my hated military school clothes, with my drunk father dressed in his tuxedo and the little monkey that Renard was, operating our boat. I believed, though, that this had to be some version of what the real thing felt like – hunting ducks with your father and a guide – and that anytime you went, even under the most perfect circumstances, there would always be something imperfect that would leave you feeling not exactly good. The trick was to get used to that feeling, or risk missing what little happiness there really was.

At a certain point when we were buzzing along the dark slick surface of the lake, Renard Junior abruptly backed off on the motor, cut his beam light, turned the motor hard left, and let the wake carry us straight into an island of marsh grass I hadn't made out. Though I immediately saw it wasn't simply an island but was also a grass-fronted blind built of wood palings driven into the mud, with peach crates lined up inside where hunters would sit and not be seen by flying ducks. As the boat nosed into the grass bank, Renard, now in a pair of hip waders, was out heeling us farther up onto the solider mud. "It's duck heaven out here," my father said, then densely coughed, his young man's smooth face becoming stymied by a gasp, so that he had to shake his head and turn away.

"He means it's the place where ducks *go* to heaven," Renard said. It was the first thing he'd said to me, and I noticed now how much his voice didn't sound much like the *yat* voices I'd heard and that supposedly sound like citizens of New York or Boston – cities of the north. Renard's voice was cultivated and mellow and inflected, I thought, like some uptown funeral director's, or a florist. It seemed to be a voice better suited to a different body than the muscular, gnarly little man up to his thighs just then in filmy, strong-smelling water, and wearing a long wavy white-trash hairstyle.

"When do the ducks come?" I said, only to have something to say back to him. My father was recovering himself, spitting in the water and taking another drink off his bottle.

Renard laughed a little private laugh he must've thought my father would hear. "When they ready to come. Just like you and me," he said, then began dragging out the big canvas decoy sacks and seemed to quit noticing me entirely.

*

Renard had a wooden pirogue hidden back in the thick grass, and when he had covered our skiff with a blanket made of straw mats, he used the pirogue to set out decoys as the sky lightened, though where we were was still dark. My father and I sat side by side on the peach boxes and watched him tossing out the weighted duck bodies to make two groups in front of our blind with a space of open water in between. I could begin to see now that what I'd imagined the marsh to look like was different from how it was. For one thing, the expanse of water around us was smaller than I had thought. Other grass islands gradually came into view a quarter mile off, and a line of green trees appeared in the distance, closer than I'd expected. I heard a siren, and then music that must've come from a car at the Reggio dock, and eventually there was the sun, a white disk burning behind the mist, and from a part of the marsh opposite from where I expected it. In truth, though, all of these things – these confusing and disorienting and reversing features of where I was – seemed good, since they made me feel placed, so that in time I forgot the ways I was feeling about the day and about life and about my future, none of which had seemed so good.

Inside the blind, which was only ten feet long and four feet wide and had spent shells and candy wrappers and cigarette butts on the planks, my father displayed the pint bottle of whiskey which was three-quarters empty. He sat for a time, once we were arranged on our crates, and said nothing to me or to Renard when he had finished distributing the decoys and had climbed into the blind to await the ducks. Something seemed to have come over my father, a great fatigue or ill feeling or a preoccupying thought that removed him from the moment and from what we were supposed to be doing there. Renard unsheathed the guns from their cases. Mine was the old A.H. Fox twenty-gauge double gun, that was heavy as lead and that I had seen in my grandmother's house many times and had handled enough to know the particulars of without ever shooting it. My grandmother had called it her "ladies gun," and she had shot it when she was young and had gone hunting with my father's father. Renard gave me six cartridges, and I loaded the chambers and kept the gun muzzle pointed up from between my knees as we watched the silver sky and waited for the ducks to try our decoys.

My father did not load up, but sat slumped against the wooden laths, with his shotgun leaned on the matted front of the blind. After a while of sitting and watching the sky and seeing only a pair of ducks operating far out of range, we heard the other hunters on the marsh begin to take their shots, sometimes several at a terrible burst. I could then see that two other blinds were across the pond we were set down on – three hundred yards from us, but visible when my eyes adjusted to the light and the distinguishing irregularities of the horizon. A single duck I'd watched fly across the sky, at first flared when the other hunters shot, but then abruptly collapsed and fell straight down, and I heard a dog bark and a man's voice, high-pitched and laughing through the soft air. "Hoo, hoo, hoo, lawd oooh lawdy," the man's voice said very distinctly in spite of the distance. "Dat mutha-scootcha was all the way to Terre Bonne Parish when I popped him." Another man laughed. It all seemed very close to us, even though we hadn't shot and were merely scanning the milky skies.

"Coon-ass bastards," my father said. "Jumpin' the shooting time. They have to do that. It's genetic." He seemed to be addressing no one, just sitting leaned against the blind's sides, waiting.

"Already *been* shootin' time," Renard Junior said, his gaze fixed upwards. He was wearing two wooden duck calls looped to his neck on leather thongs. He had yet to blow one of the calls, but I wanted him to, wanted to see a V of ducks turn and veer and come into our decoy-set, the way I felt they were supposed to.

"Now is that so, Mr. Grease-Fabrice, Mr. Fabree-chay." My father wiped the back of his hand across his nose and up into his blond hair, then closed his eyes and opened them wide, as if he was trying to fasten his attention to what we were doing, but did not find it easy. The blind smelled sour but also smelled of his whiskey, and of whatever ointment Renard Junior used on his thick hair. My father had already gotten his black and white shoes muddy and scratched, and mud on his tuxedo pants and his pink shirt and even onto his forehead. He was an unusual-looking figure to be where he was. He seemed to have been dropped out of an airplane on the way to a party.

Renard Junior did not answer back to my father calling him "Grease-Fabrice," but it was clear he couldn't have liked a name like that. I wondered why he would even be here to be talked to that way. Though of course there was a reason. Few things in the world are actually mysterious. Most things have disappointing explanations somewhere behind them, no matter how strange they seem at first.

After a while, Renard produced a package of cigarettes, put one in his mouth, but did not light it – just held it between his damp lips which were big and sensuous. He was already an odd-looking man, with his star shirt, his head too big for his body – a man who was probably in his forties and had just missed being a dwarf.

"Now there's the true sign of the *yat*," my father said. He was leaning on his shotgun, concentrating on Renard Junior. "Notice the unlit cigarette pooched out the front of the too expressive mouth. If you drive the streets of Chalmette, Louisiana, sonny, you'll see men and women and children who're all actually blood-related to Mr. Fabrice, standing in their little postage-stamp yards wearing hip boots with unlighted Picayunes in their mouths just like you see now. *Ecce Homo.*"

Renard Junior unexpectedly opened his mouth with his cigarette somehow stuck to the top of his big ugly purple tongue. He cast an eye at my father, leaning forward against his shotgun, smirking, then flicked the cigarette backward into his mouth and swallowed it without changing his expression. Then he looked at me, sitting between him and my father, and smiled. His teeth were big and brown-stained. It was a lewd act. I didn't know how it was lewd, but I was sure that it was.

"Pay no attention to him," my father said. "These are people we have to deal with. French acts, carny types, brutes. Now I want you to tell me about yourself, Buck. Are there any impossible situations you find yourself in these days? I've become expert in impossible situations lately." My father shifted his spectator shoes on the muddy floor boards, so that suddenly his shotgun, which was a beautiful Beretta over-under with silver inlays, slipped and fell right across my feet with a loud clatter – the barrels ending up pointed right at Renard Junior's ankles. My father did not even try to grab the gun as it fell.

"Pick that up right now," he said to me in an angry voice, as if I'd dropped his gun. But I did. I picked the gun up and handed it back to him, and he pinned it to the side of the blind with his knee. Something about this almost violent act of putting his gun where he wanted it reminded me of my father before a year ago. He had always been a man for abrupt moves and changes of attitude, unexpected laughter and strong emotion. I had not always liked it, but I'd decided that was what men did and accepted it.

"Do you ever hope to travel?" my father said, ignoring his other question, looking up at the sky as if he'd just realized he was in a duck blind and for a second at least, was involved in the things we were doing. His topcoat had sagged open again, and his tuxedo front was visible, smudged with mud. "You should," he said before I could answer.

Renard Junior began to blow on his duck call then, and crouched forward in front of his peach crate. And because he did, I crouched in front of mine, and my father – noticing us – squatted on his knees too and averted his face downwards. And after a few moments of Renard calling, I peered over the top of the straw wall and could see two black-colored ducks flying right in front of our blind, low and over our decoys. Renard Junior changed his calling sound to a broken-up cackle, and when he did the ducks swerved to the side and began winging hard away from us, almost as if they could fly backward.

"You let 'em see you," Renard said in a hoarse whisper. "They seen that white face."

Crouched beside him, I could smell his breath – a smell of cigarettes and sour meat that must've tasted terrible in his mouth.

"Call, goddamn it Fabrice," my father said then – shouted, really. I twisted around to see him, and he was right up on his two feet, his gun to his shoulder, his topcoat lying on the floor so that he was just in his tuxedo. I looked out at our decoys and saw four small ducks just cupping their wings and gliding toward the water where Renard had left it open. Their wings made a pinging sound.

Renard Junior immediately started his cackle call again, still crouched, his face down, in front of his peach crate. "Shoot 'em, Buck, shoot 'em," my father shouted, and I stood up and got my heavy gun to my shoulder and, without meaning to, fired both barrels, pulled both triggers at once, just as my father (who at some moment had loaded his gun) also fired one then the other of his barrels at the ducks, which had briefly touched the water but were already heading off, climbing up and up as the others had, going backwards away from us, their necks outstretched, their eyes – or so it seemed to me who had never shot at a duck – wide and frightened.

My two barrels, fired together, had hit one of Renard's decoys and shattered it to several pieces. My father's two shots had hit, it seemed, nothing at all, though one of the gray paper wads drifted back toward the water while the four ducks grew small in the distance until they were shot at by the other hunters across the pond and two of them dropped.

"That was completely terrible," my father said, standing at the end of the blind in his tuxedo, his blond hair slicked close down on his head in a way to make him resemble a child. He instantly broke his gun open and replaced the spent shells with new ones out of his tuxedo-coat pocket. He seemed no longer drunk, but completely engaged and sharp-minded, except for having missed everything.

"Y'all shot like a coupla 'ole grandmas," Renard said, disgusted, shaking his head.

"Fuck you," my father said calmly and snapped his beautiful Italian gun shut in a menacing way. His blue eyes widened, then narrowed, and I believed he might point his gun at Renard Junior. White spit had collected in the corners of his mouth, and his face had gone quickly from looking engaged to looking pale and damp and outraged. "If I need your services for other than calling, I'll speak to your owner," he said.

"Speak to yo' own owner, snooky," Renard Junior said, and when he said this he looked at me, raised his eyebrows and smiled in a way that pushed his heavy lips forward in a cruel, simian way.

"That's *enough*," my father said loudly. "That *is* absolutely enough." I thought he might reach past me and strike Renard in the mouth he was smiling through. But he didn't. He just slumped back on his peach crate, faced forward and held his newly reloaded shotgun between his knees. His white and black shoes were on top of his overcoat and ruined. His little pink carnation lay smudged in the greasy mud.

I could hear my father's hard breathing. Something had happened that wasn't good, but I didn't know what. Something had risen up in him, some force of sudden rebellion, but it had been defeated before it could come out and act. Or so it seemed to me. Silent events, of course, always occur between our urges and our actions. But I didn't know what event had occurred, only that one had, and I could feel it. My father seemed tired now, and to be considering something. Renard Junior was no longer calling ducks, but was just sitting at his end staring at the misty sky, which was turning a dense, warm luminous red at the horizon, as if a fire was burning at the far edge of the marsh. Shooting in the other blinds had stopped. A small plane inched across the sky. I heard a dog bark. I saw a fish roll in the water in front of the blind. I thought I saw an alligator. Mosquitoes appeared, which is never unusual in Louisiana.

"What do you do in St. Louis," I said to my father. It was the thing I wanted to know.

"Well," my father said thoughtfully. He sniffed, "Golf. I play quite a bit of golf. Francis has a big house across from a wonderful park. I've taken it up." He felt his forehead, where a mosquito had landed on a black mud stain that was there. He rubbed it and looked at his fingertips.

"Will you practice law up there?"

"Oh lord no," he said and shook his head and sniffed again. "They requested me to leave the firm here. You know that."

"Yes," I said. His breathing was easier. His face seemed calm. He looked handsome and youthful. Whatever silent event that had occurred had passed off of him, and he seemed settled about it. I thought I might talk about going to Lawrenceville. Duck blinds were where people had such conversations. Though it would've been better, I thought, if we'd been alone, and didn't have Renard Junior to overhear us. "I'd like to ask you . . ." I began.

"Tell me about your girlfriend situation," my father interrupted me. "Tell me the whole story there."

I knew what he meant by that, but there wasn't a story. I was in military school, and there were only other boys present, which was not a story to me. If I went to Lawrenceville, I knew there could be a story. Girls would be nearby. "There isn't any story . . ." I started to say, and he interrupted me again.

"Let me give you some advice." He was rubbing his index finger around the muzzle of his Italian shotgun. "Always try to imagine how you're going to feel *after* you fuck somebody *before* you fuck somebody. *Comprendes*? There's the key to everything. History. Morality. Philosophy. You'll save yourself a lot of misery." He nodded as if this wisdom had just become clear to him all over again. "Maybe you already know that," he said. He looked above the front of the blind where the sky had turned to fire, then looked at me in a way to seem honest and to say (so I thought) that he liked me. "Do you ever find yourself saying things in conversations that you absolutely don't believe?" He reached with his two fingers and plucked a mosquito off my cheek. "Do you," he said distractedly. "Do ya, do ya?"

I thought of conversations I'd had with Dubinion, and some I'd had with my mother. They were that kind of conversation – memorable if only for the things I didn't say. But what I said to my father was "No."

"Convenience must not matter to you much then," he said in a friendly way.

"I don't know if it does or not," I said because I didn't know what convenience meant. It was a word I'd never had a cause to use.

"Well, convenience matters to me very much. Too much, I think," my father said. I, of course, thought of my mother's assessment of him – that he was not better than most men. I assumed that caring too much for convenience led you there, and that my fault in later life could turn out to be the same one because he was my father. But I decided, at that moment, to see to it that my fault in life would not be his.

"There's one ducky duck," my father said. He was watching the sky and seemed bemused. "Fabrice, would you let me apologize for acting ugly to you, and ask you to call? How generous that would be of you. How nice." My father smiled strangely at Renard Junior, who I'd believed to be brooding.

And Renard Junior did call. I didn't see a duck, but when my father squatted down on the dirty planking where his topcoat was smeared and our empty shell casings were littered, I did too, and turned my face toward the floor. I could hear my father's breathing, could smell the whiskey on his breath, could see his pale wet knuckles supporting him unsteadily on the boards, could even smell his hair, which was warm and musty smelling. It was as close as I would come to him. And I understood that it would have to do, might even be the best there could be.

"Wait now, wait on 'im," my father said, hunkered on the wet planks, but looking up out of the tops of the eyes. He put his fingers on my hand to make me be still. I still had not seen anything. Renard Junior was blowing the long, high-pitched rasping call, followed by short bursts that made him grunt heavily down in his throat, and then the long highball call again. "Not quite yet," my father whispered. "Not yet. Wait on him." I turned my face sideways to see up, my eyes cut to the side to find *something*. "No," my father said, close to my ear. "Don't look up." I inhaled deeply and breathed in all the smells again that came off my father. And then Renard Junior said loudly, "Go on, Jesus! Go on! Shoot 'im. Shoot now. Whatchyouwaitin'on?"

I just stood up, then, without knowing what I would see, and brought my shotgun up to my shoulder before I really looked. And what I saw, coming low over the decoys, its head turning to the side and peering down at the brown water, was one lone duck. I could distinguish its green head and dark bullet eyes in the haze-burnt morning light and could hear its wings pinging. I didn't think it saw me nor heard my father and Renard Junior shouting, "Shoot, shoot, oh Jesus, shoot 'im Buck." Because when my face and gun barrel appeared above the front of the blind, it didn't change its course or begin the backward-upward maneuvering I'd already seen, which was its way to save itself. It just kept looking down and flying slowly and making its noise in the reddened air above the water and all of us.

And as I found the duck over my barrel tops, my eyes opened wide in the manner I knew was the way you shot such a gun, and yet

I thought: it's only one duck. There may not be any others. What's the good of one duck shot down? In my dreams there'd been hundreds of ducks, and my father and I shot them so that they fell out of the sky like rain, and how many there were would not have mattered because we were doing it together. But I was doing this alone, and one duck seemed wrong, and to matter in a way a hundred ducks wouldn't have, at least if I was going to be the one to shoot. So that what I did was not shoot and lowered my gun.

"What's wrong?" my father said from the floor just below me, still on all fours in his wrecked tuxedo, his face turned down expecting a gun's report. The lone duck was past us now and out of range.

I looked at Renard Junior, who was seated on his peach crate, small enough not to need to hunker. He looked at me, and made a strange face, a face I'd never seen but will never forget. He smiled and began to bat his eyelids in fast succession, and then he raised his two hands, palms up to the level of his eyes, as if he expected something to fall down into them. I don't know what that gesture meant, though I have thought of it often – sometimes in the middle of a night when my sleep is disturbed. Derision, I think; or possibly it meant he merely didn't know why I hadn't shot the duck and was awaiting my answer. Or possibly it was something else, some sign whose significance I would never know. Fabrice was a strange man. No one would've doubted it.

My father had gotten up onto his muddy feet by then, although with difficulty. He had his shotgun to his shoulder, and he shot once at the duck that was then only a speck in the sky. And of course it did not fall. He stared for a time with his gun to his shoulder until the speck of wings disappeared.

"What the hell happened?" he said, his face red from kneeling and bending. "Why didn't you shoot that duck?" His mouth was opened into a frown. I could see his white teeth, and one hand was gripping the sides of the blind. He seemed in jeopardy of falling down. He was, after all, still drunk. His blond hair shone in the misty light.

"I wasn't close enough," I said.

My father looked around again at the decoys as if they could prove something. "Wasn't close enough?" he said. "I heard the damn duck's wings. How close do you need it? You've got a gun there."

"You couldn't hear it," I said

"Couldn't hear it?" he said. His eyes rose off my face and found Renard Junior behind me. His mouth took on an odd expression. The scowl left his features, and he suddenly looked amused, the damp corners of his mouth revealing a small, flickering smile I was sure was derision, and represented his view that I had balked at a crucial moment, made a mistake, and therefore didn't have to be treated so seriously. This from a man who had left my mother and me to fend for ourselves while he disported without dignity or shame out of sight of those who knew him.

"You don't know anything," I suddenly said. "You're only . . ." And I don't know what I was about to say. Something terrible and hurtful. Something to strike out at him and that I would've regretted forever. So I didn't say any more, didn't finish it. Though I did that for myself, I think now, and not for him, and in order that I not have to regret more than I already regretted. I didn't really care what happened to him, to be truthful. Didn't and don't.

And then my father said, the insinuating smile still on his handsome lips, "Come on, sonny boy. You've still got some growing up to do, I see." He reached for me and put his hand behind my neck, which was rigid in anger and loathing. And without seeming to notice, he pulled me to him and kissed me on my forehead, and put his arms around me and held me until whatever he was thinking had passed and it was time for us to go back to the dock.

*

My father lived thirty years after that morning in December, on the Grand Lake, in 1961. By any accounting he lived a whole life after that. And I am not interested in the whys and why nots of what he did and didn't do, or in causing that day to seem life-changing for me, because it surely wasn't. Life had already changed. That morning represented just the first working out of particulars I would evermore observe. Like my father, I am a lawyer. And the law is a calling which teaches you that most of life is about adjustments, the seatings and re-seatings we perform to accommodate events occurring outside our control and over which we might not have sought control in the first place. So that when we are tempted, as I was for an instant in the duck blind, or as I was through all those thirty years, to let myself become preoccupied and angry with my father, or when I even see a man who reminds me of him, stepping into some building in a seersucker suit and a bright bow tie, I try to realize again that it is best just to offer myself release and to realize I am feeling anger all alone, and that there is no redress. We want it. Life can be seen to be about almost nothing else sometimes than our wish for redress. As a lawyer who was the son of a lawyer and the grandson of another, I know this. And I also know not to expect it.

For the record – because I never saw him again – my father went back to St. Louis and back to the influence of Dr. Carter, whom I believe was as strong a character as my father was weak. They lived on there for a time until (I was told) Dr. Carter quit the practice of medicine entirely. Then they left America and traveled first to Paris and after that to a bright white stucco house near Antibes, which I in fact once saw, completely by accident, on a side tour of a business trip, and somehow knew to be his abode the instant I came to it, as though I had dreamed it – but then couldn't get away from it fast enough, though they were both dead and buried by then.

Once, in our newspaper, early in the nineteen-seventies, I saw my father pictured in the society section amid a group of smiling, handsome crew cut men, once again wearing tuxedos and red sashes of some foolish kind, and holding champagne glasses. They were men in their fifties, all of whom seemed, by their smiles, to want very badly to be younger.

Seeing this picture reminded me that in the days after my father had taken me to the marsh, and events had ended not altogether happily, I had prayed for one of the few times, but also for the last time in my life. And I prayed quite fervently for a while and in spite of all, that he would come back to us and that our life would begin to be as it had been. And then I prayed that he would die, and die in a way I would never know about, and his memory would cease to be a memory, and all would be erased. My mother died a rather sudden, pointless and unhappy death not long afterward, and many people including myself attributed her death to him. In time, my father came and went in and out of New Orleans, just as if neither of us had ever known each other.

And so the memory was not erased. Yet because I can tell this now, I believe that I have gone beyond it, and on to a life better than one might've imagined for me. Of course, I think of life – mine – as being part of their aftermath, part of the residue of all they risked and squandered and ignored. Such a sense of life's connectedness can certainly occur, and conceivably it occurs in some places more than in others. But it is survivable. I am the proof, inasmuch as since that time, I have never imagined my life in any way other than as it is.

Reunion

When I saw Mack Bolger he was standing beside the bottom of the marble steps that bring travelers and passersby to and from the balcony of the main concourse in Grand Central. It was before Christmas last year, when the weather stayed so warm and watery the spirit seemed to go out of the season.

I was cutting through the terminal, as I often do on my way home from the publishing offices on 41st Street. I was, in fact, on my way to meet a new friend at Billy's. It was four o'clock on Friday, and the great station was athrong with citizens on their way somewhere, laden with baggage and precious packages, shouting good-byes and greetings, flagging their arms, embracing, gripping each other with pleasure. Others, though, simply stood, as Mack Bolger was when I saw him, staring rather vacantly at the crowds, as if whomever he was there to meet for some reason hadn't come. Mack is a tall, handsome, well-put-together man who seems to see everything from a height. He was wearing a long, well-fitted gabardine overcoat of some deep-olive twill – an expensive coat, I thought, an Italian coat. His brown shoes were polished to a high gloss; his trouser cuffs hit them just right. And because he was without a hat, he seemed even taller than what he was – perhaps six-three. His hands were in his coat pockets, his smooth chin slightly elevated the way a middle-aged man would, and as if he thought he was extremely visible there. His hair was thinning a little in front, but it was carefully cut, and he was tanned, which caused his square face and prominent brow to appear heavy, almost artificially so, as though in a peculiar way the man I saw was not Mack Bolger but a good-looking effigy situated precisely there to attract my attention.

For a while, a year and a half before, I had been involved with Mack Bolger's wife, Beth Bolger. Oddly enough – only because all events that occur outside New York seem odd and fancifully unreal to New Yorkers – our affair had taken place in the city of St. Louis, that largely overlookable red-brick abstraction that is neither west nor Middlewest, neither south nor north; the city lost in the middle, as I think of it. I've always found it interesting that it was both the boyhood home of T. S. Eliot, and only eighty-five years before that, the starting point of westward expansion. It's a place, I suppose, the world can't get away from fast enough.

What went on between Beth Bolger and me is hardly worth the words that would be required to explain it away. At any distance but the close range I saw it from, it was an ordinary adultery – spirited, thrilling and then, after a brief while, when we had crossed the continent several times and caused as many people as possible unhappiness, embarrassment and heartache, it became disappointing and ignoble and finally almost disastrous to those same people. Because it is the truth and serves to complicate Mack Bolger's unlikeable dilemma and to cast him in a more sympathetic light, I will say that at some point he was forced to confront me (and Beth as well) in a hotel room in St. Louis – a nice, graceful old barn called the Mayfair – with the result that I got banged around in a minor way and sent off into the empty downtown streets on a warm, humid autumn Sunday afternoon, without the slightest idea of what to do, ending up waiting for hours at the St. Louis airport for a midnight flight back to New York. Apart from my dignity, I left behind and never saw again a brown silk Hermès scarf with tassels that my mother had given me for Christmas in 1971, a gift she felt was the nicest thing she'd ever seen and perfect for a man just commencing life as a book editor. I'm glad she didn't have to know about my losing it, and how it happened.

I also did not see Beth Bolger again, except for one sorrowful and bitter drink we had together in the theater district last spring, a nervous, uncomfortable meeting we somehow felt obligated to have, and following which I walked away down 47th Street, feeling that all of life was a sorry mess, while Beth went along to see *The Iceman Cometh*, which was playing then. We have not seen each other since that leave-taking, and, as I said, to tell more would not be quite worth the words.

But when I saw Mack Bolger standing in the crowded, festive holiday-bedecked concourse of Grand Central, looking rather vacant-headed but clearly himself, so far from the middle of the country, I was taken by a sudden and strange impulse – which was to walk straight across through the eddying sea of travelers and speak to him, just as one might speak to anyone you casually knew and had unexpectedly yet not unhappily encountered. And not to impart anything, or set in motion any particular action (to clarify history, for instance, or make amends), but simply to create an event where before there was none. And not an unpleasant event, or a provocative one. Just a dimensionless, unreverberant moment, a contact, unimportant in every other respect. Life has few enough of these moments – the rest of it being so consumed by the predictable and the obligated.

I knew a few things about Mack Bolger, about his life since we'd last confronted each other semi-violently in the Mayfair. Beth had been happy to tell me during our woeful drink at the Espalier Bar in April. Our – Beth's and my – love affair was, of course, only one feature in the long devaluation and decline in her and Mack's marriage. This I'd always understood. There were two children, and Mack had been frantic to hold matters together for their sakes and futures; Beth was a portrait photographer who worked at home, but craved engagement with the wide world outside of University City – craved it in the worst way, and was therefore basically unsatisfied with everything in her life. After my sudden departure, she moved out of their house, rented an apartment near the Gateway Arch and, for a time, took a much younger lover. Mack, for his part in their upheaval, eventually quit his job as an executive for a large agri-biz company, considered studying for the ministry, considered going on a missionary journey to Senegal or French Guiana, briefly took a young lover himself. One child had been arrested for shoplifting; the other had gotten admitted to Brown. There were months of all-night confrontations, some combative, some loving and revelatory, some derisive from both sides. Until everything that could be said or expressed or threatened was said, expressed and threatened, after which a standstill was achieved whereby they both stayed in their suburban house, kept separate schedules, saw new and different friends, had occasional dinners together, went to the Opera, occasionally even slept together, but saw little hope (in Beth's case, certainly) of things turning out better than they were at the time of our joyless drink and the O'Neill play. I'd assumed at that time that Beth was meeting someone else that evening, had someone in New York she was interested in, and I felt completely fine about it.

"It's really odd, isn't it?" Beth said, stirring her long, almost pure-white finger around the surface of her *Kir Royale*, staring not at me but at the glass rim where the pink liquid nearly exceeded its vitreous limits. "We were so close for a little while." Her eyes rose to me, and she smiled almost girlishly. "You and me, I mean. Now, I feel like I'm telling all this to an old friend. Or to my brother."

Beth is a tall, sallow-faced, big-boned, ash blond woman who smokes cigarettes and whose hair often hangs down in her eyes like a forties Hollywood glamour girl. This can be attractive, although it often causes her to seem to be spying on her own conversations.

"Well," I said, "it's all right to feel that way." I smiled back across the little round blacktopped café table. It *was* all right. I had gone on.

When I looked back on what we'd done, none of it except for what we'd done in bed made me feel good about life, or that the experience had been worth it. But I couldn't undo it. I don't believe the past can be repaired, only exceeded. "Sometimes, friendship's all we're after in these sorts of things," I said. Though this, I admit, I did not really believe.

"Mack's like a dog, you know," Beth said, flicking her hair away from her eyes. He was on her mind. "I kick him, and he tries to bring me things. It's pathetic. He's very interested in Tantric sex now, whatever that is. Do you know what that even is?"

"I really don't like hearing this," I said stupidly, though it was true. "It sounds cruel."

"You're just afraid I'll say the same thing about you, Johnny." She smiled and touched her damp fingertip to her lips, which were wonderful lips.

"Afraid," I said. "Afraid's really not the word, is it?"

"Well, then, whatever the word is," Beth looked quickly away and motioned the waiter for the check. She didn't know how to be disagreed with. It always frightened her.

But that was all. I've already said our meeting wasn't a satisfying one.

*

Mack Bolger's pale gray eyes caught me coming toward him well before I expected them to. We had seen each other only twice. Once at a fancy cocktail party given by an author I'd come to St. Louis to wrest a book away from. It was the time I'd met his wife. And once more, in the Mayfair Hotel, when I'd taken an inept swing at him and he'd slammed me against a wall and hit me in the face with the back of his hand. Perhaps you don't forget people you knock around. That becomes their place in your life. I, myself, find it hard to recognize people when they're not where they belong, and Mack Bolger belonged in St. Louis. Of course, he was an exception.

Mack's gaze fixed on me, then left me, scanned the crowd uncomfortably, then found me again as I approached. His large tanned face took on an expression of stony unsurprise, as if he'd known I was somewhere in the terminal and a form of communication had already begun between us. Though, if anything, really, his face looked resigned – resigned to me, resigned to the situations the world foists onto you unwilling; resigned to himself. Resignation was actually what we had in common, even if neither of us had a language which could express that. So as I came into his presence, what I felt for him, unexpectedly, was sympathy – for having to see me now. And if I could've, I would have turned and walked straight away and left him alone. But I didn't.

"I just saw you," I said from the crowd, ten feet before I ever expected to speak. My voice isn't loud, so that the theatrically nasal male voice announcing the arrival from Poughkeepsie on track 34 seemed to have blotted it out.

"Did you have something special in mind to tell me?" Mack Bolger said. His eyes cast out again across the vaulted hall, where Christmas shoppers and over-bundled passengers were moving in all directions. It occurred to me at that instant – and shockingly – that he was waiting for Beth, and that in a moment's time I would be standing here facing her and Mack together, almost as we had in St. Louis. My heart struck two abrupt beats deep in my chest, then seemed for a second to stop altogether. "How's your face?" Mack said with no emotion, still scanning the crowd. "I didn't hurt you too bad, did I?"

"No," I said.

"You've grown a moustache." His eyes did not flicker toward me.

"Yes," I said, though I'd completely forgotten about it, and for some reason felt ashamed, as if it made me look ridiculous.

"Well," Mack Bolger said. "Good." His voice was the one you would use to speak to someone in line beside you at the post office, someone you'd never see again. Though there was also, just barely noticeable, a hint of what we used to call *juiciness* in his speech, some minor, undispersable moisture in his cheek that one heard in his *s*'s and *f* 's. It was unfortunate, since it robbed him of a small measure of gravity. I hadn't noticed it before in the few overheated moments we'd had to exchange words.

Mack looked at me again, hands in his expensive Italian coat pockets, a coat that had heavy, dark, bone buttons and long, wide lapels. Too stylish for him, I thought; for the solid man he was. Mack and I were nearly the same height, but he was in every way larger and seemed to look down to me – something in the way he held his chin up. It was almost the opposite of the way Beth looked at me.

"I live here now," Mack said, without really addressing me. I noticed he had long, dark almost feminine eyelashes, and small, perfectly shaped ears, which his new haircut put on nice display. He might've been forty – younger than I am – and looked more than anything like an army officer. A major. I thought of a letter Beth had shown me, written by Mack to her, containing the phrase, "I want to kiss you all over. Yes I do. Love, Macklin." Beth had rolled her eyes when she showed it to me. At another time she had talked to Mack on the telephone while we were in bed together naked. On that occasion, too, she'd *kept* rolling her eyes at whatever he was saying – something, I gathered, about difficulties he was having at work. Once we even engaged in a sexual act while she talked to him. I could hear his tiny, buzzing, fretful-sounding voice inside the receiver. But that was now gone. Everything Beth and I had done was gone. All that remained of it was just this – a series of moments in the great train terminal, but which, in spite of all, seemed correct, sturdy, almost classical in character, as if this later time was all that really mattered, whereas the previous, briefly passionate, linked but-now-distant moments were merely preliminary.

"Did you buy a place?" I said, and all at once felt a widely spreading vacancy open all around inside me. It was such a preposterous thing to say.

Mack's eyes moved gradually to me, and his impassive expression, which had seemed to signify one thing – resignation – began to signify something different. I knew this because a small cleft appeared in his chin.

"Yes," he said and let his eyes stay on me.

People were shouldering past us. I could smell some woman's heavy, warm-feeling perfume around my face. Music commenced in the rotunda, making the moment feel suffocating, clamorous: *We Three Kings of Orient Are, Bearing Gifts We Traverse Afar* . . .

"Yes," Mack Bolger said again, emphatically, spitting the word from between his large straight, white, nearly flawless teeth. He had grown up on a farm in Nebraska, gone to a small college in Minnesota on a football scholarship, then taken an MBA at Wharton, had done well. All that life, all that experience was now being brought into play as self-control, dignity. It was strange that anyone would call him a dog when he wasn't that at all. He was extremely admirable.

"I bought an apartment on the Upper East Side," he said and he blinked his eyelashes very rapidly. "I moved out in September. I have a new job. I'm living alone. Beth's not here. She's in Paris where she's miserable – or rather I hope she is. We're getting divorced. I'm waiting for my daughter to come down from boarding school. Is that all right? Does that seem all right to you? Does it satisfy your curiosity?"

"Yes," I said. "Of course." Mack was not angry. He was, instead, a thing that anger had no part in, or at least had long been absent from, something akin to exhaustion, where the words you say are the only true words you *can* say. Myself, I did not think I'd ever felt that way. Always for me there had been a choice.

"Do you understand me?" Mack Bolger's thick athlete's brow furrowed, as if he was studying a creature he didn't entirely understand, an anomaly of some kind, which perhaps I was.

"Yes," I said. "I'm sorry."

"Well then," he said and seemed embarrassed. He looked away, out over the crowd of moving heads and faces, as if he'd sensed someone coming.

I looked toward where he seemed to be looking. But no one was approaching us. Not Beth, not a daughter. Not anyone. Perhaps, I thought, this was all a lie, or possibly even that I'd, for an instant, lost consciousness, and this was not Mack Bolger at all, and I was dreaming everything.

"Do you think there could be someplace else you could go now?" Mack said. His big, tanned, handsome face looked imploring and exhausted. Once Beth had said Mack and I looked alike. But we didn't. That had just been her fantasy. Without really looking at me again he said, "I'll have a hard time introducing you to my daughter. I'm sure you can imagine that."

"Yes," I said. I looked around again, and this time I saw a pretty blond girl standing in the crowd, watching us from several steps away. She was holding a red nylon backpack by its straps. Something was causing her to stay away. Possibly her father had signaled her not to come near us. "Of course," I said. And by speaking I somehow made the girl's face break into a wide smile, a smile I recognized.

"Nothing's happened here," Mack said unexpectedly to me, though he was staring at his daughter. From the pocket of his overcoat he'd produced a tiny white box wrapped and tied with a red bow.

"I'm sorry?" People were swirling noisily around us. The music seemed louder. I was leaving, but I thought perhaps I'd misunderstood him. "I didn't hear you," I said. I smiled in an involuntary way.

"Nothing's happened today," Mack Bolger said. "Don't go away thinking anything happened here. Between you and me, I mean. *Nothing* happened. I'm sorry I ever met you, that's all. Sorry I ever had to touch you. You make me feel ashamed." He still had the unfortunate dampness with his *s*'s.

"Well," I said. "All right. I can understand that."

"Can you?" he said. "Well, that's very good." Then Mack simply stepped away from me, and began saying something to the blond girl standing in the crowd smiling. What he said was, "Wow-wee, boy, oh boy, do *you* look like a million bucks."

And I walked on toward Billy's then, toward the new arrangement I'd made that would take me into the evening. I had, of course, been wrong about the linkage of moments, and about what was preliminary and what was primary. It was a mistake, one I would not make again. None of it was a good thing to have done. Though it is such a large city here, so much larger than say, St. Louis, I knew I would not see him again.

Puppy

Early this past spring someone left a puppy inside the back gate of our house, and then never came back to get it. This happened at a time when I was traveling up and back to St. Louis each week, and my wife was intensely involved in the AIDS marathon, which occurs, ironically enough, around tax time in New Orleans and is usually the occasion for a lot of uncomfortable, conflicted spirits, which inevitably get resolved, of course, by good will and dedication.

To begin in this way is only to say that our house is often empty much of the day, which allowed whoever left the puppy to do so. We live on a corner in the fashionable historical district. Our house is large and old and conspicuous – typical of the French Quarter – and the garden gate is a distance from the back door, blocked from it by thick lugustrums. So to set a puppy down over the iron grating and slip away unnoticed wouldn't be hard, and I imagine was not.

"It was those kids," my wife said, folding her arms. She was standing with me inside the French doors, staring out at the puppy, who was seated on the brick pavements looking at us with what seemed like insolent curiosity. It was small and had slick, short coarse hair and was mostly white, with a few triangular black side patches. Its tail stuck alertly up when it was standing, making it look as though it might've had pointer blood back in its past. For no particular reason, I gauged it to be three months old, though its legs were long and its white feet larger than you would expect. "It's those ones in the neighborhood wearing all the black," Sallie said. "Whatever you call them. All penetrated everywhere and ridiculous, living in doorways. They always have a dog on a rope." She tapped one of the square panes with her fingernail to attract the puppy's attention. It had begun diligently scratching its ear, but stopped and fixed its dark little eyes on the door. It had dragged a red plastic dust broom from under the outside back stairs, and this was lying in the middle of the garden. "We have to get rid of it," Sallie said. "The poor thing. Those shitty kids just got tired of it. So they abandon it with us."

"I'll try to place it," I said. I had been home from St. Louis all of five minutes and had barely set my suitcase inside the front hall.

"Place it?" Sallie's arms were folded. "Place it where? How?"

"I'll put up some signs around," I said, and touched her shoulder. "Somebody in the neighborhood might've lost it. Or else someone found it and left it here so it wouldn't get run over. Somebody'll come looking."

The puppy barked then. Something (who knows what) had frightened it. Suddenly it was on its feet barking loudly and menacingly at the door we were standing behind, as though it had sensed we were intending something and resented that. Then just as abruptly it stopped, and without taking its dark little eyes off of us, squatted puppy-style and pissed on the bricks.

"That's its other trick," Sallie said. The puppy finished and delicately sniffed at its urine, then gave it a sampling lick. "What it doesn't pee on it jumps on and scratches and barks at. When I found it this morning, it barked at me, then it jumped on me and peed on my ankle and scratched my leg. I was only trying to pet it and be nice." She shook her head.

"It was probably afraid," I said, admiring the puppy's staunch little bearing, its sharply pointed ears and simple, uncomplicated pointer's coloration. Solid white, solid black. It was a boy dog.

"Don't get attached to it, Bobby," Sallie said. "We have to take it to the pound."

My wife is from Wetumpka, Alabama. Her family were ambitious, melancholy Lutheran Swedes who somehow made it to the South because her great-grandfather had accidentally invented a lint shield for the ginning process which ended up saving people millions. In one generation the Holmbergs from Lund went from being dejected, stigmatized immigrants to being moneyed gentry with snooty Republican attitudes and a strong sense of entitlement. In Wetumpka there was a dog pound, and stray dogs were always feared for carrying mange and exotic fevers. I've been there; I know this. A dogcatcher prowled around with a ventilated, louver-sided truck and big catch-net. When an unaffiliated dog came sniffing around anybody's hydrangeas, a call was made and off it went forever.

"There aren't dog pounds anymore," I said.

"I meant the shelter," Sallie said privately. "The SPCA – where they're nice to them."

"I'd like to try the other way first. I'll make a sign."

"But aren't you leaving again tomorrow?"

"Just for two days," I said. "I'll be back."

Sallie tapped her toe, a sign that something had made her unsettled. "Let's not let this drag out." The puppy began trotting off toward the back of the garden and disappeared behind one of the big brick planters of pitasporums. "The longer we keep it, the harder it'll be to give it up. And that *is* what'll happen. We'll have to get rid of it eventually."

"We'll see."

"When the time comes, I'll let *you* take it to the pound," she said.

I smiled apologetically. "That's fine. If the time comes, then I will."

We ended it there.

*

I am a long-time practitioner before the Federal Appeals Courts, arguing mostly large, complicated negligence cases in which the appellant is a hotel or a restaurant chain engaged in inter-state commerce, and who has been successfully sued by an employee or a victim of what is often some often terrible mishap. Mostly I win my cases. Sallie is also a lawyer, but did not like the practice. She works as a resource specialist, which means fund-raising, for by and large progressive causes; the homeless, women at risk in the home, children at risk in the home, nutrition issues, etc. It is a far cry from the rich, arriviste-establishment views of her family in Alabama. I am from Vicksburg, Mississippi, from a very ordinary although solid suburban upbringing. My father was an insurance-company attorney. Sallie and I met in law school at Yale, in the seventies. We have always thought of ourselves as lucky in life, and yet in no way extraordinary in our goals or accomplishments. We are simply the southerners from sturdy, supportive families who had the good fortune to get educated well and who came back more or less to home, ready to fit in. Somebody has to act on that basic human impulse, we thought, or else there's no solid foundation of livable life.

One day after the old millennium's end and the new one's beginning, Sallie said to me – this was at lunch at Le Perigord on Esplanade, our favorite place: "Do you happen to remember," she'd been thinking about it, "that first little watercolor we bought, in Old Saybrook? The tilted sailboat sail you could barely recognize in all the white sky. At that little shop near the bridge?" Of course I remembered it. It's in my law office in Place St. Charles, a cherished relic of youth.

"What about it?" We were at a table in the shaded garden of the restaurant where it smelled sweet from some kind of heliotrope. Tiny wild parrots were fluttering up in the live-oak foliage and chittering away. We were eating a cold crab soup.

"Well," she said. Sallie has pale, almost animal blue eyes and translucently caramel northern European skin. She has kept away from the sun for years. Her hair is cut roughly and parted in the middle like some Bergman character from the sixties. She is forty-seven and extremely beautiful. "It's completely trivial," she went on, "but how did we ever know back then that we had any taste. I don't really even care about it, you know that. You have much better taste than I do in most things. But why were we sure we wouldn't choose that little painting and then have it be horrible? Explain that to me. And what if our friends had seen it and laughed about us behind our backs? Do you ever think that way?"

"No," I said, my spoon above my soup, "I don't."

"You mean it isn't interesting? Or, eventually we'd have figured out better taste all by ourselves?"

"Something like both," I said. "It doesn't matter. Our taste is fine and would've been fine. I still have that little boat in my office. People pass through and admire it all the time."

She smiled in an inwardly pleased way. "Our friends aren't the point, of course. If we'd liked sad-clown paintings or put antimacassars on our furniture, I wonder if we'd have a different, *worse* life now," she said. She stared down at her lined-up knife and spoons. "It just intrigues me. Life's so fragile in the way we experience it."

"What's the point?" I had to return to work soon. We have few friends now in any case. It's natural.

She furrowed her brow and scratched the back of her head using her index finger. "It's about how altering one small part changes everything."

"One star strays out of line and suddenly there's no Big Dipper?" I said. "I don't really think you mean that. I don't really think you're getting anxious just because things might have gone differently in your life." I will admit this amused me.

"That's a very frivolous way to see it." She looked down at her own untried soup and touched its surface with the rim of her spoon. "But yes, that's what I mean."

"But it isn't true," I said and wiped my mouth. "It'd still be the thing it is. The Big Dipper or whatever you cared about. You'd just ignore the star that falls and concentrate on the ones that fit. Our life would've been exactly the same, despite bad art."

"You're the lawyer, aren't you?" This was condescending, but I don't think she meant it to be. "You just ignore what doesn't fit. But it wouldn't be the same, I'm sure of that."

"No," I said. "It wouldn't have been exactly the same. But almost."

"There's only one Big Dipper," she said and began to laugh.

"That we know of, and so far. True."

This exchange I give only to illustrate what we're like together – what seems important and what doesn't. And how we can let potentially difficult matters go singing off into oblivion.

*

The afternoon the puppy appeared, I sat down at the leather-top desk in our dining room where I normally pay the bills and diligently wrote out one of the hand-lettered signs you see posted up on laundromat announcement boards and stapled to telephone poles alongside advertisements for new massage therapies, gay health issues and local rock concerts. PUPPY, my sign said in black magic marker, and after that the usual data with my office phone number and the date (March 23rd). This sheet I Xeroxed twenty-five times on Sallie's copier. Then I found the stapler she used for putting up the AIDS marathon posters, went upstairs and got out an old braided leather belt from my closet, and went down to the garden to take the puppy with me. It seemed good to bring him along while I stapled up the posters about him. Someone could recognize him, or just take a look at him and see he was available and attractive and claim him on the spot. Such things happen, at least in theory.

When I found him he was asleep behind the lugustrums in the far corner. He had worked and scratched and torn down into the bricky brown dirt and made himself a loll deep enough that half of his little body was out of sight below ground level. He had also broken down several lugustrum branches and stripped the leaves and chewed the ends until the bush was wrecked.

When he sensed me coming forward he flattened out in his hole and growled his little puppy growl. Then he abruptly sat up in the dirt and aggressively barked at me in a way that – had it been a big dog – would've alarmed me and made me stand back.

"Puppy?" I said, meaning to sound sympathetic. "Come out." I was still wearing my suit pants and white shirt and tie – the clothes I wear in court. The puppy kept growling and then barking at me, inching back behind the wrecked lugustrum until it was in the shadows against the brick wall that separates us from the street. "Puppy?" I said again in a patient, cajoling way, leaning in amongst the thick, green leaves. I'd made a loop out of my belt, and I reached forward and slipped it over his head. But he backed up farther when he felt the weight of the buckle, and unexpectedly began to yelp – a yelp that was like a human shout. And then he turned and began to claw up the bricks, scratching and springing, his paws scraping and his ugly little tail jerking, and at the same time letting go his bladder until the bricks were stained with hot, terrified urine.

Which, of course, made me lose heart since it seemed cruel to force this on him even for his own good. Whoever had owned him had evidently not been kind. He had no trust of humans, even though he needed us. To take him out in the street would only terrify him worse, and discourage anyone from taking him home and giving him a better life. Better to stay, I decided. In our garden he was safe and could have a few hours' peace to himself.

I reached and tried to take the belt loop off, but when I did he bared his teeth and snapped and nearly caught the end of my thumb with his little white incisor. I decided just to forget the whole effort and to go about putting up my signs alone.

*

I stapled up all the signs in no time – at the laundromat on Barracks Street, in the gay deli, outside the French patisserie, inside the coffee shop and the adult news on Decatur. I caught all the telephone poles in a four-block area. On several of the poles and all the message boards I saw that others had lost pets too, mostly cats. *Hiroki's Lost. We're utterly disconsolate. Can you help? Call Jamie or Hiram at . . .*

Or, *We miss our Mittens. Please call us or give her a good home. Please!* In every instance as I made the rounds I stood a moment and read the other notices to see if anyone had reported a lost puppy. But (and I was surprised) no one had.

On a short, disreputable block across from the French Market, a section that includes a seedy commercial strip (sex shops, tee shirt emporiums and a slice-of-pizza outlet), I saw a group of the young people Sallie had accused of abandoning our puppy. They were, as she'd remembered, sitting in an empty store's doorway, dressed in heavy, ragged black clothes and thick-soled boots with various chains attached and studded wristlets, all of them – two boys and two girls – pierced, and tattooed with Maltese crosses and dripping knife blades and swastikas, all dirty and utterly pointless but abundantly surly and apparently willing to be violent. These young people had a small black dog tied with a white cotton cord to one of the boys' heavy boots. They were drinking beer and smoking but otherwise just sitting, not even talking, simply looking malignantly at the street or at nothing in particular.

I felt there was little to fear, so I stopped in front of them and asked if they or anyone they knew had lost a white and black puppy with simple markings in the last day, because I'd found one. The one boy who seemed to be the oldest and was large and unshaven with brightly dyed purple and green hair cut into a flat-top – he was the one who had the dog leashed to his boot – this boy looked up at me without obvious expression. He turned then to one of the immensely dirty-looking, fleshy, pale-skinned girls crouched farther back in the grimy door stoop, smoking (this girl had a crude cross tattooed into her forehead like Charles Manson is supposed to have) and asked, "Have you lost a little white and black puppy with simple markings, Samantha. I don't think so. Have you? I don't remember you having one today." The boy had an unexpectedly youthful-sounding, nasally Midwestern accent, the kind I'd been hearing in St. Louis that week, although it had been high-priced attorneys who were speaking it. I know little enough about young people, but it occurred to me that this boy was possibly one of these lawyers' children, someone whose likeness you'd see on a milk carton or a website devoted to runaways.

"Ah, no," the girl said, then suddenly spewed out laughter.

The big, purple-haired boy looked up at me and produced a disdainful smile. His eyes were the darkest, steeliest blue, impenetrable and intelligent.

"What are you doing sitting here?" I wanted to say to him. "I know you left your dog at my house. You should take it back. You should all go home now."

"I'm sorry, sir," the boy said mocking me, "but I don't believe we'll be able to help you in your important search." He smirked around at his three friends.

I started to go. Then I stopped and handed him a paper sign and said, "Well, if you hear about a puppy missing anywhere."

He said something as he took it. I don't know what it was, or what he did with the sign when I was gone, because I didn't look back.

*

That evening Sallie came home exhausted. We sat at the dining room table and drank a glass of wine. I told her I'd put up my signs all around, and she said she'd seen one and it looked fine. Then for a while she cried quietly because of disturbing things she'd seen and heard at the AIDS hospice that afternoon, and because of various attitudes – typical New Orleans attitudes, she thought – voiced by some of the marathon organizers, which seemed callous and constituted right things done for wrong reasons, all of which made the world seem – to her, at least – an evil place. I have sometimes thought she might've been happier if we had chosen to have children or, failing that, if we'd settled someplace other than New Orleans, someplace less parochial and exclusive, a city like St. Louis, in the wide Middlewest – where you can be less personally involved in things but still be useful. New Orleans is a small town in so many ways. And we are not from here.

I didn't mention what the puppy had done to the lugustrums, or the kids I'd confronted at the French Market, or her description of them having been absolutely correct. Instead I talked about my work on the Brownlow-Maisonette appeal, and about what good colleagues all the St. Louis attorneys had turned out to be, how much they'd made me feel at home in their understated, low-keyed offices and how this relationship would bear important fruit in our presentation before the 8th Circuit. I talked some about the definition of negligence as it is applied to common carriers, and about the unexpected, latter-day reshapings of general tort law paradigms in the years since the Nixon appointments. And then Sallie said she wanted to take a nap before dinner, and went upstairs obviously discouraged from her day and from crying.

Sallie suffers, and has as long as I've known her, from what she calls her war dreams – violent, careering, antic, destructive Technicolor nightmares without plots or coherent scenarios, just sudden drop-offs into deepest sleep accompanied by images of dismembered bodies flying around and explosions and brilliant flashes and soldiers of unknown armies being hurtled through trap doors and hanged or thrust out through bomb bays into empty screaming space. These are terrible things I don't even like to hear about and that would scare the wits out of anyone. She usually awakes from these dreams slightly worn down, but not especially spiritually disturbed. And for this reason I believe her to be constitutionally very strong. Once I convinced her to go lie down on Dr. Merle Mackey's well-known couch for a few weeks, and let him try to get to the bottom of all the mayhem. Which she willingly did. Though after a month and a half Merle told her – and told me privately at the tennis club – that Sallie was as mentally and morally sturdy as a race horse, and that some things occurred for no demonstrable reason, no matter how Dr. Freud had viewed it. And in Sallie's case, her dreams (which have always been intermittent) were just the baroque background music of how she resides on the earth and didn't represent, as far as he could observe, repressed memories of parental abuse or some kind of private disaster she didn't want to confront in daylight.

"Weirdness is part of the human condition, Bob," Merle said. "It's thriving all around us. You've probably got some taint of it. Aren't you from up in Mississippi?" "I am," I said. "Then I wouldn't want to get *you* on my couch. We might be there forever." Merle smirked like somebody's presumptuous butler. "No, we don't need to go into that," I said. "No, sir," Merle said, "we really don't." Then he pulled a big smile, and that was the end of it.

After Sallie was asleep I stood at the French doors again. It was nearly dark, and the tiny white lights she had strung up like holiday decorations in the cherry laurel had come on by their timer and delivered the garden into an almost Christmas-y lumination and loveliness. Dusk can be a magical time in the French Quarter – the sky so bright blue, the streets lush and shadowy. The puppy had come back to the middle of the garden and lain with his sharp little snout settled on his spotted front paws. I couldn't see his little feral eyes, but I knew they were trained on me, where I stood watching him, with the yellow chandelier light behind me. He still wore my woven leather belt looped to his neck like a leash. He seemed as peaceful and as heedless as he was likely ever to be. I had set out some Vienna sausages in a plastic saucer, and beside it a red plastic mixing bowl full of water – both where I knew he'd find them. I assumed he had eaten and drifted off to sleep before emerging, now that it was evening, to remind me he was still here, and possibly to express a growing sense of ease with his new surroundings. I was tempted to think what a strange, unpredictable experience it was to be him, so new to life and without essential defenses, and in command of little. But I stopped this thought for obvious reasons. And I realized, as I stood there, that my feelings about the puppy had already become slightly altered. Perhaps it was Sallie's Swedish tough-mindedness influencing me; or perhaps it was the puppy's seemingly untamable nature; or possibly it was all those other signs on all the other message boards and stapled to telephone poles which seemed to state in a cheerful but hopeless way that fate was ineluctable, and character, personality, will, even untamable nature were only its accidental by-products. I looked out at the little low, diminishing white shadow motionless against the darkening bricks, and I thought: all right, yes, this is where you are now, and this is what I'm doing to help you. In all likelihood it doesn't really matter if someone calls, or if someone comes and takes you home and you live a long and happy life. What matters is simply a choice we make, a choice governed by time and opportunity and how well we persuade ourselves to go on until some other powerful force overtakes us. (We always hope it will be a positive and wholesome force, though it may not be.) No doubt this is another view one comes to accept as a lawyer – particularly one who enters events late in the process, as I do. I was, however, glad Sallie wasn't there to know about these thoughts, since it would only have made her think the world was a heartless place, which it really is not.

*

The next morning I was on the TWA flight back to St. Louis. Though later the evening before, someone had called to ask if the lost puppy I'd advertized had been inoculated for various dangerous diseases. I had to admit I had no idea, since it wore no collar. It *seemed* healthy enough, I told the person. (The sudden barking spasms and the spontaneous peeing didn't seem important.) The caller was clearly an elderly black woman – she spoke with a deep Creole accent and referred to me once or twice as "baby," but otherwise she didn't identify herself. She did say, however, that the puppy would be more likely to attract a family if it had its shots and had been certified healthy by a veterinarian. Then she told me about a private agency uptown that specialized in finding homes for dogs with elderly and shut-in persons, and I dutifully wrote down the agency's name – "Pet Pals." In our overly-lengthy talk she went on to say that the gesture of having the puppy examined and inoculated with a rabies shot would testify to the good will required to care for the animal and increase its likelihood of being deemed suitable. After a while I came to think this old lady was probably completely loony and kept herself busy dialing numbers she saw on signs at the laundromat, and yakking for hours about lost kittens, macramé classes, and Suzuki piano lessons, things she wouldn't remember the next day. Probably she was one of our neighbors, though there aren't that many black ladies in the French Quarter anymore. Still, I told her I'd look into her suggestion and appreciated her thoughtfulness. When I innocently asked her her name, she uttered a surprising profanity and hung up.

*

"I'll do it," Sallie said the next morning as I was putting fresh shirts into my two-suiter, making ready for the airport and the flight back to St. Louis. "I have some time today. I can't let all this marathon anxiety take over my life." She was watching out the upstairs window down to the garden again. I'm not sure what I'd intended to happen to the puppy. I suppose I hoped he'd be claimed by someone. Yet he was still in the garden. We hadn't discussed a plan of action, though I had mentioned the Pet Pal agency.

"Poor little pitiful," Sallie said in a voice of dread. She took a seat on the bed beside my suitcase, let her hands droop between her knees, and stared at the floor. "I went out there and tried to play with it this morning, I want you to know this," she said. "It was while you were in the shower. But it doesn't know *how* to play. It just barked and peed and then snapped at me in a pretty hateful way. I guess it was probably funny to whoever had him that he acts that way. It's a crime, really." She seemed sad about it. I thought of the sinister blue-eyed, black-coated boy crouched in the fetid doorway across from the French Market with his new little dog and his three acolytes. They seemed like residents of one of Sallie's war dreams.

"The Pet Pal people will probably fix things right up," I said, tying my tie at the bathroom mirror. It was still unseasonably chilly in St. Louis, and I had on my wool suit, though in New Orleans it was already summery.

"If they *don't* fix things up, and if no one calls," Sallie said gravely, "then you have to take him to the shelter when you come back. Can we agree about that? I saw what he did to the plants. They can be replaced. But he's really not our problem." She turned and looked at me on the opposite side of our bed, whereon her long-departed Swedish grandmother had spent her first marriage night long ago. The expression on Sallie's round face was somber but decidedly settled. She was willing to try to care about the puppy because it suited how she felt that particular day, and because I was going away and she knew it would make me feel better if she tried. It is an admirable human trait, and how undoubtedly most good deeds occur – because you have the occasion, and there's no overpowering reason to do something else. But I was aware she didn't really care what happened to the puppy.

"That's exactly fine," I said, and smiled at her. "I'm hoping for a good outcome. I'm grateful to you for taking him."

"Do you remember when we went to Robert Frost's cabin," Sallie said.

"Yes, I do." And surely I did.

"Well, when you came back from Missouri, I'd like us to go to Robert Frost's cabin again," she smiled at me shyly.

"I think I can do that," I said, closing my suitcase. "Sounds great."

Sallie bent sideways toward me and extended her smooth perfect face to be kissed as I went past the bed with my baggage. "We don't want to abandon that," she said.

"We never will," I answered, leaning to kiss her on the mouth. And then I heard the honk of my cab at the front of the house.

*

Robert Frost's cabin is a great story about Sallie and me. The spring of our first year in New Haven, we began reading Frost's poems aloud to each other, as antidotes to the grueling hours of reading cases on replevin and the rule against perpetuities and theories of intent and negligence – the usual shackles law students wear at exam time. I remember only a little of the poems now, twenty-six years later. "Better to go down dignified / with boughten friendship at your side / than none at all. Provide, provide." We thought we knew what

Frost was getting at: that you make your way in the world and life – all the way to the end – as best you can. And so at the close of the school year, when it turned warm and our classes were over, we got in the old Chrysler Windsor my father had given me and drove up to where we'd read Frost had had his mountainside cabin in Vermont. The state had supposedly preserved it as a shrine, though you had to walk far back through the mosquito-y woods and off a winding logger's road to find it. We wanted to sit on Frost's front porch in some rustic chair he'd sat in, and read more poems aloud to each other. Being young southerners educated in the north, we felt Frost represented a kind of old-fashioned but indisputably authentic Americanism, vital exposure we'd grown up exiled from because of race troubles, and because of absurd preoccupations about the south itself, practiced by people who should know better. Yet we'd always longed for that important exposure, and felt it repre-sented rectitude-in-practice, self-evident wisdom, and a sense of fairness expressed by an unpretentious bent for the arts. (I've since heard Frost was nothing like that, but was mean and stingy and hated better than he loved.)

However, when Sallie and I arrived at the little log cabin in the spring woods, it was locked up tight, with no one around. In fact it seemed to us like no one ever came there, though the state's signs seemed to indicate this was the right place. Sallie went around the cabin looking in the windows until she found one that wasn't locked. And when she told me about it, I said we should crawl in and nose around and read the poem we wanted to read and let whoever came tell us to leave.

But once we got inside, it was much colder than outside, as if the winter and something of Frost's true spirit had been captured and preserved by the log and mortar. And before long we had stopped our reading – after doing "Design" and "Mending Wall" and "Death of the Hired Man" in front of the cold fireplace. And partly for warmth we decided to make love in Frost's old bed, which was made up as he might've left it years before. (Later it occurred to us that possibly nothing had ever happened in the cabin, and maybe we'd even broken into the wrong cabin and made love in someone else's bed.)

But that's the story. That was what Sallie meant by a visit to Robert Frost's cabin – an invitation to me, upon my return, to make love to her, an act which the events of life and years sometimes can overpower and leave unattended. In a moment of panic, when we thought we heard voices out on the trail, we jumped into our clothes and by accident left our Frost book on the cold cabin floor. No one, of course, ever turned up.

*

That night I spoke to Sallie from St. Louis, at the end of a full day of vigorous preparations with the Missouri lawyers (whose clients were reasonably afraid of being put out of business by a 250 million-dollar class action judgment). She, however, had nothing but unhappy news to impart. Some homeowners were trying to enjoin the entire AIDS marathon because of a routing change that went too near their well-to-do Audubon Place neighborhood. Plus one of the original marathon organizers was now on the verge of death (not unexpected). She talked more about good-deeds-done-for-wrong-reasons among her hospice associates, and also about some plainly bad deeds committed by other rich people who didn't like the marathon and wanted AIDS to go away. Plus, nothing had gone right with our plans for placing the puppy into the Pet Pals uptown.

"We went to get its shots," Sallie said sadly. "And it acted perfectly fine when the vet had it on the table. But when I drove it out to Pet Pals on Prytania, the woman – Mrs. Myers, her name was – opened the little wire gate on the cage I'd bought, just to see him. And he jumped at her and snapped at her and started barking. He just barked and barked. And this Mrs. Myers looked horrified and said, 'Why, whatever in the world's wrong with it?' 'It's afraid,' I said to her. 'It's just a puppy. Someone's abandoned it. It doesn't understand anything. Haven't you ever had that happen to you?'

'Of course not,' she said, 'And we can't take an *abandoned* puppy anyway.' She was looking at me as though I was trying to steal something from her. 'Isn't that what you do here?' I said. And I'm sure I raised my voice to her."

"I don't blame you a bit," I said from wintry St. Louis. "I'd have raised my voice."

"I said to her, 'What are you here for? If this puppy wasn't abandoned, why would *I* be here? I wouldn't, would I?'

"'Well, you have to understand we really try to place the more mature dogs whose owners for some reason can't keep them, or are being transferred.' Oh God, I hated her, Bobby. She was one of these wide-ass, Junior-League bitches who'd just gotten bored with flower arranging and playing canasta at the Boston Club. I wanted just to dump the dog right out in the shop and leave, or take a swing at her. I said, 'Do you mean you won't take him?' The puppy was in its cage and was actually being completely quiet and nice. 'No, I'm sorry, it's untamed,' this dowdy, stupid woman said. 'Untamed!' I said. 'It's an abandoned puppy, for fuck's sake.'

"She just looked at me then as if I'd suddenly produced a bomb and was jumping all around. 'Maybe you'd better leave now,' she said. And I'd probably been in the shop all of two minutes, and here she was ordering me out. I said, 'What's wrong with you?' I *know* I shouted then. I was so frustrated. 'You're not a pet pal at all,' I shouted. 'You're an enemy of pets.'"

"You just got mad," I said, happy not to have been there.

"Of course I did," Sallie said. "I let myself get mad because I wanted to scare this hideous woman. I wanted her to see how stupid she was and how much I hated her. She did look around at the phone as if she was thinking about calling 911. Someone I know came in then. Mrs. Hensley from the Art League. So I just left."

"That's all good," I said. "I don't blame you for any of it."

"No. Neither do I." Sallie took a breath and let it out forcefully into the receiver. "We have to get rid of it, though. Now." She was silent a moment, then she began, "I tried to walk it around the neighborhood using the belt you gave it. But it doesn't know how to be walked. It just struggles and cries, then barks at everyone. And if you try to pet it, it pees. I saw some of those kids in black sitting on the curb. They looked at me like I was a fool, and one of the girls made a little kissing noise with her lips, and said something sweet, and the puppy just sat down on the sidewalk and stared at her. I said, 'Is this your dog?' There were four of them, and they all looked at each other and smiled. I know it was theirs. They had another dog with them, a black one. We just have to take him to the pound, though, as soon as you come back tomorrow. I'm looking at him now, out in the garden. He just sits and stares like some Hitchcock movie."

"We'll take him," I said. "I don't suppose anybody's called."

"No. And I saw someone putting up new signs and taking yours down. I didn't say anything. I've had enough with Jerry DeFranco about to die, and our injunction."

"Too bad," I said, because that was how I felt – that it was too bad no one would come along and out of the goodness of his heart taken the puppy in.

"Do you think someone left it as a message," Sallie said. Her voice sounded strange. I pictured her in the kitchen, with a cup of tea just brewed in front of her on the Mexican tile counter. It's good she set the law aside. She becomes involved in ways that are far too emotional. Distance is essential.

"What kind of message?" I asked.

"I don't know," she said. Oddly enough, it was starting to snow in St. Louis, small dry flakes backed – from my hotel window – by an empty, amber-lit cityscape and just the top curve of the great silver arch. It is a nice cordial city, though not distinguished in any way. "I can't figure out if someone thought we were the right people to care for a puppy, or were making a statement showing their contempt."

"Neither," I said. "I'd say it was random. Our gate was available. That's all."

"Does that bother you?"

"Does what?"

"Randomness."

"No," I said. "I find it consoling. It frees the mind."

"Nothing seems random to me," Sallie said. "Everything seems to reveal some plan."

"Tomorrow we'll work this all out," I said. "We'll take the dog and then everything'll be better."

"For us, you mean? Is something wrong with us? I just have this bad feeling tonight."

"No," I said. "Nothing's wrong with us. But it *is* us we're interested in here. Good night, now, sweetheart."

"Good night, Bobby," Sallie said in a resigned voice, and we hung up.

*

That night in the Mayfair Hotel, with the window shades open to the early spring snow and orange-lit darkness, I experienced my own strange dream. In my dream I'd gone on a duck hunting trip into the marsh that surrounds our city. It was winter and early morning, and someone had taken me out to a duck blind before it was light. These are things I still do, as a matter of fact. But when I was set out in the blind with my shotgun, I found that beside me on the wooden bench was one of my law partners, seated with his shotgun between his knees, and wearing strangely red canvas hunting clothes – something you'd never wear in a duck blind. And he had the puppy with him, the same one that was then in our back garden awaiting whatever its fate would be. And my partner was with a woman, who either was or looked very much like the actress Liv Ullmann. The man was Paul Thompson, a man I (outside my dream) have good reason to believe once had an affair with Sallie, an affair that almost caused us to split apart without our even ever discussing it, except that Paul, who was older than I am and big and rugged, suddenly died – actually in a duck blind, of a terrible heart attack. It is a thing that can happen in the excitement of shooting.

In my dream Paul Thompson spoke to me and said, "How's Sallie, Bobby?" I said, "Well, she's fine, Paul, thanks," because we were pretending he and Sallie didn't have the affair I'd employed a private detective to authenticate – and almost did completely authenticate. The Liv Ullmann woman said nothing, just sat against the wooden sides of the blind seeming sad, with long straight blond hair. The little white and black puppy sat on the duckboard flooring and stared at me. "Life's very fragile in the way we experience it, Bobby," Paul Thompson, or his ghost, said to me. "Yes, it is," I said. I assumed he was referring to what he'd been doing with Sallie. (There had been some suspicious photos, though to be honest, I don't think Paul really cared about Sallie. Just did it because he could.) The puppy, meanwhile, kept staring at me. Then the Liv Ullmann woman herself smiled in an ironic way.

"Speaking about the truth tends to annihilate truth, doesn't it?" Paul Thompson said to me.

"Yes," I answered. "I'm certain you're right." And then for a sudden instant it seemed like it had been the puppy who'd spoken Paul's words. I could see his little mouth moving after the words were already spoken. Then the dream faded and become a different dream, which involved the millennium fireworks display from New Year's Eve, and didn't stay in my mind like the Paul Thompson dream did, and does even to this day.

I make no more of this dream than I make of Sallie's dreams, though I'm sure Merle Mackey would have plenty to say about it.

*

When I arrived back in the city the next afternoon, Sallie met me at the airport, driving her red Wagoneer. "I've got it in the car," she said as we walked to the parking structure. I realized she meant the puppy. "I want to take it to the shelter before we go home. It'll be easier." She seemed as though she'd been agitated but wasn't agitated now. She had dressed herself in some aqua walking shorts and a loose, pink blouse that showed her pretty shoulders.

"Did anyone call" I asked. She was walking faster than I was, since

I was carrying my suitcase and a box of brief materials. I'd suffered a morning of tough legal work in a cold, unfamiliar city and was worn out and hot. I'd have liked a vodka martini instead of a trip to the animal shelter.

"I called Kirsten and asked her if she knew anyone who'd take the poor little thing," Sallie said. Kirsten is her sister, and lives in Andalusia, Alabama, where she owns a flower shop with her husband, who's a lawyer for a big cotton consortium. I'm not fond of either of them, mostly because of their simple-minded politics, which includes support for the Confederate flag, prayer in the public schools and the abolition of affirmative action – all causes I have been outspoken about. Sallie, however, can sometimes forget she went to Mount Holyoke and Yale, and step back into being a pretty, chatty southern girl when she gets together with her sister and her cousins. "She said she probably *did* know someone," Sallie went on, "so I said I'd arrange to have the puppy driven right to her doorstep. Today. This afternoon. But then she said it seemed like too much trouble. I told her it *wouldn't* be any trouble for *her* at all, that *I'd* do it or arrange it to be done. Then she said she'd call me back, and didn't. Which is typical of my whole family's sense of responsibility."

"Maybe we should call her back?" I said, as we reached her car. We had a phone in the Wagoneer. I wasn't looking forward to visiting the SPCA.

"She's forgotten about it already," Sallie said. "She'd just get wound up."

When I looked in through the back window of Sallie's Jeep, the puppy's little wire cage was sitting in the luggage space. I could see his white head, facing back, in the direction it had come from. What could it have been thinking?

"The vet said it's going to be a really big dog. Big feet tell you that."

Sallie was getting in the car. I put my suitcase in the back seat so as to not alarm the puppy. Twice it barked its desperate little high-pitched puppy bark. Possibly it knew me. Though I realized it would never have been an easy puppy to get attached to. My father had a neat habit of reversing propositions he was handed as a way of assessing them. If a subject seemed to have one obvious outcome, he'd imagine the reverse of it: if a business deal had an obvious beneficiary, he'd ask who benefited but didn't seem to. Needless to say, these are valuable skills lawyers use. But I found myself thinking – except I didn't say it to Sallie – that though we may have thought we were doing the puppy a favor by trying to find it a home, possibly we were really doing ourselves a favor by presenting ourselves to be the kind of supposedly decent people who do that *sort* of thing. I am, for instance, a person who stops to move turtles off of busy Interstates, or picks up butterflies in shopping mall parking lots and puts them into the bushes to give them a fairer chance at survival. I know these are pointless acts of pointless generosity. Yet there isn't a time when I do it that I don't get back in the car thinking more kindly about myself. (Later I often work around to thinking of myself as a fraud, too.) But the alternative is to leave the butterfly where it lies expiring, or to let the big turtle meet annihilation on the way to the pond; and in doing these things let myself in for the indictment of cruelty or the sense of loss that would follow. Possibly, anyone would argue, these issues are too small to think about seriously, since whether you perform these acts or don't perform them, you always forget about them in about five minutes.

*

Except for weary conversation about my morning at Ruger, Todd, Jennings, and Sallie's re-routing victory with the AIDS race, which was set for Saturday, we didn't say much as we drove to the SPCA. Sallie had obviously researched the address, because she got off the Interstate at an exit I'd never used and that immediately brought us down onto a wide boulevard with old cars parked on the neutral ground, and paper trash cluttering the curbs down one long side of some brown-brick housing projects where black people were outside on their front stoops and wandering around the street in haphazard fashion. There were a few dingy-looking barbecue and gumbo cafés, and two tire-repair shops where work was taking place out in the street. A tiny black man standing on a peach crate was performing haircuts in a dinette chair set up on the sidewalk, his customer wrapped in newspaper. And some older men had stationed a card table on the grassy median and were playing in the sunlight. There were no white people anywhere. It was a part of town, in fact, where most white people would've been afraid to go. Yet it was not a bad section, and the Negroes who lived there no doubt looked on the world as something other than a hopeless place.

Sallie took a wrong turn off the boulevard, and onto a run-down residential street of pastel shotgun houses where black youths in baggy trousers and big black sneakers were playing basketball without a goal. The boys watched us drive past but said nothing. "I've gotten us off wrong here," she said in a distracted, hesitant voice. She is not comfortable around black people when she is the only white – which is a residue of her privileged Alabama upbringing where everything and everybody belonged to a proper place and needed to stay there.

She slowed at the next corner and looked both ways down a similar small street of shotgun houses. More black people were out washing their cars or waiting at bus stops in the sun. I noticed this to be Creve Coeur Street, which was where the *Times-Picayune* said an unusual number of murders occurred each year. All that happened at night, of course and involved black people killing other black people for drug money. It was now 4:45 in the afternoon and I felt perfectly safe.

The puppy barked again in his cage, a soft, anticipatory bark, then Sallie drove us a block farther and immediately spotted the street she'd been looking for – Rousseau Street. The residential buildings stopped there and old, dilapidated two and one story industrial uses began: an off-shore pipe manufactory, a frozen seafood company, a shut-down recycling center where people had gone on leaving their garbage in plastic bags. There was also a small, windowless cube of a building that housed a medical clinic for visiting sailors off foreign ships. I recognized it because our firm had once represented the owners in a personal-injury suit, and I remembered grainy photos of the building and my thinking that I'd never need to see it up close.

Near the end of this block was the SPCA, which occupied a long, glum red-brick warehouse-looking building with a small red sign by the street and a tiny gravel parking lot. One might've thought the proprietors didn't want its presence too easily detected.

The SPCA's entrance was nothing but a single windowless metal door at one end of the building. There were no shrubberies, no disabled slots, no directional signs leading in, just this low, ominous flat-roofed building with long factory clerestories facing the lot and the seafood company. An older wooden shed was attached on the back. And a small sign I hadn't seen because it was fastened too low on the building said: YOU MUST HAVE A LEASH. ALL ANIMALS MUST BE RESTRAINED. CLEAN UP AFTER YOUR ANIMAL. IF YOUR DOG BITES A STAFF MEMBER YOU ARE RESPONSIBLE. THANKS MUCH.

"Why don't you take him in in his cage," Sallie said, nosing up to the building, becoming very efficient. "I'll go in and start the paperwork. I already called them." She didn't look my way.

"That's fine," I said.

When we got out I was surprised again at how warm it was, and how close and dense the air felt. Summer seemed to have arrived during the day I was gone, which is not untypical of New Orleans. I smelled an entirely expectable animal gaminess, combined with a fish smell and something metallic that felt hot and slightly burning in my nose. And the instant I was out into the warm, motionless air I could hear barking from inside the building. I assumed the barking was triggered by the sound of a car arriving. Dogs trained themselves to the hopeful sound of motors.

Across the street from the SPCA were other shotgun houses I hadn't noticed. Elderly black people were sitting in metal lawn chairs on their little porches, observing me getting myself organized. It would be a difficult place to live, I thought, and quite a lot to get used to with the noise and the procession of animals coming and going.

Sallie disappeared into the unfriendly little door, and I opened the back of the Wagoneer and hauled out the puppy in his cage. He stumbled to one side when I took a grip on the wire rungs, then barked several agitated, heartfelt barks and began clawing at the wires and my fingers, giving me a good scratch on the knuckles that almost caused me to drop the whole contraption. The cage, even with him in it, was still very light, though my face was so close I could smell his urine. "You be still in there," I said.

For some reason, and with the cage in my grasp, I looked around at the colored people across the street, silently watching me. I had nothing in mind to say to them. They were sympathetic, I felt sure, to what was going on and thought it was better than cruelty. I had started to sweat because I was wearing my business suit. And I awkwardly waved a hand toward them, but of course no one responded.

When I had maneuvered the cage close up to the metal door, I for some reason looked to the left and saw down the grimy alley between the SPCA and the sailors' clinic, to where a round steel canister was attached to the SPCA building by some large corrugated aluminum pipes, all of it black and new-looking. This, I felt certain, was a device for disposing of animal remains, though I didn't know how. Probably some incinerating invention that didn't have an outlet valve or a stack – something very efficient. It was an extremely sinister thing to see and reminded me of what we all heard years ago about terrible vacuum chambers and gassed compartments for dispatching unwanted animals. Probably they weren't even true stories. Now, of course, it's just an injection. They go to sleep, feeling certain they'll wake up.

Inside the SPCA it was instantly cool, and Sallie had almost everything done. The barking I'd heard outside had not ceased, but the gamy animal smell was replaced by a loud disinfectant odor that was everywhere. The reception area was a cubicle with a couple of metal desks and fluorescent tubes in the high ceiling, and a calendar on the wall showing a golden retriever standing in a wheat field with a dead pheasant in its mouth. Two high-school-age girls manned the desks, and one was helping Sallie fill out her documents. These girls undoubtedly loved animals and worked after school and had aspirations to be vets. A sign on the wall behind the desks said *Placing Puppies Is Our First Priority*. This was here, I thought, to make people like me feel better about abandoning dogs. To make forgetting easier.

Sallie was leaning over one of the desks filling out a thick green document, and looked around to see me just as an older stern-faced woman in a white lab coat and black rubber boots entered from a side door. Her small face and both her hands had a puffy but also a leathery texture that southern women's skin often takes on – too much sun and alcohol, too many cigarettes. Her hair was dense and dull reddish-brown and heavy around her face, making her head seem smaller than it was. This woman, however, was extremely friendly and smiled easily, though I knew just from her features and what she was wearing that she was not a veterinarian.

I stood holding the cage until one of the high-school girls came around her desk and looked in it and said the puppy was cute. It barked so that the cage shook in my grip. "What's his name?" she said, and smiled in a dreamy way. She was a heavy-set girl, very pale with a lazy left eye. Her fingernails were painted bright orange and looked unkempt.

"We haven't named him," I said, the cage starting to feel unwieldy.

"We'll name him," she said, pushing her fingers through the wires. The puppy pawed at her, then licked her fingertips, then made little crying sounds when she removed her finger.

"They place sixty-five per cent of their referrals," Sallie said over the forms she was filling out.

"Too bad it id'n a holiday," the woman in the lab coat said in a husky voice, watching Sallie finish. She spoke like somebody from across the Atchafalaya, somebody who had once spoken French. "Dis place be a ghost town by Christmas, you know?"

The helper girl who'd played with the puppy walked out through the door that opened onto a long concrete corridor full of shadowy metal-fenced cages. Dogs immediately began barking again, and the foul animal odor entered the room almost shockingly. An odd place to seek employment, I thought.

"How long do you keep them?" I said, and set the puppy's cage down on the concrete floor. Dogs were barking beyond the door, one big-sounding dog in particular, though I couldn't see it. A big yellow tiger-striped cat that apparently had free rein in the office walked across the desk top where Sallie was going on writing and rubbed against her arm, and made her frown.

"Five days," the puffy-faced Cajun woman said, and smiled in what seemed like an amused way. "We try to place 'em. People be in here all the time, lookin'. Puppies go fast 'less they something wrong with them." Her eyes found the cage on the floor. She smiled at the puppy as if it could understand her. "You cute," she said then made a dry kissing noise.

"What usually disqualifies them?" I said, and Sallie looked around at me.

"Too aggressive," the woman said, staring approvingly in at the puppy. "If it can't be house-broke, then they'll bring 'em back to us. Which isn't good."

"Maybe they're just scared," I said.

"Some are. Then some are just little naturals. They go in one hour." She leaned over, hands on her lab-coat knees and looked in at our puppy. "How 'bout you," she said. "You a little natural? Or are you a little scamp? I b'lieve I see a scamp in here." The puppy sat on the wire flooring and stared at her indifferently, just as he had stared at me. I thought he would bark, but he didn't.

"That's all," Sallie said, and turned to me and attempted an hospitable look. She put her pen in her purse. She was thinking I might be changing my mind, but I wasn't.

"Then that's all you need. We'll take over," the supervisor woman said.

"What's the fee?" I asked

"Id'n no fee," the woman said and smiled. "Remember me in yo' will." She squatted in front of the cage as if she was going to open it. "Puppy, puppy," she said, then put both hands around the sides of the cage and stood up holding it with ease. She made a little grunting sound, but she was much stronger than I would've thought. Just then another blond helper girl, this one with a metal brace on her left leg, came humping through the kennels door, and the supervisor just walked right past her, holding the cage, while the dogs down the long, dark corridor started barking ecstatically.

"We're donating the cage," Sallie said. She wanted out of the building, and I did, too. I stood another moment and watched as the woman in the lab coat disappeared along the row of pens, carrying our puppy. Then the green metal door went closed, and that was all there was to the whole thing. Nothing very ceremonial.

*

On our drive back downtown we were both, naturally enough, sunk into a kind of woolly, disheartened silence. From up on the Interstate, the spectacle of modern, southern city life and ambitious new construction where once had been a low, genteel old river city, seemed particularly gruesome and unpromising and probably seemed the same to Sallie. To me, who labored in one of the tall, metal and glass enormities (I could actually see my office windows in Place St. Charles, small, undistinguished rectangles shining high up among countless others) it felt particularly alien to history and to my own temperament. Behind these square mirrored windows, human beings were writing and discussing and preparing cases; and on other floors were performing biopsies, CAT scans, drilling out cavities, delivering news both welcome and unwelcome to all sorts of other expectants – clients, patients, partners, spouses, children. People were in fact there waiting for *me* to arrive that very afternoon, anticipating news of the Brownlow-Maisonette case – where *were* things, how were our prospects developing, what was my overall *take* on matters and what were our hopes for a settlement (most of my "take" wouldn't be all that promising). In no time I'd be entering their joyless company and would've forgotten about myself here on the highway, peering out in near despair because of the fate of an insignificant little dog. Frankly, it made me feel pretty silly.

Sallie suddenly said, as though she'd been composing something while I was musing away balefully, "Do you remember after New Year's that day we sat and talked about one thing changing and making everything else different?"

"The Big Dipper," I said as we came to our familiar exit which quickly led down and away through a different poor section of darktown that abuts our gentrified street. Everything had begun to seem more manageable as we neared home.

"That's right," Sallie said, as though the words Big Dipper reproached her. "But you know, and you'll think this is crazy. It *is* maybe. But last night when I was in bed, I began thinking about that poor little puppy as an ill force that put everything in our life at a terrible risk. And we were in danger in some way. It scared me. I didn't want that."

I looked over at Sallie and saw a crystal tear escape her eye and slip down her soft, rounded pretty cheek.

"Sweetheart," I said, and found her hand on the steering wheel. "It's quite all right. You put yourself through a lot. And I've been gone. You just need me around to do more. There's nothing to be scared about."

"I suppose," Sallie said resolutely.

"And if things are not exactly right now," I said, "they soon will be. You'll take on the world again the way you always do. We'll all be the better for it."

"I know," she said. "I'm sorry about the puppy."

"Me too," I said. "But we did the right thing. Probably he'll be fine."

"And I'm sorry things threaten me," Sallie said. "I don't think they should, then they do."

"Things threaten all of us," I said. "Nobody gets away unmarked."

That is what I thought about all of that then. We were in sight of our house. I didn't really want to talk about these subjects anymore.

"Do you love me," Sallie said, quite unexpectedly.

"Oh yes," I said, "I do. I love you very much." And that was all we said.

*

A week ago, in one of those amusing fillers used to justify column space in one of the trial lawyer's journals I look at just for laughs, I read two things that truly interested me. These are always chosen for their wry comment on the law, and are frequently hilarious and true. The first one I read said, "Scientists predict that in five thousand years the earth will be drawn into the sun." It then went on to say something like, "so it's not too early to raise your malpractice insurance," or some such cornball thing as that. But I will admit to being made oddly uncomfortable by this news about the earth – as if I had something important to lose in the inevitability of its far-off demise. I can't now say what that something might be. None of us can think about 5,000 years from now. And I'd have believed none of us could *feel* anything about it either, except in ways that are vaguely religious. Only I did, and I am far from being a religious man. What I felt was very much like the sensation described by the old saying, "someone just walked on your grave." Someone, so it seemed, had walked on my grave 5,000 years from now, and it didn't feel very good. I was sorry to have to think about it.

The other squib I found near the back of the magazine behind the Legal Market Place, and it said that astronomers had discovered the oldest known star, which they believed to be 50 million light years away, and they had named it the Millennium Star for obvious reasons, though the actual Millennium had gone by with hardly any change in things that I'd noticed. When asked to describe the chemical make-up of this Millennium star – which of course couldn't even be seen – the scientist who'd discovered it said. "Oh, gee, I don't know. It's impossible to reach that far back in time." And I thought – sitting in my office with documents of the Brownlow-Maisonette case spread all around me and the hot New Orleans sun beaming into the very window I'd seen from my car when Sallie and I were driving back from delivering the puppy to its fate – I thought, "*Time*? Why does he say *time*, when what he means is space?" My feeling then was very much like the feeling from before, when I'd read about the earth hurtling into the sun – a feeling that so much goes on everywhere all through time, and we know only a laughably insignificant fraction about any of it.

*

The days that followed our visit to the SPCA were eventful days. Sallie's colleague Jerry DeFranco did, of course, die. And though he had AIDS, he died by his own dispirited hand, in his little garret apartment on Kerlerec Street, late at night before the marathon, in order, I suppose, that his life and its end be viewed as a triumph of will over pitiless circumstance.

On another front, the Brownlow appellants decided very suddenly and unexpectedly to settle our case rather than face years of extremely high lawyers' fees and of course the possibility (though not a good one) of enduring a crippling loss. I had hoped for this, and look at it as a victory.

Elsewhere, the marathon went off as planned, and along the route Sallie had wanted. I unfortunately was in St. Louis and missed it. A massacre occurred, the same afternoon, at a fast food restaurant not far from the SPCA, and someone we knew – a black lawyer – was killed. And, during this period, I began receiving preliminary feelers about a federal judgeship which I'm sure I'll never get. These things are always bandied about for months and years, all sorts of persons are put on notice to be ready when the moment comes, and then the wrong one is chosen for completely wrong reasons, after which it becomes clear that nothing was ever in doubt. The law is an odd calling. And New Orleans a unique place. In any case, I'm far too moderate for the present company running things.

Several people did eventually call about the puppy, having seen my signs, and I directed them all to the animal shelter. I went around a time or two and checked the signs, and several were still up along with the AIDS marathon flyers, which made me satisfied, but not very satisfied.

Each morning I sat in bed and thought about the puppy, waiting for someone to come down the list of cages and see him there alone and staring, and take him away. For some reason, in my imaginings, no one ever chose him – not an autistic child, nor a lonely, discouraged older person, a recent widow, a young family with rough-housing kids. None of these. In all the ways I tried to imagine it, he stayed there.

Sallie did not bring the subject up again, although her sister called on Tuesday and said she knew someone named Hester in Andalusia who'd take the puppy, then the two of them quarreled so bitterly that I had to come on the phone and put it settled.

On some afternoons, as the provisional five waiting days ticked by, I would think about the puppy and feel utterly treacherous for having delivered him to the shelter. Then, other times, I'd feel that we'd given him a better chance than he'd have otherwise had, either on the street alone or with his previous owners. I certainly never thought of him as an ill force to be dispelled, or a threat to anything important. To me life's not that fragile. He was, if anything, just a casualty of the limits we all place on our sympathy and our capacity for the ambiguous in life. Though Sallie might've been right – that the puppy had been a message left for us to ponder: something someone thought about us, something someone felt we needed to know. Who or what or in what way that might've been true, I can't quite imagine. Though we are all, of course, implicated in the lives of others, whether we precisely know how or don't.

On Thursday night, before the puppy's final day in the shelter, I had another strange dream. Dreams always mean something obvious, and so I try as much as I can not to remember mine. But for some reason this time I did, and what I dreamed was again about my old departed law partner, Paul Thompson, and his nice wife, Judy, a pretty, buxom blond woman who'd studied opera and sung the coloratura parts in several municipal productions. In my dream Judy Thompson was haranguing Paul about some list of women's names she'd found, women Paul had been involved with, even in love with. She was telling him he was an awful man who had broken her heart, and that she was leaving him (which did actually happen). And on her list – which I could suddenly, as though through a fog, see – was Sallie's name. And when I saw it there, my heart started pounding, pounding, pounding, until I sat right up in bed in the dark and said out loud, "Did you know your name's on that goddamned list?" Outside, on our street, I could hear someone playing a trumpet, a very slow and soulful version of "Nearer Walk with Thee." And Sallie was there beside me, deep asleep. I of course knew she'd done it, deserved to be on the list, and that probably there *was* such a list, given the kind of reckless man Paul Thompson was. As I said, I had never spoken to Sallie about this subject and had, until then, believed I'd gone beyond the entire business. Though I have to suppose now I was wrong.

This dream stayed on my mind the next day, and the next night I had it again. And because the dream preoccupied my thinking, it wasn't until Saturday after lunch, when I had sat down to take a nap in a chair in the living room, that I realized I'd forgotten about the puppy the day before, and that all during Friday many hours had passed, and by the end of them the puppy must've reached its destination, whatever it was to be. I was surprised to have neglected to think about it at the crucial moment, having thought of it so much before then. And I was sorry to have to realize that I had finally not cared as much about it as I'd thought.

Crèche

Faith is not driving them, her mother, Esther is.

In the car, it's the five of them. The family, on their way to Snow Mountain Highlands, to ski. Sandusky, Ohio, to northern Michigan. It's Christmas, or nearly. No one wants to spend Christmas alone.

The five include Faith, who's the motion-picture lawyer, arrived from California; her mother, Esther, who's sixty-four and has, over the years, become much too fat. There's Roger, Faith's sister Daisy's estranged husband, a guidance counselor at Sandusky JFK; and Roger's two girls: Jane and Marjorie, ages eight and six. Daisy – the girls' mom – is a presence, but not along. She's in rehab in a large Midwestern city that is not Chicago or Detroit.

Outside, beyond the long, treeless expanse of whitely-frozen winter-scape, Lake Michigan itself becomes suddenly visible, pale-blue with a thin veneer of fog just above its metallic surface. The girls are chatting in the back seat. Roger is beside them reading *Skier* magazine.

Florida would've been a much nicer holiday alternative, Faith thinks. EPCOT for the girls. The Space Center. Satellite Beach. Fresh pompano. The ocean. She's paying for everything and doesn't even like to ski. But it's been a hard year for everyone, and somebody has to take charge. If they'd gone to Florida, she'd have ended up broke.

Her basic character strength, Faith thinks, watching what seems to be a nuclear power plant coming up on the left, is the same feature that makes her a first-rate lawyer; an undeterrable willingness to see things as capable of being made better, and an addiction to thoroughness. If someone at the studio, a V.P. in marketing, for example, wishes to exit from a totally binding yet surprisingly uncomfortable obligation – say, a legal contract – then Faith's your girl. Faith the doer. Faith the blond beauty with smarts. Your very own optimist. A client's dream with great tits. Her own tits. Just give her a day on your problem.

Her sister Daisy is the perfect case in point. Daisy has been able to admit her serious methamphetamine problem, but only after her biker boyfriend, Vince, had been made a guest of the state of Ohio. And here Faith has had a role to play, beginning with phone calls to attorneys, a restraining order, then later the police and handcuffs for Vince. Daisy, strung out and thoroughly bruised, finally proved to be a credible witness, once convinced she would not be killed.

Going through Daisy's apartment with their mother, in search for clothes Daisy could wear with dignity into rehab, Faith found dildos; six in all – one even under the kitchen sink. These she put in a plastic Grand Union bag and left in the neighbor's street garbage just so her mother wouldn't know. Her mother is up-to-date, but not necessarily interested in dildos. For Daisy's going-in outfit, they eventually settled on a nice, dark jersey shift and some new white Adidas.

The downside of the character issue, the non-lawyer side, Faith understands, is the fact that she's almost thirty-seven and nothing's very solid in her life. She is very patient (with assholes), very good to help behind the scenes (with assholes). Her glass is always half full. Stand and ameliorate could be her motto. Anticipate change. The skills of the law, again, only partly in synch with the requirements of life.

A tall silver smokestack with blinking white lights on top and several gray megaphone-shaped cooling pots around it, now pass on the left. Dense, chalky smoke drifts out of each pot. Lake Michigan, beyond, looks like a blue-white desert. It has snowed for three days, but has stopped now.

"What's that big thing?" Jane or possibly Marjorie says, peering out the back-seat window. It is too warm in the cranberry-colored Suburban Faith rented at the Cleveland airport especially for the trip. The girls are both chewing watermelon-smelling gum. Everyone could get carsick.

"That's a rocket ship ready to blast off to outer space. Would you girls like to hitch a ride on it?" Roger, the brother-in-law says to his daughters. Roger is the friendly-funny neighbor in a family sit-com, although not that funny. He is small and blandly handsome and wears a brush cut and black horn-rimmed glasses. And he is loathsome – though in subtle ways, like some TV actors Faith has known. He is also thirty-seven and prefers pastel cardigans and Hush Puppies. Daisy has been very, very unfaithful to him.

"It is *not* a rocket ship," says Jane, the older child, putting her forehead to the foggy window then pulling back to consider the smudge mark she's left.

"It's a pickle," Marjorie says.

"And shut up," Jane says. "That's a nasty expression."

"No it's not," Marjorie says.

"Is that a word your mother taught you?" Roger asks and smirks. He is in the back seat with them. "I bet it is. That's her legacy. Pickle." On the cover of *Skier* is a photograph of Hermann Maier, wearing an electric red outfit, slaloming down Mount Everest. The headline says, "GOING TO EXTREMES."

"It better not be," Faith's mother says from behind the wheel. She has her seat pushed way back to accommodate her stomach.

"Okay. Two more guesses," Roger says.

"It's an atom plant where they make electricity," Faith says, and smiles back at the nieces, who are staring out at the smokestacks, losing interest. "We use it to heat our houses."

"But we don't like them," Esther says. Esther's been green since before it was chic.

"Why?" Jane says.

"Because they threaten our precious environment, that's why," Esther answers.

"What's 'our precious environment'?" Jane says insincerely.

"The air we breathe, the ground we stand on, the water we drink." Once Esther taught eighth grade science, but not in years.

"Don't you girls learn anything in school?" Roger is flipping pages in his *Skier*. For some mysterious reason, Faith has noticed, Roger is quite tanned.

"Their father could always instruct them," Esther says. "He's in education."

"Guidance," Roger says. "But touché."

"What's touché?" Jane says, wrinkling her nose.

"It's a term used in fencing," Faith says. She likes both girls immensely, and would happily punish Roger for speaking to them with sarcasm.

"What's fencing," Marjorie asks.

"It's a town in Michigan where they make fences," Roger says. "Fencing, Michigan. It's near Lansing."

"No it's not," Faith says.

"Well then, you tell them," Roger says. "You know everything. You're the lawyer."

"It's a game you play with swords," Faith says. "Only no one gets killed. It's fun." In every respect, she despises Roger and wishes he'd stayed in Sandusky. But she couldn't ask the little girls without him. Letting her pay for everything is Roger's way of saying thanks.

"So. There you are, little girls. You heard it here first," Roger says in a nice-nasty voice, continuing to read. "All your lives now you'll remember where you heard fencing explained first and by whom. When you're at Harvard . . ."

"You didn't know," Jane says.

"That's wrong. I did know. I absolutely knew," Roger says. "I was just having some fun. Christmas is a fun time, don't you know?"

*

Faith's love life has not been going well. She has always wanted children-with-marriage, but neither of these things has quite happened. Either the men she's liked haven't liked children, or else the men who loved her and wanted to give her all she longed for haven't seemed worth it. Practicing law for a movie studio has therefore become very engrossing. Time has gone by. A series of mostly courteous men has entered but then departed – all for one reason or another unworkable: married, frightened, divorced, all three together. "Lucky" is how she has chiefly seen herself. She goes to the gym every day, drives an expensive car, lives alone in Venice Beach in a rental owned by a teenage movie star who is a friend's brother and who has HIV. A deal.

Late last spring she met a man. A stock market hotsy-totsy with a house on Nantucket. Jack. Jack flew to Nantucket from the city in his own plane, had never been married at age roughly forty-six. She came east a few times and flew up with him, met his stern-looking sisters, the pretty, socialite mom. There was a big blue rambling beach house facing the sea, with rose hedges, sandy pathways to secret dunes where you could swim naked – something she especially enjoyed, though the sisters were astounded. The father was there, but was sick and would soon die, so life and plans were generally on hold. Jack did beaucoup business in London. Money was not a problem. Maybe when the father departed they could be married, Jack had almost suggested. But until then, she could travel with him whenever she could get away – scale back a little on the expectation side. He wanted children, could get to California often. It could work.

One night a woman called. Greta, she said her name was. Greta was in love with Jack. She and Jack had had a fight, but he still loved her, she said. It turned out Greta had pictures of Faith and Jack together. Who knew who took them? A little bird. One was a picture of Faith and Jack exiting Jack's building on Beekman Place. Another was of Jack helping Faith out of a yellow taxi. One was of Faith, alone, at the Park Avenue Café eating seared swordfish. One was of Jack and Faith kissing in the front seat of an unrecognizable car – also in New York.

Jack liked particular kinds of sex in very particular kinds of ways, Greta said on the phone. She guessed Faith knew all about that by now. But "best not make long-range plans" was somehow the message. Other calls were placed, messages left on her voicemail, prints arrived by Fed-Ex.

When asked, Jack conceded there was a problem. But he would solve it, *tout de suite* (though she needed to understand he was preoccupied with his father's approaching death). Jack was a tall, smooth-faced, handsome man with a shock of lustrous, mahogany-colored hair. Like a clothing model. He smiled and everyone felt better. He'd gone to public high school, Harvard, played squash, rowed, debated, looked good in a brown suit and oldish shoes. He was trustworthy. It still seemed workable.

But Greta called more times. She sent pictures of herself and Jack together. Recent pictures, since Faith had come on board. It was harder than he'd imagined to get untangled, Jack admitted. Faith would need to be patient. Greta was, after all, someone he'd once "cared about very much." Might've even married. Didn't wish to hurt. She had problems, yes. But he wouldn't just throw her over. He wasn't that kind of man, something she, Faith, would be glad about in the long run. Meanwhile, there was the sick patriarch. And his mother. And the sisters. That had been plenty.

*

Snow Mountain Highlands is a smaller ski resort, but nice. Family, not flash. Faith's mother found it as a "Holiday Getaway" in the *Erie Weekly*. The package includes a condo, weekend lift tickets, and coupons for three days of Swedish smorgasbord in the Bavarian-style lodge. The deal, however, is for two people only. The rest have to pay. Faith will sleep with her mother in the "Master Suite." Roger can share the twin with the girls.

Two years ago, when sister Daisy began to take an interest in Vince, the biker, Roger simply "receded." Her and Roger's sex life had long ago lost its effervescence, Daisy confided. They had started off well enough as a model couple in a suburb of Sandusky, but eventually – after some years and two kids – happiness ended and Daisy had been won over by Vince, who liked amphetamines and more importantly sold them. Vince's arrival was when sex had gotten really good, Daisy said. Faith believes Daisy envied her movie connections and movie lifestyle and the Jaguar convertible, and basically threw her own life away (at least until rehab) as a way of simulating Faith's, only with a biker. Eventually Daisy left home and gained forty-five pounds on a body that was already voluptuous, if short. Last summer, at the beach at Middle Bass, Daisy in a rage actually punched Faith in the chest when she suggested that Daisy might lose some weight, ditch Vince and consider coming home to her family. Not a diplomatic suggestion, she later decided. "I'm not like you," Daisy screamed, right out on the sandy beach. "I fuck for pleasure. Not for business." Then she waddled into the tepid surf of Lake Erie, wearing a pink one-piece that boasted a frilly skirtlet. By then, Roger had the girls, courtesy of a court order.

*

In the condo now, Esther has been watching her soaps, but has stopped to play double solitaire and have a glass of wine by the big picture window that looks down toward the crowded ski slope and the ice rink. Roger is actually there on the bunny slope with Jane and Marjorie, though it's impossible to distinguish them. Red suits. Yellow suits. Lots of dads with kids. All of it soundless.

Faith has had a sauna and is now thinking about phoning Jack, wherever Jack is. Nantucket. New York. London. She has no particular message to leave. Later she plans to do the Nordic Trail under moonlight. Just to be a full participant, to set a good example. For this she has brought LA purchases: loden knickers, a green-and-brown-and-red sweater knitted in the Himalayas, socks from Norway. No way does she plan to get cold.

Esther plays cards at high speed with two decks, her short fat fingers flipping cards and snapping them down as if she hates the game and wants it to be over. Her eyes are intent. She has put on a cream-colored neck brace because the tension of driving has aggravated an old work-related injury. And she is now wearing a big Hawaii-print orange muumuu. How long, Faith wonders, has she been wearing these tents. Twenty years, at least. Since Faith's own father – Esther's husband – kicked the bucket.

"Maybe I'll go to Europe," Esther says, flicking cards ferociously. "That'd be nice, wouldn't it?"

Faith is at the window, observing the expert slope. Smooth, wide pastures of snow, framed by copses of beautiful spruces. Several skiers are zigzagging their way down, doing their best to appear stylish. Years ago, she came here with her high-school boyfriend, Eddie, a.k.a. "Fast Eddie," which in some respects he was. Neither of them liked to ski, nor did they get out of bed to try. Now, skiing reminds her of golf – a golf course made of snow.

"Maybe I'll take the girls out of school and treat us all to Venice," Esther goes on. "I'm sure Roger would be relieved."

Faith has spotted Roger and the girls on the bunny slope. Blue, green and yellow suits, respectively. He is pointing, giving detailed instructions to his daughters about ski etiquette. Just like any dad. She thinks she sees him laughing. It is hard to think of Roger as an average parent.

"They're too young for Venice," Faith says, putting her small, good-looking nose near the surprisingly warm windowpane. From outside, she hears the rasp of a snow shovel and muffled voices.

"Maybe I'll take *you* to Europe, then," Esther says. "Maybe when Daisy clears rehab we can all three take in Europe. I always planned for that."

Faith likes her mother. Her mother is no fool, yet still seeks ways to be generous. But Faith cannot complete a picture that includes herself, her enlarged mother and Daisy on the Champs Elysées or the Grand Canal. "That's a nice idea," she says. She is standing beside her mother's chair, looking down at the top of her head, hearing her breathe. Her mother's head is small. Its hair is dark gray and short and sparse, and not especially clean. She has affected a very wide part straight down the middle. Her mother looks like the fat lady in the circus, but wearing a neck brace.

"I was reading what it takes to live to a hundred," Esther says, neatening the cards on the glass table top in front of her belly. Faith has begun thinking of Jack and what a peculiar species of creep he is. Jack Matthews still wears the Lobb cap-toe shoes he had made for him in college. Ugly, pretentious English shoes. "You have to be physically active," her mother continues. "And you have to be an optimist, which I am. You have to stay interested in things, which I more or less do. And you have to handle loss well."

With all her concentration Faith tries not to wonder how she ranks on this scale. "Do you want to be a hundred?"

"Oh, yes," her mother says. "*You* just can't imagine it, that's all. You're too young. And beautiful. And talented." No irony. Irony is not her mother's specialty.

Outside, one of the men shoveling snow can be heard to say, "Hi, we're the Weather Channel." He's speaking to someone watching them through another window from yet another condo.

"Colder'n a well-digger's dick, you bet," a second man's voice says. "That's today's forecast."

"Dicks, dicks, and more dicks," her mother says pleasantly. "That's it, isn't it? The male appliance. The whole mystery."

"So I'm told," Faith says, and thinks about Fast Eddie.

"They were all women, though," her mother says.

"Who?"

"All the people who lived to be a hundred. You could do all the other things right. But you still needed to be a woman to survive."

"Good for us," Faith says.

"Right. The lucky few."

*

This will be the girls' first Christmas without a tree or their mother.

Though Faith has attempted to improvise around this by arranging presents at the base of the large, plastic rubber-tree plant stationed against one of the empty white walls of the small living room. The tree was already here. She has brought with her a few Christmas balls, a gold star and a string of lights that promise to blink. "Christmas in Manila," could be a possible theme.

Outside, the day is growing dim. Faith's mother is napping. Following his ski lesson, Roger has gone down to "The Warming Shed" for a mulled wine. The girls are seated on the couch side by side, wearing their Lanz of Salzburg flannel nighties with matching smiling monkey-face slippers. Green and yellow again, but with printed white snowflakes. They have taken their baths together, with Faith to supervise, then insisted on putting on their nighties early for their nap. They seem perfect angels and perfectly wasted on their parents. Faith has decided to pay their college tuitions. Even to Harvard.

"We know how to ski now," Jane says primly. They're watching Faith trim the plastic rubber-tree plant. First the blinking lights, though there's no plug-in close enough, then the six balls (one for each family member). Last will come the gold star. Faith understands she is trying for too much. Though why not try for too much. It's Christmas. "Marjorie wants to go to the Olympics," Jane adds.

Jane has watched the Olympics on TV, but Marjorie was too young. It is Jane's power position. Marjorie looks at her sister without expression, as if no one can observe her staring.

"I'm sure she'll win a medal," Faith says, on her knees, fiddling with the fragile strand of tiny peaked bulbs she already knows will not light up. "Would you two like to help me?" She smiles at both of them.

"No," Jane says.

"No," Marjorie says immediately after.

"I don't blame you," Faith says.

"Is Mommy coming here?" Marjorie blinks, then crosses her tiny, pale ankles. She is sleepy and could possibly cry.

"No, sweet," Faith says. "This Christmas Mommy is doing *herself* a favor. So she can't do one for us."

"What about Vince?" Jane says authoritatively. Vince is ground that has been gone over several times before now, and carefully. Mrs. Argenbright, the girls' therapist, has taken special pains with the Vince subject. The girls have the skinny on Mr. Vince but want to be given it again, since they like Vince more than their father.

"Vince is a guest of state of Ohio, right now," Faith says. "You remember that? It's like he's in college."

"He's not in college," Jane says.

"Does he have a tree where he is," Marjorie asks.

"Not in any real sense, at least not in his room like you do," Faith says. "Let's talk about happier things than our friend Vince, okay?" She is stringing bulbs now, on her knees.

The room doesn't include much furniture, and what there is conforms to the Danish modern style. A raised, metal-hooded, red-enamel fireplace device has a paper message from the condo owners taped to it, advising that smoke damage will cause renters to lose their security deposit and subject them to legal actions. These partic-ular owners, Esther has learned, are residents of Grosse Pointe Farms, and are people of Russian extraction. There's, of course, no firewood except what the Danish furniture could offer. So smoke is unlikely. Baseboards supply everything.

"I think you two should guess what you're getting for Christmas," Faith says, carefully draping lightless lights onto the stiff plastic branches of the rubber tree. Taking pains.

"In-lines. I already know," Jane says and crosses her ankles like her sister. They are a jury disguised as an audience. "I don't have to wear a helmet, though."

"But are you sure of that?" Faith glances over her shoulder and gives them a smile she's seen movie stars give to strangers. "You could always be wrong."

"I'd better be right," Jane says unpleasantly, with a frown very much like her mom's.

"Santa's bringing me a disk player," Marjorie says. "It'll come in a small box. I won't even recognize it."

"You two're too smart for your britches," Faith says. She is quickly finished stringing Christmas lights. "But you don't know what *I* brought you." Among other things, she has brought a disk player and an expensive pair of in-line skates. They are in the Suburban and will be returned back in LA. She has also brought movie videos. Twenty in all, including *Star Wars* and *Sleeping Beauty*. Daisy has sent them each $50.

"You know," Faith says, "I remember once a long, long time ago, my dad and I and your mom went out in the woods and cut a tree for Christmas. We didn't buy a tree, we cut one down with an axe."

Jane and Marjorie stare at her as if they've read this story someplace. The TV is not turned on in the room. Perhaps, Faith thinks, they don't understand someone talking to them – live action presenting its own unique continuity problems.

"Do you want to hear the story?"

"Yes," Marjorie, the younger sister, says. Jane sits watchful and silent on the green Danish sofa. Behind her on the bare white wall is a framed print of Bruegel's *Return of the Hunters*, which is, after all, Christmas-y.

"Well," Faith says. "Your mother and I – we were only nine and ten – picked out the tree we desperately wanted to be our tree, but our dad said no, that tree was too tall to fit inside our house. We should choose another one. But we both said, 'No, this one's perfect. This is the best one.' It was green and pretty and had a perfect Christmas shape. So our dad cut it down with his axe, and we dragged it out through the woods and tied it on top of our car and brought it back to Sandusky." Both girls are sleepy now. There has been too much excitement, or else not enough. Their mother is in rehab. Their dad's an asshole. They're in someplace called Michigan. Who wouldn't be sleepy?

"Do you want to know what happened after that?" Faith says. "When we got the tree inside?"

"Yes," Marjorie says politely.

"It *was* too big," Faith says. "It was much, much too tall. It couldn't even stand up in our living room. And it was too wide. And our dad got really mad at us because we'd killed a beautiful living tree for a selfish reason, and because we hadn't listened to him and thought we knew everything just because we knew what we wanted."

Faith suddenly doesn't know why she's telling this story to these innocent sweeties who do not need another object lesson. So she simply stops. In the real story, of course, her father took the tree and threw it out the door into the back yard where it stayed for a week and turned brown. There was crying and accusations. Her father went straight to a bar and got drunk. Later, their mother went to the Kiwanis lot and bought a small tree that fit and which the three of them trimmed without the aid of their father. It was waiting, all lighted, when he came home smashed. The story had always been one others found humor in. This time the humor seems lacking.

"Do you want to know how the story turned out?" Faith says, smiling brightly for the girls' benefit, but feeling defeated.

"I do," Marjorie says. Jane says nothing.

"Well, we put it outside in the yard and put lights on it so our neighbors could share our big tree with us. And we bought a smaller tree for the house at the Kiwanis. It was a sad story that turned out good."

"I don't believe that," Jane says.

"Well you should believe it," Faith says, "because it's true. Christmases are special. They always turn out wonderfully if you just give them a chance and use your imagination."

Jane shakes her head as Marjorie nods hers. Marjorie wants to believe. Jane, Faith thinks, is a classic older child. Like herself.

*

"Did you know," – this was one of Greta's cute messages left for her on her voicemail in Los Angeles – "did you know that Jack hates – *hates* – to have his dick sucked? Hates it with a passion. Of course you didn't. How could you? He always lies about it. Oh well. But if you're wondering why he never comes, that's why. It's a big turn-off for him. I personally think it's his mother's fault, not that *she* ever did it to him, of course. By the way, that was a nice dress last Friday. Really great tits. I can see why Jack likes you. Take care."

*

At seven, when the girls wake up from their naps and everyone is hungry at once, Faith's mother offers to take the two hostile Indians for a pizza then on to the skating rink, while Roger and Faith share the smorgasbord coupons in the Lodge.

Very few diners have chosen the long, harshly-lit rather sour-smelling Tyrol Room. Most guests are outside awaiting the Pageant of the Lights, in which members of the ski patrol descend the expert slope each night, holding flaming torches. It is a thing of beauty but takes time getting started. At the very top of the hill a giant Norway spruce has been illuminated in the Yuletide tradition, just as in the untrue version of Faith's story. All of this is viewable from inside the Tyrol Room via a great picture window.

Faith does not want to eat with Roger, who is hungover from his gluhwein and a nap. Conversation that she would find offensive could easily occur; something on the subject of her sister, the girls' mother – Roger's (still) wife. But she's trying to keep up a Christmas spirit. Do for others, etc.

Roger, she knows, dislikes her, possibly envies her, and also is attracted to her. Once, several years ago, he confided to her that he'd very much like to fuck her ears flat. He was drunk, and Daisy hadn't long before had Jane. Faith found a way not to specifically acknowledge his offer. Later he told her he thought she was a lesbian. Having her know that just must've seemed like a good idea. A class act is The Roger.

The long, echoing dining hall has criss-crossed ceiling beams painted pink and light green and purple, a scheme apparently appropriate to Bavaria. There are long green-painted tables with pink and purple plastic folding chairs meant to promote an informal good time and family fun. Somewhere else in the lodge, Faith is certain, there is a better place to eat where you don't pay with coupons and nothing's pink or purple.

Faith is wearing a shiny black Lycra bodysuit, over which she has put on her loden knickers and Norway socks. She looks superb, she believes. With anyone but Roger this would be fun, or at least a hoot.

Roger sits across the long table, too far away to talk easily. In a room that can conveniently hold five hundred souls, there are perhaps fifteen scattered diners. No one is eating family style, only solos and twos. Young lodge employees in paper caps wait dismally behind the long smorgasbord steam table. Metal heat lamps with orange beams are steadily over-cooking the prime rib, of which Roger has taken a goodly portion. Faith has chosen only a few green lettuce leaves, a beet round, two tiny ears of yellow corn and no salad dressing. The sour smell of the Tyrol Room makes eating almost impossible.

"Do you know what I worry about?" Roger says, sawing around a triangle of glaucal gray roast beef fat, using a comically small knife. His tone implies he and Faith eat here together often and are just picking up where they've left off; as if they didn't hold each other in complete contempt.

"No," Faith says. "What?" Roger, she notices, has managed to hang on to his red smorgasbord coupon. The rule is you leave your coupon in the basket by the bread sticks. Clever Roger. Why, she wonders, is Roger tanned?

Roger smiles as though there's a lewd aspect to whatever it is that worries him. "I worry that Daisy's going to get so fixed up in rehab that she'll forget everything that's happened and want to be married again. To me, I mean. You know?" Roger chews as he talks. He wishes to seem earnest, his smile a serious, imploring, vacuous smile. This is Roger leveling. Roger owning up.

"That probably won't happen," Faith says. "I just have a feeling." She no longer wishes to look at her fragmentary salad. She does not have an eating disorder and could never have one.

"Maybe not." Roger nods. "I'd like to get out of guidance pretty soon, though. Start something new. Turn the page."

In truth, Roger is not bad-looking, only oppressively regular: small chin, small nose, small hands, small straight teeth – nothing unusual except his brown eyes are too narrow, as if he had Ukrainian blood. Daisy married him – she said – because of his alarmingly big dick. That – or more importantly, the lack of that – was in her view why many other marriages failed. When all else gave way, that would be there. Vince's, she'd shared, was even bigger. Ergo. It was to this particular quest that Daisy had dedicated her life. This, instead of college.

"What exactly would you like to do next?" Faith says. She is thinking how nice it would be if Daisy came out of rehab and *had* forgotten everything. A return to how things were when they still sort of worked often seemed a good solution.

"Well, it probably sounds crazy," Roger says, chewing, "but there's a company in Tennessee that takes apart jetliners for scrap. There's big money in it. I imagine it's how the movie business got started. Just some hair-brained scheme." Roger pokes at macaroni salad with his fork. A single Swedish meatball remains on his plate.

"It doesn't sound crazy," Faith lies, then looks longingly at the smorgasbord table. Maybe she's hungry, after all. But is the table full of food the smorgasbord, or is eating the food the smorgasbord?

Roger, she notices, has casually slipped his meal coupon into a pocket.

"Well, do you think you're going to do that?" Faith asks with reference to the genius plan of dismantling jet airplanes for big bucks.

"With the girls in school, it'd be hard," Roger admits soberly, ignoring what would seem to be the obvious – that it is not a genius plan.

Faith gazes away again. She realizes no one else in the big room is dressed the way she is, which reminds her of who she is. She is not Snow Mountain Highlands (even if she once was). She is not Sandusky. She is not even Ohio. She is Hollywood. A fortress.

"I could take the girls for a while," she suddenly says. "I really wouldn't mind." She thinks of sweet Marjorie and sweet, unhappy Jane sitting on the Danish modern couch in their sweet nighties and monkey-face slippers, watching her trim the plastic rubber-tree plant. At the same moment, she thinks of Roger and Daisy being killed in an automobile crash on their triumphant way back from rehab. You can't help what you think.

"Where would they go to school?" Roger says, becoming alert to something unexpected. Something he might like.

"I'm sorry?" Faith says and flashes Roger, big-dick, narrow-eyed Roger a second movie star's smile. She has let herself become distracted by the thought of his timely death.

"I mean, like, where would they go to school?" Roger blinks. He is that alert.

"I don't know. Hollywood High, I guess. They have schools in California. I could find one."

"I'd have to think about it," Roger lies decisively.

"Okay, do," Faith says. Now that she has said this, without any previous thought of ever saying it, it becomes part of everyday reality. Soon she will become Jane and Marjorie's parent. Easy as that. "When you get settled in Tennessee you could have them back," she says without conviction.

"They probably wouldn't want to come back by then," Roger says. "Tennessee'd seem pretty dull."

"Ohio's dull. They like that."

"True," Roger says.

No one has thought to mention Daisy in promoting this new arrangement. Though Daisy, the mother, is committed elsewhere for the next little patch. And Roger needs to get his life jump-started, needs to put "guidance" in the rearview mirror. First things first.

The Pageant of the Lights has gotten underway outside now – a ribbon of swaying torches gliding soundlessly down the expert slope like an overflow of human lava. All is preternaturally visible through the panoramic window. A large, bundled crowd of spectators has assembled at the bottom of the slope behind some snow fences, many holding candles in scraps of paper like at a Grateful Dead concert. All other artificial light is extinguished, except for the Yuletide spruce at the top. The young smorgasbord attendants, in their aprons and paper caps, have gathered at the window to witness the event yet again. Some are snickering. Someone remembers to turn the lights off in the Tyrol Room. Dinner is suspended.

"Do you downhill," Roger asks, leaning over his empty plate in the half darkness. He is whispering, for some reason. Things could really turn out great, Faith understands him to be thinking: Eighty-six the girls. Dismantle plenty jets. Just be friendly and it'll happen.

"No, never," Faith says, dreamily watching the torchbearers schussing side to side, a gradual, sinuous, drama-less tour downward. "It scares me."

"You'd get used to it." Roger unexpectedly reaches across the table to where her hands rest on either side of her uneaten salad. He touches, then pats, one of these hands. "And by the way," Roger says. "Thanks. I mean it. Thanks a lot."

*

Back in the condo all is serene. Esther and the girls are still at the skating rink. Roger has wandered back to "The Warming Shed." He has a girlfriend in Port Clinton, a former high school counselee, now divorced. He will be calling her, telling her about his new Tennessee plans, adding that he wishes she were here at Snow Mountain Highlands with him and that his family could be in Rwanda. Bobbie, her name is.

A call to Jack is definitely in order. But first Faith decides to slide the newly-trimmed rubber tree plant nearer the window, where there's an outlet. When she plugs in, most of the little white lights pop cheerily on. Only a few do not, and in the box are replacements. This is progress. Later, tomorrow, they can affix the star on top – her father's favorite ritual. "Now it's time for the star," he'd always say. "The star of the wise men." Her father had been a musician, a woodwind specialist. A man of talents, and of course a drunk. A specialist also in women who were not his wife. He had taught committedly at a junior college to make all their ends meet. He had wanted Faith to become a lawyer, so naturally she became one. Daisy he had no specific plans for, so naturally she became a drunk and sometime later, an energetic nymphomaniac. Eventually he died, at home. The paterfamilias. After that, but not until, her mother began to put weight on. "Well, there's my size, of course," was how she usually expressed it. She took it as a given: increase being the natural consequence of loss.

Whether to call Jack, though, in London or New York. (Nantucket is out, and Jack never keeps his cell phone on except for business hours.) Where is Jack? In London it was after midnight. In New York it was the same as here. Half past eight. And what message to leave? She could just say she was lonely; or that she had chest pains, or worrisome test results. (These would need to clear up mysteriously.)

But London, first. The flat in Sloane Terrace, half a block from the tube. They'd eaten breakfast at the Oriel, then Jack had gone off to work in the City while she did the Tate, the Bacons her specialty. So far from Snow Mountain Highlands – this being her sensation when dialing – a call going a great, great distance.

Ring-jing, ring-jing, ring-jing, ring-jing, ring-jing. Nothing.

There was a second number, for messages only, but she'd forgotten it. Call again to allow for a misdial. Ring-jing, ring-jing, ring-jing . . .

New York, then. East 50th. Far, far east. The nice, small slice of river view. The bolthole he'd had since college. His freshman numerals framed. 1971. She'd gone to the trouble to have the bedroom re-done. White everything. A smiling and tanned picture of herself from the boat, framed in red leather. Another of the two of them together at Cabo, on the beach. All similarly long distances from Snow Mountain Highlands.

Ring, ring, ring, ring. Then click. "Hi, this is Jack." – she almost says "Hi" back – "I'm not here right now, etc., etc., etc.," then a beep.

"Merry Christmas, it's me. Ummmm, Faith." She's stuck, but not at all flustered. She could just as well tell him everything. This happened today: the atomic energy smokestacks, the plastic rubber-tree plant, the Pageant of the Lights, the smorgasbord, Eddie from years back, the girls' planned move to California. All things Christmas-y. "Ummm, I just wanted to say that I'm . . . fine, and that I trust – make that *hope* – that I *hope* you are too. I'll be back home – at the beach, that is – after Christmas. I'd love – make that like – to hear from you. I'm in Snow Mountain Highlands. In Michigan." She pauses, discussing with herself if there was further news worth relating. There isn't. Then she realizes (too late) she's treating his voicemail like her dictaphone. There's no revising. Too bad. Her mistake. "Well, good-bye," she says, realizing this sounds a bit stiff, but doesn't revise. With them it's all over anyway. Who cares? She called.

*

Out on the Nordic Trail 1, lights, soft white ones not unlike the Christmas tree lights in the condo, have been strung in selected fir boughs – bright enough that you'd never get lost in the dark, dim enough not to spoil the mysterious effect.

She does not actually enjoy this kind of skiing either. Not really. Not with all the tiresome waxing, the stiff rental shoes, the long inconvenient skis, the sweaty underneath, the chance that all this could eventuate in catching cold and missing work. The gym is better. Major heat, then quick you're clean and back in the car, back in the office. Back on the phone. She is a sport, but definitely not a sports nut. Still, this is not terrifying.

No one accompanies her on nighttime Nordic Trail 1, the Pageant of the Lights having lured away the other skiers. Two Japanese were conversing at the trail head, small beige men in bright chartreuse Lycras – smooth, serious faces, giant thighs, blunt, no-nonsense arms – commencing the rigorous course, "The Beast," Nordic Trail 3. On their rounded, stocking-capped heads they'd worn tiny lights like coal miners to light their way. They have disappeared immediately.

Here the snow virtually hums to the sound of her sliding strokes. A full moon rides behind filigree clouds as she strides forward in the near-darkness of crusted woods. There is wind she can hear high up in the tallest pines and hemlocks, but at ground level there's none, just cold radiating off the metallic snow. Only her ears actually feel cold, that and the sweat line of her hair. Her heartbeat barely registers. She is in shape.

For an instant she hears distant music, a singing voice with orchestral accompaniment. She pauses to listen. The music's pulse travels through the trees. Strange. Possibly it's Roger, she thinks, between deep breaths; Roger on stage in the karaoke bar, singing his greatest hits to other lonelies in the dark. "Blue Bayou," "Layla," "Tommy," "Try To Remember." Roger at a safe distance. Her hair, she realizes, is shining in the moonlight. If she were being watched, she would at least look good.

But wouldn't it be romantic to peer down from these woods through the dark and spy some shining, many-winged lodge lying below, windows ablaze, like an exotic casino from some Paul Muni movie. Graceful skaters adrift on a lighted rink. A garlanded lift still in stately motion, a few, last alpinists taking their silken, torchless float before lights-out. The great tree shining from the summit.

Except, this is not a particularly pretty part of Michigan. Nothing's to see – dark trunks, cold dead falls, swags of heavy snow hung in the spruce boughs.

And she is stiffening. Just that fast. New muscles being visited. Best not to go so far.

Daisy, her sister, comes to mind. Daisy, who will soon exit the hospital with a whole new view of life. Inside, there's of course been the 12-step ritual to accompany the normal curriculum of deprivation and regret. And someone, somewhere, at some time possibly even decades back, will definitely turn out to have touched Daisy in ways inappropriate and detrimental to her well being, and at an all-too-tender age. And not just once, but many times, over a series of terrible, silent years. The culprit possibly an older, suspicious neighborhood youth – a loner – or a far too avuncular school librarian. Even the paterfamilias will come under posthumous scrutiny (the historical perspective, as always, unprovable and therefore indisputable).

And certain sacrifices of dignity will naturally be requested of everyone then, due to this rich new news from the past: a world so much more lethal than anyone believed, nothing being the way we thought it was; so much hidden from view; if anyone had only known, could've spoken out and opened up the lines of communication, could've trusted, confided, blah, blah, blah. Their mother will, necessarily, have suspected nothing, but unquestionably should've. Perhaps Daisy, herself, will have suggested that Faith is a lesbian. The snowball effect. No one safe, no one innocent.

Up ahead, in the shadows, a mile into the trek, Shelter 1 sits to the right of Nordic Trail 1 – a darkened clump in a small clearing, a place to rest and wait for the others to catch up (if there were others). A perfect place to turn back.

Shelter 1 is nothing fancy, a simple rustic school-bus enclosure open on one side and hewn from logs. Out on the snow lie crusts of dinner rolls, a wedge of pizza, some wadded tissues, three beer cans – treats for the forest creatures – each casting its tiny shadow upon the white surface.

Although seated in the gloomy inside on a plank bench are not school kids, but Roger, the brother-in-law, in his powder-blue ski suit and hiking boots. He is not singing karaoke after all. She noticed no boot tracks up the trail. Roger is more resourceful than at first he seems.

"It's eff-ing cold up here." Roger speaks from within the shadows of Shelter 1. He is not wearing his black glasses now, and is barely visible, though she senses he's smiling – his brown eyes even narrower.

"What are you doing up here, Roger," Faith asks.

"Oh," Roger says out of the gloom. "I just thought I'd come up." He crosses his arms and extends his hiking boots into the snow-light like some species of high-school toughie.

"What for?" Her knees are both knotted and weak from exertion. Her heart has begun thumping. Perspiration is cold on her lip. Temperatures are in the low twenties. In winter the most innocent places turn lethal.

"Nothing ventured," Roger says. He is mocking her.

"This is where I'm turning around," Faith ventures. "Would you like to go back down the hill with me?" What she wishes for is more light. Much more light. A bulb in the shelter would be very good. Bad things happen in the dark that would prove unthinkable in the light.

"Life leads you to some pretty interesting places, doesn't it, Faith?"

She would like to smile and not feel menaced by Roger, who should be with his daughters.

"I guess," she says. She can smell alcohol in the dry air. He is drunk and is winging all of this. A bad concurrence.

"You're very pretty. *Very* pretty. The big lawyer," Roger says. "Why don't you come in here?"

"Oh, no thank you," Faith says. Roger is loathsome, but he is also family, and she feels paralyzed by not knowing what to do – a most unusual situation. She wishes to be more agile on her skis, to leap upward and discover herself turned around and already gliding away.

"I always thought that in the right situation, we could have some big-time fun," Roger goes on.

"Roger, this isn't a good thing to be doing," whatever he's doing. She wants to glare at him, then understands her knees are quivering. She feels very, very tall on her skis, unusually accessible.

"It *is* a good thing to be doing," Roger says. "It's what I came up here for. Some fun."

"I don't want us to do anything up here, Roger," Faith says. "Is that all right?" This, she realizes, is what fear feels like – the way you'd feel in a late-night parking structure, or jogging alone in an isolated factory area, or entering your house in the wee hours, fumbling for your key. Accessible. And then, suddenly, there would be someone. Bingo. A man with oppressively ordinary looks who lacks a plan.

"Nope, nope. That's absolutely not all right." Roger stands up but stays in the sheltered darkness. "The lawyer," he says again, still grinning.

"I'm just going to turn around," Faith says, and very unsteadily begins to move her long left ski up out of its track, and then, leaning on her poles, her right ski up and out of its track. It is dizzying, and her calves ache, and it is complicated not to cross her ski tips. But it is essential to remain standing. To fall would mean surrender. What is the skiing expression? Tele . . . Tele-something. She wishes she could tele-something. Tele-something the hell away from here. Her thighs burn. In California, she thinks, she is an officer of the court. A public official, sworn to uphold the law – though not to enforce it. She is a force for good.

"You look stupid standing there," Roger says stupidly.

She intends to say nothing more. There is nothing really to say. Talk is not cheap now, and she is concentrating very hard. For a moment she thinks she hears music again, music far away. It can't be.

"When you get all the way around," Roger says, "then I want to show you something." He does not say what. In her mind – moving her skis inches at a time, her ankles heavy – in her mind she says "Then what?" but doesn't say that.

"I really hate your eff-ing family," Roger says. His boots go crunch on the snow. She glances over her shoulder, but to look at him is too much. He is approaching. She will fall and then dramatic, regrettable things will happen. In a gesture he possibly deems dramatic, Roger – though she cannot see it – unzips his blue snowsuit front. He intends her to hear this noise. She is three quarters turned around. She could see him over her left shoulder if she chose to. Have a look, see what all the excitement's about. She is sweating. Underneath she is drenched.

"Yep, life leads you to some pretty interesting situations." He is repeating himself. There is another zipping noise. This is big-time fun in Roger's world-view.

"Yes," she says, "it does." She has come almost fully around now.

She hears Roger laugh a little chuckle, an un-humorous "hunh." Then he says, "Almost." She hears his boots squeeze. She feels his actual self close beside her. This undoubtedly will help to underscore how much he hates her family.

Then there are voices – saving voices – behind her. She cannot help looking over her left shoulder now and up the trail where it climbs into the dark trees. There is a light, followed by another light, like stars coming down from on high. Voices, words, language she doesn't quite understand. Japanese. She does not look at Roger, but simply

slides one ski, her left one, forward into its track, lets her right one
follow and find its way, pushes on her poles. And in just that small
allotment of time and with that amount of effort she is away. She
thinks she hears Roger say something, another "hunh," a kind of
grunting sound but she can't be sure.

*

In the condo everyone is sleeping. The plastic rubber-tree lights are
twinkling. They reflect from the window that faces the ski hill, which
now is dark. Someone, Faith notices (her mother) has devoted much
time to replacing the spent bulbs so the tree can fully twinkle. The
gold star, the star that led the wise men, is lying on the coffee table
like a starfish, waiting to be properly affixed.

Marjorie, the younger, sweeter sister, is asleep on the orange couch,
under the Bruegel scene. She has left her bed to sleep near the tree,
brought her quilted pink coverlet with her.

Naturally Faith has locked Roger out. Roger can die alone and
cold in the snow. Or he can sleep in a doorway or by a steam pipe
somewhere in the Snow Mountain Highlands complex and explain
his situation to the security staff. Roger will not sleep with his pretty
daughters this night. She is taking a hand in things now. These girls
are hers. Though, how naive of her not to know that an offer to take
the girls would immediately be translated by Roger into an invitation
to fuck him. She has been in California too long, has fallen out of
touch with things middle American. How strange that Roger, too,
would say, "Eff-ing." He probably also says "X-mas."

At the ice rink, two teams are playing hockey under high white lights.
A red team opposes a black team. Net cages have been brought on, the
larger rink walled down to regulation size and shape. A few spectators
stand watching – wives and girlfriends. Boyne City versus Petosky;
Cadillac versus Sheboygan, or some such. The little girls' own white
skates are piled by the door she has now safely locked with a dead bolt.

It would be good to put the star on, she thinks. "Now it's time
for the star." Who knows what tomorrow will bring. The arrival of
wise men couldn't hurt.

So, with the flimsy star, which is made of slick aluminum paper and is large and gold and weightless and five-pointed, Faith stands on the Danish dining-table chair and fits the slotted fastener onto the topmost leaf of the rubber-tree plant. It is not a perfect fit by any means, there being no sprig at the pinnacle, so that the star doesn't stand up as much as it leans off the top in a sad, comic, but also victorious way. (This use was never envisioned by the Philippino tree-makers.) Tomorrow others can all add to the tree, invent ornaments from absurd or inspirational raw materials. Tomorrow Roger himself will be rehabilitated, and become everyone's best friend. Except hers.

Marjorie's eyes have opened, though she has not stirred on the couch. For a moment, but only for a moment, she appears dead. "I went to sleep," she says softly and blinks her brown eyes.

"Oh, I saw you," Faith smiles. "I thought you were another Christmas present. I thought Santa had been here early and left you for me." She takes a careful seat on the spindly coffee table, close beside Marjorie – in case there would be some worry to express, a gloomy dream to relate. A fear. She smooths her hand through Marjorie's warm hair.

Marjorie takes a deep breath and lets air go out smoothly through her nostrils. "Jane's asleep," she says.

"And how would you like to go back to bed?" Faith whispers. Possibly she hears a soft tap on the door – the door she has dead bolted. The door she will not open. The door beyond which the world and trouble wait. Marjorie's eyes wander toward the sound, then swim again with sleep. She is safe.

"Leave the tree on," Marjorie instructs, though asleep.

"Sure okay, sure," Faith says. "The tree stays. We keep the tree."

She eases her hand under Marjorie, who, by old habit, reaches, caresses her neck. In an instant she has Marjorie in her arms, pink coverlet and all, carrying her altogether effortlessly into the darkened bedroom where her sister sleeps on one of the twin beds. Carefully she lowers Marjorie onto the empty bed and re-covers her. Again she thinks she hears soft tapping, though it stops. She believes it will not come again this night.

Jane is sleeping with her face to the wall, her breathing deep and audible. Jane is the good sleeper, Marjorie the less reliable one. Faith stands in the middle of the dark, windowless room, between the twin beds, the blinking Christmas lights haunting the stillness that has come at such expense. The room smells musty and dank, as if it's been closed for months and opened just for this purpose, this night, these children. If only briefly she is reminded of Christmases she might've once called her own. "Okay," she whispers. "Okay, okay, okay."

*

Faith undresses in the Master Suite, too tired to shower. Her mother sleeps on one side of their shared bed. She is a small mountain, visibly breathing beneath the covers. A glass of red wine, half-drunk, sits on the bed table beside her molded neck brace. A picture of a white sailboat on a calm blue ocean hangs over the bed. Faith half-closes the door to undress, the blinking Christmas lights shielded.

She will wear pajamas tonight, for her mother's sake. She has bought a new pair. White, pure silk, smooth as water. Blue silk piping.

And here is the unexpected sight of herself in the cheap, wavy door mirror. All good. Just the small pale scar where a cyst was notched from her left breast, a meaningless scar no one would see. But a good effect still. Thin, hard thighs. A small nice belly. Boy's hips. The whole package, nothing to complain about.

There's need of a glass of water. Always take a glass of water to bed, never a glass of red wine. When she passes through the living-room window, her destination the tiny kitchen, she sees that the hockey game is now over. It is after midnight. The players are shaking hands on the ice, others are skating in wide circles. On the expert slope above the rink, lights have been turned on again. Machines with headlights groom the snow at treacherous angles and great risk.

And she sees Roger. He is halfway between the ice rink and the condos, walking back in his powder-blue suit. He has watched the hockey game, no doubt. Roger stops and looks up at her where she stands in the window in her white pjs, the Christmas tree lights blinking as her background. He stops and stares. He has found his black-frame glasses. His mouth is moving, but he makes no gesture. There is no room at this inn for Roger.

In bed, her mother is even larger. A great heat source, vaguely damp when Faith touches her back. Her mother is wearing blue gingham, a nightdress not so different from the muumuu she wears in daylight. She smells unexpectedly good. Rich.

How long, Faith wonders, has it been since she's slept with her mother. A hundred years? Twenty? But good that it would seem so normal.

She has left the door open in case the girls should call, in case they wake up and are afraid, in case they miss their father. The Christmas lights blink off and on merrily beyond the doorway. She can hear snow slide off the roof, an automobile with chains jingling softly somewhere out of sight. She has intended to call for messages but let it slip.

And how long ago, she wonders, was her mother slim and pretty? The sixties? Not so long ago, really. She had been a girl then. They – the sixties – always seem so close. Though to her mother probably not.

Blink, blink, blink, the lights blink.

Marriage. Yes, naturally she would think of that now. Though maybe marriage was only a long plain of self-revelation at the end of which here's someone else who doesn't know you very well. That would be a message she could've left for Jack. "Dear Jack, I now know that marriage is a long plain at the end of which there's etc., etc., etc." You always thought of these things too late. Somewhere, Faith hears more faint music, "Away in a Manger," played prettily on chimes. It is music to sleep to.

And how would they deal with tomorrow? Not the eternal tomorrow, but the promised, practical one. Her thighs feel stiff, yet she is slowly relaxing. Her mother, the mountain beside her, is facing away. How indeed? Roger would be rehabilitated tomorrow, yes, yes. There will be board games. Changes of outfits. Phone calls placed.

She will find the time to ask her mother if anyone had ever been abused, and find out, happily, not. Unusual looks will be passed between and among everyone. Certain names, words will be in short supply, for the sake of all. The girls will again learn to ski and to enjoy it. Jokes will be told. They will feel better, be a family again. Christmas takes care of its own.

Under the Radar

On the drive over to the Nicholsons' for dinner – their first in some time – Marjorie Reeves told her husband, Steven Reeves, that she had had an affair with George Nicholson (their host) a year ago, but that it was all over with now and she hoped he – Steven – would not be mad about it and could go on with life.

At this point they were driving along Quaker Bridge Road where it leaves the Perkins Great Woods Road and begins to border the Shenipsit Reservoir, dark and shadowy and calmly mirrored in the late spring twilight. On the right was dense young timber, beech and alder saplings in pale leaf, the ground damp and cakey. Peepers were calling out from the watery lows. Their turn onto Apple Orchard Lane was still a mile on.

Steven, on hearing this news, began gradually and very carefully to steer their car – a tan Mercedes wagon with hooded yellow headlights – off of Quaker Bridge Road and onto the damp grassy shoulder so he could organize this information properly before going on.

They were extremely young. Steven Reeves was twenty-eight. Marjorie Reeves a year younger. They weren't rich, but they'd been lucky. Steven's job at Packard-Wells was to stay on top of a small segment of a larger segment of a rather small prefabrication intersection that serviced the automobile industry, and where any sudden alteration, or even the rumor of an alteration in certain polymer-bonding formulas could tip crucial down-the-line demand patterns, and in that way affect the betting lines and comfort zones of a good many meaningful client positions. His job meant poring over dense and esoteric petrochemical-industry journals, attending technical seminars, flying to vendor conventions, then writing up detailed status reports and all the while keeping an eye on the market for the benefit of his higher-ups. He'd been a scholarship boy at Bates, studied chemistry, was the only son of a hard-put but upright lobstering family in Pemaquid, Maine, and had done well. His bosses at Packard-Wells liked him, saw themselves in him, and also in him saw character qualities they'd never quite owned – blond and slender callowness tending to gullibility, but backed by caution, ingenuity and a thorough-going, compact toughness. He was sharp. It was his seventh year with the company – his first job. He and Marjorie had been married two years. They had no children. The car had been his bonus two Christmases ago.

When the station wagon eased to a stop, Steven sat for a minute with the motor running, the salmon colored dash lights illuminating his face. The radio had been playing softly – the last of the news, then an interlude for French horns. Responding to no particular signal, he pressed off the radio and in the same movement switched off the ignition, which left the headlights shining on the empty, countrified road. The windows were down to attract the fresh spring air, and when the engine noise ceased the evening's ambient sounds were waiting. The peepers. A sound of thrush wings fluttering in the brush only a few yards away. The noise of something falling from a small distance and hitting an invisible water surface. Beyond the stand of saplings was the West, and through the darkened trunks,

the sky was still pale yellow with the day's light, though here on
Quaker Bridge Road it was nearly dark.

When Marjorie said what she had just said, she'd been looking
straight ahead to where the headlights made a bright path in the dark.
Perhaps she'd looked at Steven once, but having said what she'd said,
she kept her hands in her lap and continued looking ahead. She was
a pretty, blond convictionless girl with small demure features – small
nose, small ears, small chin, though with a surprisingly full-lipped
smile which she practiced on everyone. She was fond of getting a
little tipsy at parties and lowering her voice and sitting on a flowered
ottoman or a burl table top with a glass of something and showing
too much of her legs or inappropriate amounts of her small breasts.
She had grown up in Indiana, studied art at Purdue. Steven had
met her in New York at a party while she was working for a firm
that did child-focused advertizing for a large toymaker. He'd liked
her bobbed hair, her fragile, wispy features, translucent skin and the
slightly husky voice that made her seem more sophisticated than she
was, but somehow convinced her she was, too. In their community,
east of Hartford, the women who knew Marjorie Reeves thought of
her as a bimbo who would not stay married to sweet Steven Reeves
for very long. His second wife would be the right wife for him.
Marjorie was just a starter.

Marjorie, however, did not think of herself that way, only that she
liked men and felt happy and confident around them and assumed
Steven thought this was fine and that in the long run it would help his
career to have a pretty, spirited wife no one could pigeonhole. To set
herself apart and to take an interest in the community she'd gone to
work as a volunteer at a grieving-children's center in Hartford, which
meant all black. And it was in Hartford that she'd had the chance to
encounter George Nicholson and fuck him at a Red Roof Inn until
they'd both gotten tired of it. It would never happen again, was her
view, since in a year it hadn't happened again.

For the two or possibly five minutes now that they had sat on the
side of Quaker Bridge Road in the still airish evening, with the noises

of spring floating in and out of the open window, Marjorie had said nothing and Steven had also said nothing, though he realized that he was saying nothing because he was at a loss for words. A loss for words, he realized, meant that nothing which comes to mind seems very interesting to say as a next thing to what has just been said. He knew he was a callow man – a boy in some ways, still – but he was not stupid. At Bates, he had taken Dr. Sudofsky's class on *Ulysses*, and come away with a sense of irony and humor and the assurance that true knowledge was a spiritual process, a quest, not a storage of dry facts – a thing like freedom which you only fully experienced in practice. He'd also played hockey, and knew that knowledge and aggressiveness were a subtle and surprising and uncommon combination. He had sought to practice both at Packard-Wells.

But for a brief and terrifying instant in the cool padded semi-darkness, just when he began experiencing his loss for words, he entered or at least nearly slipped into a softened fugue-like state in which he began to fear that he perhaps *could* not say another word; that something (work fatigue, shock, disappointment over what Marjorie had admitted) was at that moment causing him to detach from reality and to slide away from the present, and in fact to begin to lose his mind and go crazy to the extent that he was in jeopardy of beginning to gibber like a chimp, or just to slowly slump sideways against the upholstered door and not speak for a long, long time – months – and then only with the aid of drugs be able merely to speak in simple utterances that would seem cryptic, so that eventually he would have to be looked after by his mother's family in Damariscotta. A terrible thought.

And so to avoid that – to save his life and sanity – he abruptly just said a word, any word that he could say into the perfumed twilight inhabiting the car, where his wife was obviously anticipating his reply to her unhappy confession.

And for some reason the word – phrase, really – that he uttered was "ground clutter." Something he'd heard on the TV weather report as they were dressing for dinner.

"Hm?" Marjorie said. "What was it?" She turned her pretty, small-featured face toward him so that her pearl earrings caught light from some unknown source. She was wearing a tiny green cocktail dress and green satin shoes that showed off her incredibly thin ankles and slender bare, brown calves. She had two tiny matching green bows in her hair. She smelled sweet. "I know this wasn't what you wanted to hear, Steven," she said, "but I felt I should tell you before we got to George's. The Nicholsons', I mean. It's all over. It'll never happen again. I promise you. No one will ever mention it. I just lost my bearings last year with the move. I'm sorry." She had made a little steeple of her fingertips, as if she'd been concentrating very hard as she spoke these words. But now she put her hands again calmly in her minty green lap. She had bought her dress especially for this night at the Nicholsons'. She'd thought George would like it and Steven, too. She turned her face away and exhaled a small but detectable sigh in the car. It was then that the headlights went off automatically.

George Nicholson was a big squash-playing, thick-chested, hairy-armed Yale lawyer who sailed his own Hinckley-61 out of Essex and had started backing off from his high-priced Hartford plaintiffs' practice at fifty to devote more time to competitive racket sports and senior skiing. George was a college roommate of one of Steven's firm's senior partners and had "adopted" the Reeves when they moved into the community following their wedding. Marjorie had volunteered Saturdays with George's wife, Patsy, at the Episcopal Thrift Shop during their first six months in Connecticut. To Steven, George Nicholson had recounted a memorable, seasoning summer spent hauling deep-water lobster traps with some tough old sea dogs out of Matinicus, Maine. Later, he'd been a Marine, and sported a faded anchor, ball and chain tattooed on his forearm. Later yet he'd fucked Steven's wife.

Having said something, even something that made no sense, Steven felt a sense of glum and deflated relief as he sat in the silent car beside Marjorie, who was still facing forward. Two thoughts had begun to compete in his reviving awareness. One was clearly occasioned by his conception of George Nicholson. He thought of George Nicholson as a gasbag, but also a forceful man who'd made his pile by letting very little stand in his way. When he thought about George he always remembered the story about Matinicus, which then put into his mind a mental picture of his own father and himself hauling traps somewhere out toward Monhegan. The reek of the bait, the toss of the ocean in late spring, the consoling monotony of the solid, tree-lined shore barely visible through the mists. Thinking through that circuitry always made him vaguely admire George Nicholson, and oddly, made him think he liked George even now, in spite of everything.

The other competing thought was that part of Marjorie's character had always been to confess upsetting things that turned out, he believed, not to be true: being a hooker for a summer up in Saugatuck; topless dancing while she was an undergraduate; heroin experimentation; taking part in armed robberies with her high school boyfriend in Goshen, Indiana, where she was from. When she told these far-fetched stories she would grow distracted and shake her head, as though they were true. And now, while he didn't particularly think any of these stories was a bit truer, he did realize that he didn't really know his wife at all; and that in fact the entire conception of knowing another person – of trust, of closeness, of marriage itself – while not exactly a lie since it existed *someplace* if only as an idea (in his parents' life, at least marginally) was still completely out-of-date, defunct, was something typifying another era, now unfortunately gone. Meeting a girl, falling in love, marrying her, moving to Connecticut, buying a fucking house, starting a life with her and thinking you really knew anything about her – the last part was a complete fiction, which made all the rest a joke. Marjorie might as well have *been* a hooker or held up 7-11s and shot people, for all he really knew about her. And what was more, if he'd said any of this to her, sitting next to him thinking he would never know what, she either would not have understood a word of it or simply would've said, "Well, okay, that's fine." When people talked about the bottom line, Steven Reeves thought, they weren't talking about money, they were talking about what *this* meant, *this* kind of fatal ignorance. Money – losing it, gaining it, spending it, hoarding it – all that was only an emblem, though a good one, of what was happening here right now.

At this moment a pair of car lights rounded a curve somewhere out ahead of where the two of them sat in their station wagon. The lights found both their white faces staring forward in silence. The lights also found a raccoon just crossing the road from the reservoir shore, headed for the woods that was beside them. The car was going faster than might've been evident. The raccoon paused to peer up into the approaching beams, then continued on into the safe, opposite lane. But only then did it look up and notice Steven and Marjorie's car stopped on the verge of the road, silent in the murky evening. And because of that notice it must've decided that where it had been was much better than where it was going, and so turned to scamper back across Quaker Bridge Road toward the cool waters of the reservoir, which was what caused the car – actually it was a beat-up Ford pick-up – to rumble over it, pitching and spinning it off to the side and then motionlessness near the opposite shoulder. "Yaaaa-haaaa-yipeeee!" a man's shrill voice shouted from inside the dark cab of the pick-up, followed by another man's laughter.

And then it became very silent again. The raccoon lay on the road twenty yards in front of the Reeves's car. It didn't struggle. It was merely there.

"Gross," Marjorie said.

Steven said nothing, though he felt less at a loss for words now. His eyes, indeed, felt relieved to fix on the still corpse of the raccoon.

"Do we do something?" Marjorie said. She had leaned forward a few inches as if to study the raccoon through the windshield. Light was dying away behind the slender, young beech trees to the west of them.

"No," Steven said. These were his first words – except for the words he took no responsibility for – since Marjorie had said what she'd importantly said and their car was still moving toward dinner.

It was then that he hit her. He hit her before he knew he'd hit her, but not before he knew he wanted to. He hit her with the back of his open hand without even looking at her, hit her straight in the front of her face, straight in the nose. And hard. In a way, it was more a gesture than a blow, though it was, he understood, a blow. He felt the soft tip of her nose, and then the knuckly cartilage against the hard bones of the backs of his fingers. He had never hit a woman before, and he had never even thought of hitting Marjorie, always imagining he *couldn't* hit her when he'd read newspaper accounts of such things happening in the sad lives of others. He'd hit other people, been hit by other people, plenty of times – tough Maine boys on the ice rinks. Girls were out, though. His father always made that clear. His mother, too.

"Oh, my goodness," was all that Marjorie said when she received the blow. She put her hand over her nose immediately, but then sat silently in the car while neither of them said anything. His heart was not beating hard. The back of his hand hurt a little. This was all new ground. Steven had a small rosy birthmark just where his left sideburn ended and his shaved face began. It resembled the shape of the state of West Virginia. He thought he could feel this birthmark now. His skin tingled there.

And the truth was he felt even more relieved, and didn't feel at all sorry for Marjorie, sitting there stoically, making a little tent of her hand to cover her nose and staring ahead as if nothing had happened. He thought she would cry, certainly. She was a girl who cried – when she was unhappy, when he said something insensitive, when she was approaching her period. Crying was natural. Clearly, though, it was a new experience for her to be hit. And so it called upon something new, and if not new then some strength, resilience, self-mastery normally reserved for other experiences.

"I can't go to the Nicholsons' now," Marjorie said almost patiently. She removed her hand and viewed her palm as if her palm had her nose in it. Of course it was blood she was thinking about. He heard her breathe in through what sounded like a congested nose, then the breath was completed out through her mouth. She was not crying yet. And for that moment he felt not even sure he *had* smacked her – if it hadn't just been just a thought he'd entertained, a gesture somehow uncommissioned.

What he wanted to do, however, was skip to the most important things now, not get mired down in wrong, extraneous details. Because he didn't give a shit about George Nicholson or the particulars of what they'd done in some shitty motel. Marjorie would never leave him for George Nicholson or anyone like George Nicholson, and George Nicholson and men like him – high rollers with Hinckleys – didn't throw it all away for unimportant little women like Marjorie. He thought of her nose, red, swollen, smeared with sticky blood dripping onto her green dress. He didn't suppose it could be broken. Noses held up. And, of course, there was a phone in the car. He could simply make a call to the party. He pictured the Nicholsons' great rambling white-shingled house brightly lit beyond the curving drive, the original elms exorbitantly preserved, the footlights, the low-lit clay court where they'd all played, the heated pool, the Henry Moore out on the darkened lawn where you just stumbled onto it. He imagined saying to someone – not George Nicholson – that Marjorie was ill, had thrown up on the side of the road.

The *right* details, though. The right details to ascertain from her were: *Are you sorry?* (he'd forgotten Marjorie had already said she was sorry) and *What does this mean for the future?* These were the details that mattered.

Surprisingly, the raccoon that had been cartwheeled by the pick-up and then lain motionless, a blob in the near-darkness, had come back to life and was now trying to drag itself and its useless hinder parts off of Quaker Bridge Road and onto the grassy verge and into the underbrush that bordered the reservoir.

"Oh, for God's sake," Marjorie said and put her hand over her damaged nose again. She could see the raccoon's struggle and turned her head away.

"Aren't you even sorry?" Steven said.

"Yes," Marjorie said, her nose still covered as if she wasn't thinking about the fact that she was covering it. Probably, he thought, the pain had gone away some. It hadn't been so bad. "I mean no," she said.

He wanted to hit her again then – this time in the ear – but he didn't. He wasn't sure why not. No one would ever know. "Well, which is it?" he said, and felt for the first time completely furious. The thing that made him furious – all his life, the very maddest – was to be put into a situation in which everything he did was wrong, when right was no longer an option. Now felt like one of those situations. "Which is it?" he said again angrily. "Really." He should just take her to the Nicholsons', he thought, swollen nose, bloody lips, all stoppered up, and let her deal with it. Or let her sit out in the car, or else start walking the 11.6 miles home. Maybe George could come out and drive her in his Rover. These were only thoughts, of course. "Which is it?" he said for the third time. He was stuck on these words, on this bit of barren curiosity.

"I was sorry when I told you," Marjorie said, very composed. She lowered her hand from her nose to her lap. One of the little green bows that had been in her hair was now resting on her bare shoulder. "Though not very sorry," she said. "Only sorry because I had to tell you. And now that I've told you and you've hit me in my face and probably broken my nose, I'm not sorry about anything – except that. Though I'm sorry about being married to you, which I'll remedy as soon as I can." She was still not crying. "So *now*, will you as a gesture of whatever good there is in you, get out and go over and do some-thing to help that poor injured creature that those motherfucking rednecks maimed with their motherfucking pick-up truck and then because they're pieces of shit and low forms of degraded humanity, laughed about? Can you do that, Steven? Is that in your range?" She sniffed back hard through her nose, then expelled a short, deep and defeated moan. Her voice seemed more nasal, more Midwestern even, now that her nose was congested.

"I'm sorry I hit you," Steven Reeves said, and opened the car door onto the silent road.

"I know," Marjorie said in an emotionless voice. "And you'll be sorrier."

When he had walked down the empty macadam road in his tan suit to where the raccoon had been struck then bounced over onto the road's edge, there was nothing now there. Only a small circle of dark blood he could just make out on the nubbly road surface and that might've been an oil smudge. No raccoon. The raccoon with its last reserves of savage, unthinking will had found the strength to pull itself off into the bushes to die. Steven peered down into the dark, stalky confinement of scrubs and bramble that separated the road from the reservoir. It was very still there. He thought he heard a rustling in the low brush where a creature might be, getting itself settled into the soft grass and damp earth to go to sleep forever. Someplace out on the lake he heard a young girl's voice, very distinctly laughing. Then a car door closed farther away. Then another sort of door, a screen door, slapped shut. And then a man's voice saying "Oh no, oh-ho-ho-ho-ho, no." A small white light came on farther back in the trees beyond the reservoir, where he hadn't imagined there was a house. He wondered about how long it would be before his angry feelings stopped mattering to him. He considered briefly why Marjorie would admit this to him now. It seemed so odd.

Then he heard his own car start. The muffled-metal diesel racket of the Mercedes. The headlights came smartly on and disclosed him. Music was instantly loud inside. He turned just in time to see Marjorie's pretty face illuminated, as his own had been, by the salmon dashboard light. He saw the tips of her fingers atop the arc of the steering wheel, heard the surge of the engine. In the woods he noticed a strange glow coming through the trees, something yellow, something out of the low wet earth, a mist, a vapor, something that might be magical. The air smelled sweet now. The peepers stopped peeping. And then that was all.

Dominion

Madeleine Granville stood at the high window of the Hotel Queen Elizabeth II, trying to decide which tiny car far below on Wellington Street was her yellow Saab. Henry Rothman was tying his tie in front of the mirror. Henry was catching a plane in two hours. Madeleine was staying behind in Montreal, where she lived.

Henry and Madeleine had been having a much more than ordinary friendship for two years – the kind of friendship no one but the two of them was expected to know about (if others knew, they'd decided, it didn't matter because no one *really* knew). They were business associates. She was a chartered accountant, he was an American lobbyist for the firm she worked for, the West-Consolidated Group, specializing in enhanced agricultural food additives and doing big business abroad. Henry was forty-nine, Madeleine was thirty-three. As business associates, they'd traveled together a great deal, often to Europe, staying together in many beds in many hotel rooms until late on many mornings, eating scores of very good restaurant meals, setting out upon innumerable days in bright noon sunshine, later saying their goodbyes in other hotel rooms or in airports, in car-parks, hotel lobbies, taxi stands, bus stops. While apart, which had been most of the time, they had missed each other, talked on the phone often, never written. But when they'd come each time again into the other's presence, they'd felt surprise, exhilaration, fulfillment, grateful happy relief. Henry Rothman lived in D.C., where he maintained a comfortable, divorced lawyer's life. Madeleine had settled in a tree-lined suburb with her child and her architect husband. Everyone who worked with them, of course, knew everything and talked about it constantly behind their backs. Yet the general feeling was that it wouldn't last very long; and beyond that it was best to stay out of other people's business. Conflicted gossip about people doing what you yourself would like to be doing was very Canadian, Madeleine said.

But now, they'd decided, was the time for it to be over. They loved each other – they both acknowledged that. Though they possibly were not *in* love (these were Madeleine's distinctions). Yet, they had been in *something*, she understood, possibly something even better than love, something with its own intense and timeless web, densely tumultuous interiors and transporting heights. What it exactly *was* was hazy. But it had not been nothing.

As always, other people were involved – no one in Rothman's life, it was true, but two in Madeleine's. And to these two, life had been promised a steady continuance. So either what was not just an affair ended now – they'd both agreed – or it went much much further, out onto a terrain that bore no boundaries or markers, a terrain full of terrific hazards. And neither of them wanted that.

It could as easily have stopped six months ago, in London, Henry had thought, on the plane flying in the day before yesterday. Seated together at a sidewalk café on Sloane Square one spring morning, with taxis pouring past, he and Madeleine had suddenly found they had nothing much to say at the precise moment when they'd always had something to say – an enjoyable prefiguring of their luncheon plans, rehearsing their assessments of a troublesome client, discussing reviews of a movie they might attend, or an encoded mention of lovemaking the night before – all of the engaging, short-range complications of arrangements such as theirs. Love, Henry remembered thinking then, was a lengthy series of insignificant questions whose answers you couldn't live without. And it was these questions they'd run out of interesting answers for. But to have ended it then, so far from home and familiar surroundings, would've been inconsiderate. Ending it then would've meant something about themselves neither of them would've believed: that it hadn't mattered very much; that they were people who did things that didn't matter very much; and that they either importantly did or didn't know that about themselves. None of these seemed true.

Therefore, they'd kept on. Though over the intervening months their telephone conversations grew fewer and briefer. Henry went alone to Paris twice. He began a relationship with a woman in Washington, then ended it without Madeleine seeming to notice. Her thirty-third passed unacknowledged. And then, just as he was planning a trip to San Francisco, Henry suggested a stopover in Montreal. A visit. It was clear enough to both of them.

The evening of his arrival, they'd eaten dinner near the Biodome, in a new Basque place Madeleine had read about. She dressed up in a boxy, unflattering black wool dress and black tights. They drank too much Nonino, talked little, walked to the St. Lawrence, held hands in the chill October night, while quietly observing the fact that without a patched-together future to involve and distract them, life became quite repetitious in very little time. But still, they had gone back to his room at the QE II, stayed in bed until one AM, made love with genuine passion, talked an hour in the dark, and then Madeleine had driven home to her husband and son.

Later, lying alone in bed in the warm, clocking darkness, Henry thought that sharing the future with someone would certainly mean that repetitions had to be managed more skillfully. Or else it meant that sharing the future with someone wasn't a very good idea, and he should perhaps begin to realize it.

*

Madeleine had been crying by the window (because she felt like it), while Henry had continued getting dressed, not exactly ignoring her, but not exactly attending to her either. She had re-arrived at ten to drive him to the airport. It was their old way when he came to town for business. She wore fitted blue corduroys under a frumpy red jumper with a little round white collar. She was gotten up, Henry noticed, strangely like an American flag.

In the room now neither of them ventured near the bed. They had coffee standing up, while they passed over small office matters, mentioned the fall weather – hazy in the morning, brilliant in the afternoon – typical for Montreal, Madeleine observed. She looked at the *National Press* while Henry finished in the bathroom.

It was when he emerged to tie his tie, that he noticed Madeleine had stopped crying and was studying down twelve stories to the street.

"I was just thinking," she said, "about all the interesting things you don't know about Canada." She had put on a pair of clear-rimmed glasses, perhaps to hide that she'd been crying, and that were other-wise intended to make her look studious. Madeleine's hair was thick and dark-straw colored, and tended to dry unruliness, so that she often bushed it back with a big silver clip, as she'd done this morning. Her face was pale, as if she'd slept too little, and her features, which were pleasing and soft with full expressive lips and dark, thick eye-brows, seemed almost lost in her hair.

Henry went on tying his tie. Out in the cityscape beyond the window was a big, T-shaped construction crane, the long crossing arm of which appeared to exit both sides of Madeleine's head like an arrow. He could see the little green operator's house, where a tiny human was visible inside, backed by the light of a tiny window.

"All the famous Canadians you'd never guess were Canadians, for instance." She didn't look at him, just stared down.

"*Par exemple?*" This was as much French as he knew. They spoke English here. They could speak English to him. "Name one."

Madeleine glanced at him condescendingly. "Denny Doherty, of the Mommas and the Poppas. He's from Halifax. Donald Sutherland's from the Maritimes someplace. P.E.I., I guess."

Madeleine appeared different from how she actually was – a quality he always found strangely titillating, because it made her unreadable. Generally people looked how they were, he thought. Prim people looked prim, etc. Madeleine *looked* like her name implied, slightly old-fashioned, formal, settled, given to measuring her responses, to being at ease with herself and her character assessments.

But in fact she was nothing of the kind. She was a strong farm girl from north of Halifax herself, had been a teenage curling champion, liked to stay up late having sex, laughing and drinking schnapps, and could sometimes be quite insecure. He thought this incongruity was a matter of their ages (he was sixteen when she was born), and that other people who knew her didn't find it incongruous at all. In general, he thought, younger people were more accepting now, Canadians especially. He would miss that.

Madeleine mused back out the window at the cars lined along the side of the Basiliscus de Cathedral de la Reins du Monde. "It's hazy to be flying," she said. "I'd rather just stay here."

It was eleven. The breakfast tray sat on the disheveled bed, on top of the scattered newspapers. Henry liked the Canadian papers, all the stories about things going wrong that he didn't have to care about.

Henry Rothman was a large bespectacled man, who when he was young had looked – and he'd agreed – like the actor Elliott Gould in his role, in *Bob & Carol & Ted & Alice*, though he'd always felt he was more light-hearted than the character Elliott Gould had played – Ted. Rothman was a lawyer as well as a lobbyist, and represented several big firms that did business all over the world. He was a Jew, just like Elliott Gould, but had grown up in Roanoke, gone to Virginia then Virginia Law School. His parents had been small-town doctors who now lived in Boca Grande where they were by turns ecstatic and bored in a condominium doing nothing. Henry practiced in a firm that included his two brothers, David and Michael, who were litigators. He had been divorced ten years, had a daughter living in Needham, Mass., teaching school.

Madeleine Granville knew all about the cost of things: fertilizer, train transport, container ships full of soybeans, corn, she understood futures, labor costs, currency, the price of money. She'd studied economics at McGill, spoke five languages, had lived in Greece and had dreamed of being a painter until she met a handsome young architect on a train from Athens to Sofia, and quickly married him. They'd settled in Montreal where the architect had his practice and where they liked it fine. To Rothman it seemed young, heady, exciting, but also savvy, solid, smart. He liked it very much. It seemed very Canadian. Canada, in so many ways, seemed superior to America anyway. Canada was saner, more tolerant, friendlier, safer, less litigious. He had thought of retiring here, possibly to Cape Breton, where he'd never been. He and Madeleine had discussed living together by the ocean. It had become one of those completely transporting subjects you give your complete attention to for a week – buying maps, making real estate inquiries, researching the average winter temperature – then later can't understand why you'd ever considered it.

In truth Rothman loved Washington; liked his life, his big house behind Capitol Hill, his law-school chums and his brothers, the city's slightly antic, slightly tattered southernness, his poker partners, his membership at the Cosmos Club. His access. He occasionally even had dinner with his ex-wife, Laura, who, like him was a lawyer and had remained unmarried. Who you really were, and what you believed, Rothman realized, were represented by what you maintained or were helpless to change. Very few people really *got* that; most people in his stratum thought everything was possible at all times, and so continued to try to become something else. But after a while these personal truths simply revealed themselves like maxims, no matter what you said or did to resist them. And that was that. That was you. Henry Rothman understood he was a man fitted primarily to live alone, no matter what kind of enticing sense anything else made. And that was fine.

Madeleine was writing something with her fingertip on the window glass, while she waited for him to finish getting dressed. Crying was over now. No one was mad at anyone. She was just amusing herself. Pale daylight shone through her bunched yellow hair.

"Men think women won't ever change; women think men will always change," she said concentrating, as if she were writing these words on the glass. "And lo and behold, they're both wrong." She tapped the glass with her fingertip, then stuck out her lower lip in a confirming way and widened her eyes and looked around at him. What a complicated girl she was, Henry thought; her life just now beginning to seem confining. In a year she would probably be far away from here. This love affair with him, was just a symptom. Although a painless one.

He came to the window in his starched shirtsleeves and put his arms around her from behind in a way that felt unexpectedly fatherly. She let herself be drawn in, then turned and put her face nose-first against his shirt, her arms loose about his soft waist. She took off her glasses to be kissed. She smelled warm and soapy, her skin where he touched her neck under her ear, as smooth as glass.

"What's changed, what hasn't changed?" he said softly.

"Oh," she said into his shirt folds and shook her head. "Mmmmm. I was just trying to decide . . ."

He pressed with his big fingers into the taut construction of her body, held her close. "Say," he said softly. She could speak, then he could provide a good answer. The window made the back of his hands feel cool.

"Oh well." She let out a breath. "I was trying to determine how to think about all this." She idly rubbed her shoe sole over the polished toe of his black wingtip, scuffing it. "Some things are always real-*er* than others. I was wondering if this would seem very real at a future date. You know?"

"It will," Henry said. Their thinking was not so far apart now. If they were far apart, someone might feel unfairly treated.

"You respect the real things more, I think." Madeleine swallowed, then exhaled again. "The phony things disappear." She drummed her fingers lightly on his back. "I'd hate it if this just disappeared from memory."

"It won't," he said. "I can promise you." Now was the moment to get them out of the room. Too many difficult valedictory issues were suddenly careering around. "How about getting some lunch?"

Madeleine sighed. "Oh," she said. "Yes, lunch would be superior. I'd like some lunch."

The phone on the bed table began ringing then, shrill rings which startled them both and for some reason made Henry look suddenly out the window, as if the noise came from out there. Not so far away, on a pretty wooded, urban hillside he could see the last of the foliage – deep oranges and profound greens and dampened browns. In Washington, summer was barely over.

He was startled when the phone rang a fourth time. It had not rung since he'd been in the room. No one knew he was here. Henry stared at the white telephone beside the bed. "Don't you want to answer it," she said. They were both staring at the white telephone.

The phone rang a fifth time, very loudly, then stopped.

"It's a wrong number. Or it's the hotel wanting to know if I'm out yet." He touched his glasses' frame. Madeleine looked at him and blinked. She didn't think it was a wrong number, he realized. She believed it was someone inconvenient. Another woman. Whoever was next in line after her. Though that wasn't true. There was no one in line.

When the phone rang again, he hurried the white receiver to his ear and said, "Rothman."

"Is this *Henry* Rothman?" A smirky, unfamiliar man's voice spoke.

"Yes." He looked at Madeleine, who was watching him in a way that wished to seem interested but was in fact accusatory.

"Well, is this the Henry Rothman who's the high-dollar lawyer from the States?"

"Who is this?" He stared at the hotel's name on the telephone. Queen Elizabeth II.

"What's the matter, asshole, are you nervous now?" The man chuckled a mirthless chuckle.

"I'm not nervous. No," Henry said. "Why don't you tell me who this is." He looked at Madeleine again. She was staring at him disapprovingly, as if he were staging the entire conversation and the line was actually dead.

"You're a fucking nutless wonder, that's who you are," the voice on the phone said. "Who've you got hiding in your hole there with you. Who's sucking your dick, you cockroach."

"Why don't you just tell me who this is and leave the cockroach stuff out of it," Rothman said in a patient voice, wanting to slam the phone down. But the man abruptly hung up before he could.

The big black crane with the little green house attached was still emerging from both sides of Madeleine's head. The words *Saint Hyacinthe* were written along one armature.

"You look shocked," she said. Then suddenly she said, "Oh no, oh shit, shit." She turned toward the window and put her hands to her cheeks. "Don't tell me," she said. "It was Jeff, wasn't it? Shit, shit, shit."

"I didn't admit anything," Henry said, and felt immensely irritated. Loud pounding would commence immediately from out in the hall, he supposed, then shouting and kicking, and a terrible fistfight that would wreck the room. All this, just moments before he could make it to the airport. He considered again that he *hadn't* admitted anything. "I didn't admit anything," he said again and felt foolish.

"I have to think," Madeleine said. She looked pale and was patting her cheeks softly, as if this was a way of establishing order inside her head. It was theatrical, he thought. "I just have to be quiet a moment," she said again.

Henry surveyed the cramped, odorless little room: the cluttered bed with the silver breakfast utensils, the crystal bud vase with a red rose, the dresser and the slightly dusty mirror, the arm chair with a blue hydrangea print; two reproductions of Monet's *Water Lilies* facing each other on featureless white walls. Nothing here foretold that things would work out perfectly and he would make his flight on time, or that *none* of that would happen. Here was merely a venue, a voiceless place with nothing consoling about it. He could remember when rooms felt better than this. Coming to Montreal had been peculiarly pointless – a vanity, and he was trapped in it. He thought what he often thought at moments when things went very bad – and this seemed bad: that he over-reached. He always had. When you were young it was a good quality, it meant you were ambitious, headed upward. But when you were forty-nine, it wasn't very good.

"I have to think where he might be." Madeleine had turned and was staring at the phone as if her husband were inside it and threatening to burst out. It was one of those moments when Madeleine was not how she appeared: not the formal, reserved girl in Gibson Girl hair, but a kid in a bind, trying to dream up what to do. This was less intriguing.

"Maybe the lobby," Henry said, while thinking the words: *Jeff. A man lurking in the hall outside my door, waiting to come in and make mayhem*. It was an extremely unpleasant thought, one that made him feel tired.

The telephone rang again, and Henry answered it.

"Let me speak to my wife, cockroach," the same sneering voice said. "Can you pull out of her that long?"

"Who do you want?" Henry said.

"Let me speak to Madeleine, prick," the man said.

The name Madeleine produced a tiny upheaval in his brain. "Madeleine's not here," Henry Rothman lied.

"Right. You mean she's busy at the moment. I get it. Maybe I should call back."

"Maybe you've made a mistake here," Henry said. "I said Madeleine's not here."

"*Is* she sucking your dick," the man said. "Imagine that. I'll just wait."

"I haven't seen her," Henry went on lying. "We had dinner last night. Then she went home."

"Yep, yep, yep," the man said and laughed sarcastically. "That was *after* she sucked your dick."

Madeleine was still facing out the window, listening to one half of the conversation.

"Where are you?" Henry said, feeling disturbed.

"Why do you want to know that? You think I'm outside your door calling you on a cell phone?" He heard some metal-sounding clicks and scrapes on the line, and Jeff's voice became distant and unintelligible. "Well, open the door and find out," the man said, back in touch. "You might be right. Then I'll kick your ass."

"I'll be happy to come talk to you," Henry said, then stopped himself. Why say such a stupid thing? There was no need. He caught himself in the mirror just then, a large man in shirtsleeves and a tie, with a little bit of belly. It was embarrassing to be this man. He looked away.

"So, you want to come talk to me?" the man said, then laughed again. "You don't have the nuts."

"Sure I do," Henry said miserably. "Tell me where you are. I've got the nerve."

"Then I *will* kick your ass," the man said in a haughty voice.

"Well, we'll see."

"Where's Madeleine?" the man sounded deranged.

"I have no earthly idea." It occurred to Henry that every single thing he was saying was a lie. That he had somehow brought into existence a situation in which there was not a shred of truth. How could that happen?

"Are you telling the truth?"

"Yes. I am," he lied. "Now, where are you?"

"In my fucking car. I'm a block from your hotel, asshole."

"I probably can't find you there," Henry said, looking at Madeleine, staring at him. He had things back under control, or nearly. Just like that. He could tell in her expression – a pale face, with bleak admiration in it.

"I'll be at your hotel in five minutes, Mr. big man," Madeleine's husband said.

"I'll wait for you in the lobby," Henry said. "I'm tall, and I'll be wearing –"

"I know, I know," the man said. "You'll look like an asshole no matter what you're wearing."

"Okay," Henry said.

The husband clicked off.

*

Madeleine had taken a seat on the arm of the blue-hydrangea chair, her hands clasped tightly. He felt a great deal older and also superior to her, largely, he understood, because she looked sad. He had taken care of things, as he always had.

"He thinks you're not here," Henry said. "So you'd better leave. I'm going to meet him downstairs. You have to find a back door out." He started looking around for his suit coat.

Madeleine smiled at him almost wondrously.

"I appreciate your not telling him I'm here."

"You *are* here," Henry said. He forgot his coat and began looking for his billfold and his change, his handkerchief, his pocket-knife, the collection of essential objects he carried. He would check out later. All of this was idiotic now.

"You're not a bad man, are you?" she said sweetly. "Sometimes I'll be alone, or I'll be waiting for you, and I'll just get mad and decide you're a shit. But you really aren't. You're kind of brave. You sort of have principles."

These words – principles, brave, shit, waiting – for some reason made him feel unexpectedly, heart-poundingly nervous, precisely when he didn't want to feel nervous. He was not supposed to be nervous. He felt very large and cumbersome and almost frantic in the room with her. Not superior. He could just as easily start shouting at her. The fact that she was calm and pretty was intolerable.

"I think it's time for you to leave," he said, thinking again and suddenly about his suit coat, trying to calm himself.

"Yeah, sure," Madeleine said, and reached to the side of the blue chair for her purse. She felt inside for keys without looking and produced a yellow plastic-springy car key loop, which seemed to make her stand up. "When will I see you?" she said and touched the bushed-up back of her hair. So changeable, he thought. "This is a little abrupt. I'd pictured something a little more poignant."

"It'll all be fine," Henry said and manufactured a smile that calmed him.

"Setting aside the matter of when I'll see you again."

"Setting it aside," he said, keeping the smile.

She flipped the yellow, springy key loop back and forth once across her fingers and started for the door, going past where Rothman was waiting for her to leave. No kiss. No hug. "Jeff's not violent," she said. "Maybe you two'll like each other. You have me in common, after all." She smiled as she opened the door.

"That may not be enough for a friendship."

"I'm sorry this is ending this way," Madeleine said quietly.

"Me, too," Henry Rothman said.

She smiled at him strangely and let herself out, permitting the door to shut with a soft click. He thought she hadn't heard him.

*

Waiting in the elevator vestibule, where a cigar aroma hung in the air, he began now to contemplate that he was on his way to meet the irate husband of a woman he didn't love but had nevertheless been screwing. It was like a movie. How was he supposed to think about all this? This would be a man he didn't know but who had every right to hate him and possibly want to kill him. This would be a man whose life he had entered uninvited, played fast and loose with, possibly spoiled, then ignored, but now wanted out of, thank you. Anyone could agree that whatever bad befell him was exactly what he deserved, and that possibly nothing was quite bad enough. In America, people sought damages in this sort of disagreement, but probably not in Canada. He thought about what his father would say. His father was a large man, gone bald, with a great stiffened stomach and an acerbic manner from years of treating Virginia-cracker anti-Semites with lung cancer. "At the bottom of the mine is where they keep the least amount of light," his father liked to say. Which was how he felt – in the dark without a reasonable idea for how to go about this. But not frantic now. More like engaged. He'd never been able to stay frantic.

But just blundering in as though he understood everything and letting events take place willy-nilly would certainly be the wrong course. He didn't need to know much about Jeff – it had never been necessary. But knowing nothing was unlawyerly. On the other hand, there was something so profoundly *un*serious about this whole debacle, that a sudden urge he recognized as similar to derangement made him want to break out laughing just as the mirrored elevator slid open. Still, as long as Madeleine was out of the hotel, and as long as Jeff hadn't kicked in the door and caught them in the middle of something private – which hadn't happened – then who cared who knew who? The lawyer Henry Rothman said this was all about something a man he didn't know might dream up, versus what he himself would never admit to. Nothing added to nothing. He would simply tell as many lies as necessary – which *was* lawyerly: a show of spurious good will being better than no show of any will. *Actual* good will would be represented by the trouble of inventing a lie to cancel out the bad will of having an affair with Madeleine in the first place. And since his relationship with Madeleine was now over with, Jeff could claim the satisfaction of believing he'd caused it to be over. Everybody gets to think he wins, though no one does. That was extremely lawyerly.

Stepping out into the wide, bright lobby, Henry refocused his eyes to the light and the new, congested atmosphere, a throng of hotel guests pulling suitcases on wheels toward the revolving doors and out to the street. Many were smiling, slow-moving elderlies with plastic cards strung around their necks and little fanny packs full of their valuables; most were speaking indecipherable French. He felt, he realized, absolutely calm.

The lobby otherwise offered a pleasant, inauthentic holiday-festive feel, with big gold and glass chandeliers and humming activity. It was like a stage lighted for a musical before the principals came on. He strolled out toward the middle, beyond which show-case windows of the expensive clothing stores and gift shops lined the street side, and the people gazing in the windows looked pleased and well cared for, as though they were expecting something happy to occur soon. It felt like the Mayflower in Washington, where he used to meet clients. And at the same time it felt foreign in the comfortable, half-mysterious way Canada always felt; as if the floors had been tilted three degrees off from what you were used to, and the doors opened from a different side. Nothing you couldn't negotiate. America, run by the Swiss, Madeleine said.

From the crowded middle-lobby, he observed no one who might be a Jeff. A group of small American-sounding children trooped past in a ragged line, all wearing quilted white tae kwon do uniforms and holding hands. They too were headed toward the revolving doors, followed by some large, middle-aged black ladies, eight of them, all dressed in big quilted fall frocks with matching expensive-looking feathered hats. Southerners, he realized – the ladies all talking far too loud about their bus trip down to Maine this afternoon, and about something that had happened in the night that had been scandalous and was making them laugh.

Then he noticed a man watching him, a man standing beside the entrance to the English sweater shop. He couldn't be Madeleine's husband, Henry thought. He was too young – no more than mid-twenties. The man wore black jeans, white sneakers and a black leather jacket; he had rough crew cut blond hair and was wearing yellow aviator glasses. He looked like a college student, not an architect. If the man weren't staring at him so intently, he would never have noticed him.

When Henry again caught his eye, the man abruptly began walking straight toward him, hands thrust inside his black jacket side pockets, as if he might be hiding something there, and Henry realized this man was in fact Madeleine's husband, could only be him, despite looking ten years younger than Madeleine, and twenty-five years younger than himself. This would be different from the rendezvous he'd anticipated. It would be easier. The husband wasn't even very big.

When he was ten feet away, just at the edge of the crimson carpet, the man stopped, his hands still in his pockets, and simply stared, as if something uncertain about Rothman – something unassociated in his identity – needed to be certified.

"I'm probably who you're looking for," Henry said across the space between them. He noticed again the tae kwon do kids still filing out toward the street, still holding hands.

Madeleine's husband, or the man he thought was Madeleine's husband, didn't say anything but began walking toward him again, only slowly now, as if he was trying to give the impression that he'd become intrigued by something. It was all too ridiculous. More theatricality. They should have lunch, he could tell the man a lot of lies and then pay the check. That would be good enough.

"I saw your picture," the young man said, actually seeming to sneer. He didn't remove his hands from his pockets. He was much smaller than expected, but very intense. Possibly he was nervous. His aviator glasses emblemized nervous intensity, as did this black jacket zipped up to his neck so you couldn't tell what he had on underneath it. Madeleine's husband was handsome but in a reduced, delicate, vaguely spiritless way, as if he'd once failed at something significant and hadn't altogether gotten over it. It was odd, he thought, that Madeleine could find them both – himself the big cumbersome Jew and this small, insignificant French-seeming man – attractive.

"I'm Henry Rothman." He extended his large hand, but the husband ignored it. What picture had he seen? One she'd taken, he supposed, and rashly kept. A mistake.

"Where the fuck's Madeleine," the young man said.

These were like the words he'd said on the phone, yet he didn't seem like a young man who *would* say such a thing, or whatever he'd said. Cockroach. Sucking your dick. He didn't seem that vulgar. It was absurd. He felt completely in control of things now. "I don't know where Madeleine is," he said. And it was true, which made him relax

even more. He was prepared to offer a quick trip up to the room. But
Madeleine had a habit of leaving earrings, toiletry essentials, articles
of underclothing wherever she'd been. Too risky.

"I have an eight-year-old son," the intense, bespectacled young
man said, and seemed to set his shoulders inside his bomber jacket.
He blinked at Henry and leaned forward on the balls of his feet,
making himself appear even more reduced. His eyes behind his yellow
lenses were the blandest uninflected brown, and his mouth was small
and thin. His skin was soft and olive-tinted, with a faint flush of
emotion in his cheeks. He was like a pretty little actor, Henry thought,
clean-shaven and actorishly fit-looking. Madeleine had married a
pretty boy. Why indeed *ever* have a Henry Rothman in your life if
this boy appealed to you? It made him feel his most human qualities
had been *appropriated* for purposes he didn't approve. It wasn't a
good feeling.

"I know you do," Henry said about the business of the child.

"So, I don't want to fuck with you," the young man said, redden-
ing. "I'm not about to let you fuck up my marriage and keep my
son from having two parents at home. Do you understand that? I
want you to." His soft boy's mouth became unexpectedly hard, almost
snarly. He had small, tightly-bunched square teeth that detracted
from his beauty and his anger and made him seem vaguely corrupted.
"If it wasn't for that, I wouldn't give a goddamn what you and
Madeleine did together," he went on. "Fuck in hotels rooms all
over the planet and I couldn't give a shit."

"I guess you've made your point, then," Henry said.

"Oh, am I making a point?" Madeleine's husband said, widening
his eyes behind his idiotic lenses. "I didn't realize that. I thought I was
just explaining to you the facts of life, since you're way out of touch
with them. I wasn't trying to persuade you. Do you understand?"
The boy didn't remove his eyes from Henry's. An aroma of inexpen-
sive leather had begun wafting off the black jacket, as if he'd bought
it just that day. Henry began to consider that he'd never owned a
black leather jacket. In Roanoke, well-off doctors' sons didn't go in for

those. Their style had been madras sports coats and white bucks. Jewish country club style.

"I understand what you mean," Henry said in what he assumed would seem a fatigued voice.

Madeleine's husband glared at him, but Henry realized that he himself wasn't the least bit more serious about this. Merely less engaged. And he would be willing to bet money Madeleine's husband wasn't serious either, though he perhaps didn't know it and somehow believed he felt great passion about *all* this baloney. Only neither of them were truly up against anything here. Everything they were doing, they were choosing to do – he was choosing to be here, and this Jeff was choosing to put this unconvincingly ferocious look on his face. They should talk about something else now. Ice hockey.

"I admit I may like Madeleine more than I ought to," Henry said and felt satisfied with that. "I may have acted in some ways that aren't entirely in your interest."

At this, the young man blinked his lightless brown eyes more rapidly. "Is that so?" he said. "Is this your great admission?"

"I'm afraid it is," Henry said, and smiled for the first time. He wondered where Madeleine actually *was* at the very moment he'd admitted to her boy husband, in his own fashion at least, that he'd been fucking her. He'd only done it so that something that passed between himself and this young man could have a grain of substance to it. "What kind of architecture do you do?" he asked companionably. Some people were speaking French close by. He looked around to see who. It would be so nice just to start speaking French now, or Russian. Anything. Madeleine's husband said something he wasn't sure he understood. "Excuse me." He smiled again tolerantly.

"I said fuck you," the young man said and stepped closer. "If you persist with this, I'll arrange for something really bad to happen to you. Something you don't want to happen. And don't think I won't do that. Because I will."

"Well. I certainly believe you," Henry said. "You have to believe that when someone says it. It's the rule. So, I believe you." He looked down at his own white shirt front and noticed a tiny black decoration of Madeleine's mascara from when she had pressed close to him by the window after crying. It made him feel fatigued all over again.

The young man stepped back now. His face had lost its blush and looked pale and mottled. He had never removed his hands from his pockets. He could have a gun there. Though this was Canada. No one got murderous over infidelity.

"You American assholes," Madeleine's husband said. "You've got divided inner selves. It's in your history. You have choices about everything. It's pathetic. You don't really inhabit anything. You're cynical. The whole fucking country of you." He shook his head and seemed disgusted.

"Take all the time you want. This is your moment," Henry said.

"No, that's enough," the young man said and looked tired himself. "You know what you need to know."

"I do," Henry said. "You made that clear."

Madeleine's husband turned and without speaking, strode off across the festive gilt-and-red lobby and out the revolving doors where the tae kwon do children had gone, disappearing as they had amongst the passersby. Henry looked at his wristwatch. This had all occupied fewer than five minutes.

*

Back in his room he changed his shirt and arranged his clothes and toiletries into his suitcase. The room was cold now, as though someone had shut off the heat or opened a window down a hallway. Two message slips lay on the carpet, half under the door. These would be from Madeleine, or else they were new, second-thought threats from the husband. He decided to leave them be. Though some insistent quality about the message slips triggered a sudden strong urge to make up the bed, straighten the room, set out the breakfast tray, urges which meant, he understood, that his life was becoming messy. It probably wouldn't be better until he was on the plane.

But standing exactly where Madeleine had stood earlier, he watched the big T-shaped crane slowly lift a great concrete-filled bucket toward the top of an unfinished building's high silhouette. He wondered again where, in this strange disjointed city, Madeleine was. Having a coffee with a girlfriend she could regale the day to; or waiting for her son to get out of school, or for the husband to arrive and some brittle, unhappy bickering to commence. Nothing he envied. On the window glass, he saw where she'd been writing with her finger; it showed up now that the air in the room was colder. It seemed to say Denny. What or who was Denny? Maybe the message was someone else's, some previous hotel guest.

And then, for no apparent reason he felt exhausted to the point of being dazed. Sometime, too, in the last hour, he had cracked off a sizeable piece of a molar. The jagged little spike caught at the already-tender tip of his tongue (the broken part he'd swallowed without knowing it). The day *had* worked its little pressures. He took off his glasses and lay down across the newspapers. He could hear a muffled TV in another room, a studio audience laughing. There was time to sleep for a minute or five.

About Madeleine, though: there had been a time when he'd loved her, when he'd said he loved her, felt so rather completely. None of the foolishness about love or being *in* love. One definite time he could remember had been on a pebbly beach in Ireland, near a little village called Round Stone, in Connemara, on a trip they'd made by car from Dublin, where they'd seen investors and negotiated significant advantages for the client. They'd laid a picnic on the rocky shingle and staring off into the growing evening, declared the lights they could see to be the lights of Cape Breton, where her father had been born, and where life would be better – though in true geography, they'd been facing north and were only viewing the opposite side of the bay. Behind them in the village, there'd been a little fun fair with a lighted merry-go-round and a tiny bright row of arcades that glowed upwards as the night fell. There, *that* time, he'd loved Madeleine Granville then. And there were other times, several times when he knew. Why even question it?

Even then, however, there was always the "Is this it?" issue.

Thinking of it made him think of his father again. His father had been a born New Yorker, and had retained New Yorker ways. "So, Henry. Is this it for you?" he'd say derisively. His father always felt there should be more, more for Henry, more for his brothers, more than they had, more than they'd settled for. To settle, to not over-reach was to accept too little. And so, in his father's view, even if all was exquisite and unequaled, which it might've seemed, would it still get no better than this in life? Life always *had* gotten better. There'd always been more to come. Although, he was forty-nine now, and there were changes you didn't notice – physical, mental, spiritual changes. Parts of life had been lived and never would be again. Maybe the balance's tip had *already* occurred, and something about *today*, when he'd later think back from some point further on, *today* would seem to suggest that then was when "things" began going wrong, or were already wrong, or was even when "things" were at their greatest pinnacle. And then, of course, at that later moment, you *would* be up against something. You'd be up against your destination point, when no more interesting choices were available, only less and less and less interesting ones.

Still, at this moment, he didn't know that; because if he did know it he might decide just to stay on here with Madeleine – though, of course, staying wasn't really an option. Madeleine was married and had never said she wanted to marry him. The husband had been right about choices, merely wrong in his estimation of them. Choices were what made the world interesting, made life a possible place to operate in. Take choices away and what difference did anything make? Everything became Canada. The trick was simply to find your-self up against it as little as possible. Odd, Henry thought, that this boy should know anything.

In the hall outside the room he heard women's voices speaking French very softly. The housekeepers, waiting for him to leave. He couldn't understand what they were saying, and so for a time he slept to the music of their strange, wittering language.

*

When he turned away from the cashier's, folding his receipt, he found Madeleine Granville waiting for him, standing beside the great red pillar where luggage was stacked. She'd changed clothes, pulled her damp hair severely back in a way that emphasized her full mouth and dark eyes. She looked jaunty in a pair of nicely fitted brown tweed trousers, and a houndstooth jacket and expensive-looking lace-up walking shoes. Everything seemed to emphasize her slenderness and youth. She was carrying a leather knapsack and seemed, to Henry, to be leaving on a trip. She looked extraordinarily pretty, a way he'd seen her look other times. He wondered if she was expecting to leave with him, if matters with the husband had gone that way.

"I left you two messages." She smiled in a mockingly amused way. "You didn't think I'd let you take a taxi, did you?"

Some of the same people he'd seen earlier were present in the lobby – a child sitting alone in a big throne chair, wearing his white tae kwon do get-up. A black woman in a brocaded fall suit, having a present wrapped in the sweater shop. It was past noon. He'd missed lunch.

"Are we going fox hunting?" he said, hoisting his suitcase.

"I'm taking Patrick to see the last of the fall foliage after school." Patrick was her son. She held one arm out, extended a foot stylishly. "Don't I look autumnal?"

"You're standing right where I had a truly ridiculous conversation an hour ago," he said. He looked toward the revolving doors. Traffic was silently moving on the street. He wondered if Jeff was lurking somewhere nearby.

"We'll have to erect a commemorative plaque." Madeleine seemed in gay spirits. " 'Here the forces of evil were withstood by . . . what?' " She patted her moist hair with her palm.

"I don't mind getting a taxi," Henry said.

"Screw you," she said brightly. "It's my country you've been kicked out of." She turned to go. "Come on . . . 'withstood by the forces of dull convention.' Alas."

*

From the passenger's seat of Madeleine's yellow Saab, Henry watched the big construction cranes at work – many more cranes and super-structures than had been visible from his window. The city was rising, which made it feel even more indifferent. A taxi would've been better. A taxi alone to an airport, never looking right nor left, could be a relief.

"You look all beat up, though I guess you're not," Madeleine said. Driving too fast always put her in aggressive good spirits. Together they'd always been driving someplace good. He liked speed then – but less so now, since it threatened getting safely to the airport.

There was nothing to say about looking "all beat up". He knew her, yet also now he didn't quite know her. It was part of the change they were enacting. When they were in the thick of things, Madeleine couldn't drive without looking at him, smiling, remarking about his excellent qualities, cracking jokes, appreciating his comments. Now she could be driving anybody – her mother to the beauty parlor, a priest to a funeral.

"Do you realize what the day after tomorrow is?" Madeleine said, maneuvering skillfully through the traffic's changing weave. She was wearing some sort of scent that filled the car with a dense rosy aroma he was already tired of.

"No."

"It's Canadian Thanksgiving. We have it early so we can get a jump on you guys. Canada invented Thanksgiving. Canada invented Thanksgiving, *eh*?" She quite liked making fun of Canadians and didn't like it at all if he did. He had never really thought of her as Canadian. She just seemed like another American girl. He wasn't sure how you considered someone Canadian, what important allowances you needed to make.

"Do you observe it for the same reason we do?" Henry said, watching traffic. He still felt slightly dazed.

"We just *have* it," Madeleine said happily. "Why do you have it?"

"To solemnize the accord between the settlers and the Indians who might've murdered them. Basically it's a national gesture of relief."

"Murder's your big subject down there, isn't it?" Madeleine said, and looked pleased. "We just have ours to be nice. That's enough for Canada. We're just happily grateful. Murder really doesn't play a big part."

The old buildings of the French University were passing below and to the left. The little Frogs-only fantasy world. He considered how he and Madeleine would function together after today. He hadn't really thought about it. Everybody, of course, had a past. It would be a relief to the people who knew about them to have this be over with. Plus, not having him in her life was going to be easier for her. Clear her mind. Open the world up again for both of them.

"I've got something to tell you," Madeleine said, both hands firmly on the leather steering wheel.

"I probably already know what it is," Henry said. His tongue sought the sharp little spike of his broken molar. The flesh was abraded and sore from going there. He could get it fixed in San Francisco.

"I really don't think you do," she said. A big white Japanese 747 descended slowly out of the pale sky and across the autoroute in front of them. "Do you want me to tell you?" she said. "I don't have to. It can wait forever."

"That guy wasn't your husband," Henry said and quietly cleared his throat. The thought had just come to him – why, now, he didn't know. Lawyer's intuition. "Did you think I was stupid? I mean . . ." He didn't care to finish this sentence. It finished itself. So much that was said didn't need to be.

Madeleine looked at him once, looked away then looked again. She seemed impressed. She seemed happy about feeling impressed, as if this was the best of all outcomes. The enormous jet sank from sight into an unremarkable industrial landscape. No big ball of flaming explosion followed. Everyone safe. "You're guessing," she said.

"I'm a lawyer. What's the difference?"

She liked this, too, and smiled. He understood it was impossible for her not to like him. "How'd you know?"

"Among other reasons?" The freeway traffic was standing back now

for the airport exit. "He acted more serious than he felt. Something
he said . . . 'divided inner somethings'? That wasn't right. And he
looks like an actor. Are you sleeping with him, too? I don't mean
'too.' You know."

"Not currently," Madeleine said. She touched her silver hair clip
with her little finger and cocked her head slightly. She appeared to
be realizing something. What that might be, he thought, would be
worth knowing. "I knew you'd go down there," she said. "I knew you
couldn't resist it. You always want to be so forthright and brave. It's
your disguise."

Henry watched the pleasureless freeway ambience pass slowly
along – freight depots, trucking companies, car rentals, gas stations.
The same all over. The green sign was visible. *Aerogare/Airport*. An
exertion saying everything twice.

"He's an American," Madeleine said. "His name's Bradley. He *is* an
actor. We worried you'd know he wasn't Canadian."

"Not a worry there," Henry said. She took the *Aerogare/Airport
Sortie/Exit* and looked across at him. She seemed slightly undone
now. Perhaps, he thought, she was thinking about patting her cheeks
when they were in the room, or saying, *I'd pictured something more
poignant*. That could seem excessive now.

He reached and took her hand and held it loosely. She was
nervous, her hand warm and moist. This whole business had taken
something out of her, too. They had been in love, perhaps were still
in love.

"Is someone filming all this?" he said and glanced to the side,
at a pick-up truck following along beside them on the highway.
He expected to see the truck bed full of cameras, sound equipment,
smiling young cinéastes. Everything trained on him.

"For once, no," she said.

Up ahead, *d'Embarquements/Departures* was jam-packed. Cars,
limos, taxis, people loading golf bags, collapsible cribs and taped-up
coolers from the backs of idling vans. Policemen with white over-
sleeves were flagging everyone through in a hurry. He had only a

suitcase, a briefcase, a raincoat. It had become a wonderful autumn day. Clouds and haze were being cleansed from the sky.

He continued holding her hand, and she grasped his back in a way that felt important. What would it be like finally, he wondered, to grow uninterested in women? Things he did – going here, there, deciding this, that – he'd always had a woman in mind. Their presence animated things. So much would be different without them. No more moments like this, moments of approximate truth vivifying, explaining, offering silent reason to the choices you made. And what happened to those people for whom it wasn't an issue? Who didn't think about women. Certainly they achieved things. Were they better, their accomplishments purer? Of course, when it was all out of your reach – and it would be – you wouldn't even care.

On the curb side, amid sky-caps and passengers alighting and baggage carts nosed in at reckless angles, a family – two older adults and three nearly-grown blond children – were having a moment of prayer, standing in a tight little circle, arms to shoulders, heads bowed. Clearly Americans, Henry realized. Only Americans would be so immodest about their belief, so sure a fast amen was just the thing to keep them safe – at once so careless and so prideful. Not the qualities to make a country great.

"Do you think if we asked, they'd include us in their little circle?" Madeleine said, breaking their silence as she pulled to the curb, right beside the praying Americans. She meant to annoy them.

"We're represented already," Henry said, looking at the pilgrims' hefty, strenuous backsides. "We're the forces of evil they think so much about. The terrible adulterers. We worry them."

"Life's just a record of our misdeeds, isn't it?" she said. He couldn't open his door for the pray-ers.

"I don't think that." He held her warm, soft, moist hand casually. She was just letting the other subject go free now – the lying, tricking, having a joke at his expense. Though why, for God's sake, not let it go free?

He sat a moment longer, facing forward, unable to exit. He said,

"Have you decided you don't love me?" Here was the great mystery. His version of a prayer.

"Oh, no," Madeleine said. "I wanted us to go on and on. But we just couldn't. So. This seemed like a way to seal it off. Exaggerate the difference between what is and what isn't. You know?" She smiled weakly. "Sometimes you can't believe the things that are taking place are actually taking place, but you need to. I'm sorry. It was too much." She leaned and kissed him on the cheek, then took both his hands to her lips and kissed them.

He liked her. Liked everything about her. Though now was the wrong moment to say so. It would seem insincere. Reaching for too much. Though how did you ever make a moment be worth as much as it could be, if you didn't reach?

Outside, the Americans were all hugging one another, smiling big Christian smiles, their prayers having reached a satisfactory end.

"Are you trying to think of something nice to say?" Madeleine said jauntily.

"No," Henry said. "I was trying not to."

"Well, that's just as good," she said, smiling. "It might not be good enough for everybody, but I understand. It's hard to know how to end a thing that didn't completely begin."

He pushed open the heavy door, lifted his suitcase out of the back, stepped out into the cool fall light, then looked quickly in at her. She smiled at him through the open doorway. There was nothing to say now. Words were used up.

"Wouldn't you agree with me about that, Henry?" she said. "That'd be a nice thing to say. Just that you agree with me."

"Yes, okay," Henry said. "I do. I do agree with you. I agree with you about everything."

"Then rejoin your fellow Americans."

He closed the door. She didn't look his way again. He watched her ease away, then accelerate, then quickly disappear into the traffic heading back to town.

Charity

On the first day of their Maine vacation, they drove up to Harrisburg after work, then flew to Philadelphia, then flew to Portland, where they rented a Ford Explorer at the airport, ate dinner at a Friendly's then drove up 95 as far as Freeport – it was long after dark – where they found a B&B directly across from L. L. Bean, which surprisingly was open all night.

Before getting into the rickety canopy bed and passing out from exhaustion, Nancy Marshall stood at the dark window naked and looked across the shadowy street at the big, lighted Bean's building, shining like a new opera house. At one AM, customers were streaming in and out toting packages, pulling garden implements, pushing trail bikes and disappearing into the dark in high spirits. Two large Conant tourist buses from Canada sat idling at the curb, their uniformed drivers sharing a quiet smoke on the sidewalk while their Japanese passengers were inside buying up things. The street was busy here, though farther down the block the other expensive franchise outlets were shut.

Tom Marshall turned off the light in the tiny bathroom and came and stood just behind her, wearing blue pajama bottoms. He touched her shoulders, stood closer to her until she could feel him aroused.

"I know why the store's open 'til one o'clock," Nancy said, "but I don't know why all the people come." Something about his conspicuous warm presence made her feel a chill. She covered her breasts, which were near the window glass. She imagined he was smiling.

"I guess they love it," Tom said. She could feel him properly – very stiff now. "This is what Maine means. A visit to Bean's after midnight. It's the global culture. They're probably on their way to Atlantic City."

"Okay," Nancy said. Because she was cold, she let herself be pulled to him. This was all right. She was exhausted. His cock fit between her legs – just there. She liked it. It felt familiar. "I asked the wrong question." There was no reflection in the glass of her or him behind her, inching into her. She stood perfectly still.

"What would the right question be?" Tom pushed flush against her, bending his knees just a fraction to find her. He *was* smiling.

"I don't know," she said. "Maybe the question is, what do they know that we don't? What are we doing over here on this side of the street? Clearly the action's over there."

She heard him exhale, then he moved away. She had been about to open her legs, lean forward a little. "Not that." She looked around for him. "I don't mean that." She put her hand between her legs just to touch, her fingers covering herself. She looked back at the street. The two bus drivers she believed could not see through the shadowy trees were both looking right at her. She didn't move. "I didn't mean that," she said to Tom faintly.

"Tomorrow we'll see some things we'll like," he said cheerfully. He was already in bed. That fast.

"Good." She didn't care if two creeps saw her naked; it was exactly the same as her seeing them clothed. She was forty-five. Not so slender, but tall, willowy. Let them look. "That's good," she said again. "I'm glad we came."

"I'm sorry?" Tom said sleepily. He was almost gone, the cop's blessed gift to be asleep the moment his head touched the pillow.

"Nothing," she said, at the window, being watched. "I didn't say anything."

He was silent, breathing. The two drivers began shaking their heads, looking down now. One flipped a cigarette into the street. They both looked up again, then stepped out of sight behind their idling buses.

*

Tom Marshall had been a policeman for twenty-two years. They had lived in Harlingen, Maryland, the entire time. He had worked robberies and made detective before anyone. Nancy was an attorney in the Potomac County public defender's office and did women's cases, family defense, disabled rights, children at risk. They had met in college at Macalester, in Minnesota. Tom had hoped to be a lawyer, expected to do environmental or civil rights, but had interviewed for the police job because they'd suddenly produced a child. He found, however, that he liked police work. Liked robberies. They were biblical (though he wasn't religious), but not as bad as murders. Nancy had started law school before their son, Anthony, graduated. She hadn't wanted to get trapped with too little to do when the house suddenly became empty. The reversal in their careers seemed ironic but insignificant.

In his twenty-first year, though, two and a half years ago, Tom Marshall had been involved in a shooting inside a Herman's sporting goods, where he'd gone to question a man. The officer he partnered with had been killed, and Tom had been shot in the leg. The thief was never caught. When his medical leave was over, he went back to work with a medal for valor and a new assignment as an inspector of detectives, but that had proved unsatisfying. And over the course of six months he became first bored by his office routine, then alienated, then had experienced "emotional issues" – mostly moodiness – which engendered bad morale consequences for the men he was expected to lead. So that by Christmas he retired, took his pension at forty-three and began a period of at-home retooling, which after a lot of reading led him to the idea of inventing children's toys and actually making them himself in a small work-space he rented in an old wire factory converted to an artists' co-op in the nearby town of Brunswick, on the Potomac.

Tom Marshall, as Nancy observed, had never been truly "cop-ish." He was not silent or cynical or unbending or self-justifying or given to explosive, terrifying violence. He was instead, a tall bean-poley, smilingly handsome man with long arms, big bony hands and feet, a shock of coarse black hair and a generally happy disposition. He was more like a high school science teacher, which Nancy thought he should've been, though he was happy to have been a cop once he was gone from the job. He liked to read Victorian novels, hike in the woods, watch birds, study the stars. And he could fix and build anything – food processors, lamps, locks – could fashion bird and boat replicas, invent ingenious furniture items. He had the disposition of a true artisan, and Nancy had never figured out why he'd stayed a cop so long except that he'd never thought his life was his own when he was young, but rather that he was a married man with responsibilities. Her most pleasing vision of her married self was standing someplace, *anyplace*, alongside some typical Saturday-morning project of Tom's – building a teak inlaid dictionary stand, fine-tuning a home-built go-cart for Anthony, rigging a timed sprinkling system for the yard – and simply *watching* him admiringly, raptly, almost mystically, as if to say "how marvelous and strange and lucky to be married to such a man." Marrying Tom Marshall, she believed, had allowed her to learn the ordinary acts of devotion, love, attentiveness, and the acceptance of another – acts she'd never practiced when she was younger because, she felt, she'd been too selfish. A daddy's girl.

Tom had gotten immediately and enthusiastically behind the prospect of Nancy earning a law degree. He came home on flextime to be with Anthony during his last year of high school. He postponed vacations so she could study, and never talked about his own law school aspirations. He'd rented a hall, staged a graduation party and driven her to her bar exam in the back of a police car, then staged another party when she passed. He applauded her decision to become a public defender, and didn't gripe about the low pay and long hours, which he said were the costs of important satisfactions and of making a contribution.

For a brief period then, after Tom took his retirement and began work at the co-op, and Anthony had been accepted at Goucher and was interning for the summer in D.C., and Nancy had gotten on her feet with the County, their life on earth seemed as perfect as ever could be imagined. Nancy began to win more cases than she lost. Anthony was offered a job for whenever he graduated. And Tom dreamed up and actually fabricated a toy sculpture for four-year-olds which he surprisingly sold to France, Finland and to Neiman Marcus.

One of these toys was a ludicrously simple dog shape that Tom cut out on a jigsaw, dyed yellow, red and green and drew on dog features. But he cut the shape in a way to effectively make *six* dogs that fitted together, one on the other, so that the sculpture could be taken apart and reassembled endlessly by its child owner. Tom called it Wagner-the-Dog, and made twenty thousand dollars off of it and had French interest for any new ideas. The other sculpture was a lighthouse made of balsam, which also fitted together in a way you could dismantle but was, he felt, too intricate. It sold only in Finland and didn't make any money. Maine Lighthouse he called it, and didn't think it was very original. He was planning a website.

The other thing Tom Marshall did once everything was wonderful was have an affair with a silkscreen artist who also rented space in the artists' co-op – a woman much younger than Nancy, named Crystal Blue, whose silkscreen operation was called "Crystal Blue's Creations," and who Nancy had been nice to on the occasions she visited Tom's space to view his new projects.

Crystal was a pretty little airhead with no personality of any sort, who printed Maxfield Parrish-like female profiles in diaphanous dresses, using garish, metallic colors. These she peddled out of an electric blue van with her likeness on the side, usually to bikers and amphetamine addicts at fourth-rate craft fairs in West Virginia and southern Pennsylvania. Nancy realized Crystal would naturally be drawn to Tom who was a stand-up, handsome, wide-eyed guy – the opposite of Crystal. And Tom might be naturally attracted to Crystal's cheapness, which posed as a lack of inhibition. Though only up to a point, she assumed – the point being when Tom stopped to notice there was nothing there to be interested in. Another encounter, of course. But along with that would quickly come boredom, the annoyance of managing small-change deceptions, and the silly look Crystal kept on her large, too-Italian mouth which would inevitably become irritating. Plus the more weighty issues of betrayal and the risk of doing irreparable damage to something valuable in his – and Nancy's – life.

Tom, however, managed to look beyond these impediments, and to fuck Crystal in her silkscreen studio on an almost daily basis for months, until her boyfriend figured it out and called Nancy at her office and blew Tom's cover by saying in a nasal, West Virginia accent, "Well, what're we gonna do with our two artistic lovebirds?"

When Nancy confronted Tom – at dinner in an Asian restaurant down the street from the public defender's office – with a recounting of the boyfriend's phone conversation, he became very grave and fixed his gaze on the tablecloth and laced his large bony fingers around a salad fork.

It was true, he admitted, and he was sorry. He said he thought fucking Crystal was a "reaction" to suddenly being off the force after half his life, and being depressed about his line-of-duty injury, which still caused him discomfort when it rained. But it was also a result of pure exhilaration about his new life, something he needed to celebrate on his own and in his own way – a "universe feeling" he called it, wherein acts took place outside the boundaries of convention, obligation, the past and even good sense (just as events occurred in the universe). This new life, he said, he wanted to spend entirely with Nancy, who'd sat composed and said little, though she wasn't thinking about Crystal, or Tom, or Crystal's boyfriend or even about herself. While Tom was talking (he seemed to go on and on and on), she was actually experiencing a peculiar sense of weightlessness and near disembodiment, as though she could see herself listening to Tom from a comfortable but slightly dizzying position high up around the red, scrolly, Chinese-looking crown molding. The more Tom talked, the less present, the less substantial, the less *anything* she felt. If Tom could've gone on talking – recounting his problems, his anxieties, his age-related feelings of underachievement, his dwindling sense of self-esteem since he quit chasing robbers with a gun – Nancy realized she might just have disappeared entirely. So that the problem (if that's what all this was – a problem) might simply be solved: no more Crystal Blue; no more morbid, regretful Tom; no more humiliating, dismal disclosures implying your life was even more like every other life than you were prepared to concede – all of it gone in the breath of her own dematerialization.

She heard Tom say – his long, hairy-topped fingers turning the ugly, institutional salad fork over and over like a prayer totem, his solemn gaze fastened on it – that it was absolutely over with Crystal now. Her hillbilly boyfriend had apparently set the phone down from talking to Nancy, driven to Crystal's studio and kicked it to pieces, then knocked her around a little, after which the two of them got in his Corvette and drove to Myrtle Beach to patch things up. Tom said he would find another space for his work; that Crystal would be out of his life as of today (not that she'd ever really been *in* his life), and that he was sorry and ashamed. But if Nancy would forgive him and not leave him, he could promise her that such as this would never happen again.

Tom brought his large blue cop's eyes up off the table and sought hers. His face – always to Nancy a craggy, handsome face, a face with large cheek bones, deep eye sockets, a thick chin and overlarge white teeth – looked at that moment more like a skull, a death's head. Not really, of course; she didn't see an actual death's head like on a pirate flag. But it was the thought she experienced, and the words: "Tom's face is a death's head." And though she was sure she wasn't obsessive or compulsive or a believer in omens or symbols as sources of illumination, she *had* thought the words – Tom's face is a death's head – and pictured them as a motto on the lintel of a door to a mythical courtroom that was something out of Dante. One way or another, this, the idea of a death's head, had to be somewhere in what she believed.

When Tom was finished apologizing, Nancy told him without anger that changing studios shouldn't be necessary if he could stay away from Crystal when she came back from Myrtle Beach. She said she had perhaps misjudged some things, and that trouble in a marriage, especially a long marriage, always came about at the instigation of both partners, and that trouble like this was just a symptom and not terribly important *per se*. And that while she didn't care for what he'd done, and had thought that very afternoon about divorcing him simply so she wouldn't have to think about it anymore, she actually didn't believe his acts were directed at her, for the obvious reason that she hadn't done anything to deserve them. She believed, she said, that what he'd done was related to the issues he'd just been talking about, and that her intention was to forgive him and try to see if the two of them couldn't weather adversity with a greater-than-ever intimacy.

"Why don't you just fuck *me* tonight?" she said to him right at the table. The word *fuck* was provocative, but also, she realized, slightly pathetic as an address to your husband. "We haven't done that in a while." *Though of course you've been doing it every day with your retarded girlfriend* were the words she'd thought but didn't like thinking.

"Yes," Tom said, too gravely. Then, "No."

His large hands were clasped, forkless, on the white tablecloth not far from hers. Neither moved as though to effect a touch.

"I'm so sorry," Tom said for the third or fourth time, and she knew he was. Tom wasn't a man distanced from what he felt. He didn't say something and then start thinking what it could mean now that he'd said it, finally concluding it didn't mean anything. He was a good, sincere man, qualities that had made him an exemplary robbery detective, a superb interrogator of felons. Tom meant things.

"I hope I haven't ruined our life," he added sadly.

"I hope not, too," Nancy said. She didn't want to think about ruining her life, which seemed ridiculous. She wanted to concentrate on what an honest, decent man he was. Not a death's head. "You probably haven't," she said.

"Then let's go home now," he said, folding his napkin after dabbing his mouth. "I'm ready."

Home meant he would fuck her, and no doubt do it with ardor and tenderness and take it all the way. He was very good at that. Crystal hadn't been crazy to want to fuck Tom instead of her nasal, crybaby boyfriend. Nancy wondered, though, why she herself expected that now; why *fuck me*? Probably it was *fuck me* instead of *fuck you*. Since she didn't much want that now, though it would surely happen. It made her regretful; because she was, she realized, the very sort of person she'd determined Tom was not, even though she was not an adulterer and he was: she *was* a person who said things, then looked around and wondered why she'd said them and what their consequences could be, and (often) how she could get out of doing the very things she said she desired. She'd never exactly recognized this about herself, and now considered the possibility that it had just become true, or been made true by Tom's betrayal. But what was it, she wondered, as they left the restaurant headed for home and bed? What was that thing she was? Surely it was a thing anyone should be able to say. There would be a word for it. She simply couldn't bring that word to mind.

*

The next morning, Friday – after the night in Freeport – they ate breakfast in Wiscasset, in a shiny little diner that sat beside a large greenish river, over which a low concrete bridge moved traffic briskly north and south. The gilt-edged sign outside Wiscasset said it was *The Prettiest Village in Maine*, which seemed to mean there were few houses, and those few were big and white and expensive looking, with manicured yards and plaques by the front doors telling everyone when the house was built. Across the river, which was called the Sheepscot, white summer cottages speckled out through forested riverbank. This was Maine – small in scale, profusely scenic, annoyingly remote, exclusive and crowded. She knew they were close to the ocean, but she hadn't seen it yet, even from the plane last night. The Sheepscot was clearly an estuary; gulls were flying up-river in the clear morning air, crisp little lobster craft, a few sailboats sat at anchor.

When they'd parked and hiked down toward the diner, Tom had stopped to bend over, peering into several windows full of house-for-sale pictures, all in color, all small white structures with crisp green roofs situated "minutes" from some body of water imprecisely seen in the background. All the locales had Maine-ish names. Pemaquid Point. Passamaquoddy something. Stickney Corner. The houses looked like the renter cabins across the river – places you'd get sick of after one season and then have to put back on the market. She couldn't gauge if prices were high or low, though Tom thought they were too high. It didn't matter. She didn't live here.

When he'd looked in at two or three realty windows, Tom stood up and stared down at the river beyond the diner. Water glistened in the light September air. He seemed wistful, but he also seemed to be contemplating. The salt-smelling breeze blew his hair against the part, revealing where it was thinning.

"Are you considering something 'only steps from the ocean'?" she said, to be congenial. She put her arm in under his. Tom was an enthusiast, and when a subject he wanted to be enthusiastic about proved beyond him, it often turned him gloomy, as though the world were a hopeless place.

"I was just thinking that everything's been discovered in this town," he said. "You needed to be here twenty years ago."

"Would you like to live in Wiscasset, or Pissamaquoddy or whatever?" She looked down the sloping main street – a block of glass-fronted antique shops, a chic deli, a fancy furniture store above which were lawyers' and CPA offices. These buildings, too, had plaques telling their construction dates. 1880s. Not really so old. Harlingen had plenty of buildings that were older.

"I wish I'd considered it *that* long ago," Tom said. He was wearing tan shorts, wool socks, a red Bean's canvas shirt and running shoes. They were dressed almost alike, though she had a blue anorak and khaki trousers. Tom looked like a tourist not an ex-cop, which, she guessed, was the idea. Tom liked the idea of transforming yourself.

"A vacation is *not* to regret things, or even to think about things permanently." She tugged his arm. She felt herself being herself on his behalf. The street through town – Route 1 – was already getting crowded, the bridge traffic slowing to a creep. "The idea of a vacation is to let your spirits rise on the breeze and feel unmoored and free."

Tom looked at her as though she'd become the object of his longing. "Right," he said. "You'd make somebody a great wife." He looked startled for saying that and began walking away as if embarrassed.

"I *am* somebody's wife," she said, coming along, trying to make it a joke, since he'd meant something sweet, and nothing was harmed. It was just that whatever was wrong between them caused unexpected events to point it out but not identify it. They loved each other. They knew each other very well. They were married people of good will. Everything was finally forgivable – a slip of the tongue, a botched attempt at lovemaking, a conversation that led nowhere or to the wrong place. The question was: what did all these reserves of tender feeling and kind regard actually *come to*? And not come to? Walking down the hill behind her husband, she felt the peculiar force of having been through life only once. These three days were to determine, she understood, if anything more than just this minimum made sense. It was an important mystery.

*

Inside the Miss Wiscasset Diner, Nancy perused *The Down-East Pennysaver*, which had a dating exchange on the back page. *Men seeking women. Women seeking men.* Nothing else was apparently permissible. No *Men seeking men*. Tom studied the map they'd picked up in the B&B, and which contained a listing of useful "Maine Facts" in which everything occasioned an unfunny variation on the state name: Maine Events. Mainely Antiques. Mainiac Markdowns. Maine-line

Drugs. Roof Maine-tenance. No one seemed able to get over what a neat name the place had.

Out on the river, a black metal barge was shoving a floating dredger straight up the current. The dredger carried an immense bucket suspended on a cable at the end of an articulated boom. The whole enterprise was so large as to seem ridiculous.

"What do you suppose that's for?" Nancy said. The diner was noisy with morning customers and contained a teeming greasy-bacon and buttery-toast smell.

Tom looked up from his map out at the dredger. It would not get past the bridge where Route 1 crossed the river. It was too tall. He looked at her and smiled as though she hadn't said anything, then went back to his "Maine Facts".

"If you're interested, all the women seeking men are either 'full-figure gals over fifty,'" she said, forgetting her question, "or else they're sixteen-year-olds seeking mature 'father figures.' The same men get all the women in Maine."

Tom took a sip of his coffee and knitted his brows. They had until Sunday, when they were flying out of Bangor. They knew nothing about Maine, but had discussed a drive to Bar Harbor and Mount Katahdin, which they'd heard were pretty. Nancy had proposed to visit the national park, a bracing hike, then maybe a swim in the late-lasting-summer ocean if it wasn't too frigid. They'd imagined leaves would be turning, but they weren't yet because of all the summer rain.

They were also not able to tell exactly how far anything was from anything else. The map was complicated by quirky peninsulas extending back south and the road having to go up and around and down again. The morning's drive from Freeport had seemed long, but not much distance was covered. It made you feel foreign in your own country. Though they'd always found happiness inside an automobile – as far back as when Tom played drums in a college rock band and she'd gone along on the road trips, sleeping in the car and in ten-dollar motels. In the car, who they really were became available to the other. Guards went down. They felt free.

"There's a town called Belfast," Tom said, back to his map. "It's not far up. At least I don't think it is." He looked back at where the floating dredger was making its slow turn in the river, beginning to ease back toward the ocean. "Did you see that thing?"

"I don't get what 'down-east' means," Nancy said. Everything in the *Pennysaver* that wasn't a play on "Maine" had "down-east" somehow attached to it. The dating exchange was called *'Down-East In Search Of'*. "Does it mean that if you follow one of the peninsulas as far as you can go south, you get east?"

This was a thing Tom should know. It was his idea to come here instead of the Eastern Shore place they liked. Maine had all of a sudden "made sense" to him – something hazy about the country having started here and the ocean being "primary" among experiences, and his having grown up near Lake Michigan and that never seeming remotely primary.

"That's what I thought it meant," Tom said.

"So what does Maine mean? Maine what?" she asked. Nothing was in the *Pennysaver* to explain anything.

"That I do know," Tom said, watching the barge turning and starting back downstream. "It means main *land*. As opposed to an island."

She looked around the crowded diner for their waitress. She was ready for greasy bacon and buttery toast and had wedged the *Pennysaver* behind the napkin dispenser. "They have a high opinion of themselves here," she said. "They seem to admire virtues you only understand by suffering difficulty and confusion. It's the New England spirit I guess." Tom's virtues, of course, were that kind. He was perfect if you were dying or being robbed or swindled – a policeman's character traits, and useful in many more ways than policing. "Isn't Maine the state where the woman was shot by a hunter while she was pinning up clothes on the line? Wearing white gloves or something, and the guy thought she was a deer? You don't have to defend that, of course."

He gave her his policeman's regulation blank stare across the table top. It was an expression his face could change into, leaving his real face – normally open and enthusiastic – back somewhere forgotten. He took injustice personally.

She blinked, expecting him to say something else.

"Places that aren't strange aren't usually interesting," he said solemnly.

"It's just my first morning here." She smiled at him.

"I want us to see this town Belfast." He re-consulted the map. "The write-up makes it seem interesting."

"Belfast. Like the one where they fight?"

"This one's in Maine, though."

"I'm sure it's wonderful."

"You know me," he said, and unexpectedly smiled back. "Ever hopeful." He was an enthusiast again. He wanted to make their trip be worthwhile. And he was absolutely right: it was too soon to fall into disagreement. That could come later.

*

Early in the past winter Tom had moved out of their house and into his own apartment, a grim little scramble of white, dry-walled rectangles which were part of a new complex situated across a wide boulevard from a factory-outlet mall and adjacent to the parking lot of a large veterinary clinic where dogs could be heard barking and crying day and night.

Tom's departure was calculatedly not dramatic. He himself had seemed reluctant, and once he was out, she was very sorry not to see him, not to sleep next to him, have him there to talk to. Some days she would come home from her office and Tom would be in the kitchen, drinking a beer or watching CNN while he heated something in the microwave – as though this was fine to live elsewhere and then turn up like a memory. Sometimes she would discover the bathroom door closed, or find him coming up from the basement or just standing in the backyard staring at the hydrangea beds as if he was considering weeding them.

"Oh, *you're* here," she'd say. "Yeah," he'd answer, sounding not entirely sure how he'd come to be present. "It's me." He would some-times sit down in the kitchen and talk about what he was doing in his studio. Sometimes he'd bring her a new toy he'd made – a colorful shooting star on a pedestal, or a new Wagner in brighter colors. They talked about Anthony, at Goucher. Usually, when he came, Nancy asked if he'd like to stay for dinner. And Tom would suggest they go out, and that he "pop" for it. But that was never what she wanted to do. She wanted him to stay. She missed him in bed. They had never talked about being apart, really. He was doing things for his own reasons. His departure had seemed almost natural.

Each time he was there, though, she would look at Tom Marshall in what she tried to make be a new way, see him as a stranger; tried to decide anew if he was in fact so handsome, or if he looked different from how she'd gotten used to him looking in twenty years; tried to search to see if he was as good-willed or even as large and rangy as she'd grown accustomed to thinking. If he truly had an artisan's temperament and a gentle manner, or if he was just a creep or a jerk she had unwisely married then gradually gotten used to. She considered the possibility of having an affair – a colleague or a delivery boy. But that seemed too mechanical, too much trouble, the outcome so predictable. Tom's punishment would have to be that she *considered* an affair and expressed her freedom of choice without telling him. In a magazine she picked up at the dentist's, she read that most women radically change their opinions of their husbands once they spent time away from them. Except women were natural conciliators and forgivers and therefore preferred not to be apart. In fact, they found it easy, even desirable, to delude themselves about many things, but especially about men. According to the writer – a psychologist – women were hopeless.

Yet following each reassessment, she decided again that Tom Marshall *was* all the things she'd always thought him to be, and that the reasons she'd have given to explain why she loved him were each valid. Tom was good; and being apart from him was not good, even if he seemed able to adjust to being alone and even to thrive on it. She would simply have to make whatever she could of it. Because what Nancy knew was, and she supposed Tom understood this too: they were in an odd place together; were standing upon uncertain emotional territory that might put to the test exactly who they were as humans, might require that new facets of the diamond be examined.

This was a *very* different situation from the ones she confronted at the public defender's every day, and that Tom had encountered with the police – the cut-and-dried, overdramatic and beyond-repair problems, where things went out of control fast, and people found themselves in court or in the rough hands of the law as a last-ditch way of resolving life's difficulties. If people wouldn't overdramatize so much, Nancy believed, if they remained pliable, did their own thinking, restrained themselves, then things could work out for the better. Though for some people that must be hard.

She had been quite impressed by how she'd dealt with things after Tom had admitted fucking Crystal d'Amato (her real name). Once Tom made it clear he didn't intend to persist with Crystal, she'd begun to feel all right about it almost immediately. For instance, she noticed she hadn't experienced awful stress about envisioning Tom bare-ass on top of Crystal wherever it was they'd done it (she envisioned a big paint-stained sheet of white canvas). Neither did the idea of Tom's betrayal seem important. It wasn't really a betrayal; Tom was a good man; she was an adult; betrayal had to mean something worse that hadn't really happened. In a sense, when she looked at Tom now with her benign, inquiring gaze, fucking Crystal was one of the most explicable new things she knew about him.

And yet, she realized, as spring came on and Tom remained in the Larchmere Apartments – cooking his miserly meals, watching his tiny TV, doing his laundry in the basement, going to his studio in the co-op – the entire edifice of their life was beginning to take on clearer shape and to grow smaller. Like a valuable box lost overboard into the smooth wake of an ocean liner. Possibly it was a crisis. Possibly they loved each other well enough, perhaps completely. Yet the strongest force keeping them together wasn't that love, she thought, but a matching curiosity about what the character of their situation was, and the novelty that neither of them knew for sure.

But as Tom had stayed away longer, seemingly affable and well-adjusted, she indeed had begun to feel an *ebbing*, something going out of her, like water seeping from a cracked beaker, restoring it to its original, vacant state. This admittedly did not seem altogether good. And yet, it might be the natural course of life. She felt isolated, it was true, but isolated in a grand sort of way, as if by being alone and getting on with things, she was achieving something. Unassailable and strong was how she felt – not that anyone wanted to assail her; though the question remained: what was the character of this strength, and what in the world would you do with it alone?

*

"Where's Nova Scotia?" Nancy said, staring at the sea. Since leaving Rockland, an hour back on Route 1, they'd begun glimpsing ocean, its surface calm, dense, almost unpersuasively blue, encircling large, distinct, forested islands Tom declared were reachable only by ferries and were the strongholds of wealthy people who were only there in the summer and didn't have heat.

"It's a parallel universe out there," he said as his way of expressing that he didn't approve of life like that. Tom had an affinity for styles of living he considered authentic. It was his one conventional-cop attitude. He thought highly of the Mainers for renting their seaside houses for two months in the summer and collecting fantastic sums that paid their bills for the year. This was authentic to Tom.

Nova Scotia was in her head now, because it would be truly exotic to go there, far beyond the green, clean-boundaried islands. Though she couldn't exactly tell what direction she faced out the car window. If you were on the east coast, looking at the ocean, you should be facing east. But her feeling was this rule didn't apply in Maine, which had something to do with distances being farther than they looked on the map, with how remote it felt here, and with whatever "down-east" meant. Perhaps she was looking south.

"You can't see it. It's way out there," Tom said, referring to Nova Scotia, driving and taking quick glances at the water. They had driven through Camden, choked with tourists sauntering along sunny streets, wearing bright, expensive clothing, trooping in and out of the same expensive outlet stores they'd seen in Freeport. They had thought tourists would be gone after Labor Day, but then their own presence disproved that.

"I just have a feeling we'd be happier visiting there," she said. "Canada's less crowded."

A large block of forested land lay solidly beyond a wide channel of blue water Tom had pronounced to be the Penobscot Bay. The block of land was Islesboro, and it too, he said, was an island, and rich people also lived there in the summer and had no heat. John Travolta had his own airport there. She mused out at the long undifferentiated island coast. Odd to think John Travolta was there right now. Doing what? It was nice to think of *it* as Nova Scotia, like standing in a meadow watching cloud shapes imitate mountains until you feel you're *in* the mountains. Maine, a lawyer in her office said, possessed a beautiful coast, but the rest was like Michigan.

"Nova Scotia's a hundred and fifty miles across the Bay of Fundy," Tom said, upbeat for some new reason.

"I once did a report about it in high school," Nancy said. "They still speak French, and a lot of it's backward, and they don't much care for Americans."

"Like the rest of Canada," Tom said.

Route 1 followed the coast along the curvature of high tree-covered hills that occasionally sponsored long, breathtaking views toward the bay below. A few white sails were visible on the pure blue surface, though the late morning seemed to have furnished little breeze.

"It wouldn't be bad to live up here," Tom said. He hadn't shaved, and rubbed his palm across his dark stubble. He seemed happier by the minute.

She looked at him curiously. "Where?"

"Here."

"Live in Maine? But it's mortifyingly cold except for today." She and Tom had grown up in the suburbs of Chicago – she in Glen Ellyn, Tom in a less expensive part of Evanston. Their very first agreement had been that they hated the cold. They'd chosen Maryland for Tom to be a policeman because it was unrelentingly mild. Her feelings hadn't changed. "Where would you go for the two months when you were renting the house to the Kennedy cousins just so you could afford to freeze here all winter?"

"I'd buy a boat. Sail it around." Tom extended his estimable arms and flexed his grip on the steering wheel. Tom was in dauntingly good health. He played playground basketball with black kids, mountain-biked to his studio, did push-ups in his apartment every night before climbing into bed alone. And since he'd been away, he seemed healthier, calmer, more hopeful, though the story was somehow that he'd moved a mile away to a shitty apartment to make *her* happier. Nancy looked down disapprovingly at the pure white pinpoint sails backed by blue water in front of the faultlessly green-bonneted island where summer people sat on long white porches and watched the impoverished world through expensive telescopes. It wasn't that attractive. In the public defender's office she had, in the last month, defended a murderer, two pretty adolescent sisters accused of sodomizing their brother, a nice secretary who, because she was obese, had become the object of taunts in her office full of gay men, and an elderly Japanese woman whose house contained ninety-six cats she was feeding, and who her neighbors considered, reasonably enough, deranged and a health hazard. Eventually the obese secretary, who was from the Philippines, had stabbed one of the gay men to death. How could you give all that up and move to Maine with a man who appeared not to want to live with you, then be trapped on a boat for the two months it wasn't snowing? These were odd times of interesting choices.

"Maybe you could talk Anthony into doing it with you," she

said, thinking peacefully again that Islesboro was Nova Scotia and everyone there was talking French and speaking ill of Americans. She had almost said "Maybe you can persuade Crystal to drive up and fuck you on your yacht." But that wasn't what she felt. Poisoning perfectly harmless conversation with something nasty you didn't even mean was what the people she defended did and made their lives impossible. She wasn't even sure he'd heard her mention Anthony. It was possible she was whispering.

"Keep an open mind," Tom said, and smiled an inspiriting smile.

"Can't," Nancy said. "I'm a lawyer. I'm forty-five. I believe the rich already stole the best things before I was born, not just twenty years ago in Wiscasset."

"You're tough," Tom said, "but you have to let me win you."

"I told you, you already did that," she said. "I'm your wife. That's what that means. Or used to. You win."

This was Tom's standard view, of course, the lifelong robbery-detective *slash* enthusiast's view: someone was always needing to be won over to a better view of things; someone's spirit being critically lower or higher than someone else's; someone forever acting the part of the hold-out. But she wasn't a hold-out. *He'd* fucked Crystal. *He'd* picked up and moved out. *That* didn't make her not an enthusiast. Though none of it converted Tom Marshall into a bad person in need of punishment. They merely didn't share a point of view – his being to sentimentalize loss by feeling sorry for himself; hers being to not seek extremes even when it meant ignoring the obvious. She wondered if he'd even heard her say he'd ever won her. He was thinking about something else now, something that pleased him. You couldn't blame him.

When she looked at Tom he was just past looking at her, as if *he'd* spoken something and *she* hadn't responded. "What?" she said, and pulled a strand of hair past her eyes and to the side. She looked at him straight on. "Do you see something you don't like?"

"I was just thinking about that old line we used to say when I was first being a policeman. 'Interesting drama is when the villain says something that's true.' It was in some class you took. I don't remember."

"Did I just say something true?"

He smiled. "I was thinking that in all those years my villains never said much that was true or even interesting."

"Do you miss having new villains every day?" It was the marquee question, of course; the one she'd never actually thought to ask a year ago, during the Crystal difficulties. The question of the epic loss of vocation. A wife could only hope to fill in for the lost villains.

"No way," he said. "It's great now."

"It's better living by yourself?"

"That's not really how I think about it."

"How do you really think about it?"

"That we're waiting," Tom said earnestly. "For a long moment to pass. Then we'll go on."

"What would we call that moment?" she asked.

"I don't know. A moment of readjustment, maybe."

"Readjustment to exactly what?"

"Each other?" Tom said, his voice going absurdly up at the end of his sentence.

They were nearing a town. *Belfast, Maine*. A black and white corporate-limits sign slid past. *Established 1772. A Maine Enterprise Center*. Settlement was commencing. The highway had gradually come nearer sea level. Traffic slowed as the roadside began to re-populate with motels, shoe outlets, pottery barns, small boatyards selling posh wooden dinghies – the signs of enterprise.

"I wasn't conscious I needed readjustment," Nancy said. "I thought I was happy just to go along. I wasn't mad at you. I'm still not. Though your view makes me feel a little ridiculous."

"I thought you wanted one," Tom said.

"One what? A chance to feel ridiculous? Or a period of *readjust-ment*?" She made the word sound idiotic. "Are you a complete stupe?"

"I thought you needed time to reconnoiter." Tom looked deviled at being called a stupe. It was old Chicago code to them. An ancient language of disgust.

"Jesus, why are you talking like this?" Nancy said. "Though I suppose I should know why, shouldn't I?"

"Why?" Tom said.

"Because it's bullshit, which is why it sounds so much like bullshit. What's true is that *you* wanted out of the house for your own reasons, and now you're trying to decide if you're tired of it. And me. But you want *me* to somehow take the blame." She smiled at him in feigned amazement. "Do you realize you're a grown man?"

He looked briefly down, then raised his eyes to hers with contempt. They were still moving, though Route 1 took the newly paved by-pass to the left, and Tom angled off into Belfast proper, which in a split second turned into a nice, snug neighborhood of large Victorian, Colonial, Federal and Greek Revival residences established on large lots along an old bumpy street beneath tall surviving elms, with a couple of church steeples anchored starkly to the still-summery sky.

"I do realize that. I certainly do," Tom said, as if these words had more impact than she could feel.

Nancy shook her head and faced the tree-lined street, on the right side of which a new colonial-looking two-story brick hospital addition was under construction. New parking lot. New oncology wing. A helipad. Jobs all around. Beyond the hospital was a modern, many-windowed school named for Margaret Chase Smith, where the teams, the sign indicated, were called the *Solons*. Someone, to be amusing, had substituted "colons" in dripping blood-red paint. "There's a nice new school named for Margaret Chase Smith," Nancy said, to change the subject away from periods of readjustment and a general failure of candor. "She was one of my early heroes. She made a brave speech against McCarthyism and championed civic engagement and conscience. Unfortunately she was a Republican."

Tom spoke no more. He disliked arguing more than he hated being caught bullshitting. It was a rare quality. She admired him for it. Only, possibly now he was *becoming* a bullshitter. How had that happened?

They arrived to the inconspicuous middle of Belfast, where the brick streets sloped past handsome elderly red-brick commercial edifices. Most of the business fronts had not been modernized; some were shut, though the diagonal parking places were all taken. A small harbor with a town dock and a few dainty sailboats on their low-tide moorings lay at the bottom of the hill. A town in transition. From what to what, she wasn't sure.

"I'd like to eat something," Tom said stiffly, steering toward the water.

A chowder house, she already knew, would appear at the bottom of the street, offering pleasant but not spectacular water views through shuttered screens, terrible food served with white plastic ware, and paper placemats depicting a lighthouse or a puffin. To know this was the literacy of one's very own culture. "Please don't stay mad," she said wearily. "I just had a moment. I'm sorry."

"I was trying to say the right things," he said irritably.

"I know you were," she said. She considered reaching for the steering wheel and taking his hand. But they were almost to the front of the restaurant she'd predicted – green beaverboard with screens and a big red and white *Mainely Chowdah* sign facing the Penobscot, which was so picturesque and clear and pristine as to be painful.

*

They ate lunch at a long, smudged, oil-cloth picnic table overlooking little Belfast harbor. They each chose lobster stew. Nancy had a beer to make herself feel better. Warm, fishy ocean breezes shifted through the screens and blew their paper mats and napkins off the table. Few people were eating. Most of the place – which was like a large screened porch – had its tables and green plastic chairs stacked, and a hand-lettered sign by the register said that in a week the whole place would close for the winter.

Tom maintained a moodiness after their car-argument, and only reluctantly came around to mentioning that Belfast was one of the last "undiscovered" towns up the coast. In Camden, and farther east toward Bar Harbor, the rich already had everything bought up. Any property that sold did so within families, using law firms in Philadelphia and Boston. Realtors were never part of it. He mentioned the Rockefellers, the Harrimans and the Fisks. Here in Belfast, though, he said, development had been held back by certain environmental problems – a poultry factory that had corrupted the bay for decades so that the expensive sailing set hadn't come around. Once, he said, the now-attractive harbor had been polluted with chicken feathers. It all seemed improbable. Tom looked out through the dusty screen at a bare waterside park across the sloping street from the chowder house. An asphalt basketball court had been built, and a couple of chubby white kids were shooting two-hand jumpers and dribbling a ball clumsily. There was a new jungle gym at the far end where no one was playing.

"Over there," Tom said, his plastic spoon between his thumb and index finger, pointing at the empty grassy park that looked like something large had been present there once. "That's where the chicken plant was – smack against the harbor. The state shut it down finally." Tom furrowed his thick brow as if the events were grave.

An asphalt walking path circled the grassy sward. A man in a silver wheelchair was just entering the track from a van parked up the hill. He began patiently pushing himself around the track while a little girl began frolicking on the infield grass, and a young woman – no doubt her mother – stood watching beside the van.

"How do you know about all that?" Nancy said, watching the man foisting his wheelchair forward.

"A guy, Mick, at the co-op's from Bangor. He told me. He said now was the moment to snap up property here. In six months it'll be too pricey. It's sort of a last outpost."

For some reason the wheelchair rider she was watching seemed like a young man, though even at a distance he was clearly large and bulky. He was arming himself along in no particular hurry, just making the circle under his own power. She assumed the little girl and the woman were his family, making up something to do in the empty, unpretty park while he took his exercise. They were no doubt tourists, too.

"Does that seem awful to you? Things getting expensive?" She breathed in the strong fish aroma off the little harbor's muddy recesses. The sun had moved so that she put her hand up to shield her face. "You're not against progress, are you?"

"I like the idea of transition," Tom said confidently. "It creates a sense of possibility."

"I'm sure that's how the Rockefellers and the Fisks felt," she said, realizing this was argumentative, and wishing not to be. "Buy low, sell high, leave a beautiful corpse. That's not the way that goes, is it?" She smiled, she hoped, infectiously.

"Why don't we take a walk?" Tom pushed his plastic chowder bowl away from in front of him the way a policeman would who was used to eating in greasy spoons. When they were college kids, he hadn't eaten that way. Years ago, he'd possessed lovely table manners, eaten unhurriedly and enjoyed everything. It had been his Irish mother's influence. Now he was itchy, interested elsewhere, and his mother was dead. Though this habit was as much his nature as the other. It wasn't that he didn't seem like himself. He did.

"A walk would be good," she said, happy to leave, taking a long last look at the harbor and the park with the man in the wheelchair slowly making his journey around. "Trips are made in search of things, right?" She looked for Tom, who was already off to the cashier's, his back going away from her. "Right," she said, answering her own question and coming along.

*

They walked the early-September afternoon streets of Belfast – up the brick-paved hill from the chowder house, through the tidy business section past a hardware, a closed movie theater, a credit union, a bank, a biker bar, a pair of older realtors, several lawyers' offices and a one-chair barbershop, its window cluttered with high-school pictures of young-boy clients from years gone by. A slender young man with a ponytail and his hippie girlfriend were moving large cardboard boxes from a beater panel truck into one of the glass storefronts. Something new was happening there. Next door a shoe-store space had been turned into an organic bakery whose sign was a big loaf of bread that looked real. An art gallery was beside it. It wasn't an unpleasant-feeling town, waiting quietly for what would soon surely arrive. She could see why Tom would like it.

From up the town hill, more of the harbor was visible below, as was the mouth of another estuary that trickled along an embankment of deep green woods into the Penobscot. A high, thirties-vintage steel bridge crossed the river the way the bridge had in Wiscasset, though everything was smaller here, less up-and-going, less scenic – the great bay blue and wide and inert, just another park, sterile, fishless, ready for profitable alternative uses. It was, Nancy felt, the way all things became. The presence of an awful-smelling factory or a poisonous tannery or a cement factory could almost seem like something to wish for, remember fondly. Tom was not thinking that way.

"It's nice here, isn't it?" she said to make good company of herself. She'd taken off her anorak and tied it around her waist vacationer-style. The beer made her feel loose-limbed, satisfied. "Are we down-east yet?"

They were stopped in front of another realtor's window. Tom was again bent over studying the rows of snapshots. The walk had also made her warm, but with her sweater off, the bay breeze produced a nice sunny chill.

Another Conant tour bus arrived at the stoplight in the tiny central intersection, red and white like the ones that had let off Japanese consumers last night at Bean's. All the bus windows were tinted, and as it turned and began heaving up the hill back toward Route 1, she couldn't tell if the passengers were Asians, though she assumed so. She remembered thinking that these people knew something she didn't. What had it been? "Do you ever think about what the people in buses think when they look out their window and see you?" she said, watching the bus shudder through its gears up the hill toward a blue Ford agency sign.

"No," Tom said, still peering in at the pictures of houses for sale. "I just always want to say, 'Hey, whatever you're thinking about me, you're wrong. I'm just as out of place as you are.'" She set her hands on her hips, enjoying the sensation of talking with no one listening. She felt isolated again, unapprehended – as if for this tiny second she had achieved yet another moment of getting on with things. It was a grand feeling insofar as it arose from no apparent stimulus, and no doubt would not last long. Though here it was. This beleaguered little town had provided one pleasant occasion. The great mistake would be to try to seize such a feeling and keep it forever. It was good just to know it was available at all. "Isn't it odd," she said, facing back toward the Penobscot, "to be seen, but to understand you're being seen wrong. Does that mean . . ." She looked around at her husband.

"Does it mean what?" Tom had stood up and was watching her, as if she'd come under a spell. He put his hand on her shoulder and gently sought her.

"Does it mean you're not inhabiting your real life?" She was just embroidering a mute sensation, doing what married people do.

"Not you," Tom said. "Nobody would say that about you."

Too bad, she thought, the tourist bus couldn't come by when his arm was around her, a true married couple out for a summery walk on a sunny street. Most of that would be accurate.

"I'd like to inhabit mine more," Tom said as though the thought made him sad.

"Well, you're trying." She patted his hand on her shoulder and smelled him warm and slightly sweaty. Familiar. Welcome.

"Let's view the housing stock," he said, looking over her head up the hill, where the residential streets led away under an old canopy of elms and maples, and the house fronts were white and substantial in the afternoon sun.

On the walk along the narrow, slant, leaf-shaded streets, Tom suddenly seemed to have things on his mind. He took long surveyor's strides over the broken sidewalk slabs, as though organizing principles he'd formulated before today. His calves, which she admired, were hard and tanned, but the limp from being shot was more noticeable with his hands clasped behind him.

She liked the houses, most of them prettier and better-appointed than she'd expected – prettier than her and Tom's nice blue Cape, the one she still lived in. Most were pleasant variations on standard Greek Revival concepts, but with green shutters and dressy, curved, two-step porches, an occasional widow's walk, and sloping lawns featuring shagbark hickories, older maples, thick rhododendrons and manicured pachysandra beds. Not very different from the nice neighborhoods of eastern Maryland. She felt happy being on foot where normally you'd be in the car, she preferred it to arriving and leaving, which now seemed to promote misunderstandings and fractiousness of the sort they'd already experienced. She could appreciate these parts of a trip when you were *there*, and everything stopped moving and changing. She'd continued to feel flickers of the pleasing isolation she'd felt downtown. Though it wasn't pure lonely isolation, since Tom was here; instead it was being alone *with* someone you knew and loved. That was ideal. That's what marriage was.

Tom had now begun talking about "life-by-forecast"; the manner of leading life, he was saying, that made you pay attention to mistakes you'd made that hadn't seemed like they were going to be mistakes before you made them, but that clearly *were* mistakes when viewed later. Sometimes very bad mistakes. "Life-by-forecast" meant that you tried very hard to feel, in advance, how you'd feel afterward. "You avoid the big calamities," Tom said soberly. "It's what you're supposed to learn. It's adulthood, I guess."

He was talking, she understood, indirectly but not very subtly about Crystal-whatever-her-name-had-been. Too bad, she thought, that he worried about all that so much.

"But wouldn't you miss some things you might like, doing it that way?" She was, of course, arguing *in behalf* of Tom fucking Crystal, in behalf of big calamities. Except it didn't matter so much. She was at that moment more interested in imagining what this street, Noyes Street, would look like full in the teeth of winter. Everything white, a gale howling in off the bay, a deep freeze paralyzing all activity. Unthinkable in the late summer's idyll. Now, though, was the time when people bought houses. Then was the time they regretted it.

"But when you think about other peoples' lives," Tom said as they walked, "don't you always assume they're making fewer mistakes than you are? Other people always seem to have a firmer grasp of things."

"That's an odd thing for a policeman to think. Aren't you supposed to have a good grasp on rectitude?" This was quite a silly conversation, she thought, peering down Noyes Street in the direction of where she calculated *she* herself lived, hundreds of miles to the south, where she represented the law, defended the poor and friendless.

"I was never a very good policeman," Tom said, stopping to stare up at a small, pristine Federalist mansion with Greek ornamental urns on both sides of its high white front door. The lawn, mowed that morning, smelled sweet. Lawnmower tracks still dented its carpet. A lone, male homeowner was standing inside watching them through a mullioned front window. Somewhere, on another street, a chain saw started then stopped, and then there was the sound of more than one metal hammer striking nails, and men's voices in laughing conversation at rooftop level. Preparations were in full swing for a long winter.

"You just weren't like all the other policemen," Nancy said. "You were kinder. But I do *not* assume other people make fewer mistakes. The back of everybody's sampler is always messier than the front. I accept both sides."

The air smelled warm and rich, as if wood and grass and slate walls exuded a sweet, lazy-hours ether-mist. She wondered if Tom was getting around in his laborious way to some new divulgence, a new Crystal, or some unique unpleasantness that required the ruin of an almost perfect afternoon to perform its dire duty. She hoped for better. Though once you'd experienced such a divulgence, you didn't fail to expect it again. But thinking about something was not the same as caring about it. That was one useful lesson she'd learned from practicing the law, one that allowed you to go home at night and sleep.

Tom suddenly started up walking again, having apparently decided not to continue the subject of other people's better grip on the alternate sides of the sampler, which was fine.

"I was just thinking about Pat La Blonde while we were down at the chowder house," he said, staying his course ahead of her in long studious strides as though she was beside him.

Pat La Blonde was Tom's partner who'd been killed when Tom had been wounded. Tom had never seemed very interested in talking about Pat before. She lengthened her steps to be beside him, give evidence of a visible listener. "I'm here," she said and pinched a fold of his sweaty shirt.

"I just realized," Tom went on, "all the life that Pat missed out on. I think about it all the time. And when I do, everything seems so damned congested. When Pat got killed, everything started getting in everything else's way for me. Like I couldn't have a life because there was so much confusion. I know you don't think that's crazy."

"No, I don't," Nancy said. She thought she remembered Tom saying these very things once. Though it was also possible she had thought these things *about* him. Marriage was that way. Possibly they had both felt the same thing as a form of mourning. "It's why you quit the force, isn't it?"

"Probably." Tom stopped, put his hands on his hips and took in an estimable yellow Dutch colonial sitting far back among ginkgos and sugar maples, and reachable by a curving flagstone path from a stone front wall to its bright-red, perfectly centered, boxwood-banked front door. "That's a nice house," he said. A large black Labrador had been lying in the front yard, but when Tom spoke it struggled up and trotted out of sight around the house's corner.

"It's lovely." Nancy touched the back of his shirt again, down low where it was damp and warm. The muscles were ropy here. She was sorry not to have touched his back recently. In Freeport, last night.

"I think," Tom said and seemed reluctant, "since that time when Pat was killed, I've been disappointed about life. You know it?" He was still looking at the yellow house, as if that was all he could stand.

"Or I've been afraid of being disappointed. Life was just fine, then all at once I couldn't figure out a way to keep anything simple. So I just made it more complicated." He shook his head and looked at her.

Nancy carefully removed her hand from the warm small of his back and put both her hands behind her in a protective way. Something about Tom's declaration had just then begun to feel like a prologue to something that might, in fact, spoil a lovely day, and refashion everything. Possibly he had planned it this way.

"Can you see a way now to make it *less* complicated?" she said, looking down at her leather shoe toes on the grainy concrete side-walk. A square had been stamped into the soft mortar, and into the middle of it was incised *Penobscot Concrete – 1938*. She was purposefully not making eye contact.

"I do," Tom said. He breathed in and then out importantly.

"So can *I* hear about it?" It annoyed her to be here now, to have something sprung on her.

"Well," Tom said, "I think I *could* find some space in a town like this to put my workshop. If I concentrated, I could probably dream up some new toy shapes, maybe hire somebody. Expand my output. Go ahead with the website idea. I think I could make a go of it with things changing here. And if I didn't, I'd still be in Maine, and I could find something else. I could be a cop if it came to that." He had his blue, black-flecked eyes trained on her, though Nancy had chosen to listen with her head lowered, hands behind her. She looked up at him now and created a smile for her lips. The sun was in her face. Her temples felt wonderfully warm. A man in khaki shorts was just exiting the yellow house, carrying a golf bag, headed around to where the black Labrador had disappeared. He noticed the two of them and waved as if they were neighbors. Nancy waved back and re-directed her smile out at him.

"Where do *I* go?" she said, still smiling. A brown and white Belfast police cruiser idled past, its uniformed driver paying them no mind.

"My thought is, you come with me," Tom said. "It can be our big adventure." His solemn expression, the one he'd had when he was talking about Pat La Blonde, stayed on his handsome face. Not a death's face at all, but one that wanted to signify something different. An invitation.

"You want me to move to Maine?"

"I do." Tom achieved a small, hopeful smile and nodded.

What a very peculiar thing, she thought. Here they were on a street in a town they'd been in fewer than two hours, and her estranged husband was suggesting they leave their life, where they were both reasonably if not impossibly happy, and *move* here.

"And why again?" she said, realizing she'd begun shaking her head, though she was also still smiling. The roof workers were once more laughing at something in the clear, serene afternoon. The chain saw was still silent. Hammering commenced again. The man with the golf bag came backing down his driveway in a Volvo station wagon the same bright-red color as his front door. He was talking on a cell phone. The Labrador was trotting along behind, but stopped as the car swung into the street.

"Because it's still not ruined up here," Tom said. "And because I know too much about myself where I am, and I'd like to find out something new before I get too old. And because I think if I – or if we – do it now, we won't live long enough to see everything get all fucked up around here. And because I think we'll be happy." Tom suddenly glanced upwards as if something had flashed past his eyes. He looked puzzled for an instant, then looked at her again as if he wasn't sure she would be there.

"It isn't exactly life-by-forecast, is it?"

"No," Tom said, still looking befuddled. "I guess not." He could be like an extremely earnest, extremely attractive boy. It made her feel old to notice it.

"So, am I supposed to agree or not agree while we're standing here on the sidewalk?" She thought of the woman pinning clothes to a line, wearing white gloves. No need to reintroduce that, or the withering cold that would arrive in a month.

"No, no," Tom said haltingly. He seemed almost ready to take it all back, upset now that he'd said what he wanted to say. "No. You don't. It's important, I realize."

"Did you plan all this," she asked. "This week? This whole town? This moment? Is this a scheme?" She was ready to laugh about it and ignore it.

"No." Tom ran his hand through his hair, where there were scatterings of assorted grays. "It just happened."

"And if I said I didn't believe you, what then?" She realized her lips were ever-so-slightly, dissaprovingly averted. It had become a habit in the year since Crystal.

"You'd be wrong." Tom nodded.

"Well." Nancy smiled and looked around her at the pretty, serious houses, the demure scenically-shaded street, the sloped lawns that set it all off just right for everybody. If you seek a well-tended ambience, look around you. It was not the Michigan-of-the-East. Why wouldn't one move here? she thought. It was a certain kind of boy's fabulous dream. In a way, the whole world dreamed it, waited for it to materialize. Odd that she never had.

"I'm getting tired now." She gave Tom a light finger pat on his chest. She felt in fact heavy-bodied, older even than she'd felt before. Done in. "Let's find someplace to stay here." She smiled more winningly and turned back the way they'd come, back down the hill toward the middle of Belfast.

*

In the motel – a crisp, new Maineliner Inn beyond the bridge they'd seen at lunch, where the room offered a long, unimpeded back-window view of the wide and sparkling bay – Tom seemed the more bushed of the two of them. In the car he'd exhibited an unearned but beleaguered stoicism which had no words to accompany its vulnerable-seeming moodiness. And once they were checked in, had their suitcases opened and the curtains drawn on the small cool spiritless room, he'd turned on the TV with no sound, stretched out on the bed in his shoes and clothes, and gone to sleep without saying more than that he'd like to have a lobster for dinner. Sleep, for Tom, was always profound, congestion or no congestion.

For a while Nancy sat in the stiff naugahyde chair beside a table lamp, and leafed through the magazines previous guests had left in the nightstand drawer: a *Sailing* with an article on the London-to-Cape-Town race; a *Marie Claire* with several bar graphs about ovarian cancer's relation to alcohol use; a *Hustler* in which an amateur artist-guest had drawn inky moustaches on the girls and little arrows toward their crotches with bubble messages that said *Evil lurks here*, and *Members Only*, and *Stay with your unit*. Naughty nautical types with fibroids, she thought, pushing the magazines back in the drawer.

There was another copy of the same *Pennysaver* they'd read at breakfast. She looked at more of the *Down-East In Search Of*'s. *Come North to meet mature Presque Isle, cuddly n/s, sjf, cutie pie. Likes contradancing and midnight boat rides, skinny dipping in the cold, clean ocean. Possibilities unlimited for the right sjm, n/s between 45 and 55 with clean med record. Only serious responses desired. No flip-flops or Canucks plz. English only.* Touching, she thought, this generalized sense of the possible, of what lay out there waiting. What, though, was a lonely *sjf* doing in Maine? And what could a flip-flop be that made them so unlikeable? Cuddly, she assumed, meant fat.

She wished to think about very few things for a while now. On the drive across from Belfast she'd become angry and acted angry. Said little. Then, when Tom was in the office paying for the room while she waited in the car, she'd suddenly become completely *un*-angry, though Tom hadn't noticed when he came back with the key. Which was why he'd gone to sleep – as if his sleep were her sleep, and when he woke up everything would be fixed. Peaceful moments, of course, were never unwelcome. And it was good not to complicate life before you absolutely had to. All Tom's questing may simply have to do with a post facto fear of retirement – another "reaction" – and in a while, if she didn't exacerbate matters, he'd forget it. Life was full of serious but meaningless conversations.

On the silent TV a golf match was under-way; elsewhere a movie featuring a young, smooth-cheeked Clark Gable; elsewhere an African documentary with tawny, emaciated lions sprawled in long brown grass, dozing after an off-stage kill. The TV cast pleasant watery light on Tom. Soon oceans of wildebeests began vigorously drowning in a muddy, swollen river. It was peaceful in the silence – even with all the drownings – as if what one heard rather than what one saw caused all the problems.

Just outside the window she could hear a child's laughing voice and a man's patient, deeper one attempting to speak some form of encouragement. She inched back the heavy plastic curtain and against the sharp rays of daylight looked out at the motel lawn, where a large, thick-bodied young man in a silver wheelchair, wearing a red athletic singlet and white cotton shorts – his legs thick, strong, tanned and hairy as his back – was attempting to hoist into flight a festive orange-paper kite, using a small fishing rod and line, while a laughing little blond girl held the kite above her head. Breeze gently rattled the kite's paper, on which had been painted a smiling oriental face. The man in the wheelchair kept saying, "Okay, run now, run," so that the little girl, who seemed perfectly seven, jumped suddenly, playfully one way and then another, the kite held high, until she had leaped and boosted it up and off her fingers, while the man jerked the rod and tried to wench the smiling face into the wind. Each time, though, the kite drooped and lightly settled back onto the grass that grew all the way down to the shore. And each time the man said, his voice rising at the end of his phrases, "Okay now. Up she goes again. We can do this. Pick it up and try it again." The little girl kept laughing. She wore tiny pink shorts and a bright-green top, and was barefoot and brown-legged. She seemed ecstatic.

He was the man from the park in town, Nancy thought, letting the curtain close. A coincidence of no importance. She looked at Tom asleep in his clothes, breathing noiselessly, hands clasped on his chest like a dead man's, his bare, brown legs crossed at the ankles in an absurdly casual attitude, his blue running shoes resting one against

the other. In peaceful sleep his handsome, unshaved features seemed
ordinary.

She changed the channel and watched a ball game. The Cubs
versus a team whose aqua uniforms she didn't recognize. Her father
had been a Cubs fan. They'd considered themselves northsiders.
They'd traveled to Wrigley on warm autumn afternoons like this one.
He would remove her from school on a trumped-up excuse, buy seats
on the first base line and let her keep score with a stubby blue pencil.
The sixties, those were. She made an effort to remember the players'
names, using their blue-and-white uniforms and the viny outfield
wall as fillips to memory thirty years on. She could think of smiling
Ernie Banks, and a white man named Ron something, and a tall
sad-faced high-waisted black man from Canada who pitched well but
later got into some kind of police trouble and cried about it on TV.
It was too little to remember.

Though the attempt at memory made her feel better – more settled
in the same singular, getting-on-with-it way that standing on the
sunny street corner being mis-identified by a busload of Japanese
tourists had made her feel: as if she was especially credible when
seen without the benefit of circumstance and the encumbrances of
love, residues of decisions made long, long ago. More credible,
certainly, than she was here now, trapped in East Whatever, Maine,
with a wayward husband on his way down the road, and suffering
spiritual congestion no amount of life-by-forecast or authentic
marriage could cure.

This whole trip – in which Tom championed some preposterous
idea for the sole purpose of having her reject it so he could then
do what he wanted to anyway – made her feel unkind toward her
husband. Made him seem stupid and childish. Made *him* seem
inauthentic. Not a grownup. It was a bad sign, she thought, to find
yourself the adult, whereas your lifelong love-interest was suddenly
an over-exuberant child passing himself off as an enthusiast whose
great enthusiasm you just can't share. Since what it meant was
that in all probability life with Tom Marshall was over. And not in

the way her clients at the public defender's saw things to their conclusions – using as their messenger-agents whiskey bottles, broom handles, car bumpers, firearms, sharp instruments, flammables, the meaty portion of a fist. There, news broke vividly, suddenly, the lights always harsh and grainy, the volume turned up, doors flung open for all to see. (Her job was to bring their affairs back into quieter, more sensible orbits so all could be understood, felt, suffered more exquisitely.)

For her and for Tom, basically decent people, the course would be different. Her impulse was to help. His was to try and then try harder. His perfidy was enthusiasm. Her indifference was patience. But eventually all the enthusiasm would be used up, all the patience. Possibilities would diminish. Life would cease to be an open, flat plain upon which you walked with a chosen other, and become instead cluttered, impassable. Tom had said it: life became a confinement in which everything got in everything else's way. And what you finally sought became not a new, clearer path, but a way out. Their own son no doubt foresaw life that way, as something that should be easy. Though it seemed peculiar – now that he was away – to think they even *had* a son. She and Tom seemed more like each other's parents.

But, best just to advance now toward what she wanted, even if it didn't include Tom, even if she didn't know how to want what didn't include Tom. And even if it meant she *was* the kind of person who did things, said things, then rethought, even regretted their consequences later. Tom wasn't, after all, trying to improve life for her, no matter what he thought. Only his. And there was no use talking people out of things that improved their lives. He had wishes. He had fears. He was a good enough man. Life shouldn't be always trying, trying, trying. You should live most of it without trying so hard. He would agree *that* was authentic.

Inside the enclosed room a strange, otherworldly golden glow seemed to fall on everything now. On Tom. On her own hands and arms. On the bed. All through the static air, like a fog. It was beautiful, and for a moment she wanted to speak to Tom, to wake him, to tell him that something or other would be all right, just as he'd hoped; to be enthusiastic in some hopeful and time-proven way. But she didn't, and then the golden fog disappeared, and for an instant she seemed to understand *slightly* better the person she was – though she lacked a proper word for it, and knew only that the time for saying so many things was over.

Outside, the child's voice was shouting. "Oh, I love it. I love it so much." When Nancy pulled back the curtain, the softer light fell across the chair back, and she could see that the wheelchair man had his kite up and flying, the fiberglass fishing rod upwards in one hand while he urged his chair down the sloping lawn. The barelegged child was hopping from one bare foot to the other, a smashing smile on her long, adult's face, which was turned up toward the sky.

Nancy stood and snapped on the desk lamp beside Tom's open suitcase. One bright, intact, shrink-wrapped Wagner dog and one white Maine Lighthouse were tucked among his shirts and shaving kit and socks. Here was also his medal for valor in a blue cloth case, and the small automatic pistol he habitually carried in case of attack. She plucked up only the Wagner dog, returned the room to its shadows, and stepped out the back door onto the lawn.

Here, on the outside, the air was fresh and cool and only slightly breezy, the sky now full of quilty clouds as though rain were expected. A miniature concrete patio with blue plastic-strand chairs was attached to each room. The kite, its slant-eyed face smiling down, was dancing and tricking and had gained altitude as the wheelchair man rolled farther away down the lawn toward the bay.

"Look at our kite," the little girl shouted, shading her eyes toward Nancy and pointing delightedly at the diminishing kite face.

"It's sensational," Nancy said, shading her own eyes to gaze upward. The kite made her smile.

The wheelchair man turned his head to view her. He *was* large, with thick shoulders and smooth rounded arms she could see under his red singlet. His head was round, his thick hair buzzed short, his eyes small and dark and fierce and unfriendly. She smiled at him and for no reason shook her head as though the kite amazed her. An ex-jock, she thought. A shallow-end diving accident, or some football collision that left him flying his kite from a metal chair. A pity.

The man said nothing, just looked at her without gesture, his expression so intent he seemed unwilling to be bothered. She, though, felt the pleasure to be had from only watching, of having to make no comment. The cool breeze, the nice expansive water view to Islesboro, a kite standing aloft were quite enough.

Then her mind flooded with predictable things. The crippled man's shoes. You always thought of them. His were black and sockless, like bowling shoes, shoes that would never wear out. He would merely grow weary of seeing them, give them away to someone more unfortunate than himself. Was this infuriating to him? Did he speak about it? Was the wife, wherever she might be, terribly tired all the time? Did she get up at night and stand at the window staring out, wishing some quite specific things, then return to bed un-missed. Was pain involved? Did phantom pains even exist? Did he have dreams of painlessness? Of rising out of his chair and walking around laughing, of never knowing a chair? She thought about a dog with its hind parts attached to a little wheeled coaster, trotting along as if all was well. Did *anything* work down below, she wondered? Were there understandings, allowances? Did he think his predicament "interesting"? Had being crippled opened up new and important realms of awareness? What did *he* know that she didn't?

Maybe being married to him, she thought, would be better than many other lives. Though you'd fast get to the bottom of things, begin to notice too much, start to regret it all. Perhaps while he was here flying a kite, the wife was in the hotel bar having a drink and a long talk with the bartender, speaking about her past, her father, her hometown, how she'd thought about things earlier in life, what had once made her laugh, who she'd voted for, what music she'd preferred, how she liked Maine, how authentic it seemed, when they thought they might head home again. How they wished they could stay and stay and stay. The thing she – Nancy – would not do.

"Do you want to fly our kite?" the man was saying to her, his voice trailing up at the end, almost like Tom's. He was, for some reason, smiling now, his eyes bright, looking back over his hairy round shoulder with a new attitude. She noticed he was wearing glasses – surprising to miss that. The kite, its silky monofilament bellying upward in a long sweep, danced on the wind almost out of sight, a fleck upon the eye.

"Oh do, do," the little girl called out. "It'll be so good." She had her arms spread wide and up over her head, as if measuring some huge and inconceivable wish. She was permanently smiling.

"Yes," Nancy said, walking toward them. "Of course."

"You can feel it pulling you," the girl said. "It's like you're going to fly up to the stars." She began to spin around and around in the grass then, like a little dervish. The wheelchair man looked to his daughter, smiling.

Nancy felt embarrassed. Seen. It was shocking. The spacious blue bay spread away from her down the hill, and off of it arose a freshened breeze. It was far from clear that she could hold the kite. It *could* take her up, pull her away, far and out of sight. It was unnerving. She held the toy Wagner to give to the child. That would have its fine effect. And then, she thought, coming to the two of them, smiling out of flattery, that she would take the kite – the rod, the string – yes, of course, and fly it, take the chance, be strong, unassailable, do everything she could to hold on.

ABYSS

Abyss

Two weeks before the Phoenix sales conference, Frances Bilandic and Howard Cameron drove from home – in Willamantic and Pawcatuck – met at the Olive Garden in Mystic and talked things over one more time, touching fingertips nervously across the Formica tabletop. Then each went to the restroom and made a private, lying cell phone call to account for their whereabouts during the next few hours. Then they drove across the access road to the Howard Johnson's under the Interstate, registered in as a Mr. and Mrs. Garfield, and in five minutes had chained the door, turned up the air conditioning, pulled the curtains across the sunny window and abandoned themselves to the furious passions they'd been suppressing for the month since meeting at the awards banquet, where they were named Connecticut Residential Agents of the Year.

What had occurred between them at the awards banquet was something of a mystery to them both. Seated beside each other at the head table, they'd barely spoken before being presented with their agent-of-the-year citations. But after the first course, Howard had told a funny joke about Alzheimer's disease to the person seated on his other side, and Frances had laughed. When Howard realized she thought he was funny, their eyes had met in a way Frances felt was shocking, but also undeniable, since, in her view, they'd each experienced (and fully acknowledged) a large, instinctual carnal attraction – the kind, she thought, animals probably felt all the time, and that made their lives much more bearable.

Within fifteen minutes, she and Howard Cameron had begun exchanging snickering asides about the other winners' table manners, their indecipherable wardrobe choices and probable sales etiquette, and all the while avoiding the dull, realtor shop-talk about house closings, disastrous building inspection reports, and unbelievable arguments customers routinely waged inside their cars.

By dessert, they were venturing into more sensitive areas – Frances's junior college roommate Meredith, who'd died of brain cancer in June at thirty-four (Frances's age); Howard's father's tachycardia and his unfulfilled wish to play Turnberry before he died. Napkins across their empty plates, they moved on to life's brevity and the need to squeeze every second for all its worth. And by the time decaf arrived, they'd eased over onto the subject of sex, and how misunderstood a subject it was in the culture, and how it was all the Puritans' fault that it even *was* a subject, since it should be completely natural and unstigmatized. They each spoke lovingly about their spouses, but not that much.

Seated at the long head table full of fellow award-winners and bosses, and directly in front of a Ramada Inn banquet room full of noisy, laughing people they didn't know but who were occasionally casting narrow-eyed, flaming arrows of spite through the two of them, sex infiltrated their soft-spoken conversation like a dense, rich but explosive secret they, but only they, had decided to share. And once that happened, everything – everyone in the room, everything Frances and Howard planned to do later in the evening (drive home to their spouses, Ed in Willamantic, Mary in Pawcatuck, down dark and narrow, late-night Connecticut highways; the chance visits they might have with zany colleagues at the bar; voicemail they might check for after-hours client calls) any and all thoughts about this night being normal ended.

Most Americans don't even begin to reach their sexual maturity until they're not interested in it anymore, Frances observed. The Scandinavians, indeed, had the best attitude, with sex being no big deal – just a normal human response (like sleeping) that should be respected, not obsessed over.

Americans were too hung up on false conceptions of beauty and youth, Howard agreed, sagely folding his long arms. He was six-foot five, with big pie-plate hands and had played basketball at Western Connecticut. His father had been his high school coach. Howard had dull gray, closely spaced eyes and still wore his hair in an old-fashioned buzzed-off crew cut that made him look older than twenty-nine. Orgasm was *way* overrated, he suggested, in contrast to true intimacy, which was way *under*rated.

Nothing in a marriage could ever be absolutely perfect, they agreed. Marriage shouldn't be a prison cell. The best marriages were always the ones where both partners felt free to pursue their personal needs, though neither of them advocated the open marriage concept.

The word *marriage*, Frances said, actually derived from an Old Norse word, meaning the time after the onset of a fatal illness when the disease has you in its grip but you can still walk around pretty well. This was her father's joke, though she didn't mean it to sound like a sour-puss complaint. Just a yuck, like Howard's Alzheimer's story. She found she could joke with Howard Cameron, who was witty in the blunt-to-gross way nerdy ex-jocks who weren't complete idiots could be funny. She was impressed she knew him well enough to relax, after only two hours. With Ed she hadn't gotten that far in six years.

"I'm the fifth of five. All boys," Howard said, watching the Mexican waiters collecting banquet dishes off the tables. Their own table had emptied, and the crowd was filing out through the back doors, leaving the two of them conspicuously alone behind the white-skirted dais table. People were saying good-byes and telling lame jokes about spending the night in the car on the Interstate. The lights were turned up bright to move people out, and the room smelled of sour food. He was aware they were obviously lingering. Yet he felt intimacy with Frances Bilandic. "I'm sure my parents had a solid sex life until my dad had to go on the blood thinners," Howard went on solemnly. "But then, well, I guess things changed."

"Technology took over, right?" Frances said and smirked. She was spunky and had snapping blue eyes, an attractively mannish little blond haircut and a barely noticeable overbite that displayed the bottoms of her incisors. She was the only daughter of a Polish widower from Bridgeport, had performed the balance beam in high school, and was as hard as a little brickbat. She'd probably seen plenty. Though he knew he was getting serious too fast, and that could spook her. Only she had to know what was what. It was a game. "He went on the pill? Or the pump, right?" Frances made a little up-down pumping motion with her thumb, up-down, up-down, and a little "eee-eee-eee-eee" squeaky sound. "That works out better for older people, I guess."

"He's not the type," Howard said. He thought then about his father standing sadly out in their broad, freshly mown back yard that sloped all the way to the shining Quinnebaug River, in Pomfret. It was the late-spring day his father had come back from the hospital after having his veins surgically ballooned. Geese were flying over in a V. His father had been wearing faded madras shorts and stood barefoot in the cool grass, staring off. His legs were thin and pale. It was heartbreaking.

But heartbreaking or not, Howard thought, it just showed that life had to be seized and squeezed before somebody came after you with a vein balloon. Marriage, kids – these were certainly ways you could squeeze it. His parents' way. (Though maybe they weren't so happy about that now.) But there were also alternatives, avenues that society or their employer the Weiboldt Company – red and white "For Sale" and "Sorry You Missed It" signs littering the seaboard from Cape May to Cape Ann – wouldn't necessarily condone; and avenues you definitely wouldn't start down every day of your life. Except of course those very avenues got chosen every day. Every second probably somebody somewhere was squeezing life on that alternative avenue. Probably in this very Ramada, while their banquet was ending, somebody was squeezing it. Why fight it?

"I hope I haven't made light of a serious subject," Frances said somberly referring to his parents. She was wearing a white pants suit with a green polka dot blouse that did nothing, she knew, to show off her curves. But what she had wanted tonight, her special night of recognition, was to look drop-dead gorgeous, yet also to look like business. She, after all, had sold more real estate than anybody in her part of western Connecticut, and done it by working her tail off. And not by listing water-view contemporaries and Federalist mansions in Watch Hill, but by flogging attached row-houses in Guatemalan neighborhoods, four-room Capes, and buck-and-a-half condos down-wind of the Willamantic landfill – units they buried you with in anybody else's market. And she knew business didn't take nights off, so you had to look the part. She thought of herself as a smart, tough cookie, a Polack go-getter, an early riser, a quick-study who didn't blink.

But that didn't mean you couldn't wander into some fun with a guy like this big Howard. A long, tall, galunky-jocky guy with some mischief in his eye, who could use some release from his own pressure cooker. Having an intense, private conversation with Howard Cameron was the reward for doing her job so fucking well.

"I'll bet if we adjourned to a bar where there aren't so many familiar faces, we wouldn't have to be so solemn," Frances said, touching her napkin to the corners of her mouth. She liked the sound of her voice saying this.

Howard was already nodding. "Right. I'm sure you're right." He picked up the cheap fake-wood-framed certificate he'd gotten for selling huge amounts of real estate and making everybody but himself rich. "I intend to hang this over the can at home," he said. The certificate had a stick-on gold seal below his name, and the words *In*

Hoc Signo Vinces embossed around the rim in Gothic-looking letters. He had no idea what this meant.

"I intend to lose mine someplace," Frances said. He felt her hard-as-a-board little gymnast's thigh (conceivably innocently) brush by his knee as she slid away from the long head table. "You find us a bar, okay? I'll find *you*." She placed her small hand onto his large one and squeezed. "I'm off to the whatever." She started for the rear doors, leaving him alone at the table.

A Negro woman's big round face had for a while been staring at them through the round porthole window in the kitchen door. The crew in there were wanting to go home. But when Howard caught the woman's eye, she winked a big lewd wink which he didn't appreciate.

This was how these things happened, he understood, fingering his chintzy agent-of-the-year plaque. He would see Frances Bilandic after tonight. No way it wouldn't happen. He had no pre-vision about the circumstances or what the degree of risk would be – if they'd go straight to bed or just have lunch. But in the fervid yet strangely familiar way he knew sex could make a point-of-no-return out of the most unsuspecting and innocent human interaction, nothing now seemed to make any difference but the two of them having a drink and almost certainly giving serious thought to fucking each other senseless in the not too distant future. And *she* knew it. She was definitely up for whatever this would lead to – the little brush against his leg was no mistake. Women were all different now, he thought, working women especially. A blow job meant what a handshake used to. When he'd driven down the teeming, vacationer-swarmed corridor of I-95 tonight, he'd had no idea there was even a Frances Bilandic on the planet, or that she'd be waiting for him, and that in the time it took to get designated agent-of-the-year, they'd be wandering off in search of a dark little bar for some dirty work. The world was full of wondrous surprises. And he was absolutely ready for this one, ready to find out all the mysteries and wonders it was ready to bring.

He looked back at the porthole window where the black woman's face had appeared and winked at him. He wanted to give her some kind of answering look, a look that meant he knew what she knew. But the window was empty. The light behind it had been turned off.

*

In Phoenix, the Weiboldt "Sales Festival" had taken over a towering chrome-and-glass Radisson in a crowded western foothill suburb that presented big views back toward the oppressive, boundariless city. There were two golf courses, forty-five tennis courts, a water-fun center for kids, an aquarium, a casino, an I-MAX, a multiplex with eighteen screens, a hospital, a library, a crisis counseling center and an elevated monorail that sped away someplace into the desert. All this seemed to guarantee silent and empty hallways where no one would encounter the two of them together, empty back stairways, and elevators opening on to faces neither of them would ever see again. Plus sealed, air-conditioned rooms with heavy light-proof curtains, enormous beds with scratchy sheets, giant TVs, full minibars, jacuzzis and twenty-four-hour anonymous room service.

Yet they knew they could be detected by any hint that something was funny. Following which they would immediately lose their jobs. Real estate wasn't like it used to be, when an office romance flamed up and everybody thought it was sweet and looked the other way (to gossip). Office romances, even romances that took place between offices miles apart, now landed you in Federal court for polluting the workplace with messy personal matters that interfered with the lives of loser colleagues obsessed with getting rich in a boom market and looking for an excuse for why they'd crapped out. "Personal," was now a term that meant something like criminal. Everyone was terrified.

Consequently, Howard and Frances had flown out from separate airports – Providence and Hartford – and requested rooms in different "towers". Howard had requested a smoking room, though he didn't smoke, then asked that no calls be put through. The first night, at the Platinum Club ice-breaker, they'd mingled with completely separate crowds – Frances with some high-spirited lesbian agents from New Jersey; Howard with some dreary, churchy

Mainers. Afterward, they'd gone off to different daiquiri bars, then to separate Mexican restaurants, where they made certain not to drink too much and to talk about their spouses non-stop, without once mentioning each other's name or even Connecticut.

As a result, by the end of night one, when Frances tapped lightly on Howard's door at eleven-thirty ready for fun, they each found it not immediately easy to set aside their blameless public disguises, and so had sat for an hour across a little wooden card table in uncomfortable hotel chairs, doing nothing but discussing what had happened that day, even though their days had been 100% the same.

Frances liked talking about real estate. To her surprise, she'd enjoyed her night out with the "Garden State Lesbos," had picked up on some new thinking about cold-call strategies in low-income, ethnic concentrations, and had discovered she had useful intelligence of her own to put into play about structuring earnest-money proffers so that the buyer offered full-price up-front, but was protected right to closing, and could get out without a scratch in case of buyer's remorse. She said that because her husband, Ed, had suffered an industrial accident in the indistinct past, an unspecified injury that left him not fit to work anymore (he was "older"), she'd been forced to jump into real estate as her full-time career, whereas she'd hoped to be a physiotherapist, and maybe work in France. It was a stroke of luck, she felt, that she'd turned out to be so "goddamned good at selling."

Howard, on the other hand (he'd already explained this in the dark and cozy boss-and-secretary bar they'd found after the awards banquet in August) thought of selling real estate as just a "bridging strategy" between his first job out of college (playground supervisor) and something more entrepreneurial, with travel, an incentive bonus and a company car built into the equation. His entire family were life-long Republicans, and two of his brothers were engineers in the road-paving business down in New London, and they were thinking of bringing him in. The only problem was that he didn't get along with those brothers that well, and his wife, Mary, didn't like them at all. Which was why *he* was still selling houses.

Frances had brought a bottle of not very cold, not very good Pinot Grigio, and it sat sweating on the hotel table attended by two clear-plastic bathroom cups they were drinking out of. The vast and darkened desert colossus of Phoenix lay to the east beyond the window glass – cars moving, planes descending to outlined runways, blue police flashers flashing, wide, walled neighborhoods tainting patches of the night pumpkin orange with their crime lights. It was exotic. It was the west. Neither of them had ever been here, though Howard said he'd read that Phoenix was the American city where you were most likely to get your car stolen.

Frances liked Howard Cameron. Feeling drunk, jet-lagged and talked-out, she appreciated that he could come up with this good humor, yet could also exhibit caring sensitivity – in this case, not to presume upon her for showing up in his room, though they'd been in bed together four different afternoons in four different seaside motels since the awards banquet. He understood consideration (even though she assumed he was ready to pop with desire just like she was). He also recognized the precarious situation they were in and how she might feel stressed. True, he was ready to cheat on his wife back in Pawcatuck; but he also seemed like a decent family man with a strong sense of right and wrong, and no real wish to do anybody harm. She felt the same. It was tricky. There was probably a category in some textbook for what the two of them were doing, slipping around this way, but she wasn't ready to say what it was.

She let her eyes rise woozily above the sparkling rhomboids of gaudy Phoenix and into the moonless darkness, to where the face of Howard's wife Mary, a woman she'd never seen even in a snapshot, materialized out of the dark clouds like a picture in a developer's tray. The image was of a young, sweet-faced blond like herself, whose oval face and small heart-shaped mouth bore a look of disappointment, her eyes large and doleful and unmistakably expressive of hurt.

"That's true," Frances Bilandic said. "I understand that."

"Hm?" Howard said. He looked around at the door as if someone had entered and Frances had begun talking to whomever it was. The red message bulb on the phone was blinking as it had been since he came back from dinner. Too late to call home now, he'd decided, with the time difference.

No one, however, had come into the room. It was chain latched. "Were you talking to me?"

"I guess I'm pretty whacked," she said. "I must've gone to sleep sitting up." She smiled a smile she knew was a sweet, probably pathetic smile. It was her surrender look, and she was ready for him to give up being so reserved. It hadn't been at all pleasant to see Howard's wife's face frowning out in the sky. It hadn't been the end of the world, but it had left her feeling a little dazed. But that would go away if she could get Howard to take her to bed and fuck her in the damn near frightening way they'd gone at it back home.

"I feel so free now," he said suddenly, incomprehensibly. His great, smooth, ball player's hands encircled his tiny plastic cup of cheap wine. He was looking straight at Frances, his elongated, not particularly handsome face full of wonder, his sensuous lips parted in a dopey smile. "Really. I can't explain it, but it's true."

"That's good," she said. She hoped he wouldn't give a speech now.

Howard shook his head in small amazement. "Not that I'd ever really thought different. But this is no sidetrack we're on here. This is *my* real life, you know? This is as free and as good as things ever get. I mean like – this is it." He nodded instead of shaking his buzzed head. "This is as real as marriage, for sure."

"Lots of things are *that* real."

"Okay," Howard said. "But I'm not sure I ever knew that."

"Read the fine print," Frances said. It was another of her dad's Polack maxims. Everything you either didn't like or were surprised by meant you hadn't *read the fine print*. Marriage, children, work, getting old. The fine print was where the truth was about things and it was never what you expected.

"I really like you," Howard said. "I'm not sure I exactly said that."

"I like you too," she said. "I wouldn't fuck you if I didn't like you."

"No. Of course not." His grin showed his large teeth behind his almost feminine lips. "Probably me too."

"Then why don't you just fuck me now." She intentionally widened her pretty blue eyes to indicate that was real, too.

"Okay, I will." Howard Cameron said, moving toward her, touching her knee, her breast, her soft cheeks, her lips in quick, breathless assault. "I want to," he said. "I've wanted to all day. I don't know why we waited 'til now."

"Now's okay," Frances said. "Now's perfect." Which, she felt, was only true.

*

One thing he liked about Frances Bilandic was the direct, guiltless, almost stern yet still passionate way she involved herself with screwing the daylights out of him. His sexual preference had always been for a lot of vociferous bouncing and spiritedly noisy plunging; Mary referred to their early lovemaking as *the side show,* which embarrassed him. But Frances gave fucking a new meaning. Her eyes fixed on him with an intensity that was frequently intimidating, she entered a different sexual dimension, with assertive declarations about exactly how she expected to take hold of him, and him of her, raucous tauntings in the form of instructions as to how vigorously he was expected to bring her to fulfillment; plus limitless physical stamina and perplexing orgasmic variety and originality. "That's not it, that's *not* it, no, no, no. Jesus, Jesus," she'd shout in his ear just when he thought he had her on the cusp. This insistent, uncompromising voice alone could blow the top off of him. "Don't you dare lose me, don't you lose me, god *damn* it," she'd command. "That's right. You're right. There it is. I see you now. There you are. There's no one like you, Howard. Nobody. Howard. Nobody!"

She made him think that in fact it was true. That by some amazing luck, among all men there *was* no one like Howard Cameron. He *was* as sexually insatiable as she was; he *did* possess the need, the vigor, the ingenuity – plus the equipment to do things properly. He'd never thought much about his equipment, which just seemed normal, given his height. And yet, why other men couldn't cut the mustard wasn't really a mystery. Life wasn't fair. Nobody ever said it would or should be.

Frances, however, was unqualifiedly his sexual ideal. That was irrefutable. He'd never known there was an *ideal,* or that this version was what he'd always really wanted (his sexual experience wasn't that extensive). Only here was a flat-out, full-bore sexual appetite, and with an arrogance which said that if all this wasn't absolutely fantastic she wouldn't even bother with it. Except it *was* fantastic. And he was moved by Frances, and by sex with Frances in ways he'd never in his whole life thought he'd be lucky enough to experience.

Of course, it wasn't the kind of experience that ever led to marriage, or to any lasting importance. He remembered what she'd said about the Old Norse word. She understood plenty. She and poor lame Ed probably had polite, infrequent sex, just like his parents, so that her own ravenous appetites were permanently back-burnered out of respect for whatever pitiful use he was. His own luck, Howard understood, was to play a bit part in their life's little humdrum. Though it was way too good to miss, no matter where it led to or from.

One thing had surprised him. After their first epic session at Howard Johnson's in September – this after three weeks of steamy meetings in shadowy bars and roadside cafes in little nowhere Connecticut towns between Willamantic and Pawcatuck – they had stepped out of the room into the lazer sunlight of the HoJo's parking lot, with Interstate 95 pounding by almost on top of them. He'd looked up into the pale, oxidized sky, rubbed his eyes, which had grown accustomed to the darkness of the room and, without much thought, said, "Boy, that was really something." He'd meant it as a compliment

"What do you mean, *something*?" Frances said in her husky blondie voice – a voice that electrified him in bed, a voice made for sex, but that suddenly seemed different out on the harsh, baking asphalt. She was wearing red-framed sunglasses, a short blue-leather skirt that emphasized her thighs, and what was by then an extremely wrinkled white pinafore blouse. Her hair was pressed flat on the sides and she was sweating. She looked roughed up and dazed, which was how he felt. Fucked to death would've been a way to say it.

He smiled uncomfortably. "I just mean, well . . . you're really good at this. You know?"

"I'm *not* good at this," Frances snapped, "I'm good with *you*. Not that I'm in love with you. I'm not."

"Sure. I mean, no. That's right," he said, not happy being scolded. "We don't do these things alone, do we?" He smiled, but Frances didn't.

"Some people might." She frowned from behind her shades, seeming to re-assess him all in one moment's time. It was as if there was one kind of person whom you met and maybe liked and thought was okay-looking and funny and who you fucked – one kind of Howard; but then there was another Howard, one you never liked and who immediately started comparing you to other women the moment you fucked him, and who pissed you off. She'd just met that Howard. It was her "tough cookie" side, and she was dead serious about it.

Although maybe, he thought, Frances just wanted it clear that if somebody was going to be the "tough cookie" it had to be her. Which was fine with him. If you had only *one* situation in your life with no unhappy surprises and that one worked out just halfway well – the one his parents had had for thirty years, for instance – then you were a lucky duck. His own marriage, all things taken into consideration, might be one of those rarities. He wasn't hoping to make Frances Bilandic number two. He just wished she wouldn't be so serious. They both knew what they were doing.

Frances had tiny, child's hands, but strong, with deep creases in their palms like an old person's hands. And when he'd held them, in bed in the HoJo's, they'd made him feel tender toward her, as if her hands rendered her powerless to someone of his unusual size. He reached and took both her little hands in both of his big ones, as semis pounded the girders on I-95. She was so small – a tough, sexy little package, but also a little package of trouble if you didn't exert strong force on her.

"I wish you wouldn't be mad at me," he said, bringing her in close to him. Her strong little bullet breasts greeted his maroon Pawcatuck Parks and Recreation Department tee shirt.

"I've never done this before, okay?" she said almost inaudibly, though she let herself be brought in. They didn't have to be in love, he thought, but they could be tender to each other. Why bother otherwise? (He absolutely didn't believe she'd never done this before. He, on other hand, hadn't.)

"Same here," he said. Though that didn't matter. He just wanted a chance to do it again sometime soon.

One of the tractor trailers honked from up above. They were standing out in the hot parking lot at two PM on a Tuesday in early September. It was sweet and touching but also completely stupid, since the Weiboldt Mystic office was only five blocks away. An agent could be picking up clients at the HoJos. If someone blabbed, it could be over in a flash. Boom . . . no job. Their colleagues would love nothing more than for two new agents-of-the-year to be fired and to take over their listings. And for what? For a minor misunder-standing about Frances being good in bed – which she definitely was. It made him suddenly anxious to be touching her out in the open, so that he stopped and looked around the lot. Nothing. "Maybe we ought to go back inside," he said, "we've got the room the rest of the night." He didn't really want to – he wanted to get to an appointment in White Rock. But he *would* go back if fate required it. In fact, a part of him – a small part – would've liked to have gotten in his car, piled Frances Bilandic in beside him, headed up onto the Interstate, turning south and never coming back. Leave the whole sorry shitaree in the dust. He could do that. Worry about details later. People who did that were people he admired, though you never really heard what their lives were like later.

"I'm afraid if I went back in that room I might not come out for a week," Frances said, looking around at the green door of the motel room. She put her rough little hand flagrantly against his still-stiff cock and gave it a good squeeze. "You'd probably like that, wouldn't you?"

"I guess there's your evidence," Howard said solemnly.

"Just checkin' in on Garfield," Frances said behind her shades. "I'll save him for Phoenix. How's that?"

"I can't wait." Howard realized he was grinning idiotically.

"You better," Frances said. "I'll know if you don't."

And that's how they left it.

*

The sales conference, following the first day's jet-lagged festivities and spiritless camaraderie, developed into a slog almost immediately. Frances kept running into the loud-mouth lesbians from Jersey, who kept repeating the punchline of the joke they'd told twenty times the first night. "Suck-off's just a Russian general to me, soldier." They'd bray that line in the elevator or in the ladies room or waiting for a panel to begin, then break into squalls of laughter. She couldn't remember how the joke began, so she couldn't tell it to Ed on the phone.

All the seminars, chalk-talk panels, motivational speeches and mano-a-mano sessions with the Weiboldt top management team were tedious and repetitive and usually insulting. They were aimed, she felt, at people who'd never sold a piece of real estate, instead of Platinum agents who'd spurted past four million and would've been better off at home, fielding stragglers at the end of the summer selling season.

Howard skipped most of the sessions and found some new guys from western Mass he could talk sports with – a bald Latvian he'd once played against in a state tournament in the eighties. "It comes from being one of five," he said to Frances on day three, when they'd broken their rule and allowed themselves lunch together in the hotel's food court, which had an OK Corral theme, and the servers were dressed like desperadoes with guns and fake moustaches. "I spent my youth listening to my parents telling me for the thirteenth time something I already knew." He seemed pleased, grazing at his taco salad. "I mean, I don't really mind somebody telling me how to sell a house when I've already sold five hundred of them. But I don't need to seek it out, you know?"

There were certain qualities about Howard Cameron that would never grow on you, Frances thought. He was always happy for somebody to tell him something, instead of generating important data himself. It was a passive aspect, and made him seem sensitive at first. Except it wasn't really passive; it was actually aggressive: a willingness to let somebody else say something wrong after which he could sit in judgment on the sidelines. You learned that attitude in sports: the other guy fucks up, and when he does – because he always will – then you're right there to reap the benefits. It was a privileged, suburban, cynical way of operating and passed for easy-going. And he made it work for him. Whereas someone like her had to scrap and hustle and do things in a straight-ahead manner just to get them done at all.

Of course you'd never convince him his way was wrong. He was genetically hard-wired to like things how they were. "That'll work," was his favorite expression for deciding most issues – issues such as whether to solicit a higher bid on a property after a lower one had already been accepted, or quoting a client an interest rate lower than the bank's in order to string them along. Things she would never do. Howard, however – long-armed solemn goony-faced, hard-dick Howard Cameron – *would* do them; had done them countless times, but liked to make you think that he wouldn't. It was a surprise – something learned from being alone with him two nights running – but she'd already decided that if she saw him again once they were back home, she'd be shocked. He wasn't a con man, but he wasn't much better.

Across the noisy food court she saw two of the New Jersey women waiting beside the big chrome sculpture in the middle of the room, scanning around for someone to eat lunch with, and yakking it up as usual. The food court occupied a wide, light-shot, glass-roofed atrium, architecturally grafted onto the Radisson, and rising twenty stories, with real sparrows nesting in the walls. Protruding upward fifteen stories from a central reflection pool was a huge, rectangular chrome slab that had water somehow drizzling down it. People had naturally thrown hundreds of pennies in the pool. The New Jersey realtors were looking up at it and laughing. They thought everything had a sexual significance that proved men were stupid. Frances hoped they wouldn't spot her, didn't want the Howard Cameron issue to get them going. They should never have come here together.

She had a good idea, though, that she thought she'd enlist Howard in if the two of them were still hot and heavy by mid-week. It was more fun to do things with somebody, and she still liked Howard okay, even if he had personal qualities she was starting to be sick of. "Do you know what I think we should do?" She wanted to seem spontaneous, even if the idea wasn't really original. She smiled, trying to penetrate whatever he was thinking – sports, sex, his parents, his wife – whatever.

"Let's go up to my room," Howard said. "Is that your idea?"

"No, I mean *do* in a real sense." She tapped the back of his hand with one middle finger to seize more of his attention. "I want to see the Grand Canyon," she said. "I brought a book about it. I've always wanted to. Do you want to come with me?" She tried to beam at him.

"Is it in Phoenix?" Howard looked puzzled, which was how he registered surprise.

"Not that far," Frances said. "We can get a car. Tomorrow's our free day. We can leave in an hour and be back tomorrow afternoon."

Howard shoved away the remains of his taco salad. "How long do we have to drive?"

"Four hours. Two hundred miles. I don't know. I looked at the map in the welcome kit. It's straight north. We'd have a good time. You always wanted to see it, I know you did. Take the plunge."

"I guess," Howard said, pushing out his livery lips in a skeptical way. He probably looked like his father when he did his lips that way, she thought, and he probably liked it.

"I'll drive," Frances said. "I'll rent the car. All you have to do is sit there."

"Mmmm." Howard attempted a smile, but didn't seem to share the enthusiasm. Which was, of course, his self-serving way: let the other people – his poor, innocent wife, for instance – present him with a good idea, then cast pissy doubt on it until he could let himself get talked into it, then never really seem appreciative until it turns out good, after which he takes all the credit. She could just go alone, except she didn't want to. If Ed was here, he *definitely* wouldn't go.

"Well look," she said, "if you're going, I vote we go right after the amortization panel, so we can see the desert in twilight. We can spend the night on the road, see the Grand Canyon as the sun's coming up, and be back for dinner."

"You got it all figured out," Howard said, smirking. He was beginning to go for it. In his mind, agreeing to go made it his idea.

"I'm a good planner," Frances said.

His smirk became a proprietary grin. "I never plan anything. Things just work out, whatever."

"We wouldn't make a good team, would we?" She was already standing beside the table, primed to head for the Avis desk in the lobby. She was thinking about a big red Lincoln or a Cadillac. The car could be the kick – not the company.

"I guess we might as well enjoy it," Howard said and suddenly seemed amiable. "We're out where they blew up the atom bomb, right?" He gazed at her with dumb pleasure, as if he'd forgotten he liked her, but had just suddenly remembered. Maybe he wasn't so bad. Maybe she was confusing him with Ed – lumping men in the same heap and missing their finer distinctions. Exactly like the lesbians did.

"It's New Mexico," she said, waving at the New Jersey gals, who were making gestures with their hands to indicate they thought something was up between her and whoever it was she was having lunch with. "Where they blew up the A-bomb was New Mexico."

"Well, whatever. Same desert, right? Bottom line?" He looked pleased.

"Bottom line. I guess so," Frances said. "You get to the heart of things. You probably already know that."

"I've heard it before," Howard said, and rose to head for his room.

*

In the car he wasn't on the proper side to see the sunset. Interstate 15 to Flagstaff was nothing but arid scrub, with forbidding treeless mountains on the other side of the car, where the sun *was* setting. Mostly all you saw was new development – big gas stations, shopping malls, half-finished cinema plazas, new franchise restaurant pads, housing sprawled along empty stream beds that had been walled up beside giant golf courses with hundreds of sprinklers turning the dry air to mist. There was nothing interesting or original or wild to see, just more people filling up space where formerly nobody had wanted to be. The reason to live out here, he thought, was that you *had* lived someplace worse. These were the modern-day equivalent of the lost tribes. The most curious feature of the drive were the big jackrabbits that'd gotten smacked and were littering the highway by the dozens. He quit counting at sixty. Mary believed atmospheric conditions humans weren't sensitive to made animals throw themselves in front of cars. In Connecticut it was deer, raccoons and possums. Someday it would start happening to people – maybe these people out here. Maybe they were members of a cult that was planning that.

Frances had rented a new red Town Car – the ultimate Jew canoe, she called it – a big fire chief's sedan with untouched white-leather seats, red floor mats, unspoiled ashtrays and a heavy new-car smell. He wasn't allowed to drive because he wasn't Frances's husband, which was perfect. To get comfortable, he'd ditched his conventioneer clothes for his green terry shorts, a white tee shirt and an old pair of basketball sneakers. With the seat pushed back, he could stretch his legs and doze on the headrest. The whole thing was set up right.

Frances was in high spirits behind the white leather steering wheel.

She'd brought her Grand Canyon book, her cell phone and some noisy Tito Puente CDs that featured a lot of loud bongo music. She'd changed into tight white Bermudas, a blue sailcloth blouse with a white anchor painted on the front, some tiny sapphire earrings and a pair of pink Keds with little tasseled half-socks. She'd also bought a quart of cheap gin, which they both started drinking, minus ice, out of white Styrofoam cups.

The plan was to eat dinner in Flagstaff, drive 'til after dark, then stop at whatever motel was near the canyon entrance, and be up early to see the great empty hole at daybreak, when Frances believed it would be its most spiritually potent. "I never *knew* I wanted to see it. You know?" She was driving with a cup in one hand. "But then I read about it, and knew I had to. The Indians thought it was the gateway to the underworld. And Teddy Roosevelt killed mountain lions in it." She'd already poleaxed one of the big jackrabbits. "Oooops, sorry. Shit," she said, then forgot about it. "Conquistadors came there in fifteen-ninety something," she went on, casting a mischievous eye at Howard, who was thinking about the run-over rabbit and staring moodily out at a big cinema complex built to look like an Egyptian jukebox. A vast, unlined, untenanted expanse of black asphalt lay between the theater and the highway. Soon enough, he thought, it would be stuffed with new cars and people. And then in ten years it would be gone.

"I never thought about it," he said to whatever she'd said, considering what movies the cinema would specialize in. Westerns. Space movies. Idiot comedies about golf. It was California all over again out here, just worse. "Californicate" was the word that went around realtor circles two years ago. The gin might be affecting him, he thought.

"As big as the Grand Canyon, isn't that what people say?" Frances had gone on dreamily. "My father used to say that. He was an immigrant. He thought the Grand Canyon meant something absolute. It meant everything important about America. I guess that's what it means to me."

"'In one sense it's a big hole in the ground formed by erosion.'"
He was reading aloud now off the back of her Grand Canyon guidebook. Up ahead, another big gray and white jackrabbit sat poised
on the shoulder as cars whipped past. He stared at it. The rabbit
seemed on the verge of venturing forward, but was waiting for what
it must've felt in its busy rabbit's brain to be the perfect moment. In
the opposite lane, semis were hurtling south toward Phoenix in the
twilight. This rabbit's got problems, Howard thought. Overcoming
man-made barriers. Circumventing unnatural hazards. Avoiding toxic
waste on the roadside. "Watch out for the rabbit," he said, not wanting
to seem alarmed, taking another sip of his warm gin.

"Roger. That's a copy, Houston," Frances said. She had the lip of
her white Styrofoam cup pinched between her fingers, letting the
cup dangle under the top arm of the steering wheel. She made no
effort whatsoever to steer clear of the bunny, poised on the berm. She
was drunk.

And just as the Town Car came almost abreast of the big rabbit,
a critical split second after which it would've been spared and perhaps
made it across all four lanes to sleep easily one more night in the
median strip – in that split second – the rabbit bounded forward
straight into the car's headlights, never looking right or better yet left.
And *whump*! The Lincoln sped over it, bopping whatever part of
the rabbit was highest and tumbling it senselessly across the highway.

"Ouch! Damn! Oh shit. That's two. Sor-ree little Thumper," Frances
said. "Bummer, bummer, bummer."

"Why didn't you change fuckin' lanes?" Howard said.

"I know." Frances had not even looked in the rearview. "It's on my
karma now. I'll be paying for it."

"It's really ridiculous." He glared at her, then back out into the
darkening scrub. It's fucking idiotic, he thought.

"I'll get shaped up here," she said.

"Not for that rabbit you won't."

"Nope. Not for that Mr. bunny rabbit," Frances said. "He's part
of history now."

He wished he was back at the Radisson having a glass of Pinot Grigio, not cheap warm gin he didn't even like. He could be enjoying the glowing amber grid of night-time Phoenix, and getting ready to call Mary.

"Do you think you can find something to be jovial about?" She looked at him and smiled a smile that exaggerated her face's angles. "Try to think of *one* thing."

She was hateful, he thought. Flattening a rabbit wouldn't be the half of it. It was probably how she sold houses: a steam-roller; never relenting, never seeing anything but the sale; driving buyers crazy with cell phone calls from her car; working every weekend.

"Put on some new music, why don't you, Mr. Moody?" Frances said. The insane bongo drumming had stopped miles back, rendering the car peaceful. "Put on the Rolling Stones," she said. "Do you like them? I do."

"Whatever," he said, fingering through the stack of cassettes she'd lodged on the leather seat between them. He tried to think of one Rolling Stones song but couldn't. He'd drunk too much for sure.

"Put on *Let It Bleed*, in honor of the brave rabbit who gave his life so we could see the Grand Canyon and commit adultery." She didn't even look at him.

This was fucked up, he thought. Just all of a sudden, she was a different person. The best thing would be to find the bus station in Flagstaff and let her drive off drunk into the night and never see her again. A smart man would do that.

"I was kidding about *Let It Bleed*." She sniffed. "It's not there. Put on some more Chiquita banana music and give us some gin. We'll be seeing the bright lights of Flagstaff pretty soon now. Surely something there'll make you happy. Isn't it a famous place?"

"I wouldn't know," Howard said, then under his breath added, "I hope so."

"So do I, sweetheart," Frances said, handing over her empty cup so he could fill it. "Or else, we'll just have to make it famous."

*

In Flagstaff, they found a dim little strip-mall Sushi place, facing a wide avenue clogged with evening traffic. He was tired of Mexican and spaghetti, and wanted fish even if he had to eat it raw. He would never make a westerner, he realized; he needed to see the ocean once a week and seafood was healthier. Though he also realized, as they were searching for a restaurant, traffic lights blooming into a blue-lit distance, that he'd actually been to Flagstaff – in the eighties, on a ten-day overland vacation the whole Cameron family had made to Disneyland. He'd somehow forgotten it. Though naturally, nothing looked the same. The streets were all widened twice as big and there were now a thousand motels and burger franchises and car washes. It was weird to have been in a place, and then to have blotted it out completely. It was possible, of course – and he was already beginning to forget the memory again – that he'd only dreamed about Flagstaff, or possibly seen it on TV.

From the fake teak table by the window, Frances had begun eyeing the phone booth outside in the parking lot. She wanted to call Ed. He'd be in bed soon, though the sky was still lighted over the mountaintops here. She couldn't remember when she'd called him last. And she was sorry to have gotten smashed, sorry she'd run over a rabbit, sorry to have forgotten all about her husband. It was so unusual being this free, and fucking somebody she absolutely didn't care about, or for that matter fucking anybody at all. It was disorienting and actually embarrassing.

Howard was eating sea-bass tempura and was happy for her to go make a call. She walked outside into the warm evening and stood beside the Lincoln to make the call on her cell phone. A police substation was set up in one of the empty mall store spaces. Through the windows you could see police inside sitting at desks, talking on phones and writing under fluorescent light. A young black man was also standing inside and appeared to be wearing handcuffs, his hands behind his back. Two police officers standing with him were laughing as if he'd said something funny.

"Hi, sweetie," she said brightly to Ed across the vast distance. She wanted to be upbeat. "Guess where I am? In Flagstaff."

"Yeah. So?" Ed said. "Where's that, Texas?" Ed suffered from an unusual blood disease that made his bones disintegrate from the toes up, and he was in pain a lot. He took steroids and maintained dietary restrictions that made him either hungry all the time, or else nauseated, and he was almost always in a bad mood. When she'd met Ed, who was fifteen years older, he'd been strong as a racehorse and ran his own jet-ski business. Now he couldn't work, and just watched TV and took his meds.

"No silly, it's in Arizona," Frances said. "But guess where I'm going. You won't believe it." She wondered if she'd said "guess where *we're* going."

"Bulgaria," Ed said. "Iran. I don't know. Who cares? I won't be there."

"The Grand Canyon," she said, manufacturing enthusiasm. She felt her mouth break into an involuntary smile. She was smiling for Ed, standing alongside a big red Lincoln.

Silence opened on Ed's end.

"The Grand Canyon," she said again. "Isn't that great? I'm going to see it tomorrow." She needed to be careful about particulars. She could say she was with one of the lesbians. Ed would think that was a riot.

"And what?" Ed said irritably. "You see it and then what?'

"I don't really know."

Silence again. Ed had become distracted by something in his room, possibly the Red Sox game. The thought flitted through her mind to say "I'm going to the Grand Canyon with a man I'm fucking every night and who's got a cock as hard as a hoe handle." Though it didn't make Howard any more interesting for that to be true. He might as well have not had it.

She stared at the bright-lit police substation. The uniformed police were steering the young, handcuffed black man into a wire cage in the back of the room. It was like an animal's cage. She felt suddenly dispirited and in fear of starting to cry right on the phone. Gin made women fuck, then cry, then fight, her father always said. She needed to stay away from gin. Ed, of course, was still handsome – a big, gruff blue-eyed, Boston-Irish whose life, unfortunately, hadn't made him happy. Though he loved her. That she knew. It was a shame. Lately he'd begun growing hydrangeas in the back yard, which seemed nice. "I wish you could see the Grand Canyon with me, honey."

"Maybe I'll fly out there tonight," Ed said sarcastically, and expelled a dry little cough-laugh.

"That'd be great. I'd come pick you up."

"Maybe I could just jump in," Ed said bitterly. "That'd be great, too, wouldn't it?"

"No, sweetie. That wouldn't."

Unexpectedly from across the parking lot she saw Howard emerge from the restaurant, a toothpick in his mouth. He glanced at the crowded street, then started off down the strip-mall sidewalk. He passed right in front of the police station. Two of the desk officers inside stopped what they were doing and looked out the window at him. Howard was odd looking – tall and gawky, like somebody out of the fifties.

But where was he going! She felt her heart beat three then two sudden beats. Was he taking off? Heading across to the Arco station to hitch a ride back? Her heart bumped three more percussive bumps as she watched Howard stride along in his almost-graceful gait and geek haircut (he looked ridiculous in his terrycloth shorts, big tee shirt and sockless sneakers). But she felt panicky – as if a disaster was unfolding right in front of her, and she couldn't stop it. Like running over the rabbit. Ka-thunk, ka-thunk, her heart pounded. She realized she didn't really care if he left, but the sight of his leaving made her almost paralyzed.

"Oh Jesus, don't leave," she said.

"My feet are disintegrating. I probably won't be alive in a year. That's where I'm going," Ed said.

"What's that?"

"What did I say?" Ed said. "I said . . ."

When Howard reached the asphalt apron of the Arco station, he turned left directly into the empty phone booth and began punching in numbers, though as he did it he craned his neck around in her direction, grinning at her, phone to phone – each calling his and her spouse to report where each of them was, leaving out the crucial part of the story. That absolutely wasn't how life should be, she thought. Life should be all on the up-and-up. She wished she was here alone and there weren't any lies. How good that would feel. To be all alone in Flagstaff.

"Maybe you just don't know what fuckin' fed-up is," Ed was saying angrily.

"I'm sorry, sweetheart, what is it? You're breaking up. It's way out in the prairie out here."

"Prairie schmarry," Ed snarled. Something had set Ed off. "We were already breaking up."

"You don't need to say that," Frances said. She was trying to push Howard out of her thinking, trying to concentrate on Ed her husband, furious at her for going to the Grand Canyon, furious at her for enjoying herself, or trying to, furious at her for being herself and not being him. Maybe she *didn't* know what fed-up meant. "Why don't you take a pill and let me call you later, hon, okay?" She stared at Howard, his back turned, his head bobbing back and forth. He was talking animatedly to his wife in Connecticut. Happily lying.

"*You* take a pill," Ed said, "And then disappear."

"That's not very nice."

"That's what I was just thinking," Ed said.

"I'll call you later, sweetheart," she said softly.

"I'll be asleep later."

"Sleep tight, then," she said, and folded her phone away.

*

Out again in the darkened desert, Howard ran his window down to let in the rich cooling breezes. Frances had put on some watery new-age electronic music that was making him woozy. He took his shoes off, tilted back and faced the landscape behind the barrier of the night.

A little band of nastiness which he definitely didn't appreciate had begun widening between them all the way up to Flagstaff. It was the sort of thing you suffered in the workplace. Except, precisely because it *was* the workplace and not your real life, you weren't stuck with whoever it was the way he was stuck now with nutty Frances. Which explained why being married was so good – at least the way he understood it: if you married the right person (and he had), you didn't experience unwelcome surprises and upsets. The more you got to know that right person, the better it got – not the worse and more discouraging. You liked them and you liked life. The institution took you to deeper depths, and you felt serious things you wouldn't otherwise feel. Idiotic and unnecessary escapades like this trip just didn't come up. He hadn't been married long enough to fully appreciate all this – a year, only – but he was beginning to. Of course, it was also nice to be spinning along in a big expensive car, headed for some unknown exotic place, where the night would be spent screwing an attractive woman you didn't have to take care of the rest of your life. Still, though, he was sorry not to have just gotten on a bus in Flagstaff. Frances would probably have welcomed it. He'd just forgotten.

Occasionally a dimly-lit settlement rocketed past. A scattering of lights, some shadowy men standing outside a bar or a crummy store or beside a row of pick-ups, seemingly unaware of the highway.

"Indians," Frances said authoritatively. She'd elevated her seat and re-situated closer to the steering wheel so she appeared to be a tiny pilot in a green-lit cockpit. "We're on the Hopi reservation here."

"We don't want to break down, then," Howard said.

"I'm sure they'd take good care of us."

"As soon as they finished stripping the car and killing us. That's probably true. They'd give us a decent burial up on some platform." He stared into the night, where a single socketed light glowed like a boat on the ocean. "I have Indian blood in me," he said for no particular reason. "My father was a Paiute, and my mother's named

Sue." It was a joke he'd never thought was funny before but seemed amusing now. "My mother *is* named Sue. Sue Crosby," he added, feeling better about things, including Frances. The nastiness seemed to have drifted away suddenly. Though he wasn't crazy about how she came off in her white shorts (too tight) and her blue blouse with the dopey, hand-painted anchor. She looked like a little Polack – somebody who sold cheap houses to other Polacks and bought her clothes at Target. She was too muscular, too – like somebody on the Polish gymnastics team. Somebody named Magda. Her body wasn't that great to touch. He preferred softer, less toned-up women like his wife. Though Frances was older and, he assumed, had to take better care of herself.

On an impulse, he reached across the seat, unfastened her small right hand from the steering wheel and grasped it in his own hand. "I've been wanting to do that," he said, though it wasn't true.

"Okay," she said not looking at him, just peering ahead into the tunnel of light.

"I was thinking about those Japanese in the restaurant," he said. "How weird is that? In fucking Flagstaff. Indians. Desert. Snakes. You wonder how they got there." He squeezed her hand for emphasis. He hated electronic music and switched it off before it made him carsick.

"They're everywhere now, I guess," Frances said in the new silence. "I've sold houses to them. They're nice. They take care of their stuff."

"Like lesbians," he said. "Lesbians are good home owners."

Frances sucked in her lower lip, squinted, scrunched her face up, then looked over at Howard. It was her Japanese imitation. "Condlo-min-lium," she said through her teeth.

"We want buy condlo-min-lium long time," Howard said, then they both laughed. She was funny – a side of her he hadn't seen. "You're great," he said. Then he said, "You're terrific."

"Men sometimes velly hard please," she said, still in the Japanese voice. "Too hard."

"Yeah, but it's worth it. Isn't it? Innnit?" This was his only imitation – the hair-lip. People always cracked up.

"Not know," Frances said. "Still early. Know better later."

He moved his hand up to her firm small pointed breast, then wasn't sure what to do next since she was driving and gave no sign she might want to stop the car and get something going. "If you pull this car over I'd fuck you right now in the front seat." He pushed the button to un-recline his seat, as if to make good on his word.

"Not good plan now," Frances said, still in Japanese "Hold raging dragon. Good come to mans who wait long time. Make big promise."

He caressed her breast, leaned closer, smelled the perfume she'd put on in Flagstaff. "Big promise, yeah, you bet," he said, but again wasn't sure what to do. He held her breast a few moments longer, until he began to feel self-conscious, then he re-reclined his seat and went back to staring out.

*

For a time afterwards, maybe an hour, they were encased in silence – Frances staring ahead at the illuminated highway, Howard gazing at the border of desert, beyond which in the scrubby recesses of darkness who knew what acted out an existence? He mused for a while about what sort of house Frances might live in. He'd never seen it, of course, but assumed it was a minuscule, white-shingled, green-roof Cape with fake dormers and no garage, a place she paid the note on herself. Then he thought darkly about Ed, whom he hadn't thought about all day, until he'd seen her phoning him. Frances was basically a solid, family-oriented person, no matter what she was doing with him on this escapade. She was a capable *do-er*, who took care of things, and made a good living. She just couldn't make *every* thing fit exactly for Ed's particular benefit. Fucking him, for example – that didn't fit. Though you needed to be able to do the unusual – be married and still have it be all right. Even if you had to lie about it. There was no sense hurting people for reasons they couldn't control, or that you couldn't either. Just because everything didn't always fit in the tent, you didn't throw the tent away.

He kept a pretty clear mental picture of Ed, despite having never seen him. To him Ed was a big shambling, unshaven man in gray clothing and unlaced shoes, who'd once been physically powerful, even intimidating, but was no longer the man he once was, and so had become sulky and capable of saying cruel and unfair things to innocent people, all because life hadn't been perfect. As it wasn't, of course, for anybody. The expression "block of wood" and the wounded, weathered, face of the old movie actor Lon Chaney, Junior, had become linked to Ed and with the non-existent sex Frances intimated he provided.

Whenever Howard thought about Ed, it eventually involved some imagined confrontation in which he – Howard – would be cool and collected while Ed would be seething and confused. Howard would try to be generous and friendly, but Ed inevitably would begin being cutting and sarcastic. He'd try to make Ed realize that Frances really loved him, but that sometimes other tents had to be brought in and pitched. And then it always became necessary to kick Ed's ass, though not enough to do any real damage. Later, when both their marriages had been repaired and time had elapsed, he and Ed could become grudging friends based on a shared understanding about reality and the fact that they both cared deeply for the same woman. He imagined going to Ed's funeral and standing solemnly at the back of a Catholic church.

Ahead in the pale headlights, the figures of a man and a woman appeared on the opposite shoulder – at first small and indistinct and then hyper-real as they came up out of the dark, walking side by side. Two Indians – dressed shabbily, heading the other direction. Both the man and the woman looked at the big red Town Car as it shot past. The man was wearing a bright turquoise shirt and a reddish head-band, the woman a flimsy gray dress. In an instant they were gone.

"Those were our ancient spirits," Frances said. She'd been silent, and her words carried unexpected gravity. "It's a sign. But I don't know what of. Something not good, I'd say."

He quit thinking about Ed.

"I guess if they were going in the other direction, we could've given our ancient spirits a ride. Drop them off at a convenience store."

"They were coming back from where we're going," Frances pronounced in a grave voice.

"The Grand Canyon?"

"It's a completely spiritual place. I already told you the Indians thought it was the door to the underworld."

"Maybe we'll see Teddy Roosevelt, too." He felt pleased with himself. "We oughta turn around and go back and ask them what else we need to see."

"We wouldn't find them," Frances said. "They'd be gone."

"Gone where?" he said. "Just disappeared into thin air?"

"Maybe." Frances looked at him gravely now. He knew she disapproved of him. "I want to tell you something, okay?" She looked back at the streaming white center line.

Up ahead was a string of building white lights – a motel, he hoped. It was long after eleven, and he was suddenly flattened. Those two Indians might've been phantoms of fatigue, though it was strange they'd both see them.

"If anything happens to me, you know?" Frances said, without waiting for his answer. "I mean, if I have a heart attack in the motel, or in the car, or if I just keel over dead, do you know what I expect you to do?"

"Call Ed," Howard said. "Confess everything."

"That's what I *don't* want," she said, her voice edgy with certainty. Her eyes found him again in the green-lit interior. "You understand this. You just walk away. Leave it. It'd require too much explanation. Just fade away like those Indians. I mean it. I'll be dead anyway, right?"

"What the shit," Howard said. He could see the magic letters M-O-T-E-L. "Don't get fucking weird on me. I don't know what happened when you talked to Ed, but you don't need to start planning your funeral. Jesus." He didn't want to talk about anything more serious than sex now. It was too late in the day. He was sorry all over again to be here.

"Promise me," Frances said, driving, but flicking her eyes back to him.

"I won't promise anything," he said. "Except I'll promise you a good time if we can get out of this hearse and find a bed."

Obviously she was stone serious. Except he wasn't the kind of person who walked away, and there was no use promising. His family had raised him better than that.

"You know what I'd do if you got hit by a car or struck by lightning?" Frances said.

"Let me guess."

"You don't need to. Some complications aren't worth getting into. You don't know what I mean, do you?"

The motel sign was off to the right. On the left – like a little oasis – was a bright red neon *CASINO* sign with rotating blue police lights on top, and a big red neon rattlesnake, underneath, coiled and ready to strike. Beside the snake the neon lettering said *Strike It Rich*. The casino itself was only a low, windowless cube with a single, middle door and a lot of beater cars and pick-ups and a couple of sheriff's vehicles nosed into the front. "Womans some-time velly hard to prease," Howard said in Japanese, just to break up the gloom.

"I wish you'd do what I ask you to," Frances said disappointedly, steering them into the motel's gravel lot. A lighted office building inside of which a man was visible behind a counter, talking on the phone, sat beside the highway. The units, in a row behind it, were white stucco teepees with phony lodge poles showing through phony smoke holes. There were ten teepees, each with a small round window on either side of their front door. Two other cars were parked outside individual units. Lights shone from their windows.

"If you have a heart attack," he said, "I promise I'll ride with your body back to Willamantic. Just like whoever that was. President Kennedy."

"Then you're an idiot," Frances said, stopping in front of the office, and staring ahead disgustedly.

"I'm *your* idiot, though. At least tonight," Howard said.

He was out the car door fast, his sneakers in the gravel, the sky all around suddenly dazzlingly full of pale stars, though a strong disinfectant odor was floating all through the little parking lot, and there was country music coming from the casino. Frances continued talking inside the car – more about leaving her behind – but he didn't hear. He looked up and breathed the stinging disinfectant smell all the way deep down in his lungs. This was a relief. They'd driven way too far. The whole idea sucked to begin with. But he just wanted to get her off her stupid subject – heart attacks and deaths, etc. – and back to why they'd come. People talked and talked and none of it mattered to the big picture. It was like buyer's remorse – but tomorrow would be different, no matter what you worried about today. You rode it out. He thought quite briefly about having been named Agent of the Year. It made him, for a moment, happy.

*

From the driver's seat Frances watched a large, long-tailed rat as it pestered and devilled a snake while the snake tried to make its way across the gravel from the line of teepees to the scrub ground where the desert began. The motel sign hummed and made the floodlit lot feel electrified, and kept the entire little skirmish visible. She wasn't aware things like this even occurred. The snake, she thought, was the natural enemy and physical superior to the rat. The rat had things to fear. But here was the surprising truth. As she watched out the window, several times the snake stopped, coiled and struck at the rat, who reared up on its little hind legs like a tiny stallion and danced around. Then the snake, having missed, would start to slither off again toward the vegetation and shadows. The rat pursued almost idly, nipping then hopping back, then nipping again, as if it knew the snake personally. Eventually she let the window down to hear if they were making noise – if rattles were rattling or anyone hissed or growled. But the country music from the casino was too loud. Eventually the snake found the edge of the gravel and slid away, and the rat, its work complete, scurried back across the lot and disappeared under one of the dark teepees – not, she hoped the one they'd be staying in.

She felt strange waiting here. Not really like who she was, the little agent from No-where-burg, Connecticut – *specialist* in starter homes and rehabed condos. Daughter. Wife. Holder of an associate's degree in retail from an accredited community college. In a way, though, this guy was exactly right for her, as wrong as he was. Aren't you always yourself? Is anybody you want *ever* wrong for you? She did desire him, especially after all the drinking. It was like her father had said. And anyway, why not want him? Life was sometimes a matter of ridding yourself of this or that urge, after which the rest got easier.

And adultery – she liked it when her thoughts connected up well – adultery was the act that *rid, erased*, even erased itself once the performance was over. Sometimes, she imagined, it must erase more than itself. And sometimes, surely, it erased everything around it. It was a remedy for ills you couldn't get cured any other way, but it was a danger you needed to be cautious with. In any case, she felt grateful for it tonight. And because she thought all of this, she knew she had to be right.

Howard strolled out of the motel office flipping a room key back and forth, and smirking. She wondered how often he'd done this. It seemed so natural to him, not that she gave a shit. She never had, and yet it felt perfectly familiar to do it, as if she'd been doing it forever.

"Drive down to the last teepee," Howard said, leaning in, hands on his bare knees. "And if you want to hit the casino, Big Chief Poker Face in there gave me two drinks coupons."

"I just want to get fucked, is all." She looked out the other window. "I don't like to play slot machines."

His eyes narrowed, the corners of his large unintelligent mouth turned almost imperceptibly upwards. He wasn't handsome, his hair buzzed and his ears and mouth way too big. He was clownish. Though that probably made his little wife ecstatic: a husband no one else much wanted, but who could work wonders.

Howard again put his big hand, adopting a cupping motion, in through the window, and up under one of her breasts. He didn't seem to have a purpose. Just a pointless act of uncaring familiarity. "Back this baby over across the lot and we'll do it in the car," he said in a husky, theatrical voice. His small eyes twitched to the far edge gravel. "Nobody'll see." He sniffed a little humorless laugh.

"I'll wait."

"That'll work, then," he said, standing up, sniffing again.

"Good," she said. "I'm ready for something to." She turned the key in the ignition and began backing up.

*

She knew exactly what he liked. He liked her eyes to be on him. He liked for her to slip his cock into her mouth and, just as she did it, to raise her eyes to his. "I'll do this to you now," was what that meant. Like a cheap betrothal. Otherwise he liked her voice. With her voice, with whatever she chose to say when she was whispering to him, she could make him ejaculate. Just like that. Even her breathing could do it. So she had to be careful. Though coming wasn't what he wanted. He was smart. He wanted to stay in it with her, move her where she needed to be moved around the bed, have it go and go and go until coming was just a way to end it, when they weren't interested anymore. Strange, to be so intelligent in bed, and other times not at all. It was her doing, she thought; she'd invented him, turned him into someone she had a use for. His real intelligence was not to resist.

Only in the cramped airless teepee, with the rayon portiere across the doorway and beetles crawling on the floor and the air heavy with bug dope, he wanted to take her too fast too violently – suddenly, vociferously – as if *he* meant to rid her of whatever had its grips into her, all by himself. As if it was his duty. Pounding, pounding. Like that. No time to work him with her voice, or bring him along and ease him in and out of it. Just the hard way, until it was over. And again – so odd that this man should be aware of her; knowing that something was wrong and setting out to fix it the way he knew how. That was intimacy. Of a certain kind. Yes.

Though possibly, of course – as she lay in the grainy darkness with Howard instantly, infinitely asleep beside her – possibly, she'd expressed herself perfectly in the car, and he'd just done what she told him. "I just want to get fucked." That's what she'd said. Anyone could understand what that meant. *She* had orchestrated things then, not him. She just hadn't been aware of it. He'd simply let her *employ* him – that was the word – become the implement for what she wanted fixed, emptied, ended, ridded – whatever. Really, they didn't know each other so well. She'd been mistaken about intimacy.

In the parking lot she heard men's voices, talking and laughing, followed by car doors closing and engines starting and tires rolling over gravel. Farther away there was a sudden blare of country music, as if a door had been thrown open. Then the music was muffled, so that she realized she'd been hearing it for a while without knowing it. Someone shouted, "Oooo-weee," and a car roared away. She'd brought in the bottle of gin from the car, and she reached it off the bedside table, unscrewed the cap and took a tiny sip – just to kill the stale-paper-bug-dope taste. And then she couldn't help wondering, idly, she knew: does this really come to an end now? Couldn't this go on a little longer after tonight, without the need of a fixed destination? There was a small good side to it. They both understood something. People ended things too soon, lacked patience when they could go on. If they truly erased themselves with each other, they could go on indefinitely. She could, anyway. And Howard wouldn't resist, she assumed. This was a view she was glad to have, something more than she'd expected from this night. A surprise found in the dark.

*

On the concrete stoop of their teepee lay the littered brown husks of two hundred beetles killed by the bug dope somebody'd squirted around the door after they were asleep. Unpleasant to step on them. An Indian woman was sweeping them off the other teepee steps, using a broom and a plastic dustpan. A young Indian man with a ponytail was standing beside her watching and talking softly. The only other car in the lot was a dented black Camaro with yellow flames painted on its side and a spare-tire doughnut on the back.

The morning sun was warm, though a cool autumn breeze shifted the dust across the hardtop toward the casino, where there were still some cars and trucks in front. It was eight. A small neon rectangle, previously invisible on the *Strike It Rich* sign was illuminated to say *Breakfast Now Being Served*. The blue police lights were turned off.

Breakfast was an idea, Howard thought, shirtless in the teepee doorway, his eyes aching. He couldn't find his shirt on the floor in the dark room. But it would be a relief – even without his shirt – to eat breakfast in the empty casino while Frances slept on. They'd seen it all in a casino. He could bring coffee back, pay for it with the drinks coupons.

Up behind the *Strike It Rich,* treeless brown mountains stood stark against the cool sky. These weren't available when they'd arrived last night. You definitely never got a view like this in the east – just trees there and clouds and a smaller hazy sky, even by the ocean. So this was good – the drive had brought them up to where the air was cleaner, thinner; to a beautiful wasteland no one but Indians could stand to live in. And somewhere beyond this was the Grand Canyon – the big erosion hole Frances was now sleeping through. Maybe she'd forget about it and want to drive back to the convention.

He stepped out into the lot, shirtless, in his terrycloth shorts and sneakers. Across the highway, beside the casino, was a small, new-looking, white clapboard chapel with a steeple and some plastic-looking stained glass windows, surrounded by a white picket fence that also looked plastic. For quickie marriages, Howard thought, a wife you ended up with when you got lucky in the casino. Like in Atlantic City. Indians owned it, too, he was certain. A wooden sign in the grass-less fenced yard read, "*Chris* Died For Your Sins," which put him in mind that his family had been Christians. The Camerons – Presbyterians, somewhere back in Scotland. Not Christians, *per se,* anymore. Sunday was everybody's personal day. But perfectly good people. His father was always pleased to see a church.

Except, what this crummy little chapel made him consider was that life, at best, implied a small, barely noticeable entity; and yet it was also a goddamned important entity. And you could ruin your entity before you even realized it. And further, it occurred to him, that no doubt just as you were in the process of ruining yours, how you felt at the exact moment of ruining it was probably precisely how this fucked-up landscape looked! Dry, empty, bright, chilly, alien, and difficult to breathe in. So that all around here was actually hell, he thought, instead of hell being the old version his father had told him about under the ground. The breeze moved just then across his bare chest, giving him a stiffening chill. A Greyhound rumbled past on the highway, stirring up dust, and bringing a lone man out of the casino door to stare. Just being out here, Howard thought, was enough to spook you, and make you ready to have *Chris* go to bat for you, before you fell victim to something awful – despair you wouldn't escape from *because* you were so small and insignificant. Or worse. He felt completely justified to hate it here. He was glad his father wasn't along. The Greyhound was becoming a speck on the highway heading south. He needed to get Frances to forget the Grand Canyon and get in behind that bus back to Phoenix. He'd really just come along for the ride – to keep her company. None of this was anything he'd caused.

*

When Frances stepped out of the teepee into the sharp light and cool breeze, she looked tired – her blue, anchor blouse rumpled, and her sapphire earrings missing, leaving just the little holes showing. Though she looked happy. She'd showered and slicked back her short blond hair, and had her purse and the gin bottle in hand. She looked younger and like she wasn't sure where she was, but wasn't displeased about it. Whatever last night had been hadn't left her dissatisfied, though he couldn't remember much except that it hadn't lasted very long and he'd passed out.

He'd bought Styrofoam cups of coffee in the casino and was sitting on the fender of the Lincoln, looking through her Grand Canyon book. He'd found his shirt and felt better, though he was ready to leave.

"You rarin' to go?" Frances was looking around the empty lot and up at the mountains. She smiled at the pure blue sky as she sipped her coffee. Her throat was congested and she kept clearing it. She wasn't really steady, her eyes were slits, her face puffy.

"Ready to go somewhere," he said, hoping for Phoenix, but not wanting to press it.

"Isn't it beautiful here." She blinked, her cup to her lips. "Are you happy?"

"I'm great."

"Last night?" she said. She looked confused. "You know? After you were asleep? I woke up, and I had no idea where I was. I really didn't even know who *you* were. It was weird. I guess it was the gin. But I got on my hands and knees and I stared right down into your face. I could feel your breath on my eyeballs. I just stared at you and stared at you. I'm glad you didn't wake up. You'd have thought you were in the middle of an operation."

"Or that I was dead."

"Right. Or that." She noticed all the beetle husks that had yet to be swept off the teepee steps. "Oh dear," she said. "Look-it here."

"Who'd you think I was," he said, slipping off the fender.

"I didn't know," she said looking around at the beetles all around her feet. "I didn't think you *were* anybody. You could've been an animal. You could've changed shape."

"Did you think I was Ed?"

"No." She reached into her purse for her car keys and nudged a few husks with the toe of her pink shoe. "No resemblance there."

"I wouldn't know."

"No. You wouldn't," she said and seemed annoyed, and began walking toward the car. "Come on," she said. "We're late."

*

A mile beyond the motel, a green highway sign said SOUTH RIM – 85 MILES. They turned that way, and Howard put on the Tito Puente music, then remembered what it was and turned it off as the road immediately began climbing and they began encountering campers and more tour buses creeping up and coming down. The landscape that was beginning to be below them looked flatter and smooth, pinkish like a sand sculpture, and, Howard felt, totally different from when he was on the ground in it, when it seemed spooky and uninviting. When he'd thought it was hell.

Frances produced a camera, one of the new sleek, molded operations designed by Japanese to look serious and professional, though it was actually cheap. Three times on the steep road up, she stopped the car and made them get out so she could take a picture of the desert. Twice she got him to take her picture, posing short-necked, stiff and squinting in front of a flagstone retaining wall. Once she took him, and once she got a man from Michigan to take them together with the empty sky behind. "These can be used in divorce court," Frances said when the Michigan man could still hear them. "I'll give you the negatives and you can destroy them. I just want a print."

Howard was remembering how little he liked tourist venues, how you could never see anything ten million yokels hadn't already seen and shit on and written graffiti all over before you could get there. What they were doing now really had no purpose. Purpose ended last night. They were just doing this.

Frances stood beside the car, studying her camera which she'd tried to make operate automatically but couldn't. The camera made its soft, confident whirring, clicking, sighing noise. "There's another one of my hand," she said.

"I don't think I'm going to get the Grand Canyon," Howard said. She'd gotten different again now, become businesslike. She was different every hour. You needed a program.

"You haven't experienced it yet," she said, holding her camera up, pointing back at the retaining wall and the perfect blue matte of empty space. Again it whirred, clicked and sighed. "It has to be believed to be seen. Of course, I haven't seen it either. Just pictures."

"Me not know," he said, but didn't sound Japanese. It was more like Indian, and sounded stupid.

She smiled painfully as she turned the camera upside down and read something on the bottom. "Well, you will." She shook her head and stuck the camera in her purse and started around the car to go. "Then you'll want these pictures. You'll pay me for them. You'll have been exposed to something the likes of which you'll never have seen or expected. And you'll thank me all the way back to Phoenix."

*

She loved it that the air grew cooler, and that the plant-life changed, that there were little pine trees growing right out of the dry, rocky mountain turf. She loved it that the scrub desert floor looked, from high above, like a sand painting an Indian might do – reds and pinks and blues and blacks in layers you'd never see when you were in the middle of it. This was the lesson of the outdoors, she thought: how much that actually existed was hidden in the things you saw; and, that all the things you felt so sure about, you shouldn't. It was hopeful. She would have to go outdoors more. Selling real estate wasn't really being outdoors.

She still hated it, and couldn't quit thinking about it, nearly three weeks later, that he'd said she was good in bed – like she was some carnival act he could give a score to and maybe clap for. Howard was her mistake, no matter that she'd tried to see it different, tried to make him happy. It was one thing, she thought and maybe okay, to fuck Howard in a HoJo's by the Interstate. But it was quite another thing – much less good – to move it all out to Phoenix, get to know him a lot better, risk being caught and fired, and still think it could turn out good. And it was *stupid*, *stupid* to take him to the Grand Canyon, given his little withholding, stand-on-the-sidelines, complaining self. Ed would've been better. Ed would be better because even though sex was out, Ed at least had *once* been a good sport. As a human being, Howard Cameron had been sub-par from the beginning. She hadn't read the fine print.

She glanced at him, musing away on his side about absolutely nothing, his long hairless white legs planked out in front of him like stilts, his pale knees too far below his shorts, his enormous feet with their giant gray toenails hard as tungsten, and his soft, characterless face, and his bushy unkempt eyebrows. And his basketball haircut. What had been wrong with her? He wasn't interesting or witty or nice or deep or pretty. He was a pogo stick. And up here, where everything was natural and clean and pristine, you saw it. And that it was wrong. True nature revealed true nature.

But steering the big fire chief's car up the winding, steepening road with the sheer drop to the desert twenty feet away, she understood she wasn't going to let him ruin another day with his poor-mouth, sad-sack, nothing's-perfect, pissy bad attitude. Today she felt exhilarated – it was dizzying. The feeling went right down into her middle, and set loose something else, a spirit she'd never realized was there, much less locked up and trapped. And, they were still on the road, not even to the canyon yet! How would it feel when she could get out, walk ten paces and there would be the great space stretching miles and miles and miles? She couldn't imagine it. The profound opening of the earth. Great wonders all had powers to set free in you what wasn't free. Poets wrote about it. Only the dragging, grinding minutiae of every day – cooking, driving, talking on the phone, explaining yourself to strangers and loved ones, selling houses, balancing checkbooks, stopping at the video store – all that made you forget what was possible in life.

Probably she'd faint. Certainly she would be speechless, then cry. Conceivably she'd want to move out here right away, realize she'd been living her life wrong, and begin to fix it. That's why the people she sold houses to moved – to go where they could live better. They made up their minds – at least the ones who weren't forced into it by horrible luck – that they and not somebody else ran their lives.

"Those were Navajos," Howard said, staring out at the drop-off beyond the right road shoulder. He'd been nursing his thoughts.

"Not Hopis, okay? I read it in your Grand Canyon book while you were asleep this morning."

"Whatever," she said.

"Do I scare you?" Howard said.

Frances braked as traffic on the two-lane road slowed ahead of them. "Do you scare me?" she said. "Are you supposedly threatening or something?"

"I don't know," he said.

"I really can't think of a way right at this moment that you scare me." They were already entering the village of South Rim, Arizona, which seemed to be an entirely separate town. A thousand citizens living on the edge of the Grand Canyon – going to the grocery, the dentist, watching TV, car-pooling . . . all here! Maybe it would seem like Connecticut after a month, but she couldn't see how.

"Do you think you could ever be married to me?" Howard glanced at her strangely.

"I don't think so." She was inching forward, watching traffic. "It's about the fact that I'm already married. And you're already married. And we're married to other people."

"So it's just barb-less fucking. Fuck-and-release." He wasn't paying attention, just blabbing. Bored.

"Like Etch-a-Sketch. You know?" She stared at the license plate of the Explorer ahead of them. Maine. A Natural Treasure. What was there?

"And so, do you feel guilty about it?"

"I feel . . ." She stopped. Whatever she was about to say could definitely jeopardize her first look at the Grand Canyon, simply because of whatever brainless thing he would then say back. And precious little happened for the first time anymore, so she didn't intend to fuck this one up with a lot of idiot blabbing. Why wasn't Meredith, her roommate who'd died of brain cancer, here now, instead of this guy? Meredith would've enjoyed this. "Communications are suspended for a period, okay?" She smiled over at him inhospitably. "I want to, you know, look at the Grand Canyon. *No mas preguntas este mañana."*

"That'll work. Whatever," Howard said, reaching down where he'd removed his shoe to pick at his raised, big toenail as if he was thinking of pulling it off.

She might even be harming herself by associating with this man. Possibly he posed a threat, staring at his huge toenail. What could he be thinking? Something sinister. She'd excuse herself to use the restroom the minute they were out of the car, then get away from him. Call the police and say he was stalking her. Let him find his pitiful way back to Phoenix alone. She thought of his wife's pained expression, seen like a wraith out in the night sky of Phoenix two nights ago. She could have him back.

"Do you like things complicated or simple?" Howard said, still worrying his toenail.

"Simple," she said.

"Hm. I guessed so," he said idly. "Me too."

"I've realized that."

"Yeah," he said, straightening up to stare at the traffic. "Right."

Entering South Rim Village was also entering the National Park. Cars were required to follow designated paved roads you couldn't deviate from and that wound one-way-only through pretty pine groves where traffic quickly piled up. All the drivers were patient, though, and didn't honk or try to turn around. This was the only answer to the numbers problem: orderly flow, ingress/egress, organized parking, stay in your vehicle. Otherwise people would drive straight to the rim, get out and leave their vehicles for hours, just like at the mall. When she'd imagined it, there'd been no traffic, and she'd ridden up on a palomino, stopped at the rim and stared for hours, alone with her thoughts.

"Everything's just about moving people through," Howard said. He'd run his seat forward, pushed his knees up and was watching the traffic, engrossed. "What you or I see or do is beside the point. People have to be moved or the system breaks down." He scratched his hand over the top of his bristly hair, then pulled at his ear. "Real estate's exactly the same thing. People move somewhere, and we find 'em a place. Then they move someplace else, and we find them another place. It doesn't matter where they finally *are* – which is not what we were taught to understand in school, of course. We're supposed to think where we are *does* matter. But it's like a shark's life. Dedicated to constant moving." He nodded at this conception.

"I think they come here for very good reasons," Frances said. The campers and land yachts took up *too much* space was what she was thinking. The problem was *cramped* space, not movement. The Grand Canyon was *open* space. "People don't just move to be moving. I wasn't dying to drive and somebody dreamed up a Grand Canyon for me. That's stupid."

"Civilization," Howard said dully, paying no attention, "coming up here, working up here, living up here – all these thousands of people. It's like an airport, not a real place. If we ever get to see the fucking Grand Canyon, if it's not just a myth, it'll be like being in an airport. Looking at it will be like looking at a runway where the planes are all lined up. That's why I'd rather stay home instead of getting herded here and herded there." He sniffed through his wide nostrils.

And now he *was* beginning to ruin things, just the way she'd feared but had promised herself not to let him. She looked at him and felt herself actually grimace. She needed to get away from this man. She felt willing to push him right out the door onto the road, using her foot. Though that would be hysterical, and scare him to death. She would have to try to ignore him a little longer, until they were out of the car. She produced a displeasing mental picture of Howard whamming away on her in the grubby, awful little teepee with beetles all over the floor and no TV. What had *that* been about? All those thoughts she'd thought. What was her brain doing? How desperate was she?

"There's that Indian from the motel." Howard pointed at a young man with a long black ponytail, wearing jeans and a green tee shirt. He was walking across the sunny parking lot into which a park ranger in a pointed hat, and standing beside a little hut, was flagging traffic. The Indian was in with the tourists hiking out of the lot up a paved path Frances knew had to lead to the canyon rim. This would be fine, she thought. It was too late to ruin it now. "Maybe he's one of the ancient spirit people." Howard smirked. "Maybe he's our spiritual guide to the Grand Canyon."

"Shut up," Frances said, swerving into a slot among other parked cars and campers. Families were leaving vehicles and legging it in the direction the Indian had gone. Some were hurrying as if they couldn't wait another minute. She felt that way. "Maybe you can go buy us a sandwich. I'll come find you in a while." She was looping her camera around her neck, eager to get out.

"I guess not." Howard pushed open his door with his sneaker and began unfolding his long legs. "I couldn't miss this. Haven't you ever stood beside a construction site and looked in the hole. That's what this'll be. It'll be a blast."

She looked at him coldly. A chill, pine-freshened breeze passed softly through the opened car doors. There were plenty of other people come to admire the great vista, the spiritual grandeur and the natural splendor. It was with them that she would experience the canyon. Not this loser. When it was all over, he could decide it was his idea. But in an hour he'd be history, and she could enjoy the ride back to Phoenix alone. None of this would take long.

*

Down the hill from the parking lot and through the pine trees, set away from where the tourists went, Howard could see what looked like barracks buildings with long screened windows, painted beige to blend with the landscape. These were dormitories. Like going to basketball camp in the Catskills. A boy and a girl – teenagers – were toting a mattress from one barracks building to another, and giggling. You got used to it, he imagined. Days went by probably, and you never even saw the Grand Canyon or thought a thing about it. It was *exactly* like working in an airport.

Frances was hurrying up the path, paying no attention to him.

There had to be Weiboldt people up here, he thought, folks who'd recognize them and get the whole picture in a heartbeat. They stood out like Mutt and Jeff. No way to get away with anything. His father always said it didn't matter who knew what you did, only *what* you did. And what they'd been doing was fucking and riding around in a rental car on company time – which was probably a federal crime anymore. Plus, Frances seemed not to like him much, now, though he didn't see how he'd done anything particularly wrong, except go to sleep too fast in the motel. He was perfectly happy to be up here with her, happy to take part if they didn't stay all day. He realized he was hungry.

Coming up the path, you couldn't actually tell that there was something to see up ahead, just a low rock wall where people had stopped, and a lot of blue sky behind it. An airplane, a little single-engine, puttered along through that sky.

And then, all at once, just very suddenly, he was there; at the Grand Canyon, beside Frances who had her camera up to her face. And there was no way really not to be surprised by it – the whole Grand Canyon just all right there at once, opened out and down and wide in front of you, enormous and bottomless, with a great invisible silence inhabiting it and a column of cool air pushing up out of it like a giant well. It was a shock.

"I don't want you to say one single thing," Frances said. She wasn't looking through her camera now, but had begun to stare right into the canyon itself, like she was inhaling it. Sunlight was on her face. She seemed blissed.

He did, however, expect to say *something*. It was just natural to want to put some words of your own to the whole thing. Except he instantly had the feeling, standing beside Frances, that he was already doing something wrong, had somehow approached this wrong, or was standing wrong, even looking at the goddamned canyon wrong. And there *was* something about how you couldn't see it at all, and then you completely did see it, something that seemed to suggest you could actually miss it. Miss the whole Grand Canyon!

Of course, the right way would be to look at it all at once, taking in the full effect, just the way Frances seemed to be doing. Except it was much too big to get everything into focus. Too big and too complicated. He felt like he wanted to turn around, go back to the car and come up again. Get re-prepared.

Though it was exactly, he thought, staring mutely out at the flat brown plateau and the sheer drop straight off the other side – how far away, you couldn't tell, since perspective was screwed up – it was exactly what he'd expected from the pictures in high school. It was a tourist attraction. A thing to see. It was plenty big. But twenty jillion people had already seen it, so that it felt sort of useless. A negative. Nothing like the ocean, which *had* a use. Nobody *needed* the Grand Canyon for anything. At its most important, he guessed, it would be a terrific impediment to somebody wanting to get to the other side. Which would not be a good comment to make to Frances, who was probably having a religious experience. She'd blow her top on that. The best comment, he thought, should be that it was really quiet. He'd never experienced anything this quiet. And it was nothing like an airport. Though flying in that little plane was probably the best way to see it.

The people they'd followed up the paved path were now moving on in the direction of telescopes situated in some little rocky out-crops built into the wall. They were all ooo-ing and ahh-ing, and most everybody had video equipment for taping the empty space. Farther along, he assumed, there would be a big rustic hotel and some gift shops, an art gallery and an I-MAX that showed you what you could see for yourself just by standing here.

He hadn't spoken yet, but he wanted to say something, so Frances would know he thought this was worthwhile. He just didn't want to make her mad again. It was a big deal for her. They'd gone to all this trouble and time. She should be able to enjoy it, even if he didn't particularly care. There was probably no way to get her interest in him back now; though he'd thought, while they were driving up, that they ought to at least try to keep this going back home, turn it into something more permanent, get the logistics smoothed out. That would be good. Only now it seemed like they might not even be talking on the ride back. So why bother?

Down the scenic walkway, where the other tourists were wandering toward the telescopes and restaurants, he saw the Indian boy from the motel again. He was talking into a cell phone and nodding as he walked along with the others. He was a paid guide, Howard decided, not a spiritual guide. Somebody hawking beads or trinkets to corn pones.

"What do you think about it now?" Frances finally said in a husky, reverent voice, as though she *was* in the grip of a religious experience. Her back was to him. She was still just staring out into the great silent space of the canyon. They were alone. The last three tourists were drifting away, chatting. "I thought I'd cry, but I can't cry."

"It's sort of the opposite of real estate, isn't it?" Howard said, which seemed an interesting observation. "It's big, but it's empty."

Frances turned toward him, frowning, her eyes narrowed and annoyed. "Is that what you think? Big but empty? You think it's empty? You look at the Grand Canyon and you think empty?" She looked back at the open canyon, as if it could understand her. "You'd be disappointed in heaven too, I guess."

This was clearly *not* an interesting observation, he realized. He stepped up to the stone wall, so his bare knees touched the stones and he was doing what he guessed she wanted. He could now see a little fuzz of white river far, far below, at the bottom of the canyon. And then he could see tiny people walking down the canyon's sides on trails. Quite a few of them, once you made out one – small light-colored shirts, moving like insects. Which was for the birds. You wouldn't see anything down there you couldn't better see from up here. There would be nothing down there but poisonous snakes and a killer walk back, unless somebody sent a helicopter for you. "What river is that?" he said.

"Who cares what goddamn river it is," Frances snapped. "It's the Ganges. It's not about the river. But okay, I understand. You think it's empty. To me it's full. You and I are just different."

"What's it full *of*?" Howard said. The small buzzing plane appeared again, inching out over the canyon. It was probably the police patrol, he thought. Though what could you do wrong out here?

"It's full of healing energy," Frances said. "It extinguishes all bad thoughts. It makes me not feel fed up." She was staring straight out into the cool empty air, speaking as if she was speaking to the canyon, not to him. "It makes me feel like I felt when I was a little girl," she said softly. "I can't say it right. It has its own language."

"Great," Howard said, and for some reason, he thought of the two of them together in bed last night, and how she'd fixed her eyes on his face when she took him in. He wondered if she was looking at the canyon the same way now. He hoped so.

"I've just got to do what you're not allowed to," Frances said, and took a quick, reconnoitering look to where the other visitors were occupied with their video cameras and with crowding around the brass telescopes far down the walk. "I need to get you to take my picture with just the canyon behind me. I don't want this wall in it. I want just me and the canyon. Will you do that?" She was handing him her camera and already crawling up onto the flat-topped stone retaining wall and looking around behind at the wide ledge of rubbly, rocky ground just below. "You probably can't even see the canyon from where you are, can you? You're tall but you're still too low."

He stood holding the camera, watching up at her, waiting for her to find the right place to pose.

There were plenty of hand-carved wooden signs with crisp white lettering that said, "Please do not climb on or go beyond the wall. It's dangerous. Accidents occur frequently." She could see these signs. She could read, he thought. He didn't want to start another argument.

"I'll have to break some more rules," Frances said from up on the wall, and she began to scoot down on the outside of the wall until her pink shoes touched the dirt. He looked over at her. Little pine shrubs were growing out of the arid ground, their roots broken through the dirt. Other footprints were visible. Plenty of people had walked around where she was. A small yellow film box lay half-buried in the dirt. A red and white cigarette package was wadded up and tossed. "I just want to go a step or two farther out here," Frances said, looking up at him, widening her eyes and smiling. She was happy, though she'd gotten her white shorts dirty and her pink shoes, too.

He looped the camera cord around his neck so he wouldn't drop it.

"I want just me and the canyon in the picture. Nothing else. Look through it now. See what you see when you see me." She was beaming, backing up through the little scrub pines, squinting into the morning sun. "Is it okay?"

"Be careful," Howard said, fitting the little rubber eye-cushion to his face, the camera warm against his nose.

"Okay?" she said. He hadn't found her yet. "This'll be great. This canyon's really young, it just looks old. Oh my."

He put the little black lens brackets on her, or at least on the place he thought she would be just below him – where she'd been. But where she wasn't now. Through the lens he looked left and then right, then up, then down. He lowered the camera to find where she'd moved to. "Where'd you go?" he said. He was smiling. But she was gone. The space he'd had fixed with the viewfinder was there, recognizable by a taller, jutting piece of piney scrub – *piñons*, he remembered that name from somewhere. But Frances was not occupying the space. He saw only sunny open air and, far away, the sheer brown and red and purple face of the canyon's opposite wall and the flat earth's surface atop it. A great distance. An impossible distance.

"Frances?" he said and then waited, the camera weightless in his hands. He'd hardly ever said her name, in all the times, all the hours. What had he called her? He couldn't remember. Maybe they'd never used names. "Oh my." He'd heard those words. They were in memory. He wasn't certain, though, if he hadn't said them himself. What had they meant?

He stood still and peered straight down into the space Frances Bilandic had occupied, behind which was much more vacant space.

She would appear. She would spring up. "Frances?" he said again, without completely expecting to speak, but expecting to hear her voice. He heard the far-off buzzing of the patrol plane. He looked up but couldn't see it. His knees and thighs were pressed against the rock wall. All seemed perfectly pleasant. He looked to the left and down to where he'd seen the small white-shirted humans inching along the canyon walls. One or some of them, he thought, should be looking up here. For an instant, he expected to see Frances down where they were. But she wasn't, and no one was looking up. No one there had any idea of anyone here.

And no one down the path was now walking back in his direction. He was alone here, unobserved. He put the camera on the sunny top of the wall and started crawling over, one bare knee then the other, scraping his shin but getting himself down onto the dusty ground where Frances was supposed to be, beyond where the film package and the cigarette box were. He took a step through the loose rocks – it smelled warm and familiarly like urine. But after only four cautious steps (a snake seemed possible here) he found himself at a sudden rough edge and a straight drop down.

And it was at this instant that his head began to pound and his heart jerk, and his breathing became shallow and difficult and oddly hoarse, and a roar commenced in his ears, as if he'd been running and shouting to get to here. And it was now that he got down on his knees and his fists like an animal, as though he could breathe better that way, and peered over the jagged edge and down, far down, far, far down – certainly not to where the river was shining whitely. But far. Two hundred feet, at least, to where the dirt and rock sidewall of the canyon discontinued its straight drop and angled out a few feet before breaking off again for the long, long drop to the bottom. There were rocks and more piney bushes there, and a tree – a ragged, Asiatic-looking cedar growing into the dirt and stone at an angle that would eventually cause it to fall away. And it was just there, at the up-slope base of this ancient cedar, that Frances was, two hundred feet below him.

It was her face he saw first, appearing round and shiny in the sunlight. She was staring up at him, her eyes seemingly open, though the rest of her – her white shorts and blue sailcloth top with the anchor, her bare legs and arms – these were all jumbled about her in a crazy way, as if her face had been dropped first, and then the rest of her. It actually seemed, from here, that one arm was intact but separated from her body.

And she didn't move. For a moment he thought the expression on her face changed the instant he saw her. But that wasn't likely, because it didn't change again. As poorly as he could make her out, her expression never changed.

How long did he kneel in the pine scrub and rubble and bits of paper trash and urine scent beyond the wall? He couldn't be sure. Though not long. The roar in his ears stopped first. His heart beat furiously for a time, and then seemed almost to stop beating, after which a cool perspiration rose on his neck and in his hair and stained through his tee shirt. He looked down at Frances again and, keeping a careful eye on her very white upward-turned face, he tried to think what he might do: help her, save her, comfort her, bring her back to here, give her what she needed, given where she was. Anything. All of these. What? Time did not pass slowly or quickly. Yet he seemed to have all the time he needed, alone there in the brush, to decide something.

Only, he knew that this time wouldn't last. Howard gazed up toward the telescopes, where the other visitors had wandered. Frances would not be seen at first – she was too near to the canyon wall, too hidden among the cedar branches. Too surprising. For a time she'd be mistaken for something she wasn't. An article of her own clothing. No one would *want* to see what had happened. They wanted to look at something else entirely.

Though if anyone *had* seen, they would already be coming – shouting, arms waving – the way he'd felt a moment or ten minutes ago. Other people would already be at the wall looking down. He would be seen too, hunkering like an animal, his tee shirt a white flag in the underbrush. Soon enough this would happen. Her camera was on the wall. He needed to move, now.

On his hands and knees he backed away from the edge, got turned around and crawled up through the pine roots and human debris to the piss-scented base of the wall. And as he was so tall, he simply stood and peered over, able to see all the way back down the asphalt path to the parking lot where he and Frances had followed the crowd. No one was walking up, nor was anyone coming back from the telescopes. And in that moment's recognition he leaped-hoisted himself up onto and over the wall, and in doing so kicked Frances's nice Pentax down onto the pavement.

He stood up again quickly, on the right side of the wall, the correct side, where the rest of the world was supposed to stay. And it was not, he felt, the cool breeze lifting out of the open expanse of canyon – not at all a bad feeling to be here. Whatever was bad had occurred on the other side. Now he was here. Safe.

Though all the other many phrases were about to begin now. Their exact meanings would very soon be present in his thinking. *Authorities notified. Help summoned. Frances rescued* (though of course she was dead). The forces responsible for terrible events had to be mobilized and mobilized now.

He stared at the Pentax lying on the black sequined asphalt, ruined. He tried to remember if she'd taken his picture in the car this morning, his picture in the motel last night, his picture in Phoenix, his picture at the scenic turn-out even one hour ago. But he simply couldn't remember. His mind wasn't so still that he could bring back that kind of thing, although he knew he very much wanted for the answer to be *no*, that she had not taken his picture, and for the camera to stay where it had come to rest. (Though hadn't he touched it?)

And of course *yes*, the answer was that his face *was* in the camera. More than once. That recognition did come back now. And of course he had touched it. And despite the fact that in two minutes or less he would walk quickly to the tourist center or the ranger station or to whatever there was, and make a call for emergency assistance, the camera needed to be removed. Since everything that would happen – happen to Frances, happen to him, happen to Mary, to Ed – could depend on what happened to this one camera and what it contained. Now being the significant time – he knew this from TV – with Frances suspended face-up to the empty sky and himself unscathed; *now* was the "critical period" that, in a thorough police investigation, had to be accounted for, challenged, scrutinized, gone over again and again and again. The time up to, during, and immediately after, would be considered and reconsidered to determine if he had killed Frances Bilandic and why that had suddenly become necessary. (Love gone sour? A sudden breakfast quarrel? Resentment repaid. An inexplicable act of passion or fury. A simple mistake. You could almost think you did do it, there were so many allowable reasons that you might've.)

Too bad, he thought, standing above the black camera, on its side on the black asphalt, too bad he hadn't snapped Frances just at the moment she'd gone over. So many thousands of words would be saved by that luck. "Oh my." Those were her last words to the world, apparently. He was the one who'd heard them. No one else knew that. He was very involved in this.

He grabbed the camera up then and, for a reason he wasn't at all clear about, started back from the canyon rim toward the parking lot, not toward the tourist village where help was. Newly arrived Grand Canyon tourists-enthusiasts were strolling out of the lot in shorts and bright sweaters, carrying cameras, lugging backpacks, laughing about seeing "a big hole in the ground." They would see him holding Frances's camera. But there was nothing truly suspicious about him except that he was very tall and alone. Did his face look strange? Distressed?

A pay phone sat just at the border of the prettily landscaped parking lot, at the edge of some pinewoods. Pink wildflowers still grew here. Of course he should make the call. Do that much. Call in the emergency. Though there was no such thing as an anonymous call now. Everything flashed up a screen someplace: "Howard Cameron is calling in a death." Response would be instantaneous. And then what? He needed to think, as more visitors drifted past him chatting, chuckling. Call and say what? Explain what? Own up to what? (Since he hadn't done anything but not take a picture.) Possibilities fluttered hotly in his face like cinders above a fire – none of them distinct or graspable, but all real, full of danger. And it was *so* so odd, he kept thinking: they had just arrived, and then she'd fallen in. He had wanted not to come.

He looked out across the sunny parking lot. The ranger in his campaign hat was waving vehicles past his little house, leaning in the car windows, smiling and joking with passengers. The sight of the ranger made him lonely, made him long to be miles and miles and miles from where he was – at home, or waking up, lying in bed, thinking about the day when he would sell a house, eat lunch with a friend, call his mother, drive to the playground, shoot baskets, then return at dusk to someone who loved and understood him. All that was real. All of that was possible if he didn't call.

Though all of that would soon become a dream-life he'd never live again, since eventually, somehow he'd be trapped. Reeled in. You didn't really get away with things. And he *had* come up here with Frances – if only just to fuck her; he *had* made crazy mistakes of judgment, mistakes of excess, of intemperance, of passion, of near-sightedness, of stupidity. Of course, they'd all seemed natural when he was doing them. But no one would see them that way. No one would take his part, even if it became clear and beyond any argument that he hadn't pushed Frances Bilandic off the cliff (he *was* in the camera, his hands and feet, even his toenails *had* left traces in the car's carpet, he *had* been seen with her often at the convention). Even if he was finally acquitted in court, he was still guilty of so much that he might as well have done it. Who actually *did* do it – Frances had done it to herself – was just a matter of splitting hairs. *He* did it. "A fuck-up, oh what a fuck-up." He said these words out loud as strangers walked past him. A young woman carrying a baby papoose-style glanced at him and smiled sympathetically. "I just should plan things.

I can't understand," he said in agony, because of course there was no way out of this now.

So that he simply walked to the pay phone, shining there in the morning's sun, looped the camera strap around his wrist and began to set the whole complicated machinery of responsibility into motion.

*

Later in the day, when he went to find the rental car to show the park police how they'd arrived at the Grand Canyon, it was gone. Howard stood, in his shorts and tee shirt, again in the warm parking lot, gazing at the taillights of cars and campers and vans and SUVs. He walked across into the next yellow-lined row – the one he knew was the wrong one – and looked there. Nothing he saw he recognized. The big fire chief's car was gone. It seemed unimaginable. In the sunshine, with two officers watching him, it was as though he'd invented a car. Too bad, he thought, he hadn't.

"I just don't know," he said, feeling tired, confused, but inexplicably smiling, as if he was lying. "We left it right here." He pointed to a place where someone had parked a huge white Dodge Ram Charger and emptied the contents of an ashtray on the pavement. He thought oddly about the Tito Puente CD and the bottle of gin and Frances's purse and her cell phone and her guidebook. All gone with the car.

One of the officers was a young, stiff, short-necked blond not so different in her appearance from Frances Bilandic, but dressed in a tight, high-waisted beige uniform with a clean white tee shirt under her tunic. She was carrying an absurdly large black-gripped automatic pistol high on her plump little hip. *Jorgensen* was the name on her brass nameplate. "And you *are* sure you drove up here in a rental car?" she said, looking up at Howard, her tiny periwinkle eyes blinking as though to penetrate him, see his soul, locate the well-spring cause of the profound dislike she'd begun to experience. His height, he thought, made him dislikable. Though who wouldn't doubt his story. *He* doubted it. Nothing seemed very true.

"Yes," he said, distracted. "I'm sure." He watched a crow fly across the blue pane of sky above the lot. "You can call the rental-car company. *She* rented it. Not me."

"And which rental-car company was that?" Officer Jorgensen said, continuing to ponder him, squinting.

"I don't know," he said and smiled. "I don't know very much."

"Did you notice anyone suspicious following you?" Suddenly she sounded almost sympathetic – as if no one *should've* followed him. He felt willing, since she was willing to be sympathetic, to think back through the day. Such a long day, so complicated with complex, terrible things. And now the stupid car. He could barely believe such a day had begun where it had, in the cool sunny breeze outside a teepee, watching an Indian woman sweep beetles off the stoop, while Frances slept. He remembered the Camaro with the flames on the side and the doughnut tire. And the little chapel where *Chris* died for everyone's sins. He thought a moment about Frances saying, "those were our ancient spirits," last night, but couldn't remember what had made her say that.

"No, I don't think anyone followed us," he said and shook his head. He looked back down the row of taillights. He felt he'd *have* to see the red Lincoln now. It would be there, like your wallet on the hall table – present, only for a time invisible. But no. It was far away. Something else hard to imagine.

He hadn't done what Frances told him to do, of course, as if she'd been foreseeing everything. He remembered her advice at intervals through the day, when for a time suspicion fell upon him; when he'd been informed by a rescue crew member in a plaid shirt – while he was eating a sandwich – that Frances's body had been recovered by use of a wire basket and cables, not a helicopter, and that her left arm had indeed become separated; when he'd heard her next-of-kin had been informed, using cards from a small beaded wallet she'd carried – something he didn't even know about; and when he had heard Ed's name (surprisingly, Ed's last name was Murphy); and when the name Weiboldt Company was spoken, and then the name of *his* wife and the town *he* lived in all sounding quite peculiar in the voices of strangers; on and on and on through the details of lives that now were affected, possibly spoiled, unquestionably made less good, even made impossible because of a few misguided occurrences, and by his questionable decision to stand up for them. At several intervals – sitting in a metal folding chair in a wood-paneled office with a window that looked out into the new-but-rustic visitors' center – he thought again that he'd compounded a mistake with a worse mistake, and that he should've walked away, just as Frances had said; let all he was enduring now come out not in just one day, or maybe never come out. Every single thing he'd done for two days *could've* gone unnoticed. And instead of these lengthy, wrenching moments, he could've been in Phoenix considering how best to put the day's events behind him and greet the evening. Though, of course, that might have turned out to be harder. Whereas what he had done – stayed, told, accepted – might actually be easier.

In the end, even before the afternoon was concluded, suspicion gradually lifted and settled on the concept of an accident. He had told it all, handed over the camera almost gratefully, endured the police officers' disapproval, until something about him, he thought, something actually honest in his height, something in the patient way he sat in the folding chair, elbows on his bare knees, eyes on his large soft empty hands, and explained not without emotion, what had happened – all of that just began to seem true and almost, for a fleeting instant, to seem interesting. So that finally, without even declaring so precisely, the police accepted his story. And once another hour had passed, and three documents were filled out and signed, and his address noted, and his driver's license returned, and the names of officers and telephone numbers given, he was informed he was free to go. He noticed that it was three o'clock in the afternoon.

Though not before he had spoken briefly to Ed. The police woman had asked him if he wished to when she called, and he'd felt she wanted him to, that it was his duty, after all, given his position.

"I don't really get all this," Ed had said, his voice slow and gruff with emotion. He imagined Ed sitting in a dark room, a bitter, disheveled man (more or less the man he'd imagined having a fist-fight with Lon Chaney, Junior). "What were you doing there?"

"I'm a friend," Howard said, solemnly. "We drove up together."

"Is that it?" Ed said. "A friend?"

"Yes," Howard said, and paused. "That's it. Basically."

Ed laughed a dry mirthless laugh, and then possibly – Howard wasn't sure, but possibly – he sobbed.

He wanted to say more to Ed, but neither one seemed to have any more to say, not even "I'm sorry." And then Ed simply hung up.

*

For reasons he didn't understand, a corporal from the Arizona Highway Patrol suggested they drive back down to where Howard could catch a bus back to Phoenix. The *Strike It Rich* was where the bus stopped. One would be arriving late. He had the drink coupons if there was a wait.

On the drive down, the officer wanted to talk about everything under the sun but seemed not to want to talk about what had transpired that day. He was a large, thick-shouldered, dark-haired man in his fifties, with a lined, square, attractively tanned face, whose beige uniform and pointed trooper's hat seemed to fill up the driver's seat. His name was Fitzgerald, and he was interested that Howard sold real estate, and that his deceased "friend" had too. Trooper Fitzgerald said he'd moved to Arizona from Pittsburgh many years before, because it was getting too crowded back east. Real estate, he believed, was the measure and key to everything. Everyone's quality of life was measured out in real-estate values, only it was in reverse: the higher the price, the worse the life. Though the sad truth, he believed, was that in not much time all you'd see (Officer Fitzgerald pointed straight out the windshield, down to where Howard had seen the multi-colored, multi-layered beautiful desert open up that morning, but where it now seemed purplish, smoggy gray), all that would be houses and parking lots and malls and offices and the whole array of the world's ills that come of living too near to your neighbor: crime, poverty, hostility, deceit and insufficient air to breathe. These would presently descend like a plague, and it wouldn't be long after that until the apocalypse. All the police in the world couldn't stop that onslaught, he said. He nodded his head in deep agreement with himself.

"Are you pretty religious, then, I guess?" Howard asked.

Officer Fitzgerald wore his trooper's hat set low on his big square head, almost touching his sunglasses rims. "Oh, no, no, no," he said, exposing his big straight, white teeth, and gripping his lower lip. "You don't need a book to know what's coming. You just need to be able to count the bodies."

"I guess that's right." Howard said, and suddenly felt uncomfortable wearing shorts in this man's solemn presence. He looked at his bare knees and noticed again how he'd scraped them getting back over the wall after Frances died. Trying to escape. It was embarrassing. He thought of Frances saying he'd thank her all the way back to Phoenix. He couldn't remember why she'd said that or even when. Then he thought of the night before, when he'd waked to find her on her hands and knees, staring down into his face in the dark. He'd smelled her sour breath, sensed her chest heaving like an animal's. He'd believed she intended to speak to him, feared she would say terrible things – about him – things he'd never forget. But she'd said nothing, just stared as if her open eyes no longer possessed sight. After several moments she'd lain back down on her side and said, "I don't know you, do I? I don't remember you." And he'd said, "No, you don't. We've never been introduced. But it's all right." She'd turned away from him then, faced the wall and slept. In the morning she'd remembered almost none of it. He hadn't wanted to remind her. He'd thought of it as a kindness.

What you did definitely changed things, he thought, as the powerful cruiser sped along. Even this view down the mountain was changed because of what had happened; it seemed less beautiful now. He thought about his job – that he would lose it. He'd be given the option of resigning, but there'd be no mistaking: sex with a fellow employee, a violent death, a clandestine trip on company time when other priorities were paramount – without a doubt, that didn't work. He thought about Mary – that he would tell her about none of his true emotions, would omit most of the details and the history, would try to let the subject subside and hope that would be enough. He would try to put better things in their place. His parents, too – they would all have to grow up some.

He hadn't seen Frances again after he'd seen her hung there in the little cedar tree, gazing up at him. It shocked him – that memory, and then not seeing her. It all made him feel peculiarly wronged and alone, as if he resented her absence more than he felt sorry about it. You could be happy, of course, that she'd seen the Grand Canyon before it got spoiled by houses and malls and freeways and glass office buildings. Though she'd tried to make him feel inadequate, that the things he cared about didn't matter when they were put alongside the spiritual things she was so enthused about, but had now unfortunately given her life for – the healing energy.

But those things didn't matter. Peering out the windshield at the flat, gray desert at evening, he understood that in fact very little of what he knew mattered; and that however he might've felt today – if circumstances could just have been better – he would now not be allowed to feel. Perhaps he never would again. And whatever he might even have liked, bringing his full and best self to the experience, had now been taken away. So that life, as fast as this car hurtling down the side of a mountain toward the dark, seemed to be disappearing from around him. Being erased. And he was so sorry. And he felt afraid, very afraid, even though that sensation did not come to him in the precise and unexpected way he'd always assumed it would.